Three rich, p

The Million-Dollar Catch

Three terrific, passionate novels from
favourite author Susan Mallery

Three rich, powerful men and the ultimate
wedding wager!

The Million-
Dollar Catch

three full-length romance novels from
favorite author Susan Mallery

The Million-Dollar Catch

SUSAN MALLERY

First published in Great Britain 2012
by Mills & Boon, an imprint of Harlequin (UK) Limited,
Eton House, 18-24 Paradise Road, Richmond, Surrey TW9 1SR

THE MILLION-DOLLAR CATCH
© by Harlequin Enterprises II B.V./S.à.r.l 2012

The Substitute Millionaire, The Unexpected Millionaire and *The Ultimate Millionaire* were first published in Great Britain by Harlequin (UK) Limited.

The Substitute Millionaire © Susan Macias Redmond 2006
The Unexpected Millionaire © Susan Macias Redmond 2006
The Ultimate Millionaire © Susan Macias Redmond 2007

ISBN: 978 0 263 89702 9
ebook ISBN: 978 1 408 97068 3

05-0912

Printed and bound in Spain
by Blackprint CPI, Barcelona

THE SUBSTITUTE MILLIONAIRE

BY
SUSAN MALLERY

Dear Reader,

One of my favourite things to write about is finding family. It's a constant theme for me and this series is no exception. While my three heroines, Julie, Willow and Marina, already have a great family, they've recently discovered a long-lost grandmother who very much wants to be a part of their lives.

Grandma Ruth isn't exactly the cookie-baking type. Instead she's elegant, sophisticated and rich. She also has a nephew-by-marriage she adores. She decides everything would be perfect if only one of her granddaughters would marry her favourite nephew-by-marriage. To entice the girls, she offers them each a million dollars if one of them will say, "I do".

Our heroines are both shocked and intrigued. It kind of is a lot of money. But marriage? To a perfect stranger? Well, maybe if *he* were perfect…

Welcome to *The Million-Dollar Catch,* where nothing is what it seems and falling in love is a whole lot more complicated than anyone ever imagined.

Susan Mallery

Susan Mallery is the bestselling and award-winning author of over fifty books. She makes her home in Los Angeles with her handsome prince of a husband and her two adorable-but-not-bright cats.

One

Julie Nelson's first blind date had gone so badly, she'd sworn off them for the next ten years.

The guy in question had flirted with every female *but* her at the all-you-can-eat buffet, double-dipped in their shared bowl of salad dressing and then skipped out on the bill, leaving her to pay and get herself home. She'd been sixteen and if she hadn't ended up in the emergency room with a horrible case of food poisoning, she might have been able to put the night behind her.

But throwing up all over the only cute intern had been the last straw. She'd vowed never again, for any reason imaginable in this lifetime or any to follow, to *ever* go on another blind date.

Until tonight.

"This is going to be a disaster," she muttered to

herself as she handed her car keys to the valet and made her way to the front of a trendy west side restaurant. "I'm smarter than this. What on earth am I doing here?"

Dumb question, when she already knew the answer. She and her two sisters had been faced with a choice of who got the first shot at dating the infamous Todd Aston III. Their time-honored tradition of making all of life's truly important decisions with a rousing round of Rock, Paper, Scissors had left Julie the loser, and therefore the date. She was a sucker for the scissors and her sisters knew it.

She pulled open the sleek glass door and stepped into the crowded foyer. Apparently tables at this place were as hard to come by as free parking. She wove through the well-dressed crowd until she faced a very young, very thin, very pale hostess.

"I'm meeting Todd Aston," Julie said as she fought against the need to tell the girl that a sandwich wouldn't kill her.

The young woman glanced down at her reservation book. "Mr. Aston is already here. I'll show you to his table."

Julie followed the waif to the rear of the restaurant, trying not to compare her own size-normal hips to the nonexistent ones in front of her. Although feeling inadequate was actually more fun than sweating a meeting with Todd Aston III. How did anyone live with a number after his name? It made her think of Mr. Howell on *Gilligan's Island*, a late-night favorite when she'd been growing up.

She instantly pictured a younger version of Mr.

Howell, complete with striped slacks and a white blazer and was fighting the need to laugh when the hostess stopped in front of a table tucked in the corner and pointed to someone who very definitely did *not* look like an aging, pretentious millionaire.

Todd Aston stood and smiled. "Hello. You must be Julie."

Losing Rock, Paper, Scissors had never looked so good, she thought as she took in the fact that he towered over her despite the dangerously high heels she wore. Todd was *handsome* with dark eyes and a smile that reminded her just a little of the one Big Bad Wolf must have given Red Riding Hood.

He didn't look nerdy, desperate or inbred—and she had a feeling he wouldn't be sticking her with the bill.

"Hi, Todd," she said. "Good to meet you."

He held out her chair, which was a nice and unexpected touch, then moved back to his seat. The hostess left them alone.

She studied him, taking in the dark hair, the hint of a dimple on his left cheek and the subtle power tie that had probably cost as much as her last student-loan payment.

"So, this is awkward," she said cheerfully, deciding there was no point in ignoring the obvious.

His left eyebrow rose. "No social niceties where we ask about the weather and how the traffic was on the drive over?"

"Sure, if you'd prefer. The weather is beautiful, but hey, it's Southern California and we expect that. As for the traffic, it was fine. And your day?"

He smiled again. "You're not what I expected."

She could only imagine what that would have been. "I'm not too young, too plastic and too desperate?"

He winced. "Again the lack of social niceties. Whatever would your mother say?"

Julie considered the question. "Only have one glass of wine, make sure that he's nice and if you like him, give him your number."

He laughed. The sound was low and rich and masculine. So far she'd been existing on nerves and sheer bravado, but when his smile turned into a grin, she felt the tiniest quiver somewhere behind her belly button.

Interesting. Maybe she should have given this blind-date thing a second chance a whole lot sooner.

"That's good advice," he said. "I think I like your mother."

"She's worth liking."

The waiter appeared and handed them menus, then asked for their drink orders. Todd chose an eighteen-year-old Scotch while Julie ordered a vodka tonic.

"Not following Mom's advice?" he asked when the waiter had left.

"It's been a long day."

"Doing what?"

"I'm a second-year associate at an international law firm."

"A lawyer. Pass the bar yet?"

"Of course."

He chuckled. "You sound confident."

"Confidence comes easily after the fact."

"And before?"

"Eighteen-hour workdays *and* studying. It made for a full life."

"What kind of international law? Human rights, that sort of thing?"

"*Corporate* international law," she told him. "I specialize in contracts and associations with China."

"Interesting specialty."

She loved being underestimated, especially by a man. "It was a natural fit for me. I speak Mandarin."

He was good. He only looked a little shocked and then quickly recovered. "Impressive."

"Thank you."

His gaze sharpened slighted as he studied her. "Okay, I think we should start over."

She laughed. "Why? Things are going so well."

"Sure. For you. Look, I was told by my aunt Ruth that there was a 'young lady' she wanted me to meet. I was given a time and a place and I'm here. I was expecting someone…different. You're a nice surprise."

She let her gaze linger on his broad shoulders. Either he worked out or he came from a very fine gene pool. Actually, she could accept either.

"Do you always do what Aunt Ruth says?"

"Most of the time." He shrugged. "She's really my great-great-aunt or something. But she's good to me and I care about her. She doesn't ask me much so if it's important to her, I try to say yes. This was important."

Either he was telling the truth, or he was really, really good with his lines. Right then, she wanted him to be sincere.

"You're a good surprise, too," she admitted, deciding

to trust him for now. "When I walked in, I was picturing Mr. Howell."

"From *Gilligan's Island?* Thanks."

Laughing, she asked, "Would you rather be Gilligan?"

"I'd rather be James Bond."

"You're not British."

"I can work on the accent."

She leaned toward him. "So is it the gadgets or the women that make James Bond so appealing?"

"Both."

"You're being honest."

"You sound surprised."

She was. "I can adjust," she said. "Okay, James-slash-Todd, all I know about you is you dress like a businessman and you adore your aunt Ruth. Well, and the whole number-after-your-name thing, but we probably shouldn't get into that."

"What's wrong with the number after my name?"

"Nothing. It's lovely. I always have to skip over that box when I'm registering on Internet sites, but you get to stop and put in a big three."

"The three isn't actually that big. It's the same size as all the other numbers. It wants to be big, of course, but unfulfilled fantasies are a reality of life. Three has to get used to that."

Charming, she thought happily. The man was completely charming.

The waiter appeared with their drinks. When he'd left, Todd held up his glass.

"To the unexpected pleasure of a smart, funny, beautiful woman," he said.

Okay, *that* was a line, but she was having enough fun that she would accept it in the spirit she hoped he meant it.

"Thank you." She touched her glass to his.

Somehow she misjudged and their fingers brushed. It was nothing—a brief, meaningless bit of contact. But she was oddly aware of it. Her sister Willow would tell her it was the universe giving her a message and that she should listen to it. Her sister Marina would want to know if Todd was "the one."

"So what do *you* do?" she asked.

He set down his glass. "I skywrite. You know, those horrible messages people are always leaving each other in the clouds. Barney Loves Cathy. John, Bring Home Milk."

She took another sip of her drink and waited.

He sighed. "I'm a partner in a venture capital firm. We buy into small businesses, shower them with money and expertise until they're big companies, then sell them to someone else and make an obscene amount of profit. It's disgusting. I should be ashamed."

She laughed. "I would have thought you'd be running the family foundation."

"There's a professional board that takes care of that. I'd rather build than give away."

"Sounds ruthless," she teased.

"I can be. Very. People tend to underestimate me because of the number after my name. They assume I'm useless. I'm not."

She believed him. Funny, powerful and very easy to look at. Especially now, when he stared at her so intently. She sensed she had his full attention—which was both thrilling and a little scary.

"But then they underestimate you, too," he added.

"You know this how?"

"Because I did. I assumed human-rights law when you said you were working internationally."

"It's a guy thing," she said. "The assumption that women will go for emotion rather than business."

"You get that a lot." He wasn't asking a question.

"Yes, but I don't mind. I use it. My career is very important to me. The first few years in a big law firm can be tough. I want to get ahead, but I was raised to do the right thing. So I'll take the advantage of being underestimated and run with it."

"Ruthless?" he asked.

"I flirt with ruthless, but we've never actually been a couple."

Their gazes locked. Until that moment, Julie had been enjoying her drink and the company, but suddenly tension crackled around them. She felt the hairs on the back of her neck prickle. She'd thought Todd would be prissy and he'd thought she would be an idiot. Instead she found herself rethinking her plan of no involvements until after her second year at the law firm ended. While she didn't have a lot of spare time, with the right incentive, she could make an exception.

She liked that he was smart and cynical and still paid attention to what his aunt Ruth had to say. She liked his smile and the interest flickering in his dark eyes.

For the first time in a really long time, she felt a

warmth between her thighs. Good to know that part of her wasn't completely dead.

"Tell me about the women in your life," she said.

He'd been drinking and nearly choked. "I didn't bring pictures."

"That's all right. A brief overview is plenty. I'll pass on the résumés this time."

"You're so generous." He set down his glass. "There were the twins…"

She smiled. "You don't do twins and I don't scare that easily."

"All right. No one serious at the moment." He frowned. "Make that no one at the moment. A difficult breakup last year. No ex-wives, no ex-fiancées. You?"

"One ex-fiancé from my last year of law school. No one now."

"What happened to the fool?"

Julie might not be on the dating circuit, but she knew when to sidestep a topic. There was no point in getting into her sad little story. "Things didn't work out."

The waiter appeared and asked if they had any questions about the menu.

"As that would have required us to look at them," Todd said as he grinned at her, "not yet. But we'll work on it."

Julie waited until they were alone and said, "Why bother with a menu? You're going to order steak, close to rare, and a salad. Not because you want one, but because if you don't eat a vegetable, people will think you weren't raised right."

He raised his left eyebrow. "You'll want the steak,

but there's the whole 'women don't eat on dates' thing, so you'll get fish, which you don't really like." He picked up his glass. "I take that back. You do like fish—but only in a beer batter, deep fried, with fries on the side."

"I like tuna," she said primly.

"Something from a can doesn't count."

She laughed. "All right, you win. I'll get the steak and even eat it, but you can't tell."

"Fair enough. And I'll order the damn salad." He leaned toward her. His dark gaze locked on hers. "I expected to be bored."

"Me, too. I also thought I'd feel morally and intellectually superior."

He grinned. "I'm comfortable with the moral superiority."

"But I can't be smarter?"

"I'm a pretty smart guy."

She shifted in her seat as the temperature in the room seemed to climb about sixteen degrees.

She reached for her drink, but before she could pick it up, he captured her hand in his. His fingers were warm and strong as he rubbed her knuckles. Jolts of awareness moved up her arm and from there zipped to all sorts of interesting places in her body. She felt languid and wholly feminine—an unusual combination for her. Normally she went for in charge and intimidating.

"I have a technical question," he said as he shifted his hand so his thumb could rub against the center of her palm. "It's about my aunt Ruth."

"Which is?"

"She's your grandmother."

"That's the rumor," Julie said, trying to keep her mind on the conversation rather than getting lost in the need stealing through her. She told herself her reaction to Todd was more about the fact that she hadn't been on a date in over eighteen months than anything he was doing. The problem was, she couldn't seem to convince herself.

"If she's my great-aunt and your grandmother," he said. "That makes us…"

Ah, okay. She understood his concern. "Unrelated. She was your great-uncle's second wife. They didn't have any children together. She made it a point to explain all that. She didn't tell you?"

He withdrew his hand and sat up. "No. She didn't."

"Now you know." Speaking of Grandmother Ruth, Julie was going to have to send her a big thank-you when she got home.

"Now, I do." He stood and held out his hand to her.

"What are you doing?" she asked.

"Inviting you to dance."

Dance? As in…dance? She hadn't done that since high school, and even then she hadn't been very good.

"They don't have dancing here," she said, staying firmly in her seat.

"Of course they do. And now that I know we're not cousins, let's dance."

She was torn between the fear of making a fool out of herself and the thrill of pressing her body against his. Because now that she'd bothered to notice, she could hear soft, slow music in the background. It sounded nice, but it wasn't nearly as tempting as the man standing in front of her.

"Are you going to make me beg?" he asked.

"Would you?"

One corner of his mouth turned up in a smile. "Maybe."

She rose and put her hand in his. He led her to the rear of the restaurant, where a three-piece combo played and several couples clung to each other on the small dance floor.

Before she could get her bearings, Todd pulled her against him and put his free hand on her waist. She found herself resting her fingers on his shoulder.

He was all hard, lean muscle, she thought as her thighs brushed against his. They weren't close enough for her breasts to brush against his chest, but she had a sudden wild and inappropriate desire to lean in and rub…like a lonely cat.

Too long without a man, she told herself. And wasn't this a really inconvenient time to figure that out?

"You smell good," he murmured in her ear.

"Copier toner," she whispered back. "Do you like it? I had to change the cartridge today."

He groaned. "Can't you take the compliment?"

"All right. Thank you."

"Better." He smiled at her. "You're not easy."

"Now that's a compliment I can get behind."

"You like being difficult?"

"Sometimes. Don't you?"

He moved his hand from her waist to the small of her back. "Sometimes," he said, echoing her answer.

She looked into his eyes. "You don't like people making assumptions about you."

"You made them."

"You made them as well. We're even."

"More than even, Julie. We're good."

With that, he lowered his head and lightly brushed her mouth with his. The kiss was unexpected but delicious. Her stomach clenched and her breasts began to ache. He moved back and forth, but didn't deepen the kiss.

Public place, she told herself. He didn't want to embarrass her. She should appreciate that. And she would…in time.

He straightened, then cleared his throat. "We should probably go back and order dinner. You know, be responsible."

For a heartbeat, she almost asked about the alternative. What would happen if they kept dancing and touching and kissing? Except she kind of had a feeling she knew the answer to the question.

Too much, too soon, she told herself as they stepped apart. She hadn't been doing the dating thing for a long time—taking it slow made a lot of sense. But the man did tempt her.

He kept her hand in his as they walked back to their table.

"You never told me why you're here," he said when they were seated. "I told you Aunt Ruth asked me to come. What's your excuse?"

He didn't know? Seriously? Oh, my. This could be good.

"My mother and her mother have been estranged for years. Ruth popped back into our lives a couple of months ago. My sisters and I had never met her before. Mom hadn't even mentioned her. Last week, at dinner, Ruth said she had a great nephew and suggested one of us go out with you."

"Interesting."

"More than interesting. She offered us…it's not important."

"Of course it is."

"You'll be insulted."

"I can handle the truth," he teased. "What did she offer?"

"Money."

He stared at her. "She's paying you to date me?"

"Oh, no. The dates are free. Now if I marry you, I get cash. A million dollars. Each. For me, my sisters and my mom. Pretty cool, huh."

A muscle in his jaw twitched, but otherwise, he didn't show any emotion. She couldn't begin to imagine what he was thinking.

"We were all surprised," Julie said. "We couldn't figure out what could possibly be so wrong with you that your aunt had to offer that kind of money to get someone to marry you."

"Wrong? With me?"

"Sure."

She was enjoying herself, but trying really hard to keep him from knowing.

"We decided that one of us would go on a date and figure out how truly awful you were," she continued.

"We played Rock, Paper, Scissors to determine the most likely candidate."

He actually flinched at that. "Rock, Paper…" He cleared his throat. "So you won."

She allowed herself to smile. "Oh, no, Todd. I lost."

Two

The waiter arrived to take their order. Julie placed hers, then waited while Todd did the same. He barely glanced at the menu, instead keeping his gaze fixed on her.

"You lost?" he asked, his voice slightly strangled. "As in, you didn't win?"

She allowed herself a small smile. "Uh-huh. You know how it goes. The loser has to do the icky thing. That would be this date with you. Total ick."

"You lost?"

He seemed unable to comprehend the fact that the three of them hadn't been dying to be his lady for the night. Ah, the foolishness of men.

"If it makes you feel any better," she said before taking a sip of her drink. "I'm glad I lost."

"I can't tell you how that confession moves me."

"You shouldn't take it so hard. Look at the situation from our perspective. Your own great-aunt, who has known you all your life, is willing to pay a woman to marry you. We figured at the very least you had a hump on your back and maybe some odd disease that left you twisted and bumpy. Like the Elephant Man."

He nearly choked on his drink. "You thought I was the Elephant Man?"

"It was a consideration. And yet I showed up anyway."

"You lost and I'm a mercy date. Great. I can't believe Ruth offered you a million dollars."

She thought that was odd, too, but hey, everyone had strange relatives. "Not for the date. Remember? The date is free. I have a really simple solution to the problem—don't propose."

He grinned. "Oh, sure. Easy for you to say, but now I don't have any entertainment for the dessert course."

As she laughed, she admitted to herself that he was nothing like she'd imagined. Anyone with a number after his name had to be stuffy and he wasn't. She liked him—a lot.

"You should have gotten something for the date," he told her. "Fifty thousand, at least."

"You know, I didn't even think of that. But if Grandmother Ruth mentions it again, I get a check."

He gazed into her eyes. "I'm glad you lost, too."

"Thank you. Although my losing wasn't hard to predict. I'm kind of a sucker for scissor and my sisters know. So someone is always playing the rock."

"Interesting way to determine your destiny."

She raised her eyebrows. "Destiny? Are you implying you're mine?"

She expected him to squirm, but he shrugged. "Neither of us thought things would go this well. Maybe fate had a hand in tonight."

She groaned. "No talk of fate or the universe, I beg you. My sister Willow is constantly explaining how each of us has a destiny we can't escape. She's very sweet and I love her to death, but sometimes I want to choke her. Plus, if you could see the things she eats…sprouts and tofu and slimy drinks." Julie shuddered.

He nodded sympathetically. "Vegetarian?"

"Most of the time. Although she has an entire list of foods that don't count as meat. Like hamburgers at a picnic or hot dogs at a Dodger game."

"Interesting."

"She's great. Marina is, too. She's the baby of the family. Just think, you could have been out with either of them."

"I'm happy with the sister I have."

"But you don't have me." Although he certainly could, she thought wistfully, remembering how she'd felt his in arms.

"Give me time."

Julie glanced in her rearview mirror for the hundredth time in the past seven minutes. Dinner had been fabulous. She couldn't remember a thing about the food, although she was confident that had been great. It was the conversation she remembered. The sexy banter, the laughter—the connection.

She couldn't remember the last time a man had pulled her in so completely. One minute she'd been dreading the evening and the next she'd wanted to stop time so it would never end.

Todd was amazing. Funny and smart and he got her humor, which didn't always happen. And the physical chemistry…he could make her melt just by looking at her.

All of which was really nice, but was she prepared to take things where they were obviously headed? His offer to follow her home to make sure she arrived safely was a very thin disguise for what he was really offering—naked Todd in her bed.

The question wasn't if she wanted that—she did with a desperation that left her hungry and restless. It wasn't about wanting, it was about being sensible. She hadn't had a man in her life since Garrett. Not that she was going to think about that lying bastard right now. The point was, she hadn't been playing the dating game for a long time. She was out of practice. Sure, tonight had gone well, but did that mean she should celebrate by inviting Todd in and having her way with him?

She still hadn't decided when they arrived at her place. She pulled in front of the single-car garage and climbed out of her car. The night was still and clear, not too cold because even though it was fall, it was still Los Angeles where real weather need not apply.

Nerves tingled and danced throughout her body. Every cell from her ears down begged her to take the very handsome and capable man up on his yet-to-be-made offer. Her skin ached to be touched and her feminine bits could use with a good ravishing. But her brain warned her to be careful. Sure, Todd was all things charming, but what did she really know about him? Besides, sex on the first date was so tacky.

He parked on the street and climbed out, then glanced around.

"Not what I expected," he said quietly as he approached. "I thought you'd live in something new and shiny."

The neighborhood was older, with a lot of houses having been converted into duplexes. Julie liked the settled atmosphere of the neighborhood and craftsman details inside and out.

"I'm close to work and I get to have a bit of grass," she said. "I'm not really a condo person."

He smiled down at her, then brushed her cheek with his thumb. "Good thing we didn't go to my place."

"Let me guess. It's all glass and steel."

"That, too, but mostly because it's farther."

With that, he kissed her.

His mouth was warm and firm, yet gentle. He moved slowly, as if he had all the time in the world, and she liked that. She liked how he put his hands on her waist and didn't grab for anything significant.

She stepped in a little closer and rested her fingers on his shoulders. Thank goodness her purse had a long strap, so she didn't have to waste time holding it. She wanted to have the freedom to explore his arms and back.

He was all hard muscles through the well-tailored fabric of his suit. He was also warm and alive and just tall enough that even in her heels she had to stretch a little to keep their mouths connected.

She definitely wanted the kiss to continue. Even without him deepening it, she felt tingles in all the right places and a few that surprised her. Her chest was tight, her legs kind of trembly and she had the sudden thought she was never going to be able to catch her breath again.

He drifted slightly, kissed her cheek, then along her jaw. Little brushing touches of lips on sensitized skin. He nipped her earlobe, which made her jump and shiver and need, then lightly touched the tip of his tongue to the side of her neck.

Goose bumps broke out all over. She gasped as heat poured through her. The wanting overwhelmed her until she knew that she couldn't possibly survive another second if he didn't kiss her. Really kiss her.

Fortunately Todd seemed to be a good mind reader. He brought his mouth back to hers. She parted her lips and he plunged inside of her, as if his need to take was as great as her desire to be taken.

She met him stroke for stroke, savoring the passion flaring between them. Even as his tongue mated with hers, he dropped his hands to her hips and pulled her close. She arched against him.

Two thoughts struck her at once. That the pressure of her swollen, sensitive breasts against his chest was wonderful torture, and that he was rock hard.

Images filled her brain—of them naked, touching, him filling her. She was dying from hunger and that hunger made her frantic. She tried to battle her body's desire for a man she barely knew, but it was like trying to herd cats—pointless and a little silly.

He pulled back a little and cupped her face. "This is

where I'm supposed to offer to leave," he said as he stared into her eyes. "It's how I was raised and the polite thing to do."

"Good manners are important," she murmured, pleased that she was able to speak at all. She'd wondered if it was possible, what with how every nerve was on fire.

"I agree." He drew in a ragged breath. "There is also an alternative option."

"Bad manners?"

He grinned, then lightly kissed her. "I want you, Julie. I can give you a list of really good reasons why this is a bad idea, but I want you. Desperately."

She'd never made a man desperate before, she thought as the ache between her legs grew.

"Good manners, a witty conversationalist and a great kisser," she whispered. "Who could refuse that?"

"Not me."

"Me, either."

She pulled her keys out of her purse and led the way to the front door. With each step, she braced herself for second or even third thoughts. Instead there was only a pounding rhythm urging her to hurry.

Once inside, she set her keys and her purse on the small table by the door. Todd shrugged out of what she would guess was a very expensive jacket and let it fall to the floor. Then he pulled her against him and kissed her with a thoroughness that left her weak and made her wonder how intensely he would do other things.

She kissed him just as deeply, running her hands over his chest, feeling the slick silk of his tie and the smooth cotton of his shirt. He slid one hand down to her rear, where he squeezed, and moved the other hand up until he cupped her breast.

Even through the fabric of her dress and her bra, she felt his strong fingers exploring, teasing, caressing. He lingered on her tight nipple, brushing back and forth until she wanted to rip off her clothes so he could touch her bare skin.

He nudged her backward. She reached for his tie and managed to pull it free, then she started on the buttons of his shirt. He fumbled for the zipper at the back of her dress.

They made it into the hall. She'd left a light on in the living room, but here it was dark. He kissed his way down her neck, his warm mouth making her moan. Tingles and shivers and ripples overtook her. Hunger consumed.

He made his way to the vee of her dress and his mouth settled on the curve of her breast. At the same time she found the hall light switch and he tugged down her zipper. The light came on in time for her to see as well as feel her dress fall to the floor. Todd's dark, passion-filled gaze locked with hers as he closed both hands over her breasts.

"You're beautiful," he murmured. "Hot and soft and I don't care if it *is* copier toner, you smell great."

She laughed and moaned at the same time as he rubbed her nipples. Her entire body tightened as her swollen, damp center cried out for some attention of its own.

Still touching her breasts, he leaned in for another kiss. She welcomed him, closing her lips around his tongue and sucking until he, too, shuddered.

Suddenly this wasn't enough. She wanted more—all. She wanted the weight of him on top of her. She wanted him filling her over and over again until she had no choice but to give herself up to the pleasure of her orgasm.

"Clothes," she said against his mouth. "You're wearing too many."

"Good point."

As he shrugged out of his shirt, she stepped over her dress and led the way into her small bedroom. The light from the hall was more than enough for what they were going to do. She turned to face him, only to find him staring at her.

"What?"

He swore softly. "Are you trying to kill me? You're a walking, breathing fantasy. Do the partners at your law firm know what you wear under your suits?"

She glanced down at the matching pink bra and bikini panties. They were a little lacy, but nothing special. She'd bought them on sale, but hey, guys were easy.

"They probably suspect I'm wearing underwear," she murmured as she stepped out of her high heels. "I'd rather they thought that than speculated about me wearing nothing at all. That would be tacky."

The appreciation in his gaze made her bold. Or maybe it was the fact that Todd was a sure thing that gave her confidence. Either way she slid one strap off her shoulder and smiled.

"Did you want me to take this off?"

He'd already kicked off his shoes and was in the process of lowering his slacks. As she spoke, his erection actually pulsed. She saw it through his dark briefs.

He swallowed. "That would be great."

His slacks dropped to the ground, pooling at his ankles. He didn't seem to notice. Instead his gaze fixed on her chest.

She reached behind her and unfastened her bra, then tossed it toward the dresser.

She had no idea if it actually made it because she was too caught up in the expression on Todd's face. Wonder and desire blended in a look so passionate and male that it took her breath away.

She'd been with men before and she'd been reasonably certain that they'd wanted her. After all, there had been obvious proof. But Todd stared at her as if she were his last meal. His appreciation made her feel special and exotic and more than anxious to make all his dreams come true.

He moved toward her and nearly stumbled as he got caught in his slacks. "I'm totally smooth," he muttered as he freed himself, then pulled off his socks.

She thought about mentioning the fact that she *liked* that he wasn't perfect. It made him seem more approachable somehow. But then he was pulling her close and touching her and speaking became a highly overrated activity.

His hands were everywhere—her arms, her stomach, then he cupped her bare breasts. He didn't kiss her as he explored her curves, then lightly touched her nipples with his fingers. Instead he stared into her eyes and she found herself very close to begging to be taken.

She held his gaze as long as she could, but soon sensation overwhelmed her. If was as if there were a direct line of pleasure from her breasts to between her legs. With each touch, both became more needy.

"Todd," she whispered, hoping she didn't sound as desperate as she felt.

He nudged her backward until she felt the bed behind her. Then he wrapped his arms around her, turned and lowered them both onto the mattress.

She landed on him, her legs spread, her center nestled on his arousal. He smiled up at her.

"Now I have you exactly where I want you," he whispered. "In my power."

"I'm on top," she told him. "I'm in charge."

"Wanna bet?"

He put his hands on her hips and urged her back and forth. Even through the layers of her panties and his briefs, she felt the delicious heat and friction. With a groan, she gave herself up to the sensation. It was nearly enough to get her over the edge.

"Just that like," he murmured as he began to touch her breasts.

The combination of sensations was unbelievably sensual. Tension tightened all her muscles as she felt herself racing closer and closer to her release.

Not like this, she thought frantically. Not so quickly. Not while still wearing clothes. But she also couldn't stop rubbing faster and faster.

Without warning, he rolled them both onto their sides. He removed her panties with one smooth, practiced move, then pulled off his briefs. Before she had a chance to check things out, she was on her back and his mouth was on her left breast.

He sucked and licked and teased until she thought she would go crazy from the pleasure. At the same time, he slipped his hand between her legs and explored her swollen center.

It took him less than three seconds to find that one magical spot. He circled it before settling down to a perfect, rhythmic caress that made the end inevitable.

She sank into the sensation, letting her body take over. Tension built until she could barely breathe. Her fingers curled into the blanket, her heels dug into the mattress. Todd shifted so he could claim her mouth and when his tongue touched hers, she lost herself in blissful release.

Her climax seemed to go on forever. Wave after wave of perfection rocked through her, sucking away her will to do anything but feel this forever.

Eventually, though, she became aware of his hardness pressing into her leg. She opened her eyes and found Todd smiling down at her.

"That was good," he said. "At least it was good for me. I'm thinking it was better than good for you."

"It was," she said as she traced his lower lip with her thumb. "Ready for some better than good of your own?"

"I thought you'd never ask."

He eased between her thighs, then pushed until she felt him entering her. He was big and thick, stretching her. She arched her hips toward him, wanting to take all of him. He withdrew, entered her again and she wrapped her arms round him, pulling him against her, enjoying the weight of him nearly as much as what he was doing to her body.

Because it had begun again. The sense of need and wanting. The growing heat as muscles tightened in anticipation of a spectacular ride. Faster and faster, pushing, filling. Her breathing became as ragged as his. She felt his arms begin to tremble as he sought that moment of no return.

She'd been empty for so long that she'd forgotten the glory of being filled by a man intent on pleasing them both.

He bent down and kissed her as the sensations claimed her, and then he groaned and pushed in deeper. She felt him stiffen before he stilled and shuddered.

When they'd cleaned up and slid under the covers, Julie rested her head on his shoulder. He had his arm around her, she had her thigh nestled against his. This was one of life's perfect moments, she thought happily. Those times she would look back on later and think, *That was a great night.*

"Thank you," he said as he played with her hair. "That was pretty…"

"Spectacular?" she asked, feeling content.

"I was going to say *amazing*, but *spectacular* works."

She closed her eyes and smiled. "I'm deeply out of practice. I appreciate the lesson bringing me up to speed."

"You didn't act like you were out of practice. You acted like you'd read the manual on how to push all my buttons."

The smile turned into a grin. "Really? All of them?"

"Well, maybe you missed one."

"I'll have to catch that next time."

He chuckled. "Words to make a man your love slave forever. Can I stay?"

Three little words that got her attention in a big way. She might have been out of the dating game for a while, but she remembered most of the rules. After sex, especially an encounter so unexpected, most guys preferred to dress and run. She didn't have a lot of personal experience, but she'd had enough friends cry on her shoulder to be familiar with the practice.

Todd wanted to stay? Here? With her? Tonight?

A little bubble of happiness floated up from her tummy to her chest where it gave birth to about a thousand other little bubbles.

"I had plans for later," she said, deciding going for casual was best for both of them. "I guess I can cancel them."

"I appreciate that. Do you snore?"

She laughed. "No, do you?"

"I'm a very quiet sleeper." He shifted so that he could kiss her. "Not that I expect either of us to get much sleep tonight."

Sometime after two in the morning, he watched the moonlight on Julie's face and knew he'd made a mess of things from the beginning.

It wasn't supposed to have been like this. He wasn't supposed to like her. From what he'd been told, Julie Nelson was a gold-digging bimbo who needed a good lesson and he'd been just the man to volunteer to teach it. He'd expected a vapid, over-accessorized bitch.

Instead he'd found a beautiful, funny, intelligent, sincere woman who made him laugh and want to believe in possibilities again.

Right now he should be feeling as if he'd done the world a favor. Instead he felt like a total jerk. He'd just created a hell of a mess and he had no idea how to fix it. He liked Julie. He liked her a lot.

How was he supposed to explain that he wasn't Todd Aston III, and that she'd just been set up to take a fall?

Three

Julie stood in her kitchen and held on to the edge of the counter. It wasn't that the world was spinning so much as she thought it might at any moment. She half expected a bolt of lightning to come crashing through the roof, or at the very least, hear the ghost of Christmas Past.

There was a man in her bedroom.

Right now, even while she was supposed to be making coffee, Todd lay asleep in her bed.

Until he had stepped inside last night, her place had been a man-free zone. After what had happened with Garrett, she'd wanted to keep it that way. She'd rented it after law school, furnished it with girlie stuff and her mattress had been practically virginal.

Not anymore, she thought with a grin as she reached

for the can of coffee and the scooper next to it. She had languid, morning-after glow and a couple of sore muscles to prove it.

She added water and flipped on the coffeemaker, then leaned against the counter. In theory she should probably be having regrets or even second thoughts. Last night really wasn't like her at all. She was more sensible, more careful, much less impetuous. Which she would go back to being very soon. Right now she just wanted to wallow in the hot memories of what they'd done.

She felt good—too good to feel bad.

"Morning."

She glanced up and saw Todd standing in the doorway to the kitchen. He'd pulled on his slacks and his shirt, but hadn't buttoned the latter. She could see bare skin and tapered muscles. He also looked mussed, unshaven and too sexy for words.

Unexpected shyness gripped her. "Hi," she murmured, then cleared her throat. "I'm making coffee, which you can probably guess."

"Good. Thanks."

His dark gaze settled on her face. She had to fight the need to smooth her hair, even though before entering the kitchen she'd stopped in the bathroom to wash her face, brush her teeth and make sure her hair didn't look as if it had been attacked by angry birds.

She had no idea what he was thinking. He probably did this sort of thing most mornings, woke up in a strange bed. She could let him set the tone. Except that wasn't her style. She was far more take-charge. Her sisters would be happy to provide testimony on her behalf.

"So I'm out of practice," she said with a shrug. "The whole strange-guy-in-my-bed and all that. I didn't expect last night so I certainly didn't prepare for this morning. What would you like to do? Shower? Leave? Get my phone number?"

He folded his arms over his chest and leaned against the door frame. "You're honest."

"As I was last night. It's kind of something that sticks with me. I like to think I'm a trendsetter. Plus, I've never understood the thrill of lying. The truth comes out eventually."

"Interesting point. What are your plans for the day?"

Plans? It *was* a Saturday. "I, ah, have to run some errands. I brought some work home and I'm meeting my sisters later for lunch."

"Busy lady."

"It happens. And you? What are you doing today?"

"Meeting my cousin, but that's not until later." He glanced down the hall, then back at her. "Can I take you up on that shower? Maybe borrow a toothbrush?"

"Sure."

This was so weird, she thought as she moved down the hall and opened the small linen closet by the bathroom. There was a single unwrapped toothbrush, which was, unfortunately, bright pink.

"Sorry," she murmured.

"I'll survive. Do your razors have flowers on them?"

"No, but they're mostly purple."

"Such a girl."

"Would you be more comfortable if I were a guy?" she asked.

He shuddered. "No. Although it would have made for an interesting conversation."

She handed him a couple of towels, then pointed to the bathroom. "Have at it."

"Okay, thanks."

She returned to the kitchen and reached for a mug. There was a man in her bathroom. A soon-to-be naked man who would shower and use her soap and it was all very strange. She should—

"Julie?"

She set down the mug and walked back into the hall. The bathroom door stood partially open.

"What? Is there a problem?" she asked.

"Sort of."

She paused just outside the bathroom and opened her mouth to speak. But before she could say anything, he grabbed her arm and pulled her inside.

He was naked. She grasped that much right before he drew her close and kissed her. Naked and hard and apparently still in the mood, she thought happily as she parted her lips and let the games begin. His tongue teased hers before he shifted his attention to her neck.

"You're wearing a robe," he murmured against her skin.

"Yes, I am." She sounded breathless, which made sense. She *was* breathless.

"That's gotta go."

He was a man of his word. He tugged the tie loose, then pushed the robe off her body. She was naked underneath—a good thing what with the way he immediately began to caress her breasts.

His touch was inspired, she thought as her mind began to fog as passion and need took over. In a matter of seconds she was wet and swollen and hungry for him to be inside of her.

While he bent down and licked her tight, sensitive nipples, she rubbed his shoulders, his back, then kissed the top of his head.

He straightened. "Okay, time to shower."

Shower? "What?"

He took her hand and guided her into the tub, then pulled the curtain closed. He urged her under the spray, then reached for the soap.

After lathering his hands, he began to wash her all over. The soap made her skin slick. His fingers glided and slipped as he first cleaned her, then teased her.

He washed her back, her hips, the backs of her legs, before rinsing her off. Then instead of turning her, he just moved in close and with her back pressing against his chest, began to run his hands up and down the front of her body.

He caressed her neck, then did a thorough job of cleaning her breasts. The combination of soapy fingers against her nipples and pounding hot water made her weak and hungry with need. She covered his hands with hers to keep him in place while she leaned her head against his shoulder.

"There's more," he whispered in her ear. "Much more."

Without warning, he stepped back, then turned her. He lightly kissed her on the mouth before dropping to his knees and pressing another opened-mouthed kiss to her stomach.

Her muscles clenched in anticipation. The water ran down her body. He urged her to put one foot on the edge of the tub, then he leaned in, parted her flesh and licked her. She cried out as his tongue circled the very heart of her, before moving across her swollen center. She felt his lips, his breath and the steady pressure as he pleasured her.

She had to brace herself by placing one hand on the wall. Her legs began to tremble as her muscles clenched. He moved slow, then fast, licking, sucking, forcing her higher and closer. Her breath came in pants. She was completely his to command as the promise of an incredible orgasm kept her frozen in place.

She wanted to beg. If she'd known any state secrets she would have yelled them, anything to have him keep doing what he was doing. She felt herself spiral closer and yet her release remained elusively out of reach.

More, she thought frantically, she needed more. But how?

He must have read her mind because he slipped two fingers inside of her. Even as he continued to kiss her so intimately, he filled her and the combination was too much.

She lost control right there, in the shower, with the water pounding and an incredible man between her legs. She gasped for breath and screamed and shuddered until she knew that nothing ever again would ever be this spectacular.

Her release crashed through her, leaving her exhausted and boneless. Todd stood and smiled, then pulled her close. She could barely gather the strength to hug him back.

The thought of doing to him what he'd gone to her perked her up a little. She stepped back, but before she could do anything else, he reached behind her and turned off the shower.

"We'll get cold," she told him.

"I don't think so."

He pulled open the curtains, then led her out of the shower. After spreading a towel on the counter, he lifted her onto it, parted her legs and pushed into her with one firm, demanding thrust.

She would have bet a lot of money that she was too content to even think about coming again for six or eight months. But the second he filled her, she felt tired muscles sit up and take notice. Then he kissed her and she found herself getting lost in the sensual dance of tongues and lips and need.

They were both wet and the bathroom was steamy and he hadn't had a real shower yet, but none of that mattered. Not when he slipped his hand between them and found her still-swollen center. He rubbed it gently enough not to hurt, but just enough to make her surge toward him.

She went from exhausted to take-me-now in less than fifteen seconds. She wrapped her legs around his hips and rode him until she came again—this time holding in her scream until he groaned her name and they got lost together in their mutual release.

Julie lay on her bed, her eyes closed, her long, blond hair spread out on the pillow. Ryan Bennett twisted a strand around his index finger, enjoying the softness of her hair and the way it caught the light. Her breathing was slow and steady, as if she were about to fall sleep, but the slight smile tugging at the corners of her mouth told him she might have something else on her mind.

Something he would find very appealing.

He didn't want to go. That surprised him nearly as much as anything. Normally he was a get-out-of-town-fast kind of guy, the morning after. He frequently avoided the problem by not staying at all. But he'd wanted to wake up in Julie's bed and make love with her again. He'd wanted a lot of things.

"Julie," he murmured.

She opened her eyes. Her irises were a blue with tiny flecks of green. She had freckles and a wicked smile, and she smelled like vanilla and sex and temptation.

How could she be like that and be a scheming liar? Was this all a game to her? A twisted, win-at-any-cost game?

He'd pretended not to know about Ruth's offer of a million dollars to see if she would mention it. She had, though, and in such a way that he wanted to believe it didn't matter to her. But if she didn't care about the money, why go on the date at all?

She reached up and stroked his face. "You're far too good-looking," she told him.

"That's not a bad thing."

"It could be. Handsome men don't have to try so hard."

"So you'd rather I was a troll?"

"I'd like to think you had to put a little effort into getting women into your bed. Instead, I have a feeling I'm simply one of the masses."

"I didn't get you into my bed," he said as he leaned close. "I got you into your bed."

"That's a subtlety that does nothing to weaken my point."

He rolled onto his side and supported his head with his hand. "Why do you get away with saying bad things about men, but if I were to make a crack about beautiful women, you'd accuse me of being misogynistic?"

"Because it would be true. We have centuries of inequity between the sexes to overcome. I think a little head start for the ladies is perfectly acceptable."

"So speaks the lady."

She raised her eyebrows. "We've already had the 'do you want me to be a man' conversation. Yet here we are, flirting with it again. Is there something you want to tell me?"

He rolled onto his back. "You're driving me crazy."

"It's one of my best qualities. I've turned it into an art form."

She laughed, then bent over him and brushed his mouth with hers. Her hair stroked his chest and it was all he could do not to reach out and touch her, take her, be inside of her.

Who was she, really? He'd come on the date because Todd was his cousin and he, Ryan, had been in the mood to exact a little revenge on money-hungry women, whomever they might be. He hadn't cared about Julie; in fact, he'd been prepared to dislike her on sight.

But she'd won him over and somehow made him want to believe in her.

"Tell me about your family," he said.

She raised her head. "Interesting change in topic."

"I'm curious about your grandmother. How could you not know her all these years?"

Julie curled up next to him and put her head on his shoulder. Involuntarily, he reached for her hand and laced their fingers together.

"Ruth's first husband died unexpectedly, while she was pregnant with my mom. Ruth remarried a few months after the birth to Fraser Jamison, your great-uncle. Naomi, my mom, looked on him as her father. When she was seventeen, she met Jack Nelson, my dad, and fell madly in love with him. He didn't come from money—in fact he was a bit of a loser, but charming and she couldn't help herself. She ran off and married him, and Ruth and Fraser turned their backs on her."

The story matched what Ryan had been told, although his uncle Fraser hadn't been that generous in the telling. He'd painted Naomi as an ungrateful slut who'd defied him at every turn and her husband as a money-grabbing bastard who'd been out for what he could get.

"My mom was pregnant, of course. I was born six months after the wedding. My two sisters followed very quickly. Mom got a job, Dad tried, but he wasn't the type to enjoy real work. Although he always had a scam going. Some of them even paid off. He took off for the first time when I was about eight. He'd be gone for months at a time, then show up. He'd bring us gifts and her money, then he'd leave again."

There was anger in her voice, and maybe a little pain. Was either emotion real? "That must have been hard for you," he said.

She sighed. "I wanted her to divorce him and move

on, but she wouldn't. She said he was the love of her life. I thought he was a jerk who couldn't stand to take responsibility for his family. But that's a fascinating discussion for another time. Years passed, we all grew up. Then about three months ago, Ruth appeared on our doorstep. She said that she'd been wanting to reconcile with her daughter for a long time, but Fraser had stood in the way. With him gone, she was free to do as she wanted and have her family back. So now we have a grandmother."

And a potential inheritance, he thought cynically. "She came to you?"

"That's what I heard. Mom called and asked us all to join her for dinner. We walked in and there was Ruth." She raised her head and looked at him. "It's weird to suddenly find out about relatives this long after the fact."

That he could agree with. "What do you think about her?"

"She's crusty," Julie said as she wrinkled her nose. "Very elegant, but distant and…I don't know. I don't really know her. I guess I'm mad because she turned her only daughter away. Okay, sure, she didn't approve of what my mom did, but there's a whole lot of space between not approving and never seeing her again. She turned her back on all of us. Now she says she's sorry and we're supposed to just forgive her? Pretend all those years without her didn't matter?"

He found himself in the odd position of wanting to defend his aunt. Ironic, considering he, too, thought of her as meddling and difficult. Still, he loved her.

"She's getting older," he said. "Maybe losing her husband has caused her to see what's really important."

She looked at him. "Do *not* tell me you're a middle child?"

"I'm an only child."

"You don't sound like it. Willow is the middle sister and she's forever seeing everyone else's point of view. It's an incredibly annoying characteristic."

"In my business it's important to see all sides of a situation."

"I'm not sure that's a good enough excuse."

He wanted to believe her. He hadn't expected that, but then he hadn't expected a lot of things.

"I'm not trying to jump to conclusions here," she said, "but you do realize that despite all this, we can't get involved."

Couldn't they? "Why not?"

"Because of my crazy grandmother and your crazy aunt."

"We're not related."

"It's the money. If we got involved, everyone would think it was because of the tantalizing offer of a million dollars. *You* would think that. I don't get it. You are not the kind of man who needs anyone's help to get a woman. So why would she do that?"

"Ruth has some particular ideas about life and her place in everyone else's." She always had. Maybe she genuinely thought one of her granddaughters would be able to trap Todd. Ryan was more willing to bet on his cousin. Todd wasn't interested in anything serious and no one was going to change his mind.

"Like I said. Crazy." Julie shrugged. "But now we have a problem."

Everything about her screamed that she was telling the truth. She met his gaze easily, she wasn't nervous. She'd been funny and charming and blunt ever since she'd walked up to his table in the restaurant and had compared him to Mr. Howell.

"You're saying things would be better if I was an impoverished shoe salesman?" he asked.

"In a way. Although it sounds a little nineteenth century. Couldn't you just be a high-school math teacher or an entry-level computer programmer?"

"I could be, but I'm not."

"So now what?" She reached for her robe and pulled it on, then sat up and smiled at him. "I'm presuming you want to see me again, mostly because I've given you many opportunities to bolt for freedom and you haven't taken any of them."

"Do you wish I would have?"

"No." She shrugged again. "I kind of like having you around." She laughed. "This time yesterday I was dreading meeting you. I wished that either of my sisters could have been paid to take my place. But now…" She touched his hand. "Sometimes losing is a good thing."

His chest tightened as the truth slammed into him. Whatever he and Todd had thought about Julie Nelson, they'd been wrong. She wasn't in this for the money. She wasn't in it for any reason other than she'd wanted to make her grandmother happy and she'd lost a stupid game.

The realization of what he'd done—how he'd blown it—made him sick. He'd thought she'd be a bitch—

instead she was the most amazing woman he'd ever met, and he'd screwed this up. Totally.

"Todd?" she asked. "What's wrong? You have the strangest look on your face."

"I…" He swore silently. How to explain? How to… "I'm not Todd Aston."

Four

Julie knew she was supposed to say something, but she couldn't seem to get her brain to work. Too little sleep and too much shock made thinking impossible.

"You're not Todd?" she asked, more to herself than him.

"Julie, look," he began, but she raised her hand to cut him off.

"You're not Todd," she repeated as she stared at the naked man in her bed. The man she'd made love with several times. The man she'd laughed with and joked with and had taken her clothes off for and *trusted*?

"You're not Todd?"

This time the words came out in a yell that gave voice to the fury and horror building inside of her. She scrambled off the bed and tightened the belt of her robe.

"What the hell do you mean, you're not Todd?"

"I'm his cousin, Ryan Bennett. Todd and I knew about what Ruth had done, and we figured anyone who agreed to her terms was only in it for the money. I went on this date thinking I was here to teach you a lesson. You know, pretend to be Todd and then cut out."

"His *cousin*? This was just a game to you? Is this your idea of a good time?" She glared at him and wished she worked out so she could punch him and have it hurt.

Todd or Ryan or whatever his name was climbed out of bed and stood in front of her. Naked. Gorgeous. But that shouldn't be a surprise. Why wouldn't evil, lying, snake bastards be good-looking, too?

"Julie, wait. It's not what you think."

"Don't even try," she told him, feeling light-headed from the rage coursing through her. "Don't think you can smooth talk your way out of this one."

"I don't want to talk myself out of anything—I want to explain. I didn't mean for this to happen."

This? As in the sex? The rage built and she was suddenly terrified she was going to cry. Oh, God, not that. She refused to break down in front of this weasel.

"What part didn't you mean?" she asked, her voice thick with loathing. "The part where we agreed to meet for dinner? Or was it just a slip of the tongue when you introduced yourself as Todd? Oops, silly me. I forgot my name?"

He'd been charming, she thought, just as enraged at herself as she was at him. Of course—if *she'd* fallen for him, there had to be something wrong with him. It wasn't as if she ever found someone decent. He'd been funny and smart and she'd been so attracted to him. Hadn't that been enough of a warning in her brain? But no. She had to go and think he was what he seemed. She had to go and bring him home and have sex with him.

For someone who was supposed to be so damn bright, why did she have to act so stupid?

"We thought…" he began.

"You thought what? This would be good sport? No, wait. What was it you said? You were going to teach me a lesson?" She glanced at her lamp and thought about flinging it at his head. "Who the hell are you to be judge and jury? What did I ever do to you?"

"You didn't do anything," he told her earnestly. "Nothing at all. You're the innocent party in this. I'm sorry."

"Sorry doesn't cut it."

"I know. When Aunt Ruth told Todd what she'd done, what she'd promised you and your sisters, he was furious. He always has money-hungry women chasing after him and he didn't need three more trying to marry him for his wealth."

"Todd needs to get over himself," she said bitterly. "It wasn't about the money. You know that, damn you. It was about finding out we had a grandmother and keeping things good between us. No one thought her offer was real. What's wrong with you people?"

"You have no idea what it's like," he said.

"Oh, poor little rich boy. I bleed for your pain."

He was still naked and she deeply resented that part of her brain could actually pause and appreciate the sculpted perfection of his body. Her insides quivered at the memory of being taken by him over and over again.

She sucked in a breath and pointed at the door. "Get out. Get out now."

"Julie, you have to understand. I never thought I'd be meeting *you*."

There were a thousand ways to interpret that sentence. She had a feeling it was his meager attempt to tell her that she was special, that she mattered.

Oh, please. "So if you hadn't liked me, it would have been okay to screw with me? There's a nice statement about your character."

He flinched slightly. "I didn't mean it like that."

"Sure you did. You're not sorry you tried to teach me a lesson, because even knowing nothing about me, you were confident I deserved one. No, your only problem comes from the fact that I was someone you enjoyed being with and now you've screwed things so totally I wouldn't get involved with you if you were the last man on the planet. There is nothing you can say or do to ever convince me you are anything but a lying bastard who believes he is so superior to everyone around him that he gets to cast judgment on the rest of the world. You are self-centered, egotistical, rude and twisted in ways I can't begin to comprehend. Now get the hell out of my house."

He drew in a breath, then nodded. After gathering his clothes, he walked out of the bedroom. Less than a minute later, the front door opened and he was gone.

Julie sank onto the floor. At least he was a fast

dresser, she thought as waves of pain washed over her. And he was gone.

She began to shake as she fought tears and she hated that through all of this, she'd desperately wanted him to beg. She knew it couldn't have made any difference, but she'd wanted it all the same. She'd wanted to know that last night had meant as much to him as it had to her.

Obviously, it hadn't.

Julie dressed in her tightest pair of jeans because being unable to breathe helped to keep her mind off the horrors of her morning. She'd scrubbed the shower, washed her sheets, remade the bed and had given herself a stern talking-to. None of that had worked in the least, so she'd left to go see her sisters, stopping on the way to buy the biggest latte known to man. If not breathing didn't help, maybe she could drown herself from the inside out.

It was a little after eleven when she pulled up in front of the small house where she'd grown up. The tiny lawn looked lush and green and there were flowering plants everywhere, mostly thanks to Willow's green thumb.

She glanced at the two cars already parked in front of the house and took in the empty space in the driveway, then got out and walked into the house.

"Hey, it's me," she said as she stepped into the bright living room.

Willow sat curled up in the chair in the corner, while Marina had taken a corner of the sofa. They both smiled at her.

"Hi," Willow said as she stood and hugged her sister. "Are you really going to drink all that coffee? Too much of that will kill you."

"That's the plan," Julie said, doing her best to smile as she spoke so Willow would think she was kidding.

Marina moved in for her hug. "Hi. How are things?"

"Okay. Mom at the clinic?"

"Uh-huh." Marina sat back on the sofa and patted the cushion next to her. "It's low-cost vaccination day."

"Right." Julie plopped down.

One Saturday morning a month, Dr. Greenberg, Naomi's boss, opened his offices to the neighborhood and gave low-cost vaccinations to whomever wanted them. It had been their mother's idea—part of her ongoing quest to save the world. Julie had always thought she should spend a little more time trying to save herself.

"So how are you two?" she asked.

Willow and Marina exchanged a glance. Julie immediately tensed. "What?"

Willow sighed. "We were talking about Dad."

Great. Because the day hadn't started off badly enough, Julie thought grimly.

"It's been a few months," Marina said. "He should be coming back any time now."

"How exciting," Julie muttered and sipped more coffee.

"Jules, no." Willow flipped her long blond hair off her shoulder and leaned forward. "That's not fair. You never give him a break."

"I'm sorry I don't have enough appreciation for a man who abandons his family over and over again and the mother who lets him."

Marina's mouth twisted. "That's not fair. She loves him."

Julie felt too raw to deal with the familiar argument. "Don't say he's her destiny, I beg you. He blows back into her life and ours, he's charming and adoring and then he goes away. He moves on to the next thrill and we're left picking up the pieces."

Julie's childhood had been punctuated by her father's visits and her mother's subsequent week of tears and feeble attempts to hide her pain. While her sisters were happy to remember the excitement of their father's visit, Julie always recalled the aftermath. Jack Nelson was like a big electrical storm. A lot of light and noise and an impressive show, but when it was over, someone had to handle the cleanup. That someone had usually been her.

She took another sip of her coffee. Apparently it wasn't enough to drown her, which meant she would now be completely awake to deal with the humiliation of last night and this morning.

"All men are bastards," she muttered.

Willow's blue eyes widened. "Julie, no. Not all guys are like Garrett."

Right. Her ex-fiancé. Julie groaned. She'd thought he'd been the absolute low point of her romantic life, but when compared with Todd/Ryan, he was almost a nice guy.

"Speaking of slime on two legs," she said, "I had my date with Todd last night."

"What?" Marina threw a pillow at Julie. "Are you kidding? Why didn't you say anything until now?"

"I've been here five minutes."

Willow rolled her eyes. "Oh, please. That's a walk-in announcement and you know it." She slid to the edge of the chair and grinned. "Okay, tell us everything. Start at the beginning and speak slowly. Don't leave out anything. Was he fabulous? Was he charming? Could you tell he was rich?"

Under any other circumstances, Julie would have laughed. Willow's idea of a guy with money was one who would only make her pay for her own meal instead of his as well. She tended to attract the down-and-out type, those between jobs or paychecks or even stints in jail.

"He was…"

On the way over, Julie had tried to come up with a way to make the situation into something she could laugh about instead of a pathetic statement on her luck with men. But she couldn't remember a single thing she'd planned on saying and she surprised both herself and most likely her sisters by starting to cry.

"Jules?"

They were both beside her in a heartbeat. Marina hugged her from the side and Willow knelt in front of her. Someone took her coffee from her hand, and then she was held so hard, her chest hurt. Or maybe her chest just hurt on its own.

The embrace was familiar and comforting. They'd always been there for each other, only she wasn't usually the one at the center of the healing.

Julie wiped away her tears and swallowed. "He wasn't a one-armed humpback," she said, her voice shaking a little. "He was nice. Charming and sexy and we danced and he made me laugh."

She'd already decided not to mention that she'd slept with him. No doubt she would confess all later, but right now she couldn't face admitting she'd been that much of a fool.

She'd been so careful, too. Ever since Garrett, she'd avoided men and sex and entanglements. Based on who Ryan had turned out to be, she should have stuck with being single.

"How did it go wrong?" Willow asked. "Was he secretly a woman?"

That made Julie laugh. She touched her sister's face. "No, but that would have been interesting. He lied…about everything."

She told them about him pretending to be Todd, in order to teach her a lesson.

"He assumed I was in it for the money, so his plan was to show me a good time, get me to fall for him and then tell me the truth."

"What?" Marina stood up and put her hands on his hips. "That's horrible. You didn't do it for the money. You did it for Grandma Ruth. You lost. Did you tell him you lost because you always play scissors?"

"I mentioned that."

Marina settled back beside her. "This is going to turn you off guys forever, isn't it?"

Julie nodded. "I suspect I'll have a lengthy recovery."

"Want me to hurt him for you?" Willow asked.

Julie laughed again. Willow was all of five foot three inches. She was feisty on the inside but on the outside she had a whole lot more in common with a waif than a bodybuilder.

"That's okay," Julie told her. "I appreciate the offer, but he's big and burly."

"But I have speed and the element of surprise on my side."

"I love you guys," Julie said.

"We love you, too," Marina told her. "I'm just so mad. Maybe Willow and I could take him together."

"I don't think so."

Willow leaned against Julie's shoulder. "I hate Todd, too. He's a part of this. How could Grandma Ruth want any of us to marry someone who's so jerky?"

"Maybe she doesn't know," Marina murmured.

"Maybe it's the reason she offered the money," Julie said. "It doesn't matter. It's over. I'm never going to see Ryan again."

Or think of him. Except she had a feeling that forgetting him was going to be more difficult than she wanted it to be. If only she could go back in time and never show up for that stupid date.

Willow squeezed her arm. "You want us to not tell Mom? You know how she worries."

"That would be great," Julie said. "I'll probably have to mention it eventually, but if I could wait a while, it would be easier."

"Sure," Marina said. "Whatever you want."

Julie managed a smile. "So you two feel so sorry for me I could get you to do anything, huh?"

Her sisters nodded.

If she'd been feeling better, she might have teased them or come up with a crazy task. Instead she let them comfort her and told herself that in time, she would put all this behind her and forget she'd ever known Ryan Bennett.

Julie stared out of the window of her office and did her best to get excited about the view. Sure, she could mostly see the building next door, but to the right she could see clear to Long Beach.

She'd been promoted the previous week and had moved into larger quarters. She now had a shared assistant and a nice raise. She also had big plans to celebrate this weekend with a shopping spree. Willow and Marina had already promised to come with her.

This was all good. She was smart, successful, moving upward in her chosen career. So why couldn't she stop thinking about Ryan?

It had been three weeks since that disastrous night and morning when he'd swept into her life and made her think this time things would be different. Three weeks of remembering, of dreaming about him, of wanting him.

That's what she resented most—that her own body betrayed her. She could stay sane during the day but when she finally fell asleep, he invaded her dreams as she relived what it had been like to be with him. She woke up several times a night, aroused, hungry for his touch. These were not the signs of a woman forgetting a man.

"I want him gone," she whispered into the silence.

But how to make that happen? Until she'd found out he was a lying bastard, he'd been the best night of her life.

He was also persistent. He'd phoned three times and

sent a basket filled with chocolate, wine and season one of *Gilligan's Island* on DVD.

She placed her hand on the cool glass. Things had to get better, right? She couldn't remember him forever. It was a matter of discipline and maybe a little less coffee. She could always call Willow—the queen of all things organic—and ask if there was some kind of sleep aid to get her through this rough patch.

Julie turned to return to her desk, only she didn't exactly make it. As she took a step, the room seemed to shift and sway.

Her first thought was an earthquake, but there wasn't any noise. Her second thought was that she'd never felt so dizzy in her life. Her vision narrowed and she realized she was very possibly going to faint.

Somehow she made it to her chair where she collapsed. After a couple of deep breaths, her head cleared, but now her stomach felt all queasy.

She did a quick review of what she'd eaten that day and wondered if she had food poisoning. When that seemed unlikely, she considered a quick-onset flu. It was early in the season, but it could happen.

Wasn't there a prescription she could take? Something that would cut down how long she would be sick. Eyeing the stack of work awaiting her attention, she picked up the phone and dialed a familiar number.

"Hi, Mom, it's me. I'm good. Kind of. Is there a flu going around?"

"How do you feel?" her mother asked two hours later as Julie sat in one of Dr. Greenberg's examining rooms. One of the advantages of her mother being the man's office manager was Julie and her sisters never had to wait to get an appointment.

She'd been weighed, had her blood pressure taken, peed in a cup. Talk about thorough. "I feel weird," Julie admitted. "Queasy, but otherwise fine. I keep waiting to throw up, but I don't."

"Poor girl," Naomi said soothingly as she held her hand against her daughter's forehead.

"I'm twenty-six, Mom. Not really girl material."

Her mother smiled. "You'll always be my little girl."

Julie laughed. Right now the fussing was kind of nice.

"Let me get you something carbonated," her mother said as she headed for the door. "It might settle your stomach."

Julie watched her go. All three sisters had inherited their mother's blond hair and blue eyes. They were variations on a theme, ranging from Willow's pale blond to Julie's medium, to Marina's dark gold hair. Julie and Marina had inherited their father's height, while Willow was petite.

In her high-school science class, Julie had been fascinated by how two people could have produced three daughters who were so similar in some ways and different in others.

"Here you go." Her mother returned with an iced drink in a cartoon-character paper cup. "Dr. Greenberg will be right in."

Just then the older man stepped into the room. "Julie, you never come see me anymore. What's up with that?

Now that you're a fancy lawyer, you don't have any time for a mere doctor?"

"I do move in very special circles," she said with a grin.

Her mother waved and ducked out of the room. Dr. Greenberg took Julie's hand and leaned forward to kiss her on her cheek.

"So you're not feeling too good?" he asked.

"I don't know. It's weird. I can't tell if it's food poisoning or the flu. I thought maybe you could tell me and then give me a prescription."

He scowled at her, an expression she remembered from when she'd been little and had been scratching her rampant case of poison ivy.

"Not everything can be solved with a pill, young lady."

She fingered the long sleeve of her silk blouse. "Does this make me look too young? First Mom and now you. Do I look sixteen?"

"I'm lecturing you," he said. "You could listen and pretend to be intimidated."

"Oh. Sorry."

He shook his head and settled on the stool. "You girls." She smiled.

Dr. Greenberg had been a part of their lives for as long as Julie could remember. He was a warm, caring widower. When she'd finally figured out her father would always show up only to leave again, she'd started hoping her mother would divorce him and marry Dr. Greenberg.

"All right." He flipped through her chart. "You're basically healthy. Good blood pressure. You getting enough sleep?"

She thought about the Ryan dreams. "Too much."

"Like I believe that. You work too hard, but you can slow down a little. The firm will survive."

"Slow down? Why? What's wrong with me? Is it more serious than the flu?"

He set down her chart and looked at her. "You're going to have to be the one to decide that. You're not sick, Julie. You're pregnant."

Five

"They have a unique take on the market," Todd said from his seat across the conference table. "This would be a new area for us. We've talked about expanding and—"

Todd broke off and tossed down the folder. "Am I boring you?"

Ryan glanced at his cousin, then at the paperwork in front of him. "It sounds like a great opportunity."

Todd glowered at him. "You could at least pretend to care about the damn business. What's wrong with you? It's not that Nelson woman again? It can't be. It's been too long."

Not for him, Ryan thought, feeling both angry with himself and resigned to the situation. His attempts to contact Julie had gotten him nowhere. He'd blown it and he had to accept that. The thing was, he didn't want to.

Todd leaned toward him. "Dammit, Ryan, what's the big deal? Women have been after us since we were fifteen years old. The money is just too hard to resist. We're both sick of being the catch of the day. So why now? Why this woman?"

"An excellent question," Ryan admitted. "I don't have an answer except to say she was amazing and I destroyed any chance I had with her."

"So you pretended to be me," Todd said. "What's the big deal? If she's all that, then why can't she see the humor in the situation?"

Ryan didn't answer. He'd given Todd a very abbreviated version of his date with Julie, leaving out the fact that he'd spent the night.

"I swear, Aunt Ruth can be a pain," Todd muttered. "When she suggested I marry one of her granddaughters, I wanted to choke her."

"I wanted to help," Ryan said, knowing he'd gone into the situation willingly. The idea of exacting a little revenge had been too appealing to ignore.

He'd let his pride take charge, always a dangerous decision.

"Julie didn't do anything wrong," he said, more to himself than Todd, "and I hurt her."

"She was willing to go out with a man for money," Todd pointed out. "That's something."

Despite feeling like roadkill, Ryan smiled. "The date was free. I told her she should have held out for at least fifty thousand. After all, there had to be something significantly wrong with you for your own aunt to have to pay someone to marry you."

Predictably, Todd bristled. "She's my aunt by marriage and there's nothing wrong with me."

He and Todd were enough alike that Ryan had to agree. Despite only being cousins, they were so similar in appearance that they had often been asked if they were twins. But for once, he and Todd were going to part company. On the issue of Julie Nelson, Ryan could only have regrets.

"You're going to have to forget her," Todd said.

"I will." In time. The question was, how long would it take?

"Look at the bright side. If this went as badly as you said, I don't have to worry about the other Nelson sisters wanting to marry me. So you've derailed Aunt Ruth."

"She'll come up with another plan. You know she wants to see us both married. You got picked first because you're a whole couple of months older, but my time is coming."

He had the sudden thought that if he *had* been picked first, then his date with Julie would have been real. He would have gone, expecting nothing, determined to get rid of Julie as quickly as possible, and she still would have won him over.

He felt both sad and angry at the thought. Yes, he'd screwed up. He was willing to admit that, even crawl a little. Why was she so stubborn? Was the situation really that unrecoverable?

He already knew the answer and, as he only had himself to blame, he had nowhere to put the excess emotion.

"I'm going to the gym," he said as he stood. Maybe

a couple of hours on the running track or in the weight room would allow him to sleep tonight. Or at the very least, forget for a few minutes.

But before he could leave, the door to the conference room opened and his secretary stepped in.

"Sorry to interrupt, but there's someone here to see Ryan. A Julie Nelson. She says it's important. Should I show her in?"

Todd looked at Ryan. "She must have checked out your latest financials and realized it's a hell of a lot of money."

"Shut up," Ryan said without looking at him. "Yes, Mandy, please show her in."

Seconds later Julie walked into the room. His chest tightened and he felt as stupid and clueless as a high-school sophomore on his first date. Relief, desire and excitement battled for his attention.

She was gorgeous—tall and blond with blue eyes that flashed her every emotion. Right now they held a combination of controlled rage and contempt.

"Good morning," she said, her voice as low and sexy as it had been every night in his dreams. The navy power suit she wore concealed more than it showed, but he remembered the curves and soft skin underneath. Dear God, he remembered.

She glanced from him to Todd, then smiled coldly.

"There's enough similarity in your appearance for me to know who you are," she said. "The infamous Todd Aston III. It's my lucky day. Two snakes for the price of one. The liar and the man afraid to do his own dirty work. Your mothers must be so proud."

Todd raised his eyebrows and nodded slightly. Ryan knew his cousin well enough to read his thoughts. Todd was impressed that Julie wasn't stupid and wasn't begging. If Julie had known that, she would have probably told Todd he needed to date a wider range of women.

Ryan liked that he could predict what she was going to say—only the talent wouldn't have much use. From the looks of things, she hadn't dropped in to forgive him.

"I didn't expect to see you again," Ryan told her.

"It's all about net worth," Todd said, staring at Julie. "Isn't it?"

"I'd wondered why your aunt felt it necessary to offer money to get someone to marry you," Julie said calmly. "I'd thought the reason might have something to do with a physical impairment. Now I realize the flaw is in your personality. How unfortunate and much more difficult to fix." She looked at Ryan. "I need to speak with you privately. Now is a good time for me."

Todd stood, then raised both his hands in the air. "I'll leave," he said to Ryan. "Later you can try to explain what exactly it was that you missed."

With that he left. Ryan pointed at the empty chairs around the table. "Have a seat."

She hesitated, then sat down. He could feel the anger radiating from her.

"I called," he said, knowing it was pointless, but still compelled to make the effort.

"I got the messages."

"And the basket?"

"That's not why I'm here."

"You never said thank you."

Her eyes widened in outrage. "Excuse me? You're the one who lied. You made horrible assumptions about me and you lied about who you were and what you wanted and you're trying to take me to task because I didn't send a thank-you note?"

"I…"

She stood, which forced him to his feet.

"You lied," she repeated. "I don't do liars. I could have handled pretty much anything else, but no. That would have been too easy."

"You were there because of the money," he said, in a feeble attempt to defend himself. Apologizing hadn't worked—maybe she would respond to an offense better than defense.

"Oh, please. I was there because I recently discovered I had a grandmother and I'm still thinking I want to have a relationship with her. It was never about the money and you know it." She folded her arms over her chest. "That's what gets me the most, Ryan. You know all of that. We had a great connection. That night was…" She paused and swallowed. "Forget it."

"Julie, don't do this. Don't shut me out. You're right. It *was* a great night. Magic. That doesn't happen very often in my life. What about yours? Are you really going to walk away from that because of a mistake?"

She glared at him. "A mistake is losing your keys. You lied about who you were with the express purpose of hurting me. Magic or not, those aren't qualities I look for in a man."

Right. "So why are you here?"

She sucked in a breath, then stared him in the eye. "I'm pregnant. We had sex and we didn't use anything. Didn't even discuss it, which is pretty dumb, but there we are. My excuse is I haven't been in a relationship for over a year and wasn't on anything. I won't presume to know what your excuse is."

He heard the words, but they didn't mean anything. His body froze and his brain stopped working.

Pregnant…as in *pregnant*?

"How?" he asked before he could stop himself. He shook his head. "Never mind. I know the answer to that."

"How comforting."

Pregnant. He couldn't comprehend what that meant. Sure, having kids had always been something he'd known would happen eventually, but now? Like this? With a woman who hated him?

The timing sucked the big one, but a baby? He found himself kind of liking the idea.

Julie sat down. She would have preferred to stay standing, but these days she was always at risk of being a little woozy. Some women could go their entire pregnancy without feeling symptoms. She'd managed to get her first one less than a month after conception. Was that just her luck?

Only she couldn't be upset. Even as Ryan stood there looking shocked and ready to bolt, she couldn't be unhappy. Not about having a child.

"I wasn't sure if I should even tell you," she said, probably shocking him with her honesty, but she had no choice. She was a big fan of the truth. "I've debated for the past two days. But you are the father and you have the right to know." She drew in a breath. "Just so we're all clear, I'm keeping the baby."

"I'm glad."

Really? Color her surprised. But then what did she really know about Ryan?

Except that he was a liar, of course.

"You can sign away your rights and I'll take full responsibility," she said, wondering if he would. It was the easy out, the most practical. Most men would jump at the chance. A week ago, she would have assumed *she* would have jumped at the chance.

But something had happened. The second Dr. Greenberg had said she was pregnant, Julie's heart had nearly burst with joy. She'd never much thought about having children. They had been far in her future. Yet knowing there was a life growing inside of her had changed everything. In that moment, she'd suddenly felt her life had meaning and purpose, which theoretically it had had before, but not in such a big way.

A baby. No, a miracle.

He braced his arms on the table and leaned toward her. "No," he said clearly. "I *will* be a father to my child."

Great. Because morning sickness wasn't enough of a hassle. "You don't have to do this to look good. No one needs to know."

His dark gaze locked with hers. "I will be a father to my child," he said again, his voice low and forceful. "I *want* to."

He looked good. Too good. She hated that she still found him tempting. She wanted to lean toward him as well, so their mouths were close. She wanted to breathe in the scent of him and touch him and be touched. She wanted him to make the bad parts of their last time together go away so they could have the good parts again and again.

"Obviously we'll have to work something out," she said calmly so he wouldn't guess what she'd been thinking. "As I'm less than a month along, we have time to deal with all this."

She rose and pulled a business card out of her jacket pocket. She'd put it there earlier and had written her home number on the back. Of course she'd hoped he would agree to walk away from the child, but based on how her luck was going lately, it hadn't seemed likely.

She held out the card.

"That's it?" he asked.

"What do you mean?"

"You have nothing else to say? Nothing else you want to talk about?"

She set her card on the table and shrugged. "There isn't anything else. I'm pregnant. That's for me to deal with. When there's a child, you can get involved. Between now and then, I suppose we'll talk."

"You mean I'll call and you'll ignore my messages."

She thought about the times he'd phoned her office. "I won't ignore them this time."

"I'm not sure I believe that."

She picked up her purse. "I'm not the one who lies."

"Are you ever going to let that go?"

"No."

He took a step toward her. "Julie, we're having a baby together. You have to forgive me sometime."

"Actually, I don't," she said, then turned on her heel and left.

Six

Ryan spent the afternoon in his office, not working.

Pregnant. He knew he'd been there and he knew what had happened, but it still seemed impossible that a single night could produce a baby.

Todd walked in and slumped on the leather sofa by the window.

"So what did she want?" he asked, then shook his head. "No, wait. I want to guess. She's forgiven all and desperately wants to be with you."

"Did she act like either of those was true?"

Todd shrugged. "She was mad, sure, but was it real or an act? Come on. We've seen it all. Some of them are better than others."

At one time Ryan would have agreed with his cousin.

Recently he'd become convinced there weren't any honest women left. But he'd been wrong.

"She's pregnant."

Todd straightened and stared at him. Then he swore and flopped back on the sofa. "You're totally screwed," he said glumly. "Doesn't it just figure. She wins in the end."

"No one's winning," Ryan said. "We're dealing. She asked me if I wanted to sign away rights."

"And in return she'd ask you for nothing?" Todd shook his head. "I won't believe it until I see the paperwork myself."

"I told her no."

"Of course you did."

"This isn't what I would have planned, but now that it's happened…" He didn't know what to say. In truth, the thought of a kid of his own was appealing.

Todd frowned. "Don't go all father and son on me."

"I wouldn't mind a daughter."

Todd groaned.

Ryan grinned. "Look at the bright side. I read somewhere that a child gets most of its intelligence from the mother. Julie's bright enough that her kid could grow up to save the world."

"*You* need saving right now. You barely know this woman and now you're having a baby with her? If she offered you an out, you need to think about taking it."

"No."

"Look what happened last time."

"This is different. I won't be a stepfather. I'll be involved from the beginning. We'll make decisions together."

"You sure about that?"

"Julie has every right to be pissed at me."

"I don't agree but we'll go with it," Todd said. "Fine. She's pissed and are you so sure she'll get over it? Or play straight with you? Are you even sure the kid is yours?"

Ryan stared at his cousin. "Have you always been such a cynical bastard?"

"We both are."

"Not anymore."

"No way." Todd rested one ankle on the opposite knee. "You can't tell me this changes anything. You met her, you liked her, you obviously slept with her, which I'll now point out you didn't tell me."

"It didn't seem relevant."

"All evidence to the contrary. You have no way of knowing who she was with the night or week before she met you. Okay, sure, assume it's yours, but protect yourself, Ryan. It makes sense."

It did make sense, he thought. The thing was, he knew it wasn't necessary. Something in his gut told him that Julie was telling the truth.

"Maybe she planned this," Todd said. "Maybe she set the whole thing up."

"Right. She arranged to reconcile with a grand-mother she didn't know she had, confident Ruth would insist one of the sisters go out on a date with you. Then she waited until the perfect night of her cycle, arranged the date, seduced me, dragged me home and slept with me without knowing if I would use a condom, all the while hoping she would get knocked up."

"It could happen," Todd muttered.

"You're making me rethink our partnership."

"I'm looking out for you. I know you, Ryan. You have that damned honorable streak. You keep it hidden, but I know it's there. You lied to her and even though you were justified and angry at the time, you hate that you did it. Now the woman is pregnant and you're feeling responsible. Don't be stupid."

"I won't be."

"Like I believe that. At least don't do anything until after the kid is born and you get a DNA test, okay? I can get you the name of a good lawyer."

Ryan appreciated Todd's intentions, but they weren't necessary. "Julie *is* a good lawyer."

"I meant the name of one who isn't out to screw you."

Unfortunately Ryan doubted Julie would ever want that again. He'd spent their brief meeting thinking about getting her naked again and he would bet money that she'd been planning fifty ways to skin him alive.

"Are you sure she isn't in it for the money?" Todd asked.

"Yes."

"I'm not. Ryan you're the closest thing I'll ever have to a brother. Remember what happened last time. I don't want you worked over again."

"Julie wouldn't do that."

"How do you know?"

Ryan didn't have an answer. It was something he felt, not something he could prove or explain.

In truth, Todd had a point. Ryan knew very little about Julie. It was possible she was just in it for the money. Maybe this was a game to her. But honest to God, he couldn't begin to care if she was.

Which said what about him?

"She's not like that," he said at last.

Todd shook his head. "They're all like that."

"Why am I meeting you here?" Willow asked as she climbed out of her car and glanced around at the shopping center. As Julie had requested, she'd parked in front of the office-supply store. "Is there a sale on paper clips or colored pens?"

Julie waited until her sister had joined her on the sidewalk. "I have something to tell you."

"You don't want to be a lawyer anymore? You're going into retail?"

"Almost."

"Don't make any big decisions now, while you're still in recovery from jerk-man. He's not worth it."

"I appreciate the support."

Delicate little Willow was also so passionate about everything. Unfortunately, when guys looked at her, they tended to see a best friend or a buddy. But one day the right man would open his eyes and be swept away. Julie hoped he was up for the ride.

"So I have something to tell you," Julie said as she led her sister past the office-supply center and toward the baby store next door. "I left out a small detail of my night with Ryan."

"He's a hermaphrodite?" Willow asked with a grin. "Because that would have made things really weird."

"More weird than you know." Julie faced her and

stared into blue eyes that were so much like her own. "I slept with him."

Willow surprised her by nodding slowly. "I kind of figured that."

"What? How? I didn't say anything." Julie had always thought she was *good* at keeping secrets. "I didn't even hint."

"You didn't have to. You were more upset than you needed to be and that's more my flaw or even Marina's. Not yours. So I figured there had to be a reason. Sleeping with Ryan was the most logical."

Julie sighed. Her sisters knew her and she knew them. That was at the core of their closeness. "I'd been looking forward to your shock and outrage."

"I could get huffy now, if that would help."

"I appreciate that, but I'm okay. Still, there's one more thing." She motioned to the baby store.

This time she got the reaction she'd been expecting before. Willow turned slowly, then froze in place. Her eyes widened, her mouth dropped open and she gave a strangled sound.

"You're pregnant," she breathed. "Oh no. Pregnant? Really? By Ryan?"

"Uh-huh. It was a busy night." Julie went for humor because if she actually sat down and thought about the mess she was in, she got overwhelmed.

"Pregnant." Willow reached for her hand. "What do you think? Are you happy?"

Julie smiled. "Yeah, I really am. I never thought much about kids except as something to get to later, but the second I found out, I knew I wanted this baby."

"Have you told Ryan?"

"Yesterday."

"What did he say?"

"Not much of anything. He looked a little shell-shocked, then said we needed to talk. We exchanged business cards."

Willow frowned. "That's it? Shouldn't there have been more?"

"I don't know." Julie felt unsettled about her conversation with him, but she couldn't figure out why. "He wasn't expecting to see me again, so under the circumstances he did okay. The baby threw him, but then it threw me, too. We'll deal with things when we have to. I offered to let him sign away his responsibilities, but he refused."

She hadn't really expected him to accept, which was strange. Wouldn't a man who felt comfortable lying to a woman he'd never met about whom he was and then sleeping with her seem the perfect candidate for baby abandonment?

"So you're in this together," Willow said.

"Sort of. Until there's an actual baby, I don't plan to hang out with him much."

Willow squeezed her arm. "A baby. Are you excited?"

"Yes. I am. Scared, too, but mostly excited."

"I get to be an aunt and buy presents and babysit." Willow's hold on her arm tightened. "Maybe it was supposed to happen this way. Maybe he's your—"

Julie groaned. "Don't say it, I beg you. Ryan is not my destiny."

"But you never know."

"I know. Now, come on. Let's go look at baby furniture. We have a nursery to plan."

"Your eleven o'clock is here," Leah said as she poked her head into Julie's office. "Cute guy."

Julie smiled at her assistant—the one she shared with two other second-year associates. "Do you tell that sort of thing to Mark and James?"

"Mark, no," Leah said cheerfully. "But there are rumors about James, so he might be interested if you're not."

"You're bad."

"Yes, I am. In every way possible."

Leah was a fifty-something grandmother who was also a brilliant assistant. She'd been with the firm longer than most senior partners and refused to work for any of them, contending that the associates needed her more. She'd been invaluable to Julie on more than one occasion.

Julie glanced at her calendar and saw the next hour blocked simply by a "potential client" notation. No name, no stated reason for the appointment. Interesting. Leah usually filled in the details.

Julie picked up a legal pad, her pen and BlackBerry, then walked down the long corridor to the main foyer.

As she stepped onto the polished marble floor by the round reception desk, she came to a stop so quickly, her feet nearly slid out from under her.

Ryan Bennett stood talking to Ethan Jackson, a senior partner in the firm.

Her psyche neatly split in two with her body and her emotions sighing at the sight of Ryan and her brain wanting to spit fire.

He could *not* be her potential new client, she thought frantically. How on earth could she do business with the man who had lied about who he was, slept with her and was now the father of her unborn child? That wasn't anyone's life—that was a movie-of-the-week plot.

It wasn't fair. It wasn't right. If he thought he could weasel his way into her world with a big check to her law firm then he... Damn, then he was right.

His venture-capital company was big business and it was her job to help the firm's bottom line. Second-year associates who wanted to make it to partner didn't turn down millions of dollars in billing for personal reasons. Assuming that's what he was here for.

She sucked in a deep breath, vowed she would ignore how good he looked in his suit and how much she remembered about his mouth on her body, stepped forward and smiled.

"Good morning, Ethan."

Both men turned to her.

"Julie," Ethan said as he nodded. "Good. You have a new client here. Ryan Bennett, meet Julie Nelson."

"We've met," Julie said, wanting to get everything out in the open. Well, everything except the fact that she'd slept with Ryan on their first and only date and was now pregnant. Talk about tacky.

"That's right," Ryan said easily. "We're almost related. My great-aunt by marriage is Julie's grandmother. Due to some family estrangements, we only met a few weeks ago."

Ethan gave her an approving glance. She was sure her

relationship with Ryan would be discussed at the next partner meeting and a little star would go next to her name.

"I'm here to talk about our business in China," Ryan continued. "We have several companies looking to get 'the China price' on various items, along with some companies wanting to do manufacturing there. I'm hoping your expertise can make a difference."

Ethan looked happier than Julie had ever seen him. "Then I'll leave you two to get this going. Let me know how you progress, Julie."

"Of course," she said, holding in a sigh. If Ryan was serious about bringing that much business to the firm, they would be working very closely together. The thought of that closeness made her uncomfortable and far too aware of him.

"Let's step into a conference room," she said and led the way.

When the glass paneled door was carefully shut and she'd offered both coffee and bottled water, which he refused, she took a seat across from his.

"What's this all about?" she asked, keeping her voice low, her expression controlled. This particular room had mostly glass walls. She'd chosen it deliberately, so that they would both be forced to keep things polite.

"I told you. When we had dinner, you mentioned you dealt with international concerns and that you speak Mandarin. It seemed like a good fit."

"Are you setting me up?" she asked bluntly. "Do you plan to dangle all these billable hours in front of me and one of the partners, only to pull them back later? Whatever you may think, I didn't get pregnant on purpose. If your plan is to get me fired, thinking then you'll have an easier time manipulating me, you can forget it. I'm one of the best lawyers you'll ever come up against and I won't let you mess things up for me."

He swore under his breath. "Is that what you think? That I'm doing this to set you up? That it's a joke?"

"I don't know. You're the one who decided I deserved to be taught a lesson. Why shouldn't I think the worst?"

"Did it ever occur to you I might be here to do business? That I'm accepting what I did was wrong and even though I've apologized that doesn't begin to make it right. Did it occur to you that I'm doing my best to make a difficult situation easier for both of us, but mostly you. We need a good international lawyer. Todd and I were discussing that and I thought of you. That's it. No hidden agenda."

It was a good speech, but was he telling the truth? "I want to believe you," she said.

"So give it a try." He leaned forward. "Julie, why would I want to set you up? Why would I want to hurt you any more than I have? I know this is going to be difficult for you to believe, but I'm actually a pretty decent guy."

She raised her eyebrows. "You lied."

"Yes, I did. It was a moment of bad judgment. Ever have one of those?"

She touched her stomach. "Maybe."

"You can't keep running from me."

"As you're sitting across from me," she said, "I'm not running."

"You know what I mean. Look, I'm here to talk to you about helping us out. Strictly business. I've checked around and you're good at what you do. I need someone good. If, in the process, we have a chance to get to know each other in a less charged situation, isn't that for the best?"

"I guess." He was being so logical and rational. Normally she appreciated that. But along with the wooziness, she seemed to be fighting some pretty impressive mood swings. "If you're sincere about the business—"

"I am."

"Then let's talk."

"Good. Okay."

He smiled. It shouldn't have meant anything. Men smiled all the time. But there was something about Ryan's smile, about the way he stared into her eyes, as if she had his full attention. He made her knees go weak and she wasn't even standing.

"Is that offer for coffee still open?" he asked.

"Sure. How do you take it?"

"Black."

She stood and shook her head. "Such a typical guy."

"Of course. Come on. Admit it—you'd have no respect for me if I asked for three sugars and hazelnut flavored cream."

That made her laugh. "You're right. I'll be back."

"I'll come with you."

"You don't have to." Her plan had been to escape for a minute and get herself together. Having him tag along would make the whole "get together" bit complicated.

But there was no polite way to say no, so she led him

into the break room and grabbed a clean mug from the tray by the full coffeepot.

"You don't have staff?" he asked.

"I do, but I prefer not to waste her time on errands. The other two associates I share her with don't agree with my position." She glanced at him over her shoulder. "Leah likes me much better."

"I'm sure she does."

He smiled again and Julie found herself caught up in the moment. Unfortunately, she was pouring coffee at the time and when the mug was full, the hot liquid poured over the sides and onto her hand.

"Ouch!"

She set the mug on the counter and shook off her hand, her skin burning. Suddenly Ryan was at her side. He took the pot from her, then nudged her over to the sink. While standing behind her, he took her injured hand in his and held it under the cold water.

"I didn't know you were a klutz," he said conversationally.

"I'm not usually."

She wasn't. She'd been distracted. She still was.

He stood right behind her—his front pressing against her back. She could feel the strength and power of his body, along with the heat.

Warmth seeped into her, making her want to sigh and rub and stroke. She could feel his fingers on her hand, his arm pressing against her. He was leaning forward, his face right next to hers.

If she turned just a little bit to the right, their mouths would be inches apart.

She wanted to kiss him. It didn't matter that she practically hated him, she still felt longing building up inside of her.

Just one kiss. It didn't have to last very long. Just mouths pressing, tongues stroking, bodies—

She jerked her hand free and stepped to the side. "I'm good. Thanks."

She pulled a paper towel from the holder and dried her hand, then mopped up the spill on the counter. After collecting a bottle of water for herself, she led the way back to the conference room.

Her insides felt soft and mushy. Her panties were damp and that place between her thighs was swollen and achy.

Pathetic, she thought grimly as she sat down and tried to gather her thoughts together. She was deeply pathetic. How could he have reduced her to a puddle after just one night? Sure, it had been a great night, but she'd had great nights before.

Well, not that great. But still.

She reached for her pen. "Why don't you outline what you have in mind," she said.

Ryan began to talk about the business. Julie took notes, but she wasn't really listening. How could he be so unaffected by what had just happened? Wouldn't that be horrible—if the attraction was all one-sided? Life couldn't possibly be that unfair.

"We provide venture capital and retain a major interest in each of our companies. The goal is to take them all public, but when that doesn't happen, we sometimes sell them. Right now there are three specific firms I need help with. Two are looking to do business with

China, while the third is perfect for overseas manufacturing. I assume you have contacts in China."

She looked at him. Now it was her turn to smile. "Of course. Personal as well as professional."

"Want to explain that?"

"We had a neighbor when I was growing up. Mrs. Wu had been a teacher. She retired only to discover she was bored with too much time on her hands. She taught my sisters and I Mandarin. I'm the only one who was really interested. When I was in high school, she took me to China with her to visit her family. I went back the following two summers and did a semester in China during college."

"Impressive."

"Thank you."

"What happens now?" he asked. "You'll want specific information on the companies."

"Absolutely. Also what, if anything, you've already done to establish relationships in China. We'll work on a retainer agreement, with my time billed in quarter-hour segments."

"Seems reasonable."

"I'll want a substantial sum up front."

She would ask for more than the firm usually suggested, mostly to cover her butt.

He sipped his coffee. "You still don't trust me."

"I'm willing to give you the benefit of the doubt, but I'm not willing to be stupid." No matter how her body reacted to him.

"Fair enough." His dark gaze settled on her face. "Todd and I are both only children. We grew up spending a lot of time together. We became as close as brothers."

"A bit of a non sequitur, but okay. And I already know this part. It's why you agreed to do his dirty work."

He ignored her. "We grew up rich. From the time we were teenagers there were girls, then later women, willing to do anything to get close. They weren't interested in us—they wanted the money."

"I refuse to believe every female you've ever met has ignored who you are in favor of your bank account."

"Not everyone, but enough. Under the circumstances, knowing what our aunt had promised you and your sisters, it wasn't unreasonable I think that about you."

Julie opened her mouth, then closed it. Okay, maybe she could see his point. "I know what it looks like, but that isn't the way it is."

"I believe you. Can you do the same? Can you possibly understand why Todd and I might suspect you weren't any different?"

"I don't know. Maybe. So don't go on the date. Refuse. Setting up a stranger to teach her a lesson to punish her for every other bitchy female you've met isn't right."

"Agreed. So you *can* see my side?"

He was starting to get on her nerves. What did he want? "Yes, your childhood was very tragic. Poor rich boys liked by millions for all the wrong reasons."

"You're not easy."

"I don't try to be. I've said I'll try to understand why you thought the worst of me and I'll accept your apology for what you did, but that doesn't mean I approve of it or even understand your actions. I still don't trust you."

"You're going to have to try. We'll be a family."

On what planet? "Not under any definition I can think of. We'll be co-parenting a child. That doesn't make us a family."

"You can call it what you want," he told her, "but having a baby together makes us a family. Everything has changed, Julie. There's more here than what each of us feels. There's a third life. Our child deserves the best from us. That's why I think we should get married."

Seven

"Married?" Julie sprang to her feet and stared down at Ryan. "Are you insane? *Married?* What the hell is wrong with you?"

She suddenly remembered the glass walls and sat down again. She lowered her voice, but she wasn't any less pissed off.

"If this is your idea of a joke, it's not funny. It's horrible." Married? What was he thinking? And just when she'd decided he might not be so awful after all.

"Horrible?" he asked, sounding disgustingly calm. "How so?"

"We don't even *like* each other," she muttered. "What about being married would be pleasant?"

"I do like you," he said. "Aside from a single act you

can't forgive, I think you like me. Getting married for the sake of a baby is a time-honored tradition."

"In what century?"

Had he really said he liked her? She shook her head. She had to get a grip. Who cared if he liked her? She would never marry Ryan—not in her lifetime.

"We're rational, intelligent adults," Ryan said. "We're having a baby together. We'll both want our child to have the best of everything and that means having both parents around. Do you really want to be a single mother?"

"Yes. I'm fine with it. I was raised by a single mother." Sort of. Technically there was a father, but it wasn't as if he'd ever bothered to stay more than fifteen minutes at a time.

"I think it's important to have both parents around if at all possible," he told her.

"Great, but it's not possible."

"Why?"

Why? She hated that he was sitting there, discussing this, all cool and composed while she was wishing they were in the law library so she could throw some really heavy books at his head.

"I don't want to marry you," she said, making her words as clear as possible.

"Why not?"

She was going to kill him and it wasn't going to be her fault. "I don't know you. Despite what your ego-inflated brain tells you, I don't particularly like you. I'm not interested in getting married for some arcane sociological reason and I think a single parent can do a perfectly excellent job."

"We could try."

What was with him? Why did he keep pushing? And why was she both furious and incredibly sad?

"I don't want to try. Not with you."

"Okay. So it's not me," he said. "You object to marriage in general."

"I do not. I want to get married. Someday." When men stopped lying to her. "Just not now and not to you. You're a man who assumes all women are after his money. I couldn't stand that."

"You're saying you'd object to a prenuptial agreement? Protecting my assets is only reasonable."

Right now he should be a whole lot more worried about his ass than his assets, she thought grimly as she briefly glanced around, looking for something sharp so she could stab him.

"You need to go," she said between gritted teeth. "Seriously, I have work to do. I know you don't understand how I could possibly turn down your incredibly flattering offer. Based on your view of women, there must be thousands who would take the plunge, especially after such a romantic proposal. Be still my heart. Wait. It is."

One corner of his mouth twitched, as if he found this funny. That made her want to grind him into dust.

"So much energy," he said in an infuriatingly soothing tone. "Makes me wonder what you're hiding. Getting married isn't all that unexpected a concept, Julie. So what are you really upset about?"

She stood. "This has been fabulous. We should do it again. Maybe have a party, exchange gift bags."

He stood and walked around to her side of the table, took her hand and pushed her back into a corner of the room. One where they were out of sight of anyone walking by.

"I'm not going to leave this alone," he said, staring into her eyes and making her thighs whimper. "Whatever you say, whatever you do, I'm sticking around. This is my child and my life, too. Don't think you can hide from me forever."

Then he kissed her. Right there in the office, in front of an empty conference table and a display cabinet holding some very expensive crystal pieces.

He pressed his lips to hers in a move that was both erotic and possessive. The heat was as instantaneous as it was intense. Her fingers itched to grab hold of him and never let go. The rest of her body just wanted to be naked and plastered against his.

She fought against her desire to deepen the kiss, but before she could either win or lose the battle, he stepped back.

"Have the paperwork drawn up for the retainer agreement and sent over to my office," he said. "I'll messenger it back with a check."

What? Oh, yeah. Work. "I'm not interested in working with you."

"Maybe not, but you want the account, so you'll suffer. And Julie?"

She carefully wiped her mouth with her fingers before answering. "Yes?"

"How ever much you try to deny it—I know the truth. You *do* like me."

* * *

"I love bagels," Marina said as she emptied the bag. "I love the smell of them toasting, slathering them with cream cheese, taking them out onto the patio and eating one while sipping coffee and reading the Sunday paper."

Julie glanced at Willow. "Okay, I'm suddenly hungry. How about you?"

"Starved. Mom won't be back for another half hour or so. We could snack."

"There's plenty to choose from."

In one of those unexpected quirks of fate, Julie had finished up all her work on Friday and hadn't had to go into the office on Saturday morning. With nothing to fill her time except brooding, she decided to go to the farmer's market and wander around. She'd indulged herself with tons of fresh fruits and vegetables, a sinfully gooey Danish and a baker's dozen of fresh bagels that she'd shared with her sisters.

Marina pulled out the three bagels she would take home with her and put them in a separate bag. "So how are you feeling?"

"Good."

"Not that I need to know," Marina continued as if her sister hadn't spoken. "I'm used to you keeping things from me."

Julie groaned. "I invited you to join Willow and me last week, but you had that microbiology class."

"Inorganic chemistry, but thanks for being interested."

"Marina, come on. I told you as soon as you got home."

"Yes, you did." Her sister smiled at her. "So I still love you."

"Great. Another conditional relationship. What happened to unconditional love forever?"

"We put it in the recycling bin," Willow said helpfully. "It's too late to get it back. They've already picked up." She dumped the container of blueberries that had cost a fortune from the colander into a bowl. "Berry?"

"Thanks." Julie grabbed a handful as she sank onto a stool by the center island.

"What's wrong?" Marina asked. "You seem, I don't know, not yourself."

"I'm fine. Sort of."

Willow wrinkled her nose. "That doesn't sound good. Are you sick? Too much queasiness?"

"No. I can handle that. It's just…" Julie hadn't decided if she was going to mention Ryan's stupid proposal, but suddenly she couldn't keep it to herself.

"He came to see me yesterday," she began.

"Ryan?" Marina asked helpfully.

Julie nodded. "He made an appointment. He's dangling his company's China business in front of me and I don't like it. One of the partners met him and now sees flashing dollar signs. It would be a lot in billable hours."

"Which sounds good," Willow said cautiously. "So what's the problem?"

"I don't trust him. What if he's just playing another sick, twisted game? What if he sets this all up and then disappears, taking his billable hours with him? I would look stupid in front of the partners. It wouldn't be good for my career."

Marina and Willow glanced at each other and then at her.

"Um, don't take this wrong," Willow said quietly, "but why would he do that? What does he have to gain?"

"I don't know. Just to screw with me. Don't forget this was a guy intent on teaching me a lesson, even though he'd never met me and knew nothing about me."

"That was wrong," Marina said. "But this is totally different. Julie, I can't believe he wants to hurt your career. You're having a baby together—why would he want to hurt the mother of his child?"

"To get control. That's all he cares about."

Julie knew she didn't sound exactly rational, but she couldn't seem to keep a grip on her emotions. "I just…" She swallowed and found herself fighting tears. "Okay, I'm weak. That's it, the truth in all its ickiness. I know better than to expect a guy to be decent. I know better than to dream about someone who's honest and caring. I know I should let the romantic dreams go and I try. I really try. But then when I least expect it, they pop back up and I'm hopeful and then the hopes get crushed and I want to slap myself for being so stupid in the first place."

"I love you like a sister," Willow said, which made Julie almost smile. "But what on earth are you talking about?"

"He asked me to marry him."

"Okay, then," Marina said, sliding on to the stool next to Julie's. "Start at the beginning and talk slowly."

Willow pushed aside the berries and leaned against the counter. "You have our full attention. I promise."

"There's not much to tell," Julie said with a sigh. "He came to the office yesterday."

She explained how Ryan had spoken about his three companies and how they needed help. "Then somehow we were talking about personal stuff, how he and Todd were close when they grew up and how women only wanted them for their money."

"It could happen," Marina said.

"Poor little rich boys," Willow muttered sarcastically.

"That's what I told him. Anyway, we were talking about that and then he said we should get married. That it was the best thing for the baby." She paused, then shrugged. "I didn't take it well."

"Why?" Willow asked.

"Because… He really ticked me off. You don't propose just like that. It's wrong. We barely know each other. I don't trust him and, based on how he treated me, he doesn't trust me. It's not exactly a basis for a successful marriage. I got angry."

"I get it," Willow told her. "He violated those secret dreams you're not supposed to have. It wasn't romantic and perfect and he doesn't love you."

"I refuse to have a weak side," Julie said. "I'm tough."

"You're human," Willow said.

"But it *was* romantic," Marina said.

Julie rolled her eyes. "Here we go."

"It's true," her baby sister insisted. "You get married because you have to, then you fall madly in love. It's fabulous."

"She's insane," Julie muttered.

"At least he was willing to do the right thing," Willow said. "I know he was totally in the wrong on your date. Lying like that. But you know, I kind of don't totally blame him. It's really that Todd Aston's fault. He's the one who was too big a jerk to show up and talk to you himself."

Julie thought they were both rats. "Ryan had his own agenda. Don't make him into the hero of the night."

"I won't, but maybe there's a chance he's not all bad."

"A tiny one."

"So you won't consider his proposal?" Marina asked.

"Not even on a bet. It would be dumb to marry a man I barely know just because I'm pregnant."

There was a sound from the doorway. Julie looked up to find her mother standing there.

This was *so* not how she wanted to tell the news.

Willow and Marina disappeared into the back of the house. Julie stayed on her stool and watched her mother make coffee.

"It's decaf," Naomi Nelson said as she flipped on the switch.

"Thanks."

Her mother turned to face her.

Naomi had run away with her one true love when she'd been just eighteen. She'd been pregnant and Julie's birth had been followed by two more babies in the next two years. Naomi had been all of twenty-five the first time her husband had left.

Julie remembered very little of that day, except her mother's crying. She'd been six and had just started the first grade. She'd brought home a picture she'd done in class, but her mother had been too sad to look at it. From that day on, she'd never been able to work on a school art project without remembering her mother's tears.

"So," her mother said calmly. "What's new?"

"Oh, Mom. I'm sorry. I didn't mean for you to find out that way."

"Did you mean for me to find out at all? You're pregnant, Julie, and you didn't tell me."

Naomi was slim, pretty and not yet fifty. Yet suddenly, she looked older than Julie had ever seen her. Her blue eyes were dark with emotion, but hurt rather than anger.

"I'm sorry," Julie repeated. "I was going to, I just didn't know how to say the words. I didn't plan this. In fact I messed up big time."

"Did you think I'd judge you?" her mother asked. "When have I ever done that?"

Julie shifted uncomfortably on the chair. "I don't usually screw up like this."

"Then you'll need some help getting through it. What happened?"

"I went on the date with Todd."

Her mother shook her head. "I thought you girls had decided not to do that."

"We had, but it seemed so important to Ruth and it was only one date." Julie stopped. "Mom, no one blames you for what happened with your mother."

Ruth had not approved of Naomi's relationship with Jack Nelson. When Naomi had run off with him, Ruth had cut her daughter out of her life.

"I appreciate that. I don't blame myself either. So the baby is Todd's?"

"Not exactly." Julie explained how Ryan had taken Todd's place and how she'd been swept away. "He wanted to teach me a lesson. He was playing me for a fool. Now he says he's sorry and he thinks we should try to have a relationship. Honestly, how can I ever trust the guy?"

Her mother was quiet for a few seconds. "I don't know if you can. Do you want to?"

Did she? "Maybe. Sometimes. I don't know. We're having a baby together—there's a complication." Julie stopped and smiled. "Mom, I'm having a baby."

Her mother moved close and hugged her. "I know. How do you feel? Are you happy?"

Julie leaned back and touched her arm. "I am thrilled beyond words. I never thought about having kids except in the abstract, but now that I'm pregnant, I'm really excited. I want this child. I can't believe how much."

"You were never one to explore your softer side," her mother said. "You always felt you had to be in charge and take care of everyone else. There wasn't a whole lot of energy left over for you to think about yourself. I'm glad you want the baby. You're going to be a wonderful mother."

The unexpected praise made her eyes fill with tears.

"Thanks," she murmured, feeling awkward and grateful at the same time. "You're my role model. You did great with us. We can't have been easy, what with you on your own."

As soon as she said the words, she wanted to call them back.

"I wasn't on my own," her mother said. "Your father was here."

"A few weeks a year," Julie said before she could stop herself. "Mom, come on. I know you love him, but he wasn't a good husband or a good father."

Her mother bristled. "He's still your father. You will talk about him with respect."

"Why? I don't get it. I've never understood why you let him come and go as he pleases."

"It's your father's nature. He's restless. But that doesn't make him a bad man."

"It doesn't make him a good one either."

Julie wondered why she bothered. They'd had this same discussion a hundred times before. She would never understand how her mother could give her heart to a man who thought so little of her that he would disappear for months at a time. Then he'd return with gifts and wild stories, staying just long enough to convince everyone that this time was different, that this time he would stay. Only he never did.

Julie had stopped believing in him a long time ago but her mother led with her heart.

"He's not a man to be tied down," her mother said quietly. "I've accepted that. I wish you could. This will always be his home and I will always be his wife."

"I can't do that. I can't understand him and I won't forgive him."

"Having a child changes you," her mother told her. "It changes everything."

Julie knew it wouldn't change her enough to see her father's view of the world, but that didn't matter. She shifted the subject to something less divisive.

"Ryan thinks we should get married," she said.

"What do you think?"

"That he's crazy. We've had one date. Okay, it went really well until he admitted he was a lying rat, but that's not enough to build a life on." She looked at her mother. "You're going to tell me I should marry him, aren't you?"

"I'm going to say that he's your baby's father and that you need to meet him at least halfway."

"What if I don't want to?"

Her mother smiled. "That's mature. I'm so proud."

"Mo-om."

"Julie, life is about compromise. What Ryan did was wrong. If he's really the jerk you say, then why is he going to all this trouble to convince you he's sorry? Jerks don't bother with things like that. And how is marrying you a win for him? If he was only interested in the victory, he's already slept with you."

"Ouch."

"I'm just saying that men who are into the conquest for the sake of numbers don't hang around. He's hung around. He says he wants to be a father to his child. That's not a bad thing. You don't have to marry him. You don't have to do anything. But you might want to think about getting to know him. Start there and see where it goes. Maybe he's secretly a good man."

"You think?" Julie asked. "With my luck?"

Her mother's words made sense, but Julie so didn't want to go there. She wanted to stay mad. It was safer. Getting to know Ryan meant putting herself at risk. What if she started to believe in him? He would only hurt her.

"Not every man is Garrett," her mother said.

"You want to bet?"

Eight

Ryan lived in a high rise condo that was all glass and steel. Julie was sure there had to be more to the construction because this was L.A. and earthquakes were a certainty. Regardless of what high-tech innovation kept the building standing, she was unimpressed by the modern coldness of it all. Sure, the location was great and the concierge service would take care of all the details of life, but she preferred her slightly scruffy neighborhood where lawns were normal and kids played on the sidewalk.

Of course being critical of Ryan's building was a fabulous distraction, she admitted as she stepped off the elevator and walked down the hall to his condo. She'd decided to take her mother's advice from the previous weekend and get to know the man. She'd called him and suggested they get together, and he'd offered lunch at his place.

She rang the bell. He answered right away.

He seemed taller than she remembered, but maybe her brain was fuzzy from the shock of seeing him in casual clothes. The designer suit was gone. In its place were worn and faded jeans and a long-sleeved white shirt. Both emphasized his lean strength.

His shirt was open at the collar, exposing a tanned chest and a light dusting of hair. She remembered touching him there, running her hands across his warm skin and feeling him react to her caress. Of course she'd pretty much touched him everywhere, and that memory playground was a place she wanted to avoid.

"You made it," he said. "Come on in."

"It wasn't that hard to find."

"I thought you might change your mind," he admitted. "After last time."

Right. Last time. Their fight in her office, because he'd proposed. Just thinking about it made her angry enough to spit, although honestly, she'd never spit in her life. But if anyone was going to make her, it was Ryan.

Still, she wasn't here to argue with him. "You said on the phone we could pretend that never happened."

He smiled. "You're right. So this is me pretending. Come on in."

He stepped back and she entered the foyer. The shock was instant. They were the only living things in a room of glass and metal.

"I think it's important we get to know each other," she told him, deciding it was polite to ignore the stark surroundings. "The baby isn't going away and neither are you. So here we are."

He smiled. "But you'd like me to go away."

"It would uncomplicate my life."

"Boring isn't better."

"I'm not talking boring," she said. "Just a few less surprises."

"I'll try to keep them at a minimum. So we're having a truce with lunch?"

"I'm willing. We'll think of it as a spicy side dish."

His dark gaze settled on her face. "Meaning I shouldn't mistake your pleasant conversation for forgiveness?"

She'd hoped they could avoid discussing what had happened, but maybe that was impossible. "I'm working on it."

"I understand. You're not easy. I respect that."

Despite her nervousness, she laughed. "Apparently I am easy. That's what got me into this position."

He took a step toward her and lowered his voice. "You're not easy—I'm irresistible."

"Why doesn't that make me feel any better?"

"I'm not sure," he said, leading the way through the foyer. "At least it feeds my ego, which I always appreciate."

"I can imagine," she murmured.

"Come on. I'll give you the tour."

She followed him out of the foyer and into an open living space. His unit was on the corner, so he had two walls of glass, giving him a perfect view of Hollywood, the Hollywood Hills and to the east, in the distance, the skyline of downtown.

Here the predominate color was gray, accented with wood tones and bright splashes of red and orange from a large canvas of very abstract art. The end tables and dining-area table were glass and steel. The sofa and chairs, a medium gray. The walls were a lighter shade of the same. The hardwood floors and leather ottoman provided the only hint of warmth.

"What do you think?" he asked.

She set her purse on an Ultrasuede-covered chair. "It's, um, very modern."

"Not your thing?"

"Not really." And based on the little she knew about Ryan, she would guess it wasn't his thing, either.

"I was dating a decorator when I moved in. She offered and I took the easy way out."

Ah, so it *wasn't* his style. Funny how that made her like him a little.

He led the way into the kitchen. It opened onto the rest of the room and was all hard surfaces done in gray. Concrete countertops, various shades of gray in the polished glass tile backsplash, stainless appliances.

"You need to get a couple of plants," Julie said as she took the bar stool he offered on the far side of the island. "Something green and bushy and alive. Aren't you afraid all this modern stuff is going to suck the life out of you?"

"It's okay," he said with a shrug. "It's easy to keep clean."

She grinned. "You would know this how?"

"The cleaning service has mentioned it a few times. That and the fact that I don't have pets."

"I'll bet you mostly eat out, you're rarely home, you

don't have big, loud parties. You're the perfect client for them."

He stood on the other side of the island and began removing things from the built-in refrigerator.

"How do you know I don't have big parties?"

"Your sofa and chairs are in perfect condition. Nothing crunchy or wet has been dropped on them. Parties are messy."

"Good point. You're right. No parties."

Just a parade of women, she would guess. Even ignoring his sob story about women coming on to him because of his money, Julie knew Ryan was impressive enough to entice the ladies all on his own.

He carried a package of raw chicken breasts, fixings for salad, basil, some jars and bottles she didn't recognize and—she blinked to make sure she wasn't seeing things—a cookie sheet with prepared bread dough on it.

Was he serious?

"You're cooking?" she asked, trying to sound less surprised than she felt.

"I said I'd make us lunch."

"I thought you meant reservations."

"Would you rather go out?"

"No. This is great. Shocking, but great."

"You don't cook?"

"I can prepare a few basics. I don't totally live on takeout and frozen dinners. But I don't make anything that requires baking or takes this many ingredients." She rested her forearms on the counter. "So what are we having?"

"A goat-cheese-and-arugula salad, followed by a

grilled-chicken sandwich with a pesto sauce on warm focaccia bread, with fresh berries and crème anglaise for dessert."

Color her hungry, she thought as her stomach gave a rumble.

"Impressive. Let me guess. You dated a chef."

"Hey, that's a little judgmental. The summer Todd and I were twenty, our parents took us on a Mediterranean cruise for a month. We would rather have hit Europe on our own, but they insisted, so we went. It was a small ship with not much to do and nearly everyone on it was retired. I think the captain was afraid Todd and I would start trouble because he arranged for daily cooking classes. I hated the first couple, but then I got into the whole thing. Now I cook."

Impressive, she thought. "And Todd?"

Ryan grinned. "He flirted with the cocktail waitress."

He turned on the oven, set a grill pan on the six-burner stove, then seasoned two chicken breasts. After collecting a small but powerful-looking food processor, he rinsed off the basil, then dried it with a towel.

"You're really cooking," she said. "I'm sorry, but this is very unusual for me."

"You should see what I can do with a potato."

It wasn't a side of him she would have expected. With his money and easy good looks, he could have spent his life ordering room service.

As he sprinkled various spices on the bread dough he'd flattened on a cookie sheet, she found herself getting caught up in the way he moved his hands—the confidence and finesse. Without wanting to, she remembered those hands on her body. For a guy who wore a suit and tie, he was very good at manual labor.

And she was an idiot. This was *not* a good time for R-rated flashbacks. She was here to get to know the father of her child. Oh, but if things were different she would be all over him like mascara on silk.

The bread went in the oven, the chicken went on the grill pan and then he walked to the refrigerator and pulled out a pitcher with a pinkish tea mixture, sliced lemons and ice cubes.

"Herbal," he said as he poured them each a glass. "No caffeine."

"Thanks." She sipped. The flavor was more citrus than tea, but it was nice. "It's good."

"I'm glad you like it."

"Okay, you win. I'm officially confused. Is this really you?" she asked.

"Want to see some ID?"

"You know what I mean. You're…"

"Normal?" he offered.

"Yes. Normal. Nothing like the high-powered entrepreneur who hates women."

He winced. "I don't hate women. I like them."

"As long as you can teach them lessons." She held up her hand. "Sorry. I'm breaking the rules. Let's just say this is an interesting side of you. And now we can move on to safer topics. Tell me about what your life was like growing up."

He eyed her as he tore up the arugula and dropped it into a bowl. "That could get me into trouble."

"How?"

"Let me count the ways. But I'll play along. Todd and I were born within a couple of months of each other so we've always been close. Our fathers are brothers, so we traveled together a lot, went to the same schools, hung out on vacations."

"Public school?" she asked sweetly, then sipped her drink. She had already guessed the answer, but she confessed she didn't mind seeing him defensive.

"Private. Prep."

"Ah."

He glared at her, then continued. "We both went to Stanford. There was some talk of Princeton or Yale, but we weren't interested. Our lives were in California. Snow was for ski vacations, not everyday life."

"Skiing in Gstaad?" she asked.

"All over. And before you start mocking me—"

"I would never do that!"

He ignored her. "I want to point out that Ruth came from money. This could have been your life, too."

"I can understand the words, but I'll admit I can't make the concept real. Mom always said her parents were dead and we believed her."

"But if things had been different…" he began.

She looked at him. "Then you and I would have grown up together. We would have been like brother and sister."

Ryan grimaced. Not exactly the direction he wanted them to go. He thought of Julie as many things, but a sister wasn't one of them.

As he worked, he kept getting distracted by her presence. She was so alive, so vibrant. It was as if she were the only color in the room.

He liked the way she challenged him, and how she tried to be fair. He also liked the way she looked in her soft pink sweater that just hinted at the curves beneath. Curves he remembered and ached to touch and taste again.

"Or maybe we would have been each other's first love," she said.

"I like that better," he told her.

"I can see it all now. The wonder and thrill of that first kiss. Going to each other's prom."

"You'd be attending a private girls school," he said with a grin. "In a uniform."

"I'm ignoring you. We would have parted tearfully before college, tried to keep in touch, but you were incapable of being faithful. I made a surprise trip to your dorm and found you with that redhead."

"Hey—why do I have to be the bad guy? I've never been unfaithful."

Her blue eyes widened slightly. "Why don't I believe that?"

"I don't know, but it's true. I have references."

She seemed to consider that for a second. "Okay, so we just drift apart. Then on our next holiday together, Todd comes on to me. You're crushed and while the two of you are fighting I run off with the brilliant computer-science major I met in the library."

"Do I live a life of bitterness and regret?"

"Maybe. But eventually you find someone. A spinster librarian who reads Emily Dickinson to you every night."

"Gee, thanks."

"Actually, you like it a lot."

"So you still hate me, huh?" he asked.

She tilted her head and her long, blond hair tumbled across her shoulder. "Not as much as I should."

He turned the chicken and shook his head. "I wish we'd met another way. I wish I'd run into you at the beach or the grocery store or at a party."

"Ryan, don't."

"Why not? We get along. We got along that first night, we're getting along now."

"I don't know how much of that first night was real and how much of it was your agenda. Who are you really?"

"I'm trying to show you." And to be patient. Her points were valid. As much as he didn't like it, he respected her right to be cautious.

"Okay, I'm good with that," she said. "I'm trying, Ryan. I'm not being difficult on purpose."

"It's just a happy by-product?"

"Kind of."

"So tell me about your life," he said. "You know all about the tragedy of my childhood."

She smiled and his gut tightened. Imagine what she could do to him if she worked at it.

"My sisters and I were pretty happy. There wasn't a lot of money and no private schools with or without uniforms, but that was fine with us."

"Your dad died?"

She paused and for the first time since arriving, looked uncomfortable.

"No, he's alive."

What was the problem? Divorce happened all the time.

"My parents are still married," she said. "They have a unique relationship. My dad is one of those guys who can't settle down. He's charming and funny and everyone wants to be around him."

Everyone but her, Ryan thought, watching the emotions play across her face. Her father had obviously hurt her.

"He disappears," she continued. "He'll show up for a few weeks, much to the delight of my mother who adores him. He'll shower us with presents and tell us stories and get involved in our lives and then he disappears. There's never any warning and more often than not, he cleans out my mom's bank account. A few months later, he sends a check for three or four times that amount. A few months after that, he shows up again and we're off."

"That had to be hard on you," Ryan said.

"It wasn't my favorite way of life. I wanted him to stay and if he couldn't stay I wanted him gone. For so long I hated how much I loved him when he was around and how awful I felt when he left. I hated seeing my sisters so sad and listening to my mother cry."

She stiffened, as if she hadn't meant to say that much. "It's better now," she said casually. "I don't get involved."

Was that true? Was Julie really able to cut herself off from her father or did she simply avoid any emotion where he was concerned?

"How does your mom handle it?" he asked.

"She loves him." Julie's expression was both indulgent and confused. "I don't get it, but she does. She's loved him from the moment she first saw him. She walked away from her family just to be with him. From that life of wealth and privilege, from her parents. Your uncle was her stepfather, but he'd been a part of her life since she'd been a baby. As far as she was concerned, he *was* her father. According to her, it was for the best. She's never looked back, never had regrets."

He checked on the bread, then removed the chicken from the grill. The salad was ready. Once the bread was done, he would make the pesto and they'd be ready to eat.

"I admire her ability to stand by her decision," he said. "That takes courage."

"I think being totally cut off from her family helped. It wasn't as if they would have welcomed her back."

"Her father wouldn't have," he told her. "But Ruth would have. She's a soft-hearted old bird. She'd bristly and tough on the outside, but inside, she's mush."

"I haven't seen that side of her. She was pretty intimidating when she came to visit."

He smiled. "You? Intimidated? I don't believe it."

She laughed. "Okay, I was nervous. You obviously care about her. I can hear it in your voice. I mean this in the nicest possible way—why? She tried to get one of us to marry your cousin by bribing us. That's not exactly sweet."

"But it's vintage Ruth. She loves to meddle, but she's also always been a big part of my life. Our parents traveled constantly and when they were gone, Todd and I lived with Ruth. She had an incredible old house in Bel Air. The grounds were massive, two or three acres at least. We'd spend summers getting lost in the gardens. When we were at school, she'd show up for no reason, pull us out of classes and take us to the beach or Disneyland."

"That sounds nice." Doubt filled her voice.

"It was. You'll have to get to know her."

"I can't wait. At least the house will be cool if she asks me to visit."

"She doesn't live there anymore. She gave it to her daughter, who's the oldest of the two sisters and she passed it along to Todd."

Julie stared at him. "Todd lives in an old Bel Air mansion?"

"Does that change anything? Are you sorry he wasn't the one on the date?"

She laughed. "No. It makes him even more mockable. What's a single guy doing with a house like that? It must be a museum."

"It is. Why do you find that so funny?"

"I don't know, but I can't wait to tell my sisters. Okay, my good manners are kicking in. How can I help?"

"You could set the table."

"Great. Show me where to wash my hands?"

"Sure."

He led her to the guest bathroom off the dining area. She glanced around at the white tile, marble floor and white fixtures, then returned her attention to him.

"You really need to work on saying no to your interior decorator."

"I know. It's a disaster."

"You could get snow blindness in here."

"If you think this is bad," he teased, "you should see the bedroom. It's all done in black and purple."

In less than a heartbeat, the entire mood shifted. Tension crackled between them. Ryan couldn't look away from her mouth, and the need to kiss her and hold her attacked him like a semiautomatic.

Julie opened her mouth, then closed it. "This is awkward," she said at last.

"It doesn't have to be." Although it nearly killed him, he took a step back. He'd given in to temptation at the law office and it hadn't furthered his cause. He tried never to make the same mistake twice. "See. All better."

It wasn't. At least not for him. The more he was with her, the more he wanted her, but for right now, he was going to ignore the heat and desire. He had to think long-term. He and Julie needed to establish a comfortable relationship so they could get to know each other. Then, when he'd softened her up, he would propose again. Because one way or the other, they were going to be married.

No child of his was going to be born without legally joined parents at his or her side. So he was willing to do whatever it took to convince Julie that she could take a chance on him—even not give in to the only thing they could agree on.

Sex.

Nine

This was her weekend for fancy lunches, Julie thought as she pulled into the circular drive in front of a large Beverly Hills estate. Yesterday she'd been at Ryan's for a surprisingly delicious meal and kind of pleasant conversation. She'd returned home to find a message from Ruth asking her to stop by this afternoon for a late lunch. The invitation had sounded very much like a command.

Julie had considered refusing for about three seconds, but then had called back to confirm. She wanted to get to know her grandmother. Ryan had painted a very different picture from the woman she'd met all of three times in her life. Maybe this visit would show her which Ruth was real.

She walked up to the impressive double doors and

rang the bell. A maid answered. When Julie gave her name, she was escorted through a foyer as large as her entire house, then into an equally large living room.

There were several sofas, close to a dozen chairs, tables, sideboards, artwork that belonged in a gallery and a man standing in front of the fireplace.

Her heart began to race even before he turned, so she actually wasn't all that startled to see it was Ryan.

Obviously he hadn't been briefed as to her arrival, she thought as he raised his eyebrows and smiled.

"Julie?"

The pleasure in his voice did something to her insides. Yesterday she'd had the chance to get to know the man. Despite everything, he was making a good case for himself. But seeing him so happy to see her gave him bonus points.

"Ruth asked me to lunch," she said.

"Me, too." He lowered his voice. "A command performance."

"Both of us together? Should I be worried?"

"I don't think so." He walked over and took one of her hands in his, then leaned in and kissed her cheek. "Regardless of why you're here, I'm happy to see you. Lunch yesterday was good."

So was he, she thought as she stared into his eyes and felt herself begin to tingle all over. His fingers were warm and her cheek burned from the light brush of his lips on her skin.

"I had a nice time," she admitted, suddenly wishing they weren't going to be disturbed.

She'd been involved with guys before, she'd even

been engaged, but she'd never had such a visceral reaction to a man.

"Oh, good. You're both here."

Ruth Jamison walked into the living room, her arms wide open, a smile on her carefully made-up face.

"Ryan, darling, how good of you to come." She hugged him and kissed him, then turned to Julie. "I still can't believe I have such lovely granddaughters."

Julie got her own hug and kiss, then Ruth linked arms with them both and led them to one of the sofas. When they were seated, she took a chair opposite.

"I know this was last minute," she told them, "so I appreciate you indulging an old woman."

"A sly old woman," Ryan said. "What's this all about, Ruth?"

"Does it have to be about anything?"

"Knowing you? Yes."

She smiled at him, then turned to Julie. "Don't listen to him. He'd have you believe I'm a terrible person, which I'm not. I'm very sweet. I'm also concerned. I heard that you went out with Ryan instead of Todd, dear. Is that true?"

The question was so unexpected, Julie didn't know what to say. How on earth had she found that out? Had Ryan told her? Ruth continued talking.

"While Ryan is a wonderful man and I'm desperate to see him settled as well, Todd's the oldest. He should be married first."

"He's older by a couple of months," Ryan said easily. "You don't really care about that sort of thing, do you?"

"Not generally, but this is different. This is family.

Your great-uncle had some very particular ideas and I intend to see them followed out. Todd marrying first was one of them. So what happened?"

"Ruth, this isn't your business," Ryan said gently, answering Julie's question about whether or not he'd been his aunt's source. But if he wasn't, who was?

"Of course it is."

Julie sensed danger ahead. She didn't want Ryan admitting the truth about their first meeting for a lot of reasons. She had the feeling that he was torn between wanting to answer his aunt and wanting to protect Julie. Rather than see where it would all go, she plunged into the conversation.

"I set up the date with Todd as you suggested," Julie said quickly. "Then he got tied up with some business and Ryan stopped by to tell me he was running late. He stayed for a drink and we ended up having dinner together."

Ryan shot her a grateful look. "That's right. Todd couldn't make it."

"I see." Ruth sighed. "So now what? Will you be going out with Todd?"

Oh, God. Because she needed more stress in her life? "No, I won't."

Ruth stared at her. "It's a million dollars, Julie. Do you know what you could do with that money?"

"I have a fair idea, but I'm good. Thanks for asking."

Later, when lunch was over, Julie and Ryan left together. When they stepped out into the cool afternoon, Julie turned to him.

"I can't figure out if she's just a crazy old woman or if she's the devil."

He shook his head. "Normally I'd take her side, but she's acting very strange. What's up with grilling us like that? And how the hell did she find out we had dinner instead of you and Todd?"

"I have no idea. Although I did think it was you."

"It wasn't."

"I got that."

He looked back at the house. "She's not usually like that. Maybe having granddaughters has gone to her head."

"We didn't come with any special powers. She seemed upset about me not wanting to go out with Todd. I'm going to have to warn Willow and Marina that she'll be coercing them next. Not that she'll have any luck with Willow. My sister is feeling very protective of me these days. The only thing she wants from Todd is the chance to yell at him."

Ryan stopped beside her car. "We've got a mess here."

"Oh, yeah. I totally blame you, by the way."

He chuckled. "How do you figure?"

"You have really good swimmers. Otherwise I wouldn't be pregnant."

"I think it's all your fault."

She leaned against the driver's door and faced him. "Really? So guy-like."

"I'm a guy. It's your fault because you were smart and sexy and funny and you smelled good."

"The copier toner."

"Whatever. I didn't have a chance to escape."

"Did you want one?"

His eyes darkened with something that looked very much like desire.

She shivered. This was a dangerous game. She and Ryan were supposed to be in the "get to know you" stage of their relationship. Some people got to know each other *before* having a baby, but why be conventional?

Still, the smartest thing to do was pull back. To step away from the sexy man and drive home. But she couldn't seem to move, a little because the sexy man was so intriguing but also because she'd started to like him.

"It was a great night," he said. "You were amazing."

"You were adequate."

"Thanks."

She smiled. "You're very welcome."

He put his hand on her shoulder. A casual touch, she told herself. It meant nothing. So why was it suddenly so hard to breathe?

"We have to keep Ruth from finding out about the baby, at least for a while," he said. "In her present state, I'm not sure what she'd do with the information."

"The thought *is* a little scary."

"We also have a business meeting in a couple of days."

"I know. I put it on my calendar myself."

"Todd will be there."

"I have no words to describe my joy." Was it her imagination or was he moving closer?

"He's not such a bad guy."

"So you say." Ryan was definitely closer. Funny how she liked that.

"I'm not such a bad guy either."

She opened her mouth to say something back and he kissed her. He wrapped his arms around her, tilted his head and pressed his mouth to hers.

She meant to be affronted or at least crabby. Instead she parted her lips instantly, even as she pressed her body against his and clung to him.

Their tongues tangled in a sea of hunger and need. Wanting poured through her, making it impossible to care that they were in her grandmother's driveway. His kiss was hot and familiar and arousing and nothing mattered except that he never stop.

He ran his hands up and down her back. He cupped her rear and squeezed, causing her to surge against him. When she pressed against his hardness, she whimpered.

Oh, yes. That was exactly what she wanted—him hard and inside of her. Arms and legs tangling, bodies reaching, him filling her until she had no choice but to give in to the rising desire. Then they would—

No! She couldn't give in. Not again. Not until she'd figured out who he was and how she felt about him. Getting naked was a complication she didn't need.

It took all her strength, but she forced herself to step to the side.

"We have to stop," she told him, sounding more breathless than stern.

"No, we don't."

"I was just beginning to like you. Don't press your luck."

One corner of his mouth quirked up. "You like me?"

"A little. Maybe. Don't annoy me or the feeling will fade."

He grinned, then took a step back. "You are your own woman, Julie Nelson. You're definitely a hell of a ride."

The last time Julie had been at Ryan's office, she'd been too angry to pay attention to the elegant surroundings, but this morning she could appreciate the subtle blending of colors and the expensive but comfortable furnishings.

"Ryan should have slept with this decorator instead of the one who did his place," she murmured to herself as she walked into the reception area and gave her name to the woman behind the desk.

She was shown back to the conference room immediately. As her heels sank into the plush carpet, she reminded herself that this was strictly business. The kiss she and Ryan had shared a few days before was totally out of her mind. She was determined to be the best damn lawyer they'd ever had and to win them over. Ryan had offered three small companies to her firm. She'd done her research and knew there was a whole lot more where that had come from. She intended to walk away with it all.

She walked into the paneled conference room. Both men stood and smiled at her, but her gaze didn't see past Ryan. While she was aware that Todd was also in the room, she couldn't seem to convince herself that he mattered.

She stared into Ryan's eyes and he stared back and she would have sworn that time stood still. The ever-present need exploded, but she was practically used to that by now. She ignored the way her breasts got sensitive, and the sense of heat and dampness between her legs.

"Good morning," she finally forced herself to say.

"Morning." Ryan smiled. "It's really good to see you."

"Disgusting," Todd muttered.

Julie remembered where she was and forced herself to look away from the man who mesmerized her.

"Gentlemen." She put down her briefcase, refused an offer of tea, coffee or water, and took a seat at the small conference table. Todd and Ryan were across from her. "Let's talk business."

"We're ready," Ryan said.

She smiled at him, then turned her attention to Todd. "I don't think you are."

Todd, nearly as good-looking as his cousin, leaned back in his chair and shook his head. "What makes you say that, Ms. Nelson?"

"The way you run things around here." She'd decided on a blunt attack to set up her position, then she would drown them in facts to get them to agree with her. "You say you're interested in doing business in China, but your actions don't support that. You came to me for help with three very small businesses, but you're sitting on millions with your other holdings. I've been doing my research and you're getting screwed. Your deals are standard at best. At worst you're being taken. Your contracts don't protect you and your entire liaison staff is receiving kickbacks. I have the numbers to prove my position, if you'd like to see them."

She reached into her briefcase and pulled out several folders. Todd and Ryan looked at each other, then at her.

She continued. "I know I was offered a couple of

accounts as a peace offering and while I appreciate the gesture, I've decided I want all your business. Not for any reason other than you won't find a law firm that's better. You need more than advice, you need a partner. We don't farm out our contacts. They're all carefully screened. I speak with the Chinese liaisons myself. No one can claim a translation error."

"What the hell are you talking about?" Todd demanded.

She smiled. "I speak Mandarin."

"Yeah," Ryan said. "I guess I forgot to mention that."

"I learned from a neighbor," Julie said. "I spent several summers in China and did a semester of college there. I'm fluent."

"Interesting," Todd said. "If you'll excuse me for a moment."

Ryan watched his cousin walk out of the conference room, then he turned to Julie.

She looked amazing, but then she always did. Smart and sexy. How'd he get so lucky? If only he could convince her to marry him.

He had the feeling he was making progress, which was good. The more time he spent with her, the more he enjoyed her company, which was better.

"It wasn't mercy business," he said.

She shrugged. "Whatever. It was a very small slice of the pie."

"You want the whole thing?"

"Of course. Why would you think otherwise?"

"I have no idea. This would be a big deal for you. It's a senior-partner-level account."

"I actually know that." She smiled. "I'm capable."

She also understood how the game was played, he thought. "It would smooth things over with the partners when they find out you're pregnant."

"I know. It's part of my motivation, but not the biggest part." She leaned toward him. "Ryan, I'm really good. I know what I'm doing. If we were talking about Europe or Russia or South America, I wouldn't be pushing this hard. But I know this part of the world."

Her eyes were bright with excitement and conviction. Just once he'd like to see her eyes light up when she saw him. That would—

Whoa. Where had that come from? He wanted to marry Julie for the sake of his child. There were no other reasons. Sure, she was great and sexy and he wanted her, but this wasn't about having a relationship. He'd given up on those about six months ago. He was never risking his heart again.

Todd returned to the conference room with a Chinese woman. Ryan groaned.

"You're kidding, right?" he asked.

Todd ignored him. "Mrs. Lee, this is Julie Nelson."

Mrs. Lee bowed, then began to speak in what Ryan guessed was Mandarin.

Ryan narrowed his gaze. "You couldn't just trust her?" he asked Todd in a low voice.

"You wouldn't have trusted anyone else. If we're serious about giving her business, then she'd better be the right person." Todd frowned. "You used to be as much of a cynical bastard as I am. Don't tell me that's gone."

"Not gone," Ryan said as Julie and Mrs. Lee chatted about who knew what. "Shifted."

"Because of a woman?" Todd sounded incredulous.

Fortunately Mrs. Lee turned to him just then. "Her Mandarin is good and clear and she understands nuance." She smiled. "Her accent needs work."

Julie laughed. "I know. I try."

"You do very well."

Todd shrugged. "Okay, then I guess we have some things to talk about."

The conference door opened and Ryan's assistant stepped in. "Ryan, it's that call from the bank. The one you've been waiting for."

"Thanks."

He looked at Todd and Julie. "I have to take that. I'll be about five minutes. Try not to kill each other."

"We won't," Julie said cheerfully.

Ryan thanked Mrs. Lee for her assistance, then walked her out.

Julie glanced at Todd. "Speaking Mandarin is an odd thing to lie about."

"It's business."

"I understand." In his position, she probably would have done the same thing. Not that she was going to tell him that. "So, I have a question."

"Which is?"

"Your aunt offered a million dollars for me or one of my sisters to marry you. What's wrong with you that she would do that? Aside from the obvious."

She'd expected Todd to get angry, or at the very least, all puffed up and manly. Instead, he laughed.

"I'm starting to get what Ryan sees in you," he admitted.

"Which is charming but doesn't answer my question."

"My aunt has some interesting ideas about relationships. This is one of them." He leaned toward her. "I know you're still angry about that first date, Julie, but it's not all Ryan's fault."

"Oh, I know you're to blame, too."

"How refreshing. But that's not what I meant." He glanced at the door, then back at her. "Ryan had a rough time a few months ago. A complicated relationship."

As Julie had recently had one of her own, she understood how that sort of thing happened.

"Ryan's always been cautious," Todd continued. "We both have. But he met this woman and she seemed to be perfect. She wasn't interested in his money, she insisted on paying her way. She was a working single mother and he respected that. He was also crazy about her little girl."

Julie felt a twinge inside and this one had nothing to do with being enchanted by Ryan. Instead of heat, she felt cold and something heavy in her stomach.

She could do the translation for what Todd was so politely understating. Ryan had fallen madly in love with both the woman and her child.

Julie started to say she didn't care about that. She barely cared about Ryan herself. But somehow she couldn't seem to form the words.

"I met her and I thought she was great, too," Todd said. "I was a little worried because Ryan seemed to be more excited about being a father than being a husband, but I figured it would all even out. Things were getting serious when Ryan overheard her talking to her girlfriend. She said when she'd first gotten pregnant, she'd thought it was a disaster, but after her daughter was born, she'd discovered rich guys were suckers for cute little girls. They all imagined themselves playing daddy. The relationship itself was boring, but she would marry Ryan, wait two years, then leave and take a big chunk of cash with her. After all, he would have bonded with the kid, and he wouldn't want her to suffer."

The chill increased. Julie felt sick and for once it had nothing to do with her pregnancy.

"That's horrible," she murmured.

"And a whole lot more. Ryan was okay. He got out in time. But the experience battered him and made him feel stupid. Not something guys enjoy."

No one wanted to be an idiot, but in this case, Ryan had done nothing wrong. Sort of like her situation with Garrett.

"I can guess the rest," she said. "A few months later your aunt sprung her deal. Both of you saw me and my sisters as more of the same."

"That's it. I was telling Ryan about the situation and he offered to take my place."

"To teach me a lesson."

"It wasn't personal," Todd told her.

Funny how it had still hurt.

"I wanted you to know why he did it," Todd said. "You're having a baby with him. Ryan's a good guy. He made a mistake and he regrets it. That should count for something."

"It does," she said slowly. "But he still lied in a huge way. While I appreciate the situation the two of you are in, it doesn't give you the right to mess with innocent parties. I didn't do anything wrong. I wasn't her."

"He screwed up. Give him a break. If he'd known he was going to fall for you, he wouldn't have done it."

Fall for her? As in *fallen*? As in he *cared*?

Julie didn't want the words to mean anything, but they did. She wanted Ryan to like her and respect her, although why his opinion should mean anything, she couldn't say.

Ryan walked back into the conference room. "Sorry about that. So what did I miss?"

"We were just talking," Todd said.

They returned their attention to business and wrapped things up in an hour. Ryan walked Julie to the elevator.

"The partners will be happy," he said.

"I think they might even dance. I'm good at my job. You won't be disappointed."

"I know. How are you feeling?"

"Good. Still woozy a lot of the day, but I'm learning to live with it."

The polite conversation made her crazy. She really wanted to ask about what Todd had said. Had Ryan fallen for her and if he had, what did that mean? Was any of this real or was he still trying to convince her to marry him? And was marrying the father of her child be such a horrible thing?

"Have you told your family?" he asked.

"Everyone except my dad. I have no idea where he is." Not that she would waste any time tracking him down.

"I haven't told my parents. They're in Europe. They don't get back to the States very often, but you'll meet them when they do."

She had a vision of her very pregnant self waddling to meet a couple straight from the pages of *Town & Country* magazine.

"Great," she muttered.

"I should meet your family, as well," he said.

"What?"

"Don't you want me to?"

It was a trick question. No, she really didn't want him to meet them. It would be awkward and strange and…awkward. But to refuse when they were having a baby together?

"That would be fun," she managed to say.

"I'm free this weekend."

How lucky for her. "Okay. Um, sure. I'll, ah, set something up."

"Good."

He leaned forward and kissed her lightly.

There was none of the passion or power of their last kiss, but it still rocked her to her toes. He straightened and smiled.

"Until this weekend, then."

"Sure. I'll be the one with the pickle cravings."

Ten

The house was modest at best, one in blocks and blocks of starter homes. Ryan parked and tried to take in the fact that while he'd grown up in a world of wealth and privilege, Ruth's granddaughters had grown up here.

He climbed out of his sports car and walked to the front door. Julie already had it open. She leaned against the door frame.

"Are you braced? You should be braced."

"Your sisters can't be that bad," he told her as he approached. "I'll be fine."

"Silly, silly man." But she was smiling as she spoke.

He slipped past her, then turned around and kissed her. She didn't react, but he caught the sudden surge in heat and tension. They might have other issues, but

connecting sexually wasn't one of them. Maybe he'd
been too quick when he'd decided that his plan would
progress better if they weren't physically involved.

"My mom's at work," Julie said when he straightened. "She's in charge of a low-cost vaccine clinic one
Saturday a month, but she'll be by later. In the
meantime I have my sisters here to grill you—ah, keep
you entertained."

He chuckled. "They can grill me. I can handle it."

"So you think."

The morning was warm, with the promise of a hot
day—the kind that pops up every now and then in the
fall. Julie wore some kind of filmy, lacy blouse, with a
loose neckline and tiny sleeves that left her arms bare.
Instead of jeans, she had on a skirt that sort of floated
around her calves. Her feet were bare, her hair hung
loose. She looked like a wanton fairy princess.

Ryan stopped in the middle of the living room. A
wanton fairy princess? What the hell was wrong with
him?

"This way," Julie said from a few feet in front of him.
"No backing out now."

"I don't plan to."

She led him through the kitchen and out into a
backyard that was far more paradise than he ever would
have expected. There were plants everywhere, a big
patio with a table and chairs at one end and a barbecue
and fire pit at the other. There were candles and things
that spun in the wind and gauzy, hanging fabric that
served no purpose he could see.

There were also two women, both blond and blue-eyed, with Julie's features and identical "you're going to have to prove yourself" expressions.

"My sisters," Julie said. "Willow and Marina."

Willow was fairly petite, delicate and pretty. Marina was the tallest of the three sisters, and a beauty as well. Great gene pool, he thought. At least their kid had a fighting chance at being cute.

"Nice to meet you," he said and smiled. "Julie's told me a lot about you."

"Did she mention how we wanted to take you down?" Willow asked. "Not just you, either. I still want to march over to that house and give Todd Aston a piece of my mind. You wouldn't happen to have the address, would you?"

Ryan cleared his throat. "I, ah, the backyard looks great. There are so many plants. You have a very special place here."

"Not exactly a smooth change of subject," Marina said, her arms folded over her chest. "I doubt you're seriously interested in the landscaping, but in case you're not just jerking us around, Willow's the one who does all that."

Ryan held in a groan. They were going to be a tough crowd.

Julie urged him to sit and took the chair across from his. "Willow can grow anything. She's into herbs and all things organic. She has a line of candles that are very popular in some of the health-food stores and she writes a comic strip."

He looked at Willow. "Impressive. Do you have any of your comics here? I'd like to read one."

She picked up a slim magazine from the glass-topped table and tossed it to him.

"About eight pages in," she muttered.

He flipped through the pages of the publication. There were articles on organic gardening, an essay on surviving cold-and-flu season and a pull-out diagram on how to get the most from your compost.

Then he saw the small six-panel comic. There were two squash talking about a shoe sale. Judging from the bows on their heads and their high heels, they were girl squash. Okay, then.

He read the panel and forced himself to chuckle at the end, even though he had no idea what the punch line meant.

When he'd finished, he said, "That's great. Is this syndicated?"

"In a couple of small-town newspapers. The major publications aren't interested in organic humor."

"They're missing a growing market."

Willow eyed him as if trying to figure out if he was patronizing her. He was about to launch into a conversation on the phenomenal growth of the organic market—one of their start-ups was in the business— when Willow and Marina stood.

"We'll go get snacks," Marina said.

When they'd left, he turned to Julie. "I don't get it," he whispered, waving the magazine. "Explain it to me."

She leaned close. "I can't. I don't get it, either. Maybe you have to be a vegan to understand, I don't know. For a while I thought maybe Willow's comics just weren't funny. But she's in more and more magazines all the time, so it must be me. Well, and Marina and my mom."

"And me," he said.

She smiled at him and he grinned back.

The sisters returned.

"Mango lemonade," Willow said, handing him a glass.

Marina put a plate of cookies on the table.

Mango lemonade? He took a sip. It wasn't half-bad.

Marina and Willow sat back down.

"Have you ever been married?" Willow asked.

"No."

"Engaged?" This question came from Marina.

"No."

"Any children, other than the one Julie is carrying? And please don't say 'not that I know about.' That just makes guys look stupid."

So the grilling had begun. "No other children."

They were thorough. They covered everything from his relationship with his mother to asking about his financial situation and whether he paid his taxes on time. Through it all, Julie sat back and watched him, as if judging him by his answers.

He was good with that. He had nothing to hide. So he answered their questions without stumbling, right up until Willow said, "How could you be so weaselly to lie about who you were with the express purpose of hurting that person?"

The patio got very quiet.

He started to say he hadn't thought Julie would get hurt, but that didn't sound right. Saying he'd assumed she was incapable of emotion wasn't smart. He could explain how he'd been hurt badly and why he'd felt the need to get back at someone. Only Julie hadn't been the one to hurt him. In the end, he went with the truth.

"I was wrong," he told Willow. "There's no excuse for my behavior and I won't try to make one."

Marina and Willow looked at each other, then at Julie. Willow gave a slight shrug.

He felt that something important had just happened, but he wasn't sure what. At times, women were a serious mystery.

"When we were little, Julie was really bossy," Marina said. "Especially to me."

Julie groaned. "I was not bossy at all. However, our mother worked and someone had to be in charge. I was the oldest."

Willow leaned toward him. "Bossy. Big time."

"I'm ignoring you," Julie said as she stood and walked around the table so she could pour herself a glass of the mango lemonade. But instead of sitting back in her original chair, she settled in the seat next to his.

He made the mistake of glancing at her bare feet when she crossed her legs. Dear God—she painted her toes bright pink and wore a toe ring. It was about the sexiest thing he'd ever seen.

Focus on the plan, he reminded himself. He had a plan to get Julie to marry him. For the sake of the child.

But right then, the child didn't seem very real. All Ryan could think about was that he liked Julie and her sisters and that their cozy house was a home in ways his had never been.

"You didn't buy this, did you?" Julie asked as Ryan pulled up in front of a massive Beverly Hills estate. The wrought-iron gates swung open, exposing a three-story house, manicured lawns and lawn art. Who owned lawn art?

"I grew up here."

"What?" She stared at him. "You lived here? With your parents? You told me to dress casual. You said we'd probably be getting dusty. I can't meet your parents looking like this."

She was in jeans and a T-shirt she'd been about to toss in her "donate" bag. She hadn't bothered with makeup or washed her hair.

"They're not here," he said as he parked by the front steps that led to the huge double front door and turned off the car. "They're in Europe. I brought you here so we could go through the attic. I thought there'd be some stuff there you'd like."

Her panic faded. "Oh. Okay. An attic sounds intriguing." She climbed out of the car and looked around. "Very stylish. Nothing like my house."

He moved next to her and unlocked the front door. "I liked your house. It was warm and homey. This place isn't."

They stepped inside and he pushed buttons on a keypad that had been concealed behind a panel. Julie took in the soaring ceilings, the hardwood floors and impressive artwork. Hey, and this was only the entryway.

"No staff?" she asked.

"There's a live-in housekeeper. Today's her day off. I told her we were stopping by but that she didn't need to be here. We have the house to ourselves."

Ryan led the way up a grand, curving staircase, then along a hallway flanked by bedrooms.

"So how big is this place?" she asked. "Ten thousand square feet?"

"I think closer to fifteen."

"That's a lot of vacuuming."

He grinned. "I wouldn't know."

"It would be a full-time job. I can't believe your parents own this place and they're never here."

"They like to travel."

Julie rubbed the long, smooth banister. "My sisters and I could have had a lot of fun on this thing. Who would need to go to a theme park? You did good with them, by the way. Did I mention that? You nearly won them over."

They reached the landing and he looked at her. "I did win them over. There's no *nearly* about it."

"Cocky, aren't we?"

"With cause."

Danger signs flashed all around them. She knew better than to be charmed but she couldn't seem to help herself. The guy was pretty cool.

At the end of the hallway, they took another, slightly less impressive, staircase to the third floor. Instead of more bedrooms, there were several large, open areas, giving the space a loft-like feel. Windows let in massive amounts of light.

"I love this," she murmured. "It makes me wish I was a painter or something creative. Wouldn't this be a great studio?"

"Todd and I played up here when we were young. We had the whole floor to ourselves."

"Kid heaven."

Tucked in the corner was a third set of stairs. These were narrow and steep. Julie followed Ryan up and found herself in a musty attic.

It was something out of a PBS original movie—with exposed beams, furniture covered with sheets and dusty windows. There were boxes everywhere, along with trunks and hanging racks.

How was it possible that she and Ryan had grown up less than twenty miles from each other and had lived such different lives? How could this world be real?

Ryan walked around and pulled off a few sheets. "Todd and I spent a lot of time up here. We dug through nearly everything. Most of it was pretty boring for a couple of boys, but I remember…"

He crossed the dusty wood floor and moved a few boxes, then beckoned her forward.

"I know how you feel about ultra modern. Is this more your style?"

He'd promised her a surprise. She hadn't been sure what to expect, but it hadn't been a beautiful carved bassinet.

She dropped to her knees and sucked in a breath as she touched the smooth finish. Angels and hearts and flowers adorned the piece. It was a little battered, but mostly incredible.

"Oh, Ryan. It's stunning."

"I'm glad you like it. We can get it refinished or painted or whatever. There's a matching dresser." He sat down beside her. "This stuff is maybe a hundred and fifty years old. There's no changing table, but we could get one made. The same with a crib."

"That sounds great. How did you know I would love this?"

His dark gaze settled on her face. "I just knew."

She would have guessed he was the kind of guy to give traditional, expected gifts, but she was wrong—and happy to be so. Not that she would be keeping the pieces. They were family heirlooms. But she would be delighted to use them while the baby was young.

"You're unexpectedly thoughtful," she said. "Thank you. These are amazing."

"Good. I've been doing some reading online. About babies. They need a lot of stuff."

"It is hard to believe something so small needs so many accessories."

He leaned against a chest and stretched out his legs in front of him. "Can you feel anything yet?"

She touched her stomach. "Just faint queasiness. No movement. It's going to be a couple of months before that."

"You're barely showing."

"I have a tummy." She'd been about to say he should see her naked, but that would lead them to places probably best left unvisited.

"When are you telling the partners?" he asked.

"Soon. I have to. There are a lot of details I'm going to have to work out, but I'll make it work. It's so strange. Until I found out I was pregnant, my career was the most important part of my life. I lived for work. I was determined to get ahead, no matter what. A baby is really going to mess that up and I can't seem to mind."

"You won't be making the decisions alone," he told

her. "I'll be participating. I'm going to be a present parent, Julie. I want to be there for my child."

He sounded determined and intense. "I'm good with that," she said. "We can both interview prospective nannies."

She'd meant it as a joke, but he grimaced.

"I had a nanny."

As big as the house was, and as much money as his family had, she shouldn't have been surprised. Yet she was. "Interesting. Was she nice?"

"I had several and they were all fine. My parents preferred to avoid the hands-on aspect of raising a kid. They took me when they traveled, but we weren't ever together. I don't remember them taking me places themselves or sharing meals with me. I had my own suite at the hotel, with my nanny, sometimes Todd, if his folks were along."

That was so not the picture of his childhood she'd expected. She'd imagined something far more perfect and loving.

"Sounds lonely," she said.

"Sometimes it was. I did better as I got older and was able to get out on my own. I could meet other kids. Once I was in school, I was safe, except for the summer. We were always flying off somewhere."

Julie remembered her childhood summers as long, lazy days spent in the garden. She and her sisters would invent elaborate games that took days to play out.

"Todd helped," Ryan continued. "We were there for each other. Like you and your sisters."

"They're important to me," she agreed.

"I want more for our baby, Julie. I want our child to

know we're both there, that we both care. I want us to create a family. I want the family I never had."

He sounded both determined and painfully sad. She ached for the small boy who'd had so many things and yet so little of what really mattered.

"I don't think we can go back and give you that family," she said. "I know I don't want to re-create mine. But we can build something new, that works for us."

He nodded. "I'd like to try that." He looked at her. "Does your dad know about the baby yet?"

She wrinkled her nose. "I certainly haven't told him. If my mom spoke to him recently, then she might have mentioned it."

"You don't like him. I can hear it in your voice."

"I can't forgive him," she admitted. "He hurts her over and over again. I know she has some responsibility in that—she keeps letting him come back. I just wish she would dump him once and for all and find a good guy. But she claims to love him."

"You don't believe her?"

"I don't think love is supposed to hurt that much."

He reached out and took her hand. Of course there was the usual array of tingles and tightening and desire. Julie had the feeling she would always experience that when Ryan was around. But there was also something different. Something warm and comforting. As if she could trust him to be there.

Not likely, she told herself. But it was nice to pretend.

She shifted so she sat crossed-legged. "I was engaged once," she said quietly. "His name was Garrett and he was very charming. We met in law school."

"I hate him," Ryan said lightly.

She smiled. "That is a testament to your excellent taste." She shrugged. "I keep looking back, trying to figure out where I went wrong and no matter how many times I go over the material, I can't figure it out. I don't see what clues I missed. I like to think there weren't any, but who knows. Anyway, we started dating, we fell in love, or so I thought, we got engaged."

She looked at Ryan. "He was already married. His wife, a very sweet young woman, lived back in New Mexico with her family. She was working two jobs to pay for his education. They'd decided it would be cheaper for her to stay with them, while he got a studio apartment here and went to UCLA."

Ryan's hold on her hand tightened slightly. He swore.

"My thoughts exactly," she murmured, fighting emotions she didn't want to feel again. She'd been a fool, it was over, move on. "So we were engaged and planning a post-graduation wedding. The only reason I found out about his wife was that she won the lottery." Julie managed a smile. "Nothing big—about thirty thousand dollars. But it meant she could move out and be with him and only have to work one job. She showed up without warning. All three of us got a really big shock."

Ryan pulled her close. She stiffened, then relaxed into his embrace. She knew her life was better with Garrett out of it, but still, the hug felt good.

"I don't know what he planned to do," she said, her head resting on his shoulder. "Was he going to be a bigamist? Was he going to wait until the last minute to tell me? Was he going to disappear? I don't know and I didn't stay long enough to find out. I got the basic facts and I took off."

She closed her eyes. "I hated how stupid I felt. Even more than missing him and still loving him, the stupidity of it all killed me. I'd always thought of myself as so smart, and yet he'd fooled me totally."

"He was a bastard and a liar. I'm sorry you had to go through that."

She opened her eyes and looked at him. "Yes, well, now you can see why your little stunt might have pushed a button with me. Besides the obvious reasons."

He grabbed her by the shoulders and shifted so that he could look into her eyes. "I've apologized. I think you believe me. So here's what I want to know—are you ever going to be able to let it go?"

Interesting question. It all came down to whether or not she wanted to. Was she willing to accept that he'd had momentary bad judgment, that it hadn't been personal and that if he could take it back, he would? How long did she want him punished?

"I'm getting closer," she admitted. "A lot closer. But you need to back off on the whole getting-married thing."

"Hey, I mentioned it once. And for the record, you seriously overreacted."

"Oh, please. It was a terrible way to propose. Besides, once was enough."

"You don't want to get married?"

She wondered what he was thinking. Was he relieved that she'd refused or had he really meant that they should get married? She wasn't sure which she wanted it to be.

"Eventually," she said. "But because I want to, not out of duty."

"A romantic. I never would have guessed."

"Not a romantic. I just want to find someone special. The right guy for me."

He dropped his hands to her knees. "So what's he like, this right guy?"

"I don't know—I haven't met him yet."

"So you're available."

What? "Are you planning to set me up with one of your friends? Do you have someone in mind?"

"Of course," he said as he leaned close. "Someone charming and successful and very good-looking."

She could feel his breath on her face. Anticipation swept through her. "Let me guess. Someone we both know?"

"Uh-huh. Me."

"Why am I not surprised?"

But he didn't answer, which was fine with her. Because he kissed her instead.

Eleven

Ryan wrapped both arms around her and slowly lowered her to the floor. At the same time, his mouth claimed hers in a kiss that stirred her to her soul. She felt weak and hungry, powerful and on fire. Her body ached for possession and her heart wanted to open and accept this man inside.

Only her brain wasn't sure if, after all this time, he could be trusted. Still, right now Julie was far less concerned about trust than feeling his hard body pressed against hers. Sometimes, you just had to go with the moment.

His tongue swept leisurely through her mouth, teasing, exploring, exciting. He lowered one hand to her hip and slid his palm across the slight swell of her belly before climbing higher. Her muscles clenched in anticipation of him touching her breasts. Her breath caught in her throat until the weight of his palm settled on her curves.

She was more sensitive than she'd been before, she thought as he lightly brushed against her nipples. More sensitive, but in an amazing, connected, oh-God-I-might-come-right-now sort of way. Sensation shot through her, burning down to her fingers and toes. Between her legs, she felt both heat and dampness.

He broke the kiss and smiled down at her. "I used to dream about this when I was in high school. A sexy woman in my attic. I'd nearly forgotten about it, but suddenly the memories are very clear."

"Did it ever happen?"

"Not until today."

"So I'm about to fulfill an erotic adolescent fantasy."

"That would be my preference."

She pretended to consider the matter. "It's interesting, I suppose. So what exactly did you want to do to this mystery woman?"

His smile turned wicked. "Everything."

She shivered in anticipation. "Can you be more specific?"

"Of course."

But instead of telling her, he bent down, pushed up her T-shirt and pressed an open-mouthed kiss to her belly. After unfastening her jeans and pulling them open, he used his tongue to tease her belly button.

Even as her insides clenched and she fought against begging to be taken right then, she managed to kick off her shoes so he could tug her jeans down and toss them aside. Her T-shirt followed.

He supported himself on one elbow. With his other hand, he traced patterns on her rib cage. "Your skin is so soft. I used to wonder what it would be like to touch a woman. How she would be different. I read a lot, I listened to other guys talk, I imagined, but I wasn't prepared for the softness."

She liked knowing he hadn't always been so experienced and together. "So how fast was that first time?"

He chuckled. "An eighth of a second. I just wanted to be inside and finally do it. I didn't appreciate the subtleties until later."

"Subtleties?"

He unfastened the front hook of her bra with a quick movement of his fingers. "The way a slow build can make the end result even better. How I can know what you like by the way you react to my touch."

The air in the attic was warm, yet goose bumps broke out on her skin.

"If I do this…" He slipped his index finger across her tight, sensitive nipple.

Instinctively, she closed her eyes and arched her body toward him, silently asking for more.

"See," he murmured. "You react."

He bent low and took the same nipple in his mouth. The combination of wet heat and gentle sucking made her gasp. Ribbons of need flowed down her body. She ran her fingers through his hair, then squeezed his shoulders as he shifted to her other breast.

He circled her, then drew her deeply into his mouth.

He trailed one of his hands down her stomach and slipped his fingers under her panties into the waiting dampness below.

She parted her legs for him and let her eyes sink closed. Yes, she thought hazily. This was what she wanted.

He explored her, dipping a single finger inside of her before settling on that one hypersensitive spot. Then he began a dance designed to send her screaming into her release. But just as she settled in to enjoy the ride, he straightened and removed his hands.

Her eyes popped open. "Are you all right?"

"I'm fine." He began unfastening his shirt.

Oh, good—live entertainment, she thought as she slipped off her panties, then stretched back out and watched Ryan undress.

He worked efficiently, first shrugging out of his shirt, then kicking off his athletic shoes and tugging at his socks. He moved to his jeans next. Her gaze focused on the impressive bulge there. All that for her?

"It must be difficult to have your interest out there," she said as he stepped out of his jeans and colored briefs. She reached toward him and stroked his arousal. "There's nothing subtle going on. Women can pretend interest we don't feel. Guys can't."

"We're more honest," he said as he knelt next to her and bent down to nibble on her neck.

"You're not more honest," she said, her voice breathless. "But it could get really awkward to be hard in a situation where you don't want to be. Plus, we always know if you come. Women can fake it."

He raised his head and looked at her. "I'd know."

"I'm not so sure. Some women fake it really well."

"I'd know," he insisted stubbornly, then he smiled. "We'll test your theory. Go ahead and try to fake it. See if I'm fooled."

He shifted so that he was between her thighs, then parted her gently and gave her an intimate kiss that took her breath away.

She had no time to prepare, no time to brace herself for the arousing sensation of lips and tongue against her body. She went from "this is nice" to "I need this or I'll die" in less than a heartbeat. Her body was on fire, her muscles trembled and all she could do was lie there and feel what he was doing to her.

He moved slowly at first. Exploring, tasting, making her shake and gasp and moan. He circled her center with his tongue before gently sucking.

She wanted to scream out her pleasure. She wanted this to never, ever end. Instead she parted her legs as wide as she could and pushed herself against him.

He moved faster against her—stroking up and down, over and over again. He slipped a finger inside of her, moving at the same pace, the same intensity, pushing her forward until she had no choice but to let herself fall.

Her climax began deep inside of her as muscles began to clench and release in a rhythm as old as time. She gave herself up to the waves of pleasure, calling out his name, surrendering everything.

Her orgasm went on and on for what seemed like an hour. When the last waves faded away, he shifted and plunged inside of her.

The unexpected penetration thrilled her. She held on to him, wrapping her legs around his hips, pulling him in closer. He filled her over and over, driving deeper.

She came again, only this time he was with her. He stiffened and groaned. She took all of him, wanting it to always be like this—the connection. The perfect moment.

He opened his eyes and looked down at her. "You weren't faking it."

She gave a strangled laugh. "I know."

Later that week, Julie stopped by her mom's house. It was nearly nine, but she'd been caught up in a brief that had taken way too long to pull together. Still, her mother had said any time before ten was fine, and Julie took her at her word.

She parked in the driveway, then walked to the back door, knocked once and pushed it open.

"It's me," she called, before being led inside by the delicious smell of baking chocolate. "What is that?"

Her mother looked up from the pan in front of her and smiled. "Perfect timing. The brownies are cool enough to serve. I know you want one."

Julie's stomach growled. "I'm starved."

Her mother glanced at the clock on the stove. "Didn't you eat dinner?"

"No. I meant to, but I got busy. Then I came straight here. I'll grab something when I get home."

"Julia Marie Nelson, you know better than that. You're pregnant. You can't go around skipping meals."

Great—talk about feeling as if she were eleven again. "Mom, I know I need to eat regular healthy meals. I've been doing really well. But tonight got away from me. I'll do better."

"All right. Save the brownie. I'll make you something for dinner, first." Her mother walked over to the refrigerator and stuck her head inside. "I have lasagna."

"Yours or Willow's?"

"Willow's." A vegetarian, all the time. "I'd kinda like something with meat. Anything else?"

"Some roast from last Sunday. How about a sandwich and a salad?"

"Sounds great."

While her mother removed various items from the refrigerator, Julie collected a plate, napkin and a knife until her mother shooed her away.

"Go sit. I'll bring you the sandwich."

"Mom, I'm pregnant, not dying."

"I know, but sometimes I like to baby my girls."

As Julie's feet hurt and her back was a little achy, she wasn't about to push the point. Instead she claimed a seat at the island—a tiny version of the massive one in Ryan's ultra-modern kitchen.

Ryan. Just thinking about him made her smile. She hadn't seen him since Sunday when they'd made love in the attic of his old house. That unexpected event had been followed by an evening at her place, which had turned into a very nice sleepover. When he'd left just before sunrise, she'd had to hold back the need to say "we should do this again." Not because she didn't want to but because everything was confusing.

Her life had changed so completely, so quickly. She

didn't know what was happening with him, or what she wanted to happen.

"Have you been to a doctor?" her mother asked.

"I have my first appointment next week. I'll be seeing the same ob-gyn I've been using. I like her and I've heard she's great through the whole pregnancy."

"Is Ryan going with you?"

Interesting question. "I don't know. I haven't asked him."

"You should," her mother told her. "He seems like a nice young man." Naomi stopped and winced. "Tell me I didn't just say that. Nice young man? I sound like my mother. Worse! I sound like *her* mother."

Julie laughed. "It's okay. I won't tell anyone you've entered your dotage."

"If I'm in my dotage, what does that make your grandmother?"

Julie hesitated, then said, "Not the nicest person on the planet."

Naomi finished with the sandwich. She opened a plastic container and dumped a prepared salad into a bowl.

"What do you mean? I thought you liked your grandmother."

"I don't know her," Julie said, hedging. "She's a little scary. At first I thought the whole 'marry my nephew' bit was charming, but when I really go over what she said, it's creepy. She can't control us with money."

"I don't think she was trying to. It was her way of connecting two families. If she'd simply asked you to meet Todd, would you have agreed?"

"Probably. Just to be nice."

Of course without the million dollars on the line, Todd wouldn't have freaked and Ryan wouldn't have stepped in. So she would have gone on her date with Todd, been pleasant and it would have all ended very differently. How long would it have been, under those circumstances, before she'd even have met Ryan?

She was surprised by the panic and regret that seized her. As if not meeting Ryan, not getting involved with him, would be something to grieve.

She didn't want to think about that so she turned to a slightly safer subject.

"Grandma had Ryan and I stop by recently," she said. "She wanted to know how I'd ended up on the date with Ryan instead of Todd and did I have plans to go out with Todd in the future."

Her mother sighed. "She always did love to meddle."

"Apparently. I don't know what has happened to her in her life and I'm sure deep down she's a lovely person, but I have trouble accepting what she did to you. You were seventeen, Mom. She threw you out and turned her back on you."

Naomi set the food on the island. "It's not her fault. I disappointed both my parents."

"Disappointed, yes. Became an ax murderer, not so much. You're her only daughter. I can see having a big fight, not speaking for a while, but twenty-six years? That's excessive."

"Fraser was a difficult man," Naomi murmured.

"He sounds like a tyrant. But here's what I don't get. From what I've seen, Ruth is a really strong woman. If that's right, she could have stood up to him and insisted on seeing her child." Julie touched her mother's arm. "You did an incredible job with all of us. I don't regret anything about my childhood. But it makes me crazy that you had to work so hard and suffer so much and they were only a few miles away, ignoring you and us."

"I wouldn't have taken anything from them."

"I'm not talking about money. You could have used someone to talk to or with babysitting so you could have an evening by yourself."

Her mother smiled. "I love my girls and I'm very happy with my life."

"I'm glad. I just don't understand your mother. I can't figure out if she's a victim or the devil."

"She's not the devil."

"Maybe. But she does have to take responsibility for actions, or lack of action. We all do."

"Even me?" her mother asked quietly.

Julie looked at her. "What do you mean? Leaving with Dad? Mom, you were seventeen. You're allowed to be impulsive."

"I didn't mean that so much as what's happened since then. I know you don't approve of me."

Julie set down her sandwich. Suddenly she wasn't so hungry. "Mom, I love you and I only want you to be happy. It's not my place to approve or disapprove. You've made your choices."

"Which you don't understand."

Julie shrugged. "I don't. He's my father and I love him." Sort of, she thought. "But I don't forgive him. He has no right to appear and disappear from our lives on a whim. Family is about more than that. Family is about taking responsibility."

"He loves us."

"He has a funny way of showing it," Julie muttered. "I can't stand it when he shows up and you're so happy. I know what's coming. Sure enough, he sticks around just long enough for us all to believe in him again, then he's gone. He breaks your heart over and over and you let him."

"He's a good man and a good father."

"He wasn't a good father to me."

"Oh, Julie. You're going to have to learn to be a little more tolerant of people and their flaws."

"What? A flaw is leaving toothpaste in the sink or being chronically late. Abandoning your family over and over is a little more than a flaw. You're so great and pretty and there are wonderful men out there who would love to have you in their lives. They would treat you like a princess."

"I just want to be Jack's wife," her mother said sadly. "I wish I could make you understand that loving someone doesn't mean you get to change him. You accept the good with the bad."

"His bad is too big for me," Julie told her.

"But not for me."

Julie thought about pointing out that there were other women when her father left, but why state the obvious and cause pain?

"Sometimes loving someone means forgiving over and over," her mother said. "You pick what you can live with. I can live with this. I have to. He is, as your sister would say, my destiny."

"Oh, please." Julie gave a strangled laugh.

"I'm serious. Don't you think I've tried to get over him? When you were younger, after he'd stayed nearly three months and I was sure that this time he'd changed, but he hadn't, I decided I wasn't going to do that anymore. I wasn't going to get my heart broken again. So I started dating. I went out with several men. One of the relationships even got a little serious."

"Mom! You wild woman. You never said anything." Julie hadn't had a clue.

"I didn't know how it was going to work out and I didn't want you girls to be disappointed by another man. I thought it best to wait until I was sure."

"I'm guessing it didn't work out."

Her mother shook her head. "I wanted to love him, but I couldn't. For better or worse, I love your father. I've learned I would rather be missing him than trying to love someone else."

Julie didn't know what to say to that. Talk about a sad choice.

"He's older now," her mother continued. "He'll be settling down soon. And when he does, it will be here. With me. We'll grow old together."

Julie tried to understand, but she couldn't. "Wouldn't you have rather had a whole life instead of just the end of his?"

"I'm content, Julie. You may not understand that, but you need to accept it. This is what I want."

"I know, Mom. I'll let it go."

"I hope you can. I hope you can find someone who makes you happy. Is that person Ryan?"

"I don't know," she admitted.

"He's the father of your child," her mother said gently.

Julie looked at the woman who had been so important to her for so long. "You'd like me to just forgive him and move on," she said. "You'd like to see us married."

"I'd like to see you happy. I worry about all my girls. Marina, because she leads with her heart. Willow, because she finds men who need rescuing, and once they're healed, they move on to someone else. And you because—"

"Because I'm stubborn and difficult and don't trust easily."

"You because you've been hurt and you don't trust yourself to pick a good man."

"Same thing." Julie poked at her salad.

"Does Ryan make you happy?" her mother asked.

"Sometimes. Maybe. He's not so bad."

"I'm sure he'll want you to be in charge of his ad campaign if he ever runs for public office," Naomi teased.

Julie smiled. "You know what I mean. If I pretend we met a different way, then he's amazing. He's smart and caring and yeah, I like him."

"You can't change the past."

"I know, but occasionally I try to argue with it."

Her mother grinned. "Does that work?"

"Not as well as I'd like. I just wish things were different."

"Events can't be undone. People are who they are. He's a good man, and the father of your child. You're starting to care about him. Isn't all that what you want?"

"You'd think so," Julie said with a shrug. "But in my gut, I'm still afraid he's lying or holding back or there's some big secret and when it all comes out, my heart will be broken again."

"Getting involved is a risk. For what it's worth, you survived Garrett."

"True." Julie drew in a breath. "But getting over Garrett was a lot easier than it should have been. I'm terrified I won't be able to get over Ryan."

"You're falling for him," her mother told her.

"Apparently. And I don't think I want to."

"Can you stop those feelings from growing?"

Not if they continued to spend time together, Julie thought, remembering the previous weekend. It wasn't just about the sex. It was about the way they talked together and laughed together. It was how he made her feel, and how much she wanted to trust him.

"I refuse to fall in love," Julie said.

Her mother nodded. "I thought you might decide that. On the one hand, I think you've made an incredibly sad choice. On the other hand, I don't think anyone, even you, has that much control. Ryan isn't going away. He will always be the father of your child and in your life. Can you resist him forever?"

Julie already knew the answer to that was no. So if falling for him was inevitable, why was she struggling so hard to resist him now?

Julie made a note on her pad. She needed a couple more citations and then she'd be ready to write up her brief. There was a knock on her open door. She glanced up.

"Come in," she said to the short, older man standing there.

He was dressed in jeans and a sweater, nothing fancy. He looked especially nondescript.

"Julie Nelson?" he asked.

"Yes."

"Julia Marie Nelson?"

She didn't like people using her full name. It reminded her too much of when her mother was mad at her. "May I help you?"

He handed her a thick envelope. "You've been served." With that, he was gone.

Julie stared at the envelope, then opened it. The accompanying letter was from a law firm in the next high-rise over. As she scanned the contents, she felt her entire body grow cold. Her heart cried out in protest, her brain muttered, "I told you so," and her chest tightened until it was nearly impossible to breathe.

Ryan was offering an official prenuptial agreement and a proposal of marriage valid only after the baby was born and his paternity was proven by DNA testing. If she refused either the proposal or the test, then he would sue her for custody of the child. Permanent and total custody. He would have her or she would have nothing.

Twelve

Julie stormed into the offices of Aston and Bennett, ignored the receptionist and stalked down the hall to Ryan's office. She found him on the phone.

He looked up when she entered and smiled. Dammit all to hell if she didn't feel a kind of quiver. Crap, she thought grimly. It was all crap.

She jerked the phone from his hand and hung up, then tossed the papers in his face.

"How could you?" she demanded, her voice loud and angry, but not nearly as loud and angry as she felt on the inside. "How could you? I trusted you. I believed you. That's what kills me. I was starting to think I'd been wrong about you. That I'd misjudged you. That it had all been a simple mistake. But it wasn't, was it? You were your own true self that first night we were together. You were a snake then and you're a snake now."

Ryan grabbed the papers and stood. "Julie, what are you talking about?"

"That." She pointed at the papers. "You think you've won, but you are sorely mistaken. I'm a better lawyer than you'll ever be able to hire. You won't get anything, you hear me? You're going to lose. You're going to lose big time and then you're going to have nothing. Not this baby and not me. Let me be clear. I will never marry you. Never. The next time I see you, we'll be in front of a judge. I will eviscerate you. I will leave you broken and bleeding and then I'm going to kick you while you're down. You're a lying bastard and I can't tell you how much I wish I'd never met you. I can't believe I thought I was in love with you."

With that, she turned and left.

Ryan stared after her, stunned by her attack. He couldn't think, couldn't feel, couldn't understand what was going on. He opened the envelope and read the paperwork. Horror filled him.

"No," he said between clenched teeth. "Julie, no. I didn't do this."

He went after her, but it was too late. The elevator doors had closed and she was gone.

Now what? How could he explain he hadn't done this? And who the hell had?

But he already knew that answer. He walked into Todd's office and closed the door.

"What are you doing?" he demanded. "This is crazy.

Why would you go behind my back? Do you know how you've screwed up things?"

Todd frowned and reached for the papers. He scanned them, then groaned. "Oh, God, Ryan, I'm sorry. I never meant for this to go out to her. Did Julie see this?"

"Based on what she just said to me, yeah. She was served earlier today. What the hell were you thinking?"

"I wanted to protect you. I went to see our lawyer after she came by for the first time. Before I knew anything about her. I just told him I wanted you protected and that you wanted to marry her, which I thought was crazy." Todd looked at him. "I didn't do any more. He wasn't supposed to do anything but draw up papers. I swear."

Ryan believed him. Todd was looking out for his back. If their situations had been reversed, Ryan might have done exactly the same thing.

But the plan had backfired. Instead of covering his back, the papers had ripped him open and destroyed any chance he had of getting Julie ever to trust him. He was empty inside and he had a bad feeling that later he was going to long to feel nothing more than empty. Because when reality hit, it was going to be grim.

"We hired a shark on purpose," he said with a meager attempt at lightness. "He just made a kill."

"He wasn't supposed to kill you."

"Killing Julie isn't a good idea, either."

She'd said she loved him. He'd wanted to hear those exact words from her…just not in that context.

"You'll make her understand it wasn't you," Todd said. "Tell her. Hell, I'll tell her."

"Why would she believe either of us?" Ryan asked wearily. "I wouldn't. Would you? I lied to her when we first met. I lied and I hurt her. I've been working my ass off to regain her trust and now this. She's going to think it was all a game."

"You love her," Todd said. "You can't just let her go."

"I won't," Ryan said. "I'll win her back…just as soon as I figure out how."

Julie lay curled up on her sofa. She'd been unable to face the thought of going back to work, so she'd come home. She'd managed to maintain something close to control until she'd been in the door, then the tears had poured down her face and the sobs had choked her throat.

She cried so hard, she felt she would soon break in two. This couldn't have happened. Ryan couldn't have lied about all of it…but he had.

Garrett's betrayal had been impossibly harsh and unexpected, yet after her initial shock, she'd thought only about getting as far away from him as possible. But now, even though she hated Ryan and wanted him punished and humiliated, she was just as upset at the thought that she would never see him again.

"I'm mentally uns-stable," she said, her voice breaking on another sob. "I need professional help."

Someone knocked on the door.

She stiffened, then covered her mouth with her hand. She wasn't going to answer that. Odds were it was Ryan and she wasn't interested in talking to him now or ever.

The bell rang, followed by more knocking.

"It's Todd. I know you're in there, Julie. Your car's

in the driveway and the hood is still warm. You just got here. Let me in. We have to talk."

"We don't have to do anything," she yelled as she stood and glared at the door. "You're just like him. You're a complete bastard. Go away or I'm calling the cops."

"I'm not leaving. You can let me inside, or I can yell your personal business loud enough to keep the neighbors talking for weeks. Let me in. You'll want to hear what I have to say."

"I doubt that," she muttered and put her hand on the lock. Let him in? Why not? There was nothing he could say that would change her mind.

She opened the door.

Todd stepped inside. He looked enough like his cousin to make her stomach clench. She fought against tears, not wanting to cry in front of him. Kind of pointless, she admitted to herself. She already looked like a wreck.

"Why are you here?" she demanded. "Go away."

"I just got inside," he told her. "Hear me out. Then you can kick my ass."

If only, she thought bitterly. Why hadn't she learned some karate method? Hearing a couple of bones snap right now would be very satisfying.

He pointed at the sofa. "May I sit down?"

"No."

"You're pregnant and upset. You should sit. I'll stand."

"I'm fine." She folded her arms over her chest. "Start talking."

Todd drew in a breath. "Okay, but once I start, you have to let me finish. No interruptions."

She glared at him. "Excuse me? Who do you think

you are? You don't get to set the rules here. Your cousin screwed me, in more ways than one. You don't get to set anything, you jerk."

"Fine. I'll talk fast. It wasn't Ryan, it was me. Ryan didn't know I went to see our lawyer and he doesn't know I'm here now. I have the bill to prove my point— about the lawyer, not about me being here now. It shows I consulted with our attorney for over an hour about you two. I was trying to protect my cousin because he was in no position to protect himself. All he could think about was how he'd blown it with you. He felt horrible about what had happened."

It hadn't been Ryan? Julie walked to the sofa and sat down. Was that possible? Was this an elaborate trick?

"Ryan would never do that," Todd told her. "I wouldn't now, either, but I didn't know you then. I thought you were just in it for the money and that you'd tricked Ryan into getting you pregnant."

"I'm flattered."

"I apologize, but there have been plenty of women who would do just that. At the time, I needed to make sure you weren't one of them. Look, Ryan is the only real family I have. I would do anything for him. I just wanted to make sure he was okay. But I messed up. You're blaming him and because of what I did, you don't trust him. It's not him, Julie. He's a great guy. I'm the bastard. Hate me."

What she hated was how much she wanted to believe him. Based on what she knew about Todd, this was exactly something he would do in the name of protecting his buddy. But was it possible Ryan knew nothing about it?

"It's just too much," she said quietly. "All of it. The ride's been too much, too fast. I need time."

The front door opened and Ruth stepped inside.

"You simply leave your house unlocked?" the older woman asked as she shut it behind her. "Not a very safe way to live." She glanced at Todd. "You're an unexpected visitor."

Julie rose to her feet. "So are you, Grandmother."

"I know. I phoned your office, but your assistant said you'd gone home ill. I came to check on you, and my great-grandchild."

Okay, and the hits just kept on coming. "You know about the baby?"

"I know everything. Well, not everything. I didn't know you were going to go on that date with Ryan instead of Todd. If so, I would have stepped in. Todd is the oldest and I did so want to see him married first."

Julie's head was spinning. She had just enough brain power left to invite Ruth to sit before she collapsed back on the sofa.

"How did you know about the baby?" Julie asked.

Ruth glanced at Todd, who still stood in front of the sofa. "Are you lurking, dear boy? Don't lurk."

He took a step back.

Ruth turned to Julie. "The young woman who comes to my house and does my nails has a sister who works in a law firm. It's the same one where Ryan and Todd do business. I've used her from time to time, just to keep in touch with their business. Those boys tell me nothing. She told me about those papers. A little harsh, perhaps, but they get the job done."

Julie didn't know what to react to first. The fact that Ruth was spying on her own nephews—which really put the whole marry-Todd-for-a-million-dollars thing in perspective—or that a secretary in a law firm was giving out privileged information.

She looked at Todd who looked as angry as she felt.

"I'll have her fired," he said.

"Of course you will," Ruth said breezily. "I've already arranged for her to have a wonderful new job, so run off and take care of things while I talk to Julie."

Todd hesitated. Julie sensed that he was actually going to stay to make sure things were all right with her.

"I'm good," she told him. "You can go."

"If you're sure?"

She nodded.

Todd left, closing the door behind him. Julie turned to her grandmother.

"You've been busy."

"I need to stay involved with my family."

Julie realized she'd had enough meddling and controlling and lies and subterfuge to last five lifetimes.

"Okay, Grandma, here's the thing," she said. "You can't do this. You can't spy and trick people. That isn't how you treat family and it's not any way to get family to want to be around you. I know you're old and I should respect that, but I can't forgive you for what you did to my mom. She was seventeen and you threw her out."

Ruth stiffened. "Your mother chose to leave. It was her decision and she knew the consequences."

"You made her choose. My father was the first man she ever loved—apparently the only man she'll ever love—and you made her take sides. What did you expect her to do?"

"Her duty."

"Isn't it a mother's duty to love her children no matter what? But apparently that's not your way. I guess in your world, people get to mess up one time, and then you turn your back on them. Well, here's a news flash. Don't bother caring about me because I'm going to mess up big time. I'm going to disappoint you. It's inevitable. I'd rather you knew that now and got out of my life. That would be easier. I don't want to care about you only to find out there are strings and conditions on your affection."

Ruth paled. "How dare you talk to me this way?"

"Someone has to. Why do you hold on so tight to Ryan and Todd, yet you let my mother go so easily? Are you…" Julie opened her mouth, then closed it. Of course, she thought as the truth dawned on her.

"You're sorry about what happened," she said slowly. "You have nothing but regrets where she's concerned. But you never knew how to make it right with her— either because of your pride or your husband. You were afraid she'd reject you again, so you didn't try. But you had Ryan and Todd and they almost made up for it. So you clung to them, torn between loving them and needing to control them so they wouldn't disappear the way your daughter had."

Tears filled Ruth's eyes, but her expression remained stern and disapproving. "I have no idea what you're talking about, but I can see your mother did a terrible job in raising you. You're rude and unprofessional."

"Unprofessional?" Julie actually smiled. "This is a personal conversation. I don't have to be professional."

"Fine. Be what you want, but know this, young lady. You're having my great-grandchild and you will be marrying Ryan Bennett."

"No, she won't."

Julie looked up and saw Ryan had stepped into her house. He ignored her and turned to Ruth.

"Julie isn't going to do anything she doesn't want. No one is going to make her. Not you, not me, not anyone. I want her happy—that's *all* I want. If she can be happy with someone else, then I'll step aside."

Julie stared at him, not totally sure she believed him, although she was disgustingly thrilled to see him.

"You're being ridiculous," Ruth told him, her voice sharp. "I won't stand for this."

"Then take a seat, because it's what's going to happen."

"But you love her," Ruth said. "I can tell because you've never been this stupid about a woman before. It's not like you to be a fool."

He looked at Julie and gave her a rueful smile. "I don't care. I just want you not to hurt anymore. I can't seem to stop screwing up."

She stood and took a step toward him. Seeing him felt so right. She could believe that Todd had made a mess of things, and now Ruth was here, butting in. Did any of that matter? Weren't she and Ryan the ones who had to make the decision about what was right for them?

Then Ruth's words really sank in. Love? Did Ryan love her? Her soul brightened at the thought. Her heart beat faster. Could he? Did he?

"Propose," Ruth instructed. "Propose now and we'll have this business done."

"No," Ryan told her. "I won't marry Julie. It's the only way I can make sure she's happy."

"What?" both women asked together.

He grabbed Julie's hands and stared into her eyes. "I made you cry. I never want to do that again. I never want you to doubt me or us or my motives. I only know one way to do that. Not to marry you. Because that's what I've wanted this whole time. Us, together. At first it was about the baby, but now it's more. It's about you."

He drew in a breath. "I hate how we met. It was the best and worst night of my life. By the time I realized what I was doing and how great you were, it was too late to start over. Then you were hurt and angry and I knew I'd blown it. But the baby gave us a second chance. You *had* to deal with me and I thought maybe, with time, you'd start to like me. Only then I proposed and that set you off again and I was back where I'd started."

The words were magic. They were warm and loving and everything about this moment was so perfect, except maybe for Ruth being there.

"I love you," he said as he smiled at her. "I love you and I will never make you do anything you don't want to do. We'll co-parent, I'll buy the house next door. You just tell me and I'll be there. I swear, Julie. I had nothing to do with those papers. I would never, ever do that to you."

"I know," she said breathlessly. "I know. I just reacted and then I didn't know how to un-react when Todd told me the truth."

"Todd was here?"

"I haven't had this many people through the house since my last Christmas party." Her eyes burned with more tears, but these were happy ones. "I believe him and I believe you, Ryan. When I hurt so much, thinking you'd lied and tricked me, I realized I love you, too."

Julie braced herself for Ruth's instant criticism that if they loved each other and were having a baby together that getting married seemed the sensible solution. Only there wasn't a sound.

She turned and saw the older woman had slipped away. The front door was closed and she and Ryan were alone.

"I wouldn't have thought she was that sensitive," she admitted.

"Me, either. Todd, Ruth and I are going to have a long talk about her way of keeping in touch."

"She's alone and holding on too tight," Julie said, surprising herself and possibly him. "Be kind."

"I will." He kissed her fingers. "I do love you."

"I love you, too." She tilted her head and fought a smile. Suddenly she felt as if she were channeling Ruth. "Which does beg an interesting point. We *are* having that baby together."

"Yes, we are."

"Traditionally, couples prefer to be married."

"I've heard that." He released one of her hands to touch her face. "Are you saying you'd be *willing* to marry me? Despite everything?"

Julie smiled. "I'd actually be honored."

He pulled her close and kissed her. She wrapped her arms around him and hung on. He was the kind of man who would always be there for her, just as she would always be there for him.

"We're going to make a great team," she murmured.

"Go us," he said as he nibbled his way down her neck.

"I'm serious. We'll be one of those wildly efficient couples who has everything done on time. We'll have to move, of course. This place is too small and your condo, well, I can't even imagine living there. We'll need a house."

He raised his head and smiled at her. "My parents would give us theirs if you wanted."

"Maybe just the attic. I had a good time there."

"I always have a good time with you." He kissed her again. "We actually owe Ruth for bringing us together. If we have a girl, we could name her after her great-grandmother."

Julie winced. "Tell me you're kidding."

He drew her toward the bedroom.

"Ryan! Wait! We're *not* naming our daughter Ruth. I won't have it. Do you hear me? What happened to whatever I want? What happened to me being in charge?"

"I never said you were in charge." He tugged her blouse out of her skirt.

"It was implied."

"This is a partnership. Equal votes."

"Fine. As long as mine counts just a little bit more."

He laughed, then kissed her again and suddenly she didn't care about being in charge or baby names or anything but the amazing man who had claimed her heart and changed her world forever.

* * * * *

THE UNEXPECTED
MILLIONAIRE

BY
SUSAN MALLERY

Dear Reader,

The fun of THE MILLION-DOLLAR CATCH series
continues with Willow's story. Willow has possibly the
worst taste in men ever. Seriously. She finds guys who
need rescuing, fixes them up and then they leave her.
Not a well-thought-out plan on her part. So when she
literally stumbles into the arms of Kane Dennison, she
has no idea what she's getting herself into.

Kane is a warrior in every sense of the word. He's
dark, he's dangerous, he's unbelievably sexy. He's also
as determined to avoid Willow as she is to be a part of
his life. But honestly, how can one powerful, wealthy,
alpha male expect to stand up against a petite, semi-
vegetarian, cartoonist gardener who simply won't go
away? The poor man doesn't know what hit him.

Willow is exactly what our solitary hero needs. He just
hasn't realised it yet. *The Unexpected Millionaire* is
delicious, hot, sexy fun with plenty of twists and turns.
I hope you enjoy the ride.

Susan Mallery

One

About eight seconds too late, Willow Anastasia Nelson realized there was a massive flaw in her plan.

She'd driven over to Todd Aston the Third's embarrassingly huge estate to give the slimy, no-good weasel a piece of her mind. But she'd never actually met the man, so she didn't know what, exactly, he looked like.

She had an idea, of course, sort of. Tallish, handsomeish, rich. But wasn't his hair dark and weren't his eyes brown? Why hadn't she thought to look him up on the Internet? He was probably on the front page of "JerksMonthly.com."

And if Todd Aston defined the whole tall, dark and yucky scenario, then who was the blond hunk and a half standing in front of her?

"Oh, hi," she said, smiling at the man who'd opened the front door and hoping she didn't look as out of place as she felt. "I was hoping to have a word with Todd. This is his house, right? My sister mentioned he lived here and…"

Willow groaned. That hadn't come out right. She sounded like a groupie.

"My sister knows him," she added helpfully.

Blond guy didn't step aside to let her in, although he did fold his arms over his chest in a move that got her attention. The man was *big*—really muscled, but not in a too-buff, action hero kind of way. This guy looked powerful, like a jaguar. She would bet he could snap her forearm without breaking a sweat.

His eyes were green and kind of catlike, she thought absently, continuing the whole "powerful cat" analogy. He had a good face—handsome, but also trustworthy. Not that she knew anything about him. He could be… She shook her head. She had to focus on her mission.

"Look," she said as forcefully as she could, determined to sound in charge and unintimidated by the burly guy's presence. "I need to talk to Todd. I'd like to do more, of course. He totally messed things up for my sister. Everything turned out in the end, but what if it hadn't? I get so mad when I think about it, I just want to pop his pointy little head. And that's the least of it."

The man in the doorway raised one eyebrow, then pushed aside the front of his suit jacket. Willow felt all the blood rush out of her head—no doubt fleeing to somewhere much safer than her body.

The man had a gun.

She could see it just inside his coat, tucked under her arm in some kind of holster. It was almost like in the movies, except for the cold knot of terror in her stomach.

"What is your business with Mr. Aston?" the man asked in a low voice that sent chills tripping down her spine.

So he wasn't Todd. She'd sort of guessed that, but now she knew for sure. "I, ah, he…"

The smartest move would be to leave. She wanted to yell at Todd, not get shot. But some stubborn streak made her plant her feet more firmly on the oversize and pillared porch.

"I think you're overreacting," she muttered, forcing herself to look away from the gun, back to the man threatening her with it. Well, not *threatening*, but intimidating. Something he was doing really, really well.

"I get paid to overreact."

"Has weasel-man already left for the office?" she asked sweetly. "I'll catch him there."

"You won't be catching him anywhere. Who are you and what do you want with Mr. Aston?" As he spoke, he reached out to grab her arm.

Willow had tried out every year of high school for the cheerleading squad. But in a world of amazons, she'd been too short. No matter how well she knew the routine, putting her in the lineup made them look off balance. Still, she'd been good at tumbling and turning and ducking.

The skills came back to her now as she faked a spin to the left, instead went to the right, then ducked under the big guy's arm. Suddenly she was inside the house.

Elation filled her. If Todd was here, she would find him. Then she would yell at him and her world would be set to rights.

She sprinted down the wide entryway, Mr. Big Gun and Cranky right behind her, then ran through huge rooms with soaring ceilings. This place was more like a museum than a house, she thought as she raced through what looked like a study and came out in a long hallway. She heard the man with the gun running behind her. She was fairly confident he wouldn't actually shoot her, but just in case, she wove back and forth and kept close to walls.

"Todd," she yelled as she ran. "Are you home? You need to get your lying, slimy butt down here. You don't have the right to mess with people's lives. It's wrong. You should know better."

Perhaps not words to put fear into his heart, but they would have to do.

She heard footsteps closing in and righteous anger gave her a burst of speed. Unfortunately that burst led her into a room with no other exits.

Panic energized her. She spun quickly, looking for a door, a big window, anything. Then she stared at the floor to ceiling drapes and headed in that direction.

Victory! A French door that led onto a patio as big as her elementary school had been. She burst outside and glanced around.

The grounds were stunning. The patio led to stairs that flowed into a terraced garden that reminded her of the grounds around Versailles. Beyond them was a forest of trees.

Didn't Todd know he was in the middle of Los Angeles?

"Stop," Burly Guy demanded as he ran out of the house after her. "Stop, or I'll make you stop!"

Ha! He hadn't been able to stop her yet, had he? But had he already called the police? Willow didn't wait to ask. She bolted for the trees.

Unfortunately the open ground gave her pursuer the advantage, mostly because his legs were a lot longer than hers. That combined with her erratic commitment to physical fitness and any sort of regular exercise program meant he gained on her far too quickly.

She dug down for more righteous indignation to give

her speed, or slow him down or something, but there wasn't anything left. Her breath came in pants, the sound of her rapid heartbeat filled her ears, and she felt the chilling fingers of defeat reaching for her.

"I will not be taken alive," she gasped as she surged forward, straining to reach the trees. Once there, she might have a chance. As for not being taken alive, okay, yeah, she had a slight dramatic streak.

She felt him reach for her and darted to the left, where a tree root jutted out of some grasses. She tripped over it, lost her balance and started to go down.

As she did, several things happened at once. There was an awful sensation of pain from her left ankle, she saw something gray and white and furry in a hollowed-out base of the tree, and what felt like a tank plowed into her from the rear.

She hit the ground, all the air rushed out of her lungs, and there were actual spinning lights where the rest of the world should have been.

She resurfaced to someone rolling her onto her back and telling her to take a breath.

Breath? She couldn't breathe. She really was not going to get out of here alive. Oh, God—she'd been kidding. She didn't want to die here. Now. Like this.

"Take a breath," the man repeated. "You're fine."

How did he know that? How could he be sure?

Willow opened her mouth and sucked in air. It filled her lungs. She did it again and again until the lights faded and she could focus on everything around her.

Gun Guy sat next to her. He'd removed his jacket. The good news was she could see he was all muscle and it was pretty impressive. The bad news was his gun was totally exposed and she couldn't pretend it wasn't there.

"Who *are* you?" he asked. "Some crazy ex-girlfriend? I usually know them, but every now and then…"

Willow raised herself up on one elbow. "Ex-girlfriend? No way. I wouldn't date Todd if the continuation of the entire planet depended on it. Well, okay, if it would save some endangered species, maybe. We all have to do our part. It's important for us to realize that for the planet to continue to be a renewable resource, there are some basic rules we need to follow."

He held up his hands in the shape of a T. "Time-out. Who are you?" he asked again.

"Oh. Sorry. Willow. My sister is Julie Nelson. She's engaged to Ryan, Todd's cousin. But rat fink Todd did everything he could to keep them apart and I can't let that go. I know I should just accept it and move on, but it was wrong. He thinks because he's so rich, he's king of the world or something. Idiot. Who are you?"

"Kane Dennison. I'm in charge of security."

"Here at the house?"

His expression hardened, as if she'd just insulted him. "For the entire company."

"Oh, sure. That explains the gun." She pushed herself into a sitting position and brushed at the grass stains on her sweater. "I wasn't going to hurt him, you know. I mean come on, look at me. Do I look dangerous? Seriously?"

He tilted his head as if considering the question. "You're short and scrawny, so I guess not."

The short she could handle—it was a reality she couldn't change. But scrawny?

"Excuse me? I'm petite."

"Is that what they call it?"

"I have curves," she said, really annoyed and just a little hurt. Maybe she didn't have big curves or a lot of them, but they were there. "It's the sweater. It's bulky, so you can't see what's underneath, but I'm very sexy."

She wasn't—not really. She tried, of course. But it was a losing cause. Still, to have this man just dismiss her like that was more than annoying.

"I'm sure you're stunning," Kane muttered, suddenly looking as if he wished he were anywhere but here. "I'm sorry you're mad at Todd, but you can't show up at the man's house and threaten him. It's wrong and it's illegal."

"Really?" She'd broken the law? "Are you going to have me arrested?"

"Not if you leave quietly and never come back."

"But I *have* to talk to him. It's just one of those things. He needs a good talking to."

One corner of Kane's mouth turned up. "You think you can scare him?"

"Maybe." Although in truth she'd kind of lost her passion for the job. "I could come back later."

"I'm sure Todd would be delighted to hear that. You have a car?"

"What?" she asked. "Of course I have a car."

"Then let's get you to it and we'll pretend this never happened."

A course of action that made sense. There were only a couple of problems standing in the way. Standing, or not standing being the main one.

"I can't," she said and rotated her foot. Instantly pain shot through her ankle and made her clench her teeth. "I think I broke my ankle when I fell."

Kane muttered something under his breath and shifted so that he was by her foot. He lifted it gently and held it in one hand while untying the laces with the other.

She wore size six shoes, which, considering she was

only five foot three, wasn't all that dainty. Still, his large hand nearly dwarfed her foot. Wasn't there some old wives' tale about guys and big hands?

Willow didn't know whether to laugh or blush at the thought, so she let it go and watched him carefully remove her athletic shoe.

"Move your toes," he said.

She did. The pain made her wince.

He peeled off her sock and began to examine her foot. Willow winced again, but this time it had nothing to do with pain. Even with her total lack of medical training, she could see her ankle swelling.

"That can't be good," she murmured. "I'm going to walk with a limp for the rest of my life."

He looked at her. "You sprained your ankle. You'll need to rest it and ice it for a couple of days, then you'll be fine."

"How do you know?"

"I've seen enough sprains."

"There's a lot of that in the security business? You work with especially clumsy people?"

He drew in a long breath. "I just know, okay?"

"Hey, I'm the one with the potentially life-threatening injury here. If anyone gets an attitude, it's me."

He muttered something that sounded like "Why me?" then he moved next to her and before she realized what was happening, picked her up in his arms.

The last time Willow had been carried anywhere, she'd been seven and throwing up from too much junk at the county fair. She shrieked and wrapped her arms around Kane's neck.

"What are you doing?" she demanded. "Put me down."

"I'm taking you inside so we can ice your ankle. Then I'll wrap it and figure out a way to get you home."

"I can drive."

"I don't think so."

"You said it wasn't that bad," she reminded him as she noticed he seemed to carry her effortlessly. Apparently the muscles were for real.

"You're in some kind of shock. You shouldn't be driving."

Shock or not, she didn't like the sensation of being swept away. She preferred to be in charge of her own destiny. Besides, there were other considerations.

"You left my shoe and sock back there," she said. "And your jacket."

"I'll get them when you're settled."

"What about the cat?"

Her rescuer gave her a look that told her he was questioning her grip on reality. She really hated when that happened.

"The one in the tree. I think she's giving birth. I saw her when I was falling—I'm good at multitasking that way. It's cold. We can't leave her out there. Do you have a box and some old towels? Or newspaper first, maybe towels later. Isn't birth messy? I know it's a part of the cycle of life and all, but there are fluids."

He stepped onto the stone path and walked toward a gatehouse. Willow let the cat issue drop as she stared at the pretty structure. It was all windows and wood, perfectly suited for the surroundings. But it wasn't the main house.

"Hey, where are you taking me?" she demanded, having sudden visions of a dark dungeon with chains and handcuffs on the walls.

"My house. I have first-aid supplies here."

Oh, right. That made sense. "You live on the property?"

"It's convenient."

"It shortens the commute, if nothing else." She glanced around at the gardens. "Nice southern exposure. You could grow anything here." Gardening was a favorite hobby. Her fingers itched to be in the soil and planting.

"If you say so."

He slowly lowered her to the ground, but kept an arm around her and supported most of her weight. She leaned on him, her body nestled close.

He had to be well over six feet and a couple hundred pounds. He felt as solid as a building and she had the thought that whatever happened, this was a man who could keep a woman safe.

He dug keys out of his trouser pocket, then unlocked the door and carried her inside.

"If we were dating, this would be romantic," she said with a sigh. "Can we pretend?"

"To be dating? No."

"But I'm injured. I may die and, frankly, it's your fault. Is it because you're married?"

He lowered her into the chair by the fireplace, then put her injured foot on the ottoman.

"You're the one who ran," he said. "It's your fault. I'm not married and don't move."

He disappeared into what Willow suspected was the kitchen. All right, so Kane didn't mind doing the rescue thing, but he wasn't exactly friendly about it. She could handle that.

She looked at the room, liking the high beamed ceiling and the earth tones. The space was bigger than she would have thought, yet still cozy. The large windows that faced south cried out for a few planter boxes, though.

On the table next to her was a book on the Middle East. Financial magazines littered the coffee table in front of the sofa. Interesting reading for a security guy.

"Engaged?" she yelled.

He mumbled something she couldn't hear, then said, "No."

"So the lack of pretending is a personal thing. Are you getting ice?"

"Yes."

"Don't forget the box for the cat."

"There's no cat."

"Oh, there's a cat. It's too cold. Even if she'd be okay, what about her kittens? They're newborn. We can't just leave them to die."

"There's no damn cat."

There was a cat, Kane thought grimly as he stared into the hollow of the tree. A gray and white one with three tiny kittens. Despite having been pregnant until a couple of hours ago, the cat looked skinny and bedraggled.

A stray, he thought, wondering what he'd done to deserve this. He was a decent guy. He tried to do the right thing. All he asked was that the world leave him alone. For the most part, the world agreed. Until today.

As the odds of the cat getting into the box were close to zero, he set it on the ground and studied the situation. He wasn't a pet person, but he knew enough to know cats had claws, teeth and miserable dispositions. However, this cat had recently given birth, so maybe it was weak and therefore feeling more cooperative. It was also a new mother and likely to be protective.

One way or the other, he knew there was going to be blood spilt and it was going to be his.

He reached inside the hollow and closed his hand around the first kitten. The mother cat stared at him and put her paw on top of his hand. As he began to move the impossibly small ratlike baby, claws sank into his skin. Oh, yeah, a real good time.

"Look. I've got to get you and the kittens inside. It's cold and it'll be foggy tonight. I know you're hungry and tired so just shut up and cooperate."

The cat blinked slowly. The claws retracted.

He scooped up the kittens and set them in the nest of towels he'd folded in the box, then reached for the mother cat. She hissed, then rose and jumped gracefully onto the towels and curled up around her babies.

Kane grabbed his coat, Willow's shoe and sock and the box, then headed back to his place.

This wasn't how his day was supposed to go. He lived a quiet life by choice. He liked his place—it was secluded and he didn't get visitors. Solitude was his friend and he didn't need any others. So why did he have an uncomfortable sensation that everything was about to change?

He walked into the gatehouse and found Willow on the phone.

"Gotta go," she said. "Kane's back with the cat and her kittens. Uh-huh. No, that's great. Thanks, Marina. I appreciate it."

"You called someone?" he asked as he set the box by the fireplace.

"You gave me the phone. Was I not supposed to use it?"

"It was for emergencies."

"You didn't say that. Anyway, the call was local. I phoned my sister. She's bringing over cat food and a litter box. Oh, and some dishes, because I didn't think you'd want to use yours for the cat food. I'd put money on her calling Mom and telling her what happened, which means Dr. Greenberg is probably going to want to check me out before I can move."

"You have a doctor who makes house calls?"

"My mom's worked for him for years. He's great." She glanced at her watch. "We should have this all wrapped up by two or three. Really. But if you have to be somewhere, don't let me keep you."

As if he was going to leave her alone in his place. "I can work from home today."

"So that's all good."

She smiled at him, as if all this was normal. As if *she* was normal.

"You can't do this," he told her. "You can't invade my life."

"I didn't invade it. I stumbled into it. Literally."

There was that smile again—the one that transformed her from pretty to beautiful and made her eyes twinkle. As if there was a joke that only she got. Which, based on her loose grasp of reality, was probably true.

"Who the hell are you?" he demanded.

"I told you. Julie's sister."

"Why aren't you at work?"

"Oh, I work from home, too. I'm a cartoonist, actually. I have my own comic strip. I'm syndicated. Do you have anything to eat? I'm starved."

He didn't keep much food around. It was always easier to grab a meal on his way home from work. But there had to be something.

"I'll go look." He stalked toward the kitchen.

"Nothing with meat. I'm a vegetarian."

"Of course you are," he muttered.

The cat had followed him into the kitchen. He searched his bare pantry and found a can of tuna. After opening it, he dumped the contents on a plate and set it on the floor. The cat gulped down the food.

"She must have been starving."

He looked up and saw Willow standing in the doorway. She was balanced on one foot, holding on to the door frame, her gaze focused on the stray.

"Poor thing. All alone in the world and pregnant. You know whoever the guy cat is, he didn't bother to stick around. It's just so typical. A real statement on our society today."

Kane rubbed his temples as he felt the beginnings of a headache.

"You should be sitting," he said. "You need to ice your ankle."

"I'm getting cold from the ice. Do you have any tea?"

He wanted to snap back that this wasn't the kitchen at the Four Seasons and no he didn't have any damn tea. That she should be grateful he hadn't left her and the stupid cat out there to freeze to death.

Except this was Los Angeles and it never got close to freezing and there was something in Willow's blue eyes, an expectation of goodness and trust, that stopped him.

She was the kind of woman who expected the best from people and would bet a large portion of his considerable bank account that she'd been disappointed more often than not.

"No tea."

She nodded. "Not the tea type, huh? You're too macho for that."

"Macho?"

"Manly, virile, whatever."

"Virile?"

"I'm just guessing on that one. It might not be true. You don't seem to have a woman in your life."

He felt an unusual need to growl at her. "You screw with my day, threaten my boss, run from me, blame me because you tripped and now you're questioning my…my…"

"Manhood?" she offered helpfully. "Am I making you

crazy? It happens. I try not to do that to people and I don't always know when I'm doing it."

"You're doing it now."

"Then I'll stop. Would it help if I hopped back to my chair?"

"More than you know."

"Okay."

She turned, then swayed and grabbed on to the door frame to keep her balance. He swore and stepped over the cat to pick her up.

"It's just the blood loss," she said as she rested her head on his shoulder. "I'll be fine."

"Especially considering you haven't lost any blood."

"But I could have."

He turned his head to look at her. It was only then that he realized how close their mouths were. His gaze locked on the curve of her lips and he had a pressing need to rest his mouth there. Just for a second. To know what she felt like and how she tasted.

He shouldn't. He would only hurt her—it was as inevitable as the sunrise and yet he was tempted.

"I wouldn't mind," she whispered. "I know I'm not your type but I wouldn't ever tell anyone."

He didn't know what she was talking about and he didn't care. Because for once in his life, he was going to do the one thing he knew he shouldn't.

He was going to kiss her.

Two

Kane claimed Willow with a kiss that took her breath away. Powerful, sensual, erotic. She couldn't say what was different, how his mouth pressing against hers was unlike any other kiss, but it was.

His lips were firm and demanding, but with a gentleness that made her want to give him anything he wanted. She knew he could just claim her—he was more than capable of taking, but the fact that he didn't seemed to make him even more powerful and appealing.

She clung to him, her arms around his neck. Her body straining to be closer. He touched his tongue to her lower lip and she parted for him instantly.

When he swept into her mouth, she felt heat pouring through her body. Need made her quiver and if she'd been standing, she would have collapsed.

His tongue explored her, teased her, excited her. He

tasted of coffee and some exotic flavor that left her hungry for more. She kissed him back with an enthusiasm that probably should have embarrassed her, but as she figured this was a one time thing, why not go for it.

The kiss went on and on until various parts of her body began complaining that they, too, wanted some of that. Her breasts ached and between her legs she felt a distinct longing.

Finally he raised his head and looked at her. Passion darkened his eyes to the color of storm clouds, which was something she'd never been able to think before. The wanting tightened his features and made him look predatory.

"You want to have sex with me!" she announced, so pleased she nearly kissed him again.

He muttered something under his breath and carried her back to the chair on the living room.

"We're *not* having sex," he told her.

"Oh, I know. I don't know you and that would make it tacky, but you were interested. Plus, you held me for a long time without breaking a sweat. So you must work out."

He shook his head. "I've never understood why anyone would want to bang his head against a wall, but now I get it."

She ignored that. "Kane?"

He glanced at her.

Her breath caught. It was still there—the need. Men had offered to take her to bed before, but they'd never *needed* her. Not sexually.

"Wow. I'm not imagining it. You are so incredibly sweet. Thank you."

"I'm not sweet. I'm a cold son of a bitch."

Oh, please. She smiled. "You've made my whole day. Guys don't ever want me. Not really."

He looked her up and down in a blatantly sexual way.

She supposed that to be a fully realized woman, she should be insulted, but in truth, it was thrilling.

"Trust me—guys want you. You're just not paying attention."

"No, they don't. I'm the warm, caring type who takes in strays. I give them a home—well, not literally. I mean they don't come live with me. But I rescue them. You know, patch them up, give them support, care about them and then they leave. But they never...you know."

"Wanted to sleep with you?" he asked bluntly.

She winced. "Not usually. Which is fine. Some are just friends, but others..." She shrugged. "It's kind of the way my life goes."

She could deal with that—it was her destiny to fix the guys and send them on their way. But sometimes she wished they would see her as something other than a good friend. There had been a couple she'd wanted to stick around.

"Just so we're clear," he said. "I don't need rescuing."

She wasn't sure she believed him, but she was willing to let it go for now. Mostly because the wanting thing was so incredible.

"You're so good-looking and powerful," she said with a sigh. "Not my type at all, not that I'm complaining."

"Good to know," he said dryly.

"You could kiss me again. I wouldn't mind."

"While that's a pretty irresistible invitation, I'll find you something to eat instead."

She was kind of hungry. "But you do still want me, right? That hasn't faded."

He looked into her eyes and she felt the pull of his need. Her insides got all hot and quivery.

"Wow," she breathed as he turned away. "You're good."

"I live to serve."

He crossed to the kitchen where she heard him opening cupboard doors. She glanced at the mother cat licking her babies.

"I think you're going to be really happy here," she whispered. "Kane is nice and gentle. He'll be a good owner."

Or he *would* be, once she convinced him that he wanted to keep the mother cat and her kittens. He was at heart, she believed, a decent man. With her need to rescue, she didn't find decent very often.

There was a knock on the door.

"I'll get that," she said as she slid to the edge of the chair and prepared to stand on one leg.

"This is my place and I'll get it," he told her as he walked across the hardwood floor. "Sit. Stay."

"You kiss too good for me to be scared of you," she told him.

He ignored her and opened the door. "Yes?"

"I'm Marina Nelson. I'm here to see my sister." She thrust a bag into his arms. "There are more in the car."

Willow twisted in her seat and waved. "You came."

"Of course I came. You said you'd fallen and broken your ankle."

"I called Marina because I knew she was home this morning," Willow said to Kane, "Julie's at work. Are you going to step aside so she can come in?"

"I haven't decided."

"You could push past him," Willow told her sister.

Marina shook her head. "He looks burly."

Willow opened her mouth to say that he wasn't all that tough and that he was an amazing kisser, then she thought better of it. It was really the sort of information she needed to keep to herself.

"You look alike," Kane said.

Willow sighed. Obviously he was going to be difficult. "All three of us do. It's quite a gene pool. Are you going to let her in?"

"Do I have a choice?"

"If I leave now, I'll only come back with reinforcements," Marina told him.

"Right."

He moved aside and Marina slipped past him. She rushed to the chair and hugged Willow.

"What on earth happened? What are you doing here? What did you do to your poor foot?" Marina sank onto the ottoman and leaned forward. "Start at the beginning and tell me everything."

Kane took the single bag into the kitchen, then disappeared outside.

"So talk," Marina said.

"I haven't been able to forget about Todd," Willow began. "I kept getting madder and madder. Or is it more mad? Anyway, when I woke up this morning, I just couldn't stand it anymore."

Marina looked at her. "Tell me you didn't come over here to take him on."

"That's exactly what she did," Kane said as he walked in with an armful of bags. "Are there more in the trunk?"

"No, just those in the backseat. Thanks."

He grunted, then disappeared into the kitchen.

Willow watched him go, admiring the way his slacks tightened around his butt as he moved. She'd never been one of those women who admired men's rears before, but then she'd never seen one this good.

"Willow," Marina said impatiently.

"What? Oh, sorry. So I came over here to yell at Todd. He nearly broke up Julie and Ryan and I couldn't stand thinking about that. I mean who does he think he is? Plus there's the whole million dollar thing just hanging out there and he's so self-centered and egotistical you just know he's thinking we're dying to meet him now that Julie's engaged. I just want to beat him with a stick."

"For someone who's a vegetarian and so into being one with nature, you're surprisingly violent," Kane called from the kitchen.

"I'm not violent," she yelled back. "I wasn't the one flashing a gun around. Where is it, by the way?"

"Somewhere you can't get it."

Marina's eyes widened. "He had a gun?"

"Yes, but don't worry about it. So I came here and Kane answered the door and I guess he thought I was a serious threat because he tried to grab me."

"What?"

"It's his job. He's in charge of security for all of Todd and Ryan's companies. You have to be clear on that. He's a little touchy about people thinking he's only in charge of the house or something."

"I'm not touchy."

The words were a little garbled, as if he were speaking through clenched teeth.

She leaned forward and lowered her voice. "He really is. Who knew? Okay, so he tried to grab me, I ran and got through the house, but he caught up with me on the grounds. Then I tripped, and as I went down, I not only ripped off my ankle, I saw the cat there giving birth. So here we are."

Marina covered her mouth, then dropped her hand to her lap. "I swear, I don't know if I should laugh or shriek. Only you, Willow, only you."

Kane walked out of the kitchen, holding a litter box in his hand. "Is this what I think it is?"

"Only if you think it's a cat box," Marina said, then turned back to her sister. "It's completely disposable and biodegradable. Cool, huh?"

"Very. Thanks for that. Where do you think we should put it?"

Marina glanced around the living room. "Somewhere a little more private."

Kane stared from the women to the litter box and back. What the hell had happened? When had he lost control of the situation, not to mention his life?

"I'll go find a place," Marina said. She stood and took the box from him, then smiled. "It's kind of a lot to take in. You probably need a minute to recover."

He watched her walk out of the living room and down the hallway. Great, Willow thought he needed rescuing and her sister was convinced he was an idiot.

"Is there a scooper?" Willow asked him. "You'll want that by the box, along with some paper towels.

He started to ask for what, then stopped himself. Right— it was basically a cat's bathroom. There would be deposits.

"She'll know how to use it, right?" he asked as he jerked his head toward the cat.

"Oh, sure. We'll just show her where it is."

Marina returned without the litter box. "The bathroom off the second bedroom seems like a good bet. I put it there." She walked to her sister, bent over and said in a low voice, "It doesn't look like he has women here on a regular basis, so that's something."

He was equally outraged and admiring. "I'm standing right here."

Willow smiled at him. "We know."

"He seems okay," Marina continued. "But given your history with guys…"

"It's true," Willow said sadly. "Maybe he's different."

"Still standing here," he announced.

"You could feed the cat," Willow said. "You'll probably be more comfortable in the kitchen while we're talking about you behind your back."

In a scary, twisted way, her words made sense. He retreated to the kitchen, all the while wondering what had happened. This morning everything about his life had been normal and pleasantly solitary. Somewhere along the way, he'd been invaded. There were people here—he didn't do people.

He went through the bags. There was canned cat food, a bag of dry and three bowls. He filled one with water and the other with dry food. The mother cat rushed into the kitchen and fell on the food. When he dished up some canned, she abandoned the dry to feast on that.

While she ate, he checked out the rest of the bags. Marina had brought over bread, honey, several packages of frozen soup, bags of cookies, apples, pears, some girly soap and the latest issue of a celebrity gossip magazine. Did she think her sister was moving in?

He felt something brush against his leg. When he glanced down he saw the mother cat rubbing her leg against him. She looked up, purring.

Feeling awkward and stupid and like he was being taken, he bent over and patted the top of her head. She turned and rubbed her jaw against his fingers. He could feel the vibration of her purring.

He'd never been one for pets. As a kid, it was all he could do to feed himself. Plus caring about anything only made you a victim. In the army, there had always been guys who kept dogs around, but he wasn't one of them.

He straightened. He could hear Willow and Marina

talking in the living room, although he couldn't hear the words, thank God. So now what? Where did he go? This was supposed to be his house, but he suddenly felt like he didn't belong.

There was another knock on the door. Before he could say anything, Marina yelled that she was getting it. He walked into his living room in time to see an older version of Willow stepping into his house, along with a fiftysomething guy in a suit.

"Mom, you didn't have to come," Willow said. "I'm fine."

Willow's mother handed Marina a casserole, then rushed to Willow's side. "You're not fine. You hurt yourself. What was I supposed to do? Just let you lie here in pain?"

"Oh, Mom."

The man approached Kane. "I'm Dr. David Greenberg, a friend of the family."

"Kane Dennison." They shook hands.

Dr. Greenberg moved over to the ottoman. "All right, Willow, let's see what you've done."

Willow's mother moved back. Marina touched her arm. "This is Kane, Mom."

The older woman smiled at him. "Hi. Naomi Nelson. She said you carried her here and saved her life."

Willow had managed to make a number of phone calls and pass on a lot of information in the short time he'd been gone, he thought, not sure if he should punish her or be impressed.

"I don't think she was all that near death," he said.

"Mom, there are kittens," Willow said. She pointed at the box.

"Oh, they're just born."

While Naomi went to coo over the kittens, Marina murmured something about putting the casserole in the refrigerator. Kane watched as the doctor examined Willow's ankle.

"Does this hurt?" he asked as he manipulated her foot. "Does this?"

She answered his questions, then looked at Kane. He felt the impact of her gaze all the way down to his groin. Funny how Marina was similar in appearance, but nothing about her turned him on. Yet with Willow, all it took was a look.

Dr. Greenberg continued his exam for a couple more minutes, then patted her knee. "You'll live. It's a minor sprain. You have some swelling, which should go away in the next couple of days. Keep doing what you're doing. Elevation and ice. You'll be better in the morning."

"It hurts," Willow said with a soft whimper.

The doctor smiled. "I remember how badly you handle pain. You're the one who cried before I ever gave you a shot when you were little." He dug around in his case and handed her a sample pack of pills. "These will help. Take them now and then don't even think about driving until tomorrow. You're going to be out of it."

She smiled. "You've been very good to me."

"I know." He stood, bent over and kissed her cheek. "Try not to be such a klutz."

"I didn't do this on purpose."

"But you still do it."

Naomi hurried over. "Thank you so much for coming."

The doctor shrugged. "I've known them nearly all their lives. They're like my girls, too. I'm going back to the office."

"I'll be there within the hour," Naomi promised.

Both women fluttered around, bringing Willow water so she could take her pill, more ice, a snack. Kane stayed in the background, watching them move so easily through his place—as if they'd been here before. Or maybe that was the way of nurturers. They were comfortable wherever they went.

At last Marina left, leaving only Willow and her mother. Naomi beckoned him into the kitchen.

"Thank you for all your help," she began. "I'm sorry we've all invaded you like this."

"It's fine," he said, when what he was thinking was more along the lines of "you could be gone now."

"I'll just get her things and take her home."

Kane eyed the woman. She was about five-five and in decent shape, but there was no way she could carry her daughter.

"I'll do that," he said, knowing it was the only way. "You can't carry her inside."

"Oh." Naomi looked concerned. "I hadn't thought about that. With her foot and all… Can she hop?"

"Not well. Don't worry. I'll get her home."

"If you're sure…" She glanced at her watch and he knew she was thinking she had to get back to work.

"Ask Willow if she's comfortable with that arrangement," he said.

Naomi nodded, then walked back into the living room. Kane followed her and watched as Willow and her mother spoke.

"I'll be fine," Willow said, glancing at him, her blue eyes bright with anticipation and humor.

He narrowed his gaze. What the hell was she planning now?

Naomi hugged her daughter, then walked over to him and held out her hand. "You've been very kind. I don't know how to thank you."

"Not a problem."

"Good luck with the cat and her kittens. They're going to be a handful."

As they wouldn't still be here while they were growing up, he didn't care.

Then she was gone and he was alone with Willow.

"Sorry about everyone coming by," she said.

"No, you're not. You invited them all. You wanted them to come."

"Okay. Maybe. I had to be sure I wasn't dying."

"Sprained ankles are rarely fatal."

"At least they brought food." She smiled. "You like food."

"How do you know?"

"You're a guy. It's a guy thing."

"I'm going to get the cat food," he said and turned back to the kitchen.

"You haven't fed her yet?" Willow sounded outraged.

He held in a groan. "Of course I fed the cat. I'm going to collect the food so you can have it."

"I don't eat cat food."

She was doing this on purpose. He knew that. She thought baiting him was a fun, new game.

"It's for the cat," he said patiently.

"The cat's not coming home with me. My building doesn't allow pets, which is one of the reasons I rented there. That and the amazing backyard. I turned it into a garden and it's so beautiful. But there are a lot of plants that would be poisonous to a kitten. Not that I wouldn't love one. But I know better. If I rescue one cat, soon I'll want to rescue them all. Then there are dogs and birds and it could really turn into a disaster."

He rarely got headaches, but he could feel one coming on.

"I'm *not* keeping the cat."

"You have to," she told him. "The kittens are too young

to be moved. They have to be warm and they need their mom. Oh, do you have a hot water bottle to put in the box, because that would be great."

He could hear a strange buzzing in his ears. "Aren't there rescue places?"

"Sure, but they're already busy with real strays. This cat has a home, at least until the babies are older."

"They don't have a home here."

She stared at him, wide-eyed. He knew he was being manipulated and knew he wasn't going to give in.

"I don't do cats," he said firmly. "Not this one, not any one."

"That's so mean."

She spoke softly. He barely heard the words, yet it was as if she'd slapped him. Her blue eyes darkened with disappointment and she seemed to shrink into the chair.

"All right," she told him. "Just get the cat supplies together. I'll figure out something."

He'd led men into more dangerous parts of the world than most people knew about. He'd killed to stay alive and had been left for dead more than once. Yet never had he felt so out of his element than he did at this moment.

What the hell did he care what this woman thought of him? It was a damn cat. Let her take it.

He went into the kitchen and put the food into a grocery bag, then carried it into the living room. But when he glanced at Willow, he saw she'd fallen asleep.

Her head lay on the armrest, her long blond hair a contrast to the dark leather. One leg curled up under her while the other one was stretched out, ice still strapped to her injured ankle.

"Willow?"

She didn't stir. In addition to being a wimp about pain,

she was also a lightweight when it came to painkillers. No wonder the doctor had told her not to drive after taking it.

The room was silent, except for the quiet purring of the mother cat and loud thudding of his own heart.

Willow woke up and had no idea where she was. As if that had never happened to her before, she immediately sat up and thought about panicking. But before the adrenaline could really get pumping, she remembered the whole Kane-ankle-cat thing and decided she was probably still in his house.

A quick glance at the clock on the nightstand told her it was nearly midnight. Wow—that pill had knocked her out for hours. She sat up and looked around. A night-light from the bathroom allowed her to see the shapes of the furniture, including the bed she'd slept on. The guest room, she thought, noting the bed wasn't huge and the furniture looked more neutral than masculine. Too bad. She really wouldn't have minded waking up in his bed…with him.

Smiling at the thought, she looked down at herself and saw that except for her shoes, she was completely dressed. Kane had been a gentleman. Wasn't that just her luck?

Willow sighed. She was never really like this about guys. But there was just something about Kane that got to her and made her want to be wild. Maybe because being around him felt safe. As if no matter what she did or how she acted, nothing bad would happen to her. He would be there, protecting her.

No one had ever been safe before.

She swung her feet over the side of the bed and stood carefully. While her ankle was still sore, it was a ton better. She could almost walk normally.

After visiting the bathroom—where she found a brand-new toothbrush and toothpaste conveniently waiting—she made use of the facilities, washed her face, brushed her teeth, then went in search of her host.

Kane was in the living room, reading. He glanced up as she entered.

"Sorry," she said. "The pill knocked me out."

"I noticed."

"So, you, um, carried me to bed."

"Yes."

"I slept through that."

"Apparently."

"You kept my clothes on."

"It seemed the polite thing to do."

"Okay."

One corner of his mouth twitched. "Should I have stripped you naked and taken you while you were unconscious?"

"Of course not. It's just…"

He kissed her before. Hadn't he meant it?

He stood and walked over to her. In less than a second, the humor was gone and he looked…predatory.

"You're playing a dangerous game," he told her. "You don't know anything about me."

It was true. The sensible part of her brain told her to quietly back away, retreat to the guest room and lock the door behind her. Only, he'd wanted her before. Really wanted her. The sensible part of her brain needed to remember how rare that was.

He reached up and fingered a strand of her hair. "Like silk," he murmured.

And then it was back—the fire that had thrilled her so much. She felt the heat burn between them, drawing her closer, making her promises, tempting her into the path of possible destruction.

Three

"I don't get it," Willow said. "I'm not your type."

"You said that before. How do you know?"

"I'm not anyone's type."

Kane shook his head. "I don't believe that."

"It's true. I have the sad, painful romantic history to prove it. I'm the best friend, the one guys confide in."

"I don't confide in anyone," he told her.

"You should. It's very healthy. Sharing problems make them seem more manageable."

"You know this how?"

"I read it in a magazine somewhere. You can learn a lot from magazines."

His dark gaze never left her face. "Go back to bed. I'll take you home in the morning."

No! She didn't want to be sent to bed like a child. "But then where will you sleep?"

"You're in the guest room. I still have my own bed."

"See, that was flirting. I was flirting. Wouldn't it be nice if you just went with it?"

He moved so fast, he was like a human blur. One second he was several feet away and the next he was right in front of her, one hand on her waist, the other wrapped around her hair. He eased forward that last inch, so they were touching everywhere.

She had the feeling he was trying to intimidate her and it would have worked, except she couldn't seem to be afraid of him.

"You won't hurt me," she whispered.

"Your faith is foolish and misplaced. You don't know what I'll do."

He bent his head and claimed her with a hard, demanding kiss. He pushed into her mouth and stroked her tongue, then sucked on her lower lip.

She wrapped one arm around his neck and gave as good as she got, stealing into his mouth and dueling right back. She felt him stiffen with surprise. He pulled her hard against him and she went willingly. The hand holding her hair tightened, drawing her head back.

He broke the kiss and stared into her eyes.

"I am dark and dangerous and I don't play the games you know," he said. "I'm not anyone you want to get involved with. I'm not nice, I don't call the next day and I'm never interested in more than a single night. You can't fix me, reform me, heal me or change me. You are so far out of your league, you don't know enough to run scared, but you should. Trust me on that."

His words made her tremble.

"I can't be afraid of you," she told him again.

"Why the hell not?"

She smiled and rubbed her index finger against his lower lip. "I'll agree that you're tough and you probably scare other people, but Kane, you rescued me and kittens and you were nice to my mom and my sister and when you put me to bed, you didn't even think about taking advantage of me. What's not to like?"

He closed his eyes and groaned. She had a feeling the sound wasn't about being turned on.

He opened his eyes. "You're impossible."

"I've heard that before."

"You're just about irresistible."

She sighed. "That's a new one. Can you say it again?"

He backed her up until she was trapped between him and the wall. She felt his body—and his arousal—pressing against her.

"I want you," he said in a low growl. "I want you naked and begging and desperate. I want to bury myself inside of you until you forget who you are. But you're a fool if you take me up on that. This is not a fun trip to the dark side. If you expect anything of me, you *will* be hurt. I'm going to walk away, Willow. I can walk away now or later. It's your choice."

She saw the truth reflected in his eyes. Once again the sensible part of her brain pointed out that the guest room was the best option. Only Willow had never met anyone like Kane before and she was unlikely to ever again. He claimed to be incredibly tough and maybe he was, but she had a feeling there was more to him than he wanted her to see.

Walk away? Not possible. Maybe he would hurt her, but maybe he wouldn't. She was willing to take the risk. She had to. There was something about him that called to her.

Besides, the guy could make her quiver with just a look.

"For a man so intent on insisting he doesn't care, you're

going out of your way to warn me off," she said. "Maybe you should stop talking and kiss me instead."

"Willow."

"See? You're doing it again. I understand the rules, I'm willing to play by them and you're still talking. You know what? I think it's all an act. I don't think you have any real intention of doing anything at all. I think—"

He grabbed her and kissed her. There were no preliminaries, just him wrapping his arms around her as he claimed her mouth with his own. He kissed her deeply, passionately, with no pause for breath or social niceties. He took, sweeping past her lips to stroke her tongue, circling her, claiming her. His possessive acts thrilled her and she freed her arms so she could hang on for the ride.

There was no fear, she thought as her body heated and her muscles lost their ability to support her. However much he threatened, he still held her gently. His hands moved up and down her back, exploring her, touching her, but there was nothing harsh about the contact.

She put her hands on his shoulders and leaned into him. His body supported hers. The combination of hard muscles and warmth thrilled her. She tilted her head and closed her lips around his tongue so she could suck.

He stiffened, then took a step back and stared at her. There was shock, pleasure and need in his eyes—an irresistible combination.

"I don't scare easily," she said with a shrug.

He shook his head, then bent down, gathered her in his arms and carried her down the hall.

They moved into a bedroom illuminated by a single lamp on a nightstand. Here the design was totally masculine with large pieces of dark furniture lining the walls. The bed could sleep twenty, and suited Kane completely.

He set her on the mattress and looked at her.

She felt the challenge of his gaze and refused to look away—even when he began unfastening the shirt he wore. When he'd removed that, he pulled off a T-shirt, exposing his bare chest.

Her breath caught. He was as muscled as she'd first thought, but there were also scars...dozens of them. Small irregular circles and long, jagged lines. Scars from surgeries and from wounds that made her ache inside.

What had happened to this man? Who had hurt him and why?

But there was no time for questions. He pulled off his loafers, then his socks. Trousers quickly followed, along with dark briefs.

And then he was naked. Beautiful and hard and ready. His body should be immortalized in marble, she thought. A master should sculpt him. Not that Kane would ever agree to pose.

He put his hands on his hips and stared at her. "You can still run," he told her.

"Not with my ankle."

"You know what I mean."

"Yes, I do. And I'm not going anywhere."

He took a step toward the bed, then stopped. "Dammit, Willow," he began.

She pulled her sweater up and over her head, then tossed it onto the floor. "So what, exactly, does a girl have to do to get your attention?"

He made a sound in his throat that was part growl, part groan. Then he was on the bed, on top of her, rolling with her so that she ended up sprawled across him. He tangled one hand in her hair and claimed her with a kiss that made her toes curl.

She parted for him, welcomed him. Their tongues danced. He stroked her bare back, his fingers moving slowly over her skin. When he reached the waistband of her jeans, he slipped his hands over the curve of her rear and squeezed.

She could feel his arousal pressing into his stomach. Her skin was hot and hungry for his touch. She wanted his hands everywhere, touching her, taking her, claiming her.

He shifted so she was on her back. His dark eyes stared into hers.

"You are so beautiful," he whispered before reaching behind her to unfasten her bra.

His words delighted her, but they weren't nearly as thrilling as his mouth on her bare breast. One moment there was fabric, then a whisper of cool air followed by the warm, wet sensation of lips and tongue.

He suckled her and she felt the pull through her belly and between her legs. His teeth scraped her nipple, then he licked that tight point until she felt a scream building up inside of her.

The wanting grew until it was unbearable. Her legs moved restlessly. She wanted to rip off the rest of her clothes and feel their naked bodies press together.

He turned his attention to her other breast and repeated his attentions. She stroked his shoulders, his back, then ran her fingers through his short hair. Sensations swept through her. Pleasure and tension and a deep hunger for more and more and more.

He began to drift lower, kissing her ribs, then her belly. He unfastened her jeans and continued to kiss as he went. Soft kisses, wet kisses, nibbling kisses. He anointed her with his mouth and tongue, driving her need higher and higher.

He grabbed the waistband of her jeans and drew them off in one easy, practiced movement. Her bikini panties went with them, leaving her as naked as he. Then he continued kissing his way down and down and down.

When he was inches from the promised land and she thought she might die if he didn't finally touch her *there*, she eased her thighs open and braced herself for the assault.

It was amazing. Hot and wet and fast and slow and everything in between. He licked all of her, teased her, made her whimper with gentle sucking before settling down into a rhythm designed to make her beg for him to never stop.

He moved his tongue back and forth, drawing her in deeper, pushing her to the edge, then pulling her back. Twice she was sure she was going to come, then he slowed and she lost it.

Her breath came in quick pants. She clutched at the sheets and dug her heels into the mattress. He picked up the pace again and she found herself straining toward her release. His tongue moved back and forth, taking her higher and higher. She was so close...so incredibly close.

"Kane," she breathed.

He stopped. He actually stopped. She felt her release slipping away and nearly cried in frustration. Then he pushed a single finger inside of her. In and out, circling. A deep, pulsing began building through her body, the intensity stunning her. She could barely breathe from all the powerful sensations. He put his mouth on her most swollen, sensitive spot and sucked. At the same time, he touched her with the very tip of his tongue.

Without warning, she exploded into her release. One second there was nothing, the next, her whole body was shaking from the powerful waves crashing through her. It was incredible and nearly violent and unlike anything she'd experienced.

The pleasure seemed to go on forever. Finally it began to fade and he raised his head to look at her.

There was still hunger in those dark eyes, but also satisfaction. She couldn't find it in her heart to even mind. The man had earned it.

"I'm boneless," she whispered.

"That was the point."

"You're really good at that."

"You're easy."

She smiled. "Words every woman longs to hear."

He knelt between her legs and reached for the nightstand drawer. "You're sexually responsive."

"Better."

He pulled out a condom, put it on and then eased between her thighs. His dark eyes were bright with wanting and need and desire. Willow reached down to guide him inside of her, then gasped as he filled her, stretching her with his hard thickness.

But instead of thrusting inside and having his way with her, he moved slowly, giving her time to adjust and appreciate their differences.

She tightened around him, wanting the experience to be as good for him as it had been for her. He groaned in appreciation, then shifted so he could touch her while he continued to move in and out.

She opened her eyes and prepared to ask him what he was doing, only at that exact moment, his fingers came in contact with her center.

She was already sensitive from what he'd done before and the combination of his skilled touch and his arousal pushing into her quickly took her to the edge of another release. She'd planned to focus on him and his pleasure, but soon it was all she could do to keep breathing.

He rubbed faster and faster, keeping the exact amount of pressure, while the pace of him moving in and out remained steady.

There was too much going on, she thought frantically. She didn't know where to focus her attention. It was all so good, so incredible, so...

Her release swept through her, making her body burn as it shuddered in waves of perfect pleasure. Kane leaned forward so he could brace himself above her and began to pump his hips. The movement was enough to keep her own climax going on and on, seemingly endless.

Nothing had ever been like this. She hadn't known her body was capable of these kinds of sensations. She clung to him, giving herself up to him, feeling him get closer and closer until he groaned and was still.

Willow tried to catch her breath. If she'd been boneless before, she was positively two-dimensional now. She would never be able to walk again, but that was okay. She would have the memories of this night to sustain her.

He rolled off her onto his back, then wrapped an arm around her and pulled her close.

She snuggled up against him and rested her head on his shoulder. She could feel the rapid beat of his heart and his heavy breathing.

"Not bad for a rookie," she said.

He laughed. "Gee, thanks."

She smiled. "You know your stuff. You could probably heal a few diseases with that technique."

"Like I said, you're easy."

If being easy meant feeling like this, she was all for it. Until tonight she'd been able to count her physical experiences on two fingers. Neither encounter had prepared her for Kane's mastery.

His heartbeat had slowed, as had his breathing. She could feel herself getting sleepy. The part of her brain that could still function wondered if she should offer to head back to the guest room bed. But then she reminded herself this was Kane. If he wanted her gone, he would have no problem telling her exactly that.

So much for being a big, bad tough guy, she thought as she snuggled closer and closed her eyes.

Kane woke shortly before dawn and knew there were two things wrong—the woman in his bed and the intruder moving through his bedroom.

He knew the woman was Willow and someone he could deal with later. First there was the matter of the intruder. But before he could slip out of bed and attack, a skinny cat jumped on his chest and meowed in his face.

"Good morning to you, too," he muttered and raised his hand. She rubbed against his fingers before settling down on his chest and purring loudly.

He shifted her onto the bed and got up. After grabbing a robe, he walked into the kitchen and started the coffee machine. The cat followed. When he'd flipped on the machine, he checked out her food. The bowl of canned was licked clean and most of the dry was gone. He gave her more of both, then walked into the living room.

The kittens were still in their box. One was awake and mewing for its mother. He bent over and stroked the tiny body. The kittens were blind and defenseless. In the wild, they'd be dead within hours. There were plenty of small predators on the grounds to deal with them. It was just the ugly side of life.

He could see that and accept it, but not Willow. She wanted to save the world. Funny how she hadn't learned that a lot of the world wasn't worth saving.

Willow awoke to sunlight spilling into the bedroom and the smell of coffee filling the house. A quick glance at the clock on the nightstand told her it was after eight and she was still in Kane's bed. Not to mention…naked.

She smiled as she stretched, feeling sore muscles protest. It had been some workout. Make that workouts with an *S*, because sometime well after three in the morning, Kane had done the whole thing again.

She stood and strolled into the bathroom where she found her clothes all neatly folded. After showering, she dressed and was able to get her foot in her shoe with no problem. The swelling was nearly gone and her ankle barely hurt at all. She walked into the kitchen and poured herself coffee, then headed for the living room.

Kane sat at a desk in the corner, facing his laptop. He, too, had showered and dressed, mostly likely in the guest room because she hadn't heard him.

He looked up at her, but didn't speak. He looked dark and dangerous and there wasn't a hint of desire or softness in his eyes.

"Don't panic," she said with a smile. "I'm leaving as soon as I'm done with my coffee, so you can afford to be pleasant. I promise, you won't have to resort to scaring me off."

"Why should I believe you? You settle in very easily."

His voice was familiar and sexy. She liked the way it played in her mind, the low notes making her shiver.

"I have things to do," she told him. "Important things."

"I can only imagine."

She walked closer to the desk. "What are you doing? Work stuff?"

"I finished that earlier. This is personal."

"Ooh. An online girlfriend."

He shook his head and turned the computer toward her. She saw a picture of a beautiful island. The sky was an impossible shade of blue, the sands nearly white. In her next life, when she was rich, she would hang out in places like that.

"Vacation?" she asked.

"Retirement. I'll be ready in eight years. Five if my investments continue to pay off better than I expect."

Retire? She frowned. "But you're barely in your thirties."

"Thirty-three."

She sank into the club chair by the desk. "Why would you want to retire?"

"Because I can. I've done as much as I want to do."

And she'd barely started on *her* life. "Like what?"

He leaned back in his chair. "I lied about my age, faked a birth certificate and joined the army when I was sixteen. I was there for ten years, eight of them in Special Forces."

Which explained the scars, she thought. A warrior. Her heart gave a little shimmy.

"After I got out, I spent four years protecting rich people in dangerous parts of the world. The money was good, but I got tired of being shot at. I took the job with Todd and Ryan because I get in on the ground floor with a lot of start-ups. It's a good way to make a fortune."

"Is that what you need? A fortune?" If he was planning on retiring in five to eight years, he probably already had one.

"I need several."

"For what?"

He jerked his head at the computer screen. "Privacy and solitude don't come cheap. I want a place that's isolated and easy to defend. Where there aren't many people but there are things I like to do."

While she could respect the desire for a fortune or two—frankly, a third of a fortune would be enough for her—she didn't understand the need to be alone.

"What about family?" she asked. "A wife, kids? You can't keep them isolated."

"Not interested."

She tightened her grip on her coffee. "But then you'll be alone."

"Exactly."

"But that's not a good thing."

He looked at her. "I told you, Willow. I don't get involved. Ever."

It was like he was speaking a foreign language. "But family is everything to me," she told him. "I'd be lost without them. Everyone needs to belong, even you."

"You're wrong."

He spoke with a confidence that made her want to believe him. But she couldn't get her mind around the fact that he was planning to spend the rest of his life by himself.

"Last night was so intimate," she murmured.

"It was sex."

"Is that the only way you feel comfortable connecting? Sexually?"

He looked more amused than annoyed. "Don't try to analyze me. It won't work. I'm not broken—I don't need fixing."

"You need more in your life than just you, Kane." But he wasn't going to believe her. She looked across the room toward the basket where the mother cat licked her kittens. "Do you want me to call the rescue place about the cats?"

"They can stay for a couple of weeks. I looked online

and by then they'll have their eyes open and be moving around. I'll take them in after that."

She wanted to take heart in the fact that he was accepting pets into his life, but she knew he meant what he said. That it was only temporary.

"Do you, ah, want help with them?" she asked. "I can come by and feed them and stuff."

"I'm good."

There was something about his tone more than his words that made her feel as if he were slipping away. As if the connection had ceased to exist between them.

"Do you mind if I come visit them before you take them to the rescue place?" she asked.

"That would be fine."

She wanted to think he meant something significant by that, but somehow she couldn't convince herself. "Okay, then I should be going."

"I moved your car around back," he said, returning his attention to the computer screen. "It's just outside the front door."

"Thanks."

She took the coffee cup back into the kitchen and rinsed it out. After collecting her purse, she walked to the front door. "I guess I'll see you around."

"Goodbye, Willow."

"Bye." She opened the door, then hesitated. "Do you want my phone number?"

He looked at her then, his dark gaze locking with hers. She searched for some hint of the fire she'd seen before, but it was so gone, it was as if it had never been.

"No, you don't," she whispered, and left.

Four

Kane finished his presentation on security for the company's latest acquisition. Todd and Ryan glanced at each other.

"Remind us not to get involved with anything this proprietary again," Ryan said. "It's a real pain."

Kane thought about the executive detail he'd had to protect for two months in Afghanistan. Compared to that, this was something he could do with his eyes closed. "It's not that difficult. I'll handle it. As long as everyone follows procedure, we're protected."

"And if they don't?" Todd asked with a grin.

"Then they answer to me," Kane said.

Todd looked at Ryan. "This is why I like him."

"Right back at you."

Todd turned back to Kane. "I heard there was some trouble at the house yesterday. I go away for one day and all hell breaks loose?"

Kane had a sudden image of Willow in his bed, her body flushed, her eyes glazed and her long, blond hair spread out on the pillow. His groin tightened, but he ignored the flash of need, not to mention the pictures in his brain. It had happened, it was over, end of story.

Still, he couldn't stop wondering why she'd wanted to be with him. He would bet a large portion of his considerable bank account that she was the type who led with her heart. So why take on a guy just for the night?

"It was Willow," Ryan said. "Julie told me last evening. Apparently Willow's still a little annoyed that you got between me and Julie."

Todd grimaced. "I didn't get between you. I was looking out for a friend. You're happy now—that's the end of it." He returned his attention to Kane. "Should I be worried?"

Kane held in a smile. "I think you could take her."

"That's not what I meant. Is she crazy?"

"No. She wanted to tell you off because you'd messed with her sister."

"It's the money," Todd grumbled. "If Aunt Ruth hadn't offered her granddaughters a million dollars to marry me, none of this would have happened."

Kane raised his eyebrows. "I didn't know you were looking for a wife."

"I'm not." Todd sighed. "Aunt Ruth is our late uncle's second wife, so we're not actually related. Ruth had a daughter who ran off when she was seventeen and got married. Ruth and our uncle cut her off and apparently never had anything to do with her until a few months ago. Our uncle died. Ruth missed her daughter and got in touch with her only to discover there were three granddaughters she'd never met. Somewhere along the way, she got it in her head that life would be perfect if one of her granddaughters married me. She offered them each a million dollars if one of them would take me on."

Todd glared at Ryan. "Do you know how insulting that is? The assumption she has to pay someone to marry me?"

Ryan grinned. "Actually it's kind of funny."

"So says the man who's getting married."

Ryan turned to Kane. "I went on the first date to throw the sisters off the path. I met Julie and after a few complications, we got engaged."

Kane knew that Julie was also pregnant, but he wasn't about to say anything. Being in charge of security meant keeping secrets—and he was good at that.

"So everything worked out," Todd said. "Willow should just let it go."

"I don't think she'll be back," Kane told him. "Although there were a few interesting events." He explained about Willow running through the grounds and spraining her ankle. He left out the cat, the kittens and the sex.

Both his bosses stared at him. "You didn't just leave her there, did you?" Todd asked.

"I took her home and iced her ankle."

"To your house," Ryan confirmed.

"Uh-huh."

"You don't usually invite people to your house," Todd said.

"I didn't invite Willow. It just happened." Which was true. If only he had an excuse for what he'd done last night…and again this morning.

She'd been a hell of a temptation, but he'd been tempted before. And resisted. There was just something about her…

"Be careful," Ryan said with a grin. "The Nelson women are complicated. Just when you least expect it, they've invaded your world and changed everything."

"I'm not worried," Todd said confidently. "I'm not

marrying either one of them. They'll have to find their million dollars elsewhere."

"I was thinking more of Kane," Ryan said with a grin. "Willow's a pretty lady."

Todd looked at Kane. "Intrigued?"

Not in the way they meant. "I don't do relationships. Don't worry about me."

She was gone and he would never see her again, which was exactly how he liked things. But as the day wore on, he found himself remembering her smile, her laugh and the way she'd felt in his arms. It was as if she were a song he couldn't shake from his brain. One that played over and over and wouldn't go away.

Willow showed up on Saturday morning without warning because she didn't have Kane's phone number and naturally Mr. Macho Security Man wasn't listed. She'd even Googled him and had come up with nothing. It was as if he didn't exist.

But she knew he was real. Elusive and possibly dangerous to her emotional well-being but real. He was an interesting combination of contrasts. A tough man who knew how to be tender. A rich man who chose to live simply.

She'd told herself to forget him, but that wasn't happening anytime soon. All she had to do was close her eyes to remember how she'd felt when he touched her. Last night she'd even dreamed about him.

So she braced herself for possible rejection, grabbed the tote bag on the passenger seat and climbed out of her car. She was halfway up the walk when the front door to the gatehouse opened.

He wore jeans and a long-sleeved shirt and looked sexy enough to melt chocolate.

"You came back," he said, his voice, not to mention his expression, giving nothing away.

"I'm here to see the cats, not you," she said with a smile, hoping he wouldn't guess that was a big, fat lie. "You don't have to panic."

"I don't panic."

Her smile widened. "I can think of a few girly conversations that would make you sweat. Want to test my theory?"

One corner of his mouth twitched. "Not especially."

"I didn't think so." She held her tote in both hands. "I would have called first, but you didn't give me your number. And don't bother telling me you didn't give it to me on purpose. I already know that. You were afraid I'd turn into stalker girl."

"I'm not afraid of you."

She walked toward him and braced herself for the impact of seeing those dark eyes and that mouth up close.

"You could be, and you know it," she said cheerfully. "Now let me inside."

She was operating mostly on bravado, but either he didn't know that or he was just going with it. He stepped aside to let her in.

She walked into the living room and was assaulted by memories. There was the chair where he'd carried her when she'd first hurt her ankle and that was the doorway to the hall that led to the bedroom.

Her skin heated as she remembered him touching her. She swung to face him, prepared to mention how it had been, but the words died unspoken.

His expression was one of polite interest—nothing more. There was no humor, no flash of fire, no *need*. It was as if it had never been.

He hadn't been kidding about the one night, she thought

sadly. If she were someone else, she might have tried tempting him, but hey, this was her. What was the point? Instead she would have to be happy for what they'd had and remind herself that at least he'd wanted her once.

She dropped her tote on the ottoman and crossed to the box by the fireplace. The mother cat was curled up with her three kittens. She purred as Willow approached.

"Hi, sweetie," Willow murmured. "How have you been? Your babies are bigger. Look at how big they're getting. Are you doing all right?"

The cat rubbed her head against Willow's hand. "Is she still eating well?" she asked.

"About twice what I think she should," he told her. "Stuff comes out the other end really regularly, too."

She smiled. "At least we know she's healthy. That's something. Have you thought of a name?"

"I'm not naming the damn cat."

"But you have to. She needs an identity."

"She's a stray."

Willow sat on the carpet and looked up at him. She had to tilt her head back until she could meet his gaze. "Everyone deserves to have a name."

His mouth tightened. "Fine. You name her."

"Okay." She looked back at the gray and white cat. "How about Muffin."

"Not Muffin."

"Why not?"

"It's a food. You don't name a cat after something you eat."

So he had opinions, she thought as she held in a smile. "Then Pookey."

Kane made a strangled sound. "No."

"You've made it very clear this isn't your cat. Why do you get veto power?"

"It's living in my house. I'll have to call it by the name. Not Pookey."

He could barely say the word. Willow ducked her head so he wouldn't see her grinning.

"Jasmine? Snowflake? Princess Leia?"

"Princess Leia?"

"I'm a *Star Wars* fan. More the first three than the last three, but I like them all."

"Good to know. I can live with Jasmine."

"Not Snowflake?"

"She's not white."

"Snow can be gray."

He made a sound that was more strangled groan than growl, but she couldn't be totally sure about that.

"Then Jasmine," she said as she stood. "Hi, Jasmine. Welcome to the family." And before Kane could point out they weren't a family, she grabbed her tote and headed for the kitchen. "I'm going to make cookies."

He followed her. "Here? In my kitchen?"

"In your oven, actually," she said as she set the temperature. "My powers of cooking through psychic energy aren't what they used to be."

"What if I don't want cookies?"

She looked at him. "Everyone wants cookies. They're chocolate chip. What's not to like?"

She pulled a baking pan out of her tote along with a package of premade cookie dough. All she had to do was break off the little squares, put them on the pan and stick them in the oven. Nearly instant fresh-baked cookies.

When the pan was ready, she leaned against the counter and looked at him. He looked good...too good. He made her wish things could be different, that he was secretly desperate to have her again. If only there was a scrap of evidence, she would cling to that fantasy, but so far…not so much.

She also knew that he could throw her out in a heart-beat, if that was what he really wanted. The cookies wouldn't matter to him. But as he made no move to bodily remove her, she settled in for a little visit.

"So," she said, "how are things?"

"It's not going to work," he told her.

"What isn't?"

"You're not going to convince me to get involved with you."

"I kind of know that. The cookies are just my way of being nice." And maybe hanging around for a little longer, which made her pathetic, but she could live with that.

His dark gaze settled on her face. She felt the weight of his attention down to her toes, which chose that moment to curl ever so slightly.

He was as big as she remembered. Big and powerful and totally masculine. Kane was not the kind of guy to get in touch with his feminine side. He was more likely to get a knife and cut it away.

"Why did you do it?" he asked. "Why did you sleep with me? I made the rules very clear and you're not that kind of woman."

She sighed. "Slutty, you mean? I know. I've never done that before. I mean sex, sure. A couple of times. But meeting a guy and jumping into bed with him…not ever. I think it was the blood loss. My brain wasn't working right."

That earned her a smile, which, unfortunately, faded quickly. "You weren't slutty. I still want to know why you did it."

"Do I confuse you?" she asked, hoping that was it because confusing and intriguing weren't all that different.

"A little. I know there's more going on than I can see." Yeah!

He waited expectantly. She shifted, then folded her arms across her chest.

"It's kind of embarrassing," she said.

"I won't laugh."

She drew in a deep breath. He'd been honest about what he wanted and didn't want, so maybe she should be honest about why she'd done it…

"You wanted me," she said simply. "I liked you and trusted you. Being with you made me feel safe, but what pushed me over the edge was how much you wanted me."

He frowned. "You're available to any guy who's interested?"

She laughed. "No. Well, probably not. I don't know. Guys don't want me."

"You've said that before and it's crap. Of course they do. Look in the mirror. You're beautiful and funny. A little strange, but not psycho."

Compliments? Compliments before he'd even had cookies? She wanted to bask in the moment, but he looked impatient.

"I'm the best friend," she said. "I'm the one guys confide in, the one they tell their troubles to. I fix them and they go out and fall in love with someone else. I couldn't figure out what was wrong, then a couple of years ago I was at a party. I heard a group of guys talking. They were pretty drunk and going on about which of the girls at the party they'd like to sleep with. When they got to me, they all said they liked me, thought I was sweet, but I wasn't the kind of girl they wanted to…you know."

That was the easy part. She looked out the window over the sink and steeled herself to tell the rest. "I'd gone out with one of the guys and we'd…been together. He'd kind of been my first. I thought we were in love, but then he broke up with me and never really said why. That night he said he'd slept with me because he'd owed me. He'd been doing me a favor."

It still hurt. Not in the bone-crushing way it had at first, but enough to make her catch her breath.

"The second guy I was with said all the right things, but after the first time, he was never very interested in sex. He said it was me, that he'd never had any problems with other women."

"It wasn't you," Kane said flatly.

"You don't know that."

"Willow, I've seen you naked. I've touched you every-where possible. I've kissed you and tasted you and watched you come apart in my arms. It wasn't you."

Her eyes widened. He was good. Better than good. She felt her battered ego heal a little.

"But those guys, the things they said…"

Kane shook his head. "You're complicated. Guys, es-pecially young guys, want things simple. You scare them off. Or you take care of them so much they think you're their mother. But there's nothing wrong with you."

"But…"

He cut her off with a look. "Did I fake it?"

She smiled. "No. You were very clear about what you wanted."

"What did I want?"

"Me?" The single word came out in a squeak.

"You. Now let it go. You're fine."

Just then the oven dinged. She put in the pan of cookies and set the timer.

If only he wanted her again, she thought. But he'd been

clear about that, too. One night. She decided not to push her luck and instead changed the subject.

"How's Todd?" she asked.

"Why do you want to know?"

"Just making conversation. Does he know I was here?"

"I told him."

She laughed. "Was he scared?"

"No."

"Couldn't you have told him I was really scary?"

"No."

"Typical. I think he's safe. Julie and Ryan are so happy together, and he wasn't able to break them up, so I'm losing energy about the whole telling him off thing."

"Any plans to date him?" Kane asked.

"What?"

"I know about the million-dollar offer on the table."

Ah, yes. It was more than a fortune, she thought. "My grandmother is an interesting woman. I don't know why she made that ridiculous statement, but now we all have to deal with it. I'm not interested in marrying someone for money."

"It's a lot of money."

"I believe in falling in love. That my soul mate is my destiny. Money doesn't matter."

He shook his head. "Money always matters."

"That's cynical and sad."

"That's realistic."

"You've never been married, have you?"

"I don't do relationships, remember?"

Which was more than sad, she thought. It was tragic. "You have to connect to someone."

"Why?"

"It's how people are. We are the sum of our experiences,

our relationships. You can't tell me you're totally happy living on your own."

"I am, but you won't believe me."

"Kane, be serious. Don't you ever want more?"

He stunned her by walking toward her and crowding her back against the counter. He was close enough for her to feel the heat of his body. Close enough for her to see the various shades of brown and gold that made up the color of his eyes. Close enough for her to begin to melt with longing.

"This isn't going to work," he said in a low voice. "You can prance around all you want, but it's not going to change anything."

"Prance? I don't prance."

"You move, you sway, you glide, you intrigue. But I will not be tempted. This is over. We do not have nor will we ever have a relationship. It was a great night. Maybe the best night. If I were ever to reconsider my position, you'd be the one I'd do it for. But it's not going to happen. I will not let you in."

She opened her mouth, then closed it. He still wanted her. She could see the fire back in his eyes. Desire was there, but so was determination. She was thrilled and confused.

"Why not?" she asked. "What's so scary about a relationship?"

"I don't trust anyone," he said flatly. "I learned early that everyone was in it for himself. The only person I can depend on is me."

He was wrong—so wrong. But she didn't know how to convince him otherwise.

"What happened to you?" Had his parents abused him? Had a friend died?

His dark gaze locked with hers and she had a feeling she wasn't going to like what he had to say.

"I lived on the streets when I was a kid. Just me. I joined a gang to stay alive and they became my family. When I was sixteen, my girlfriend fell for a guy in a rival gang. She kept the relationship a secret. To prove her loyalty, she set me up. I was shot three times and left for dead by the only person I'd ever loved."

"What do you mean dead?" Marina asked as she passed the basket of rolls.

Willow took one and offered the rest to Julie who shook her head. "Her boyfriend shot Kane and drove off. Someone called for an ambulance and somehow he survived." Willow still couldn't believe that had happened, but she'd seen those scars on his body.

The sisters had met for lunch near Julie's office. It was one of those warm fall days that makes people in snow country think about moving to Los Angeles.

"I know what you're thinking," Marina told her. "That you can save him."

"Don't go there," Julie added. "He's not like the guys you usually rescue. He's dangerous."

Which made him even more appealing, Willow thought humorously. "He's alone. I think he needs someone in his life."

Marina looked at Julie then shook her head. "Let me guess. You're volunteering. Willow, sometimes guys mean what they say. He's not looking for any kind of relationship. You can't change him."

"But if he could just let himself risk it, he would be so much better off," Willow said.

Julie touched her arm. "You know I love you and I'll be there for you, no matter what, but why do you do this to yourself? You're always setting yourself up."

"It's just who I am," Willow said. "I want things to be different. I want a guy to love me and want to be with me forever. Maybe Kane's that guy."

"Maybe he's going to trample all over your heart," Julie said gently. "I hate to see you hurt again."

"I know."

Willow had possibly the worst luck in men. She fell for guys who weren't attracted to her. She saved them, healed them and they moved on to someone else.

"This is different," she said.

"Is it?" Julie asked. "How? No, wait. Don't answer that. Have you ever considered that you get involved with men you can never have so you don't have to risk falling in love? You say you want happily-ever-after, but you seem to go out of your way to make sure it never happens."

Willow looked from her to Marina. "I don't do that."

Marina sighed. "I'd have to agree with Julie on this one. You avoid normal men. Men who want to get married and have kids."

Willow opened her mouth, then closed it. She wanted to tell them both that they were wrong. She wasn't like that—except maybe she was.

Suddenly she was seventeen again, standing in her bedroom, getting ready for a date. She was fussing with her hair when her father walked in. He wasn't around much, so having him home was a big deal. She remembered putting down her brush and spinning in a circle.

"What do you think, Daddy? Am I pretty enough?"

Her father had looked at her for a long time. "You'll never be as smart and pretty as your sisters, but I'm sure you'll find someone to take care of you. Just don't aim too high, kid."

His words had cut through to her soul. She'd gone on

the date, but she remembered nothing about the night. Her father's words had burned themselves in her brain and left her gasping with pain.

She'd known that Marina and Julie were more beautiful and that she had to work harder in school to get lesser grades, but she'd never thought that mattered. Until that moment, she'd always believed she was special.

But if her own father didn't think so, maybe she wasn't. She'd never felt special again…until that night in Kane's arms.

"Willow?" Marina leaned toward her. "Are you okay?"

"I'm fine." She took a deep breath as the truth settled in her brain. "You're right. Both of you. I avoid regular guys because I'm afraid to take a chance on falling in love for real and being rejected. What was I thinking? I can't fix Kane. He doesn't want to have anything to do with me and I'm going to let him go. It's the right thing to do."

Julie bit her lower lip. "Are you all right? I didn't mean to hurt your feelings."

"You didn't. You're looking out for me and that's good."

"I love you," Julie said sincerely.

"Me, too," Marina added.

Willow felt their affection and it eased the hurt inside. Whatever else happened, she could count on her sisters to be there for her. As for Kane…she was going to let him go. He didn't want her around. The man couldn't have been more clear in his meaning.

Maybe it was time to stop chasing after the moon and settle here on earth where she belonged. Find a normal guy. So what, exactly, did normal look like?

Five

Kane walked into his house and heard the kittens crying. Usually they were silent, contentedly sleeping or nursing or being groomed by their mother. He dropped his briefcase onto a kitchen chair and moved into the living room where he found the kittens in their box, but no mother cat.

He quickly searched the house and there was no sign of her. But the window he'd left open for fresh air had been pushed open wider and the screen lay on the ground below. The mother cat was gone.

He swore under his breath and looked at the mewing kittens in the box. Now what? Was the mother cat gone for good? Had she abandoned her family? He did not need this crap in his life, he thought as he grabbed the phone, then realized he didn't have the number.

Three minutes later, he was dialing. His security

programs meant, with his trusty computer and decent Internet access, he could find anyone anywhere.

"Hello?"

He frowned. The voice wasn't familiar. "Willow?"

There was a sniff, followed by a shaky, "Yes."

Something was wrong. He didn't actually want to know what right now but knew it was polite to ask. Screw it, he thought a second later. "It's Kane."

She made a noise that sounded a lot like a sob. "What's wrong?" she asked, her voice thick with what he had a bad feeling was tears. "You wouldn't be calling if there wasn't something wrong."

She told the truth and he was good with that. So why did he feel a flash of guilt from her words?

"The cat is gone."

"Jasmine?"

Who the hell was... Oh, yeah. She'd named the cat. "Yes, Jasmine. I left a window open to get some air in this place. She managed to push out the screen and escape. The kittens are crying and I don't know what to do."

"Not leaving the window open would be a start," she said quietly. "I'll be right over."

Willow did her best to get control. She was not a pretty crier. There were no delicate tears rolling down a perfectly pale cheek. Instead she got blotchy, her eyes swelled and her nose wouldn't stop running. But even more importantly, she didn't want Kane to think she was crying over him. She wasn't. Her current pothole in the road of life had nothing to do with him. But men had such big egos. He would assume he'd crushed her.

She parked her car and used the last of her tissue to wipe her face. Then she blew her nose and drew in a breath. She ignored how she looked. What was important was finding Jasmine.

She stepped out of the car, prepared to call for the cat, but before she could say a word, Jasmine came strolling out of the bushes and meowed.

Willow crouched down and patted her. "Did you just need some alone time?" she asked. "Were the kids getting to you?"

Jasmine meowed again and rubbed against her fingers. The front door opened.

Willow straightened and braced herself for the impact of seeing Kane again. The man still looked good and her entire body sighed in appreciation. He was big and strong and looked as if he could take on the world.

Was it just a size thing, she wondered. If she were taller, would she be able to take on the world? Not that she was interested in all of it. But some control over her little corner would be nice.

"She's back," she said, pointing at Jasmine. "I think she just wanted to get out for a while. Did you try opening the door and calling for her?"

"Ah, no. I didn't think of that. I'm not a pet person."

"Obviously."

Kane stared from her to the cat and back. He shifted on his feet. If she didn't know better, she would think he felt a little foolish.

Maybe it was wrong, but that made her feel better. "I would suggest you check to make sure your screens are secure. Also, it wouldn't be a bad idea to let her out every morning, just so she can be on her own for a while. I'm sure it's draining to look after three babies all at once."

"Okay. Thanks. I will."

He stared at her. She had no idea what he was thinking and, at that moment, she didn't much care. She hurt from the inside out and it wasn't a pain that any pill could help. She'd been rejected in such a fundamental way. The worst part was, she hadn't been prepared. The news had come from nowhere.

"You want to come in?" he asked.

"Are there any cookies left?"

He nodded.

"Okay." Maybe chocolate would help.

She walked into the house. Jasmine came with her and gracefully jumped into the box with her kittens. They mewed frantically, until she licked each of them and they got quiet. Everything was all right in their world now, Willow thought, envious of their simple needs. Maybe she should have been a cat instead of a person. It looked like a better life.

"Have a seat," Kane said, motioning to the sofa.

Willow perched on a cushion. How strange to be back here. She'd already decided she would never see him again and here she was. While she could appreciate the thrill of watching his powerful body move through the room, she couldn't help thinking this was another place she'd been rejected. When she got home she would have to check her charts and see if Mercury was in retrograde.

Kane returned with a plate of her cookies and a bottle of water.

Despite the knot in her chest, she looked up at him and smiled. "Cookies and water? You know how to treat a girl right."

"Sorry. I don't have anything else to drink."

"It's fine."

As she spoke, a single tear ran down her cheek. That would have been okay, but she could feel others building up inside. She swallowed.

"Could you, um, get me some tissues?"

"Sure."

He bolted from the room. At any other time, his panic would have been amusing. Now she couldn't seem to find humor in anything.

When he returned with a box of tissues, she grabbed a couple and blotted her face.

"You don't have to get your panties in a twist," she said before blowing her nose. "This isn't about you."

"My panties?"

"You know what I mean. I'm not crying over you. I lost my syndication deal." Just saying it out loud made her start to cry again. "There'd been no warning. I thought things were going great. Then I got a call that they were dropping me. Too many people wrote in and said the comic strip wasn't funny or that they didn't get it."

She sucked in a breath and looked at him. He still hovered in front of the sofa, as if not sure where he should go.

"There were three girl squash. They were friends and dated and shopped. It was a lot like *Sex and the City*, only without the sex…or the city part, either. My girls lived on a farm. But not a real one. There was a mall and restaurants. They dated other vegetables. It was funny."

She ducked her head as more tears spilled down her cheeks. "How could people not get it? I worked so hard, too." That's what killed her. How she'd poured so much of herself into the comic strip.

"Are there other places you could sell it?" Kane asked.

"I don't think so. I was mostly in vegetarian magazines and newspapers. You know, the weekly kind. A few organic-focused newsletters picked me up, too. The girls were really into the organic, holistic lifestyle. They were very spiritual."

"The squash?"

She nodded. "It wasn't a lot of money, you know. I wasn't in a big magazine, but still. The money from that and the candle sales was enough for me to get by."

"You sell candles?"

"Uh-huh." She choked down a sob. "I know I'm not like my sisters, but I thought my life was really good. Small, but good. I had my candles and the girls. But now they're gone and I don't know what I'm going to do. Plus, they just called and said it wasn't funny and people didn't get it. Goodbye. Just like that. Not that they were sorry or that they knew how hard I worked. Do you know how many hours I spent on it each week? A lot."

Kane sat on the sofa and looked at her. "I'm sorry."

"Thanks. It's not you. It's just everything right now. I had lunch with my sisters a couple of days ago. They said I avoid normal men because I'm afraid to have a real relationship and I think they might be right. So I'm not just a failure, I'm emotionally stunted, too."

"You're not a failure. You had a setback."

That nearly made her laugh. "A setback? I have a crushed and broken career. Do you know my sister Julie passed the bar exam the first time? She works for a very high-powered international law firm and she's on the partner track. Marina, my younger sister, is so smart, she graduated from high school when she was fifteen and went to UCLA on a full scholarship. She got three different degrees in chemistry and physics. I don't even know exactly what they are. I think one is in inorganic chemistry, but I don't even know what that is. How lame is that? She has all kinds of grad schools begging her to attend. I mean begging. They came to the house and everything. Do you know what she's doing now?"

She looked at him. He was a little blurry around the edges, which was probably just her tears. "Do you?"

He shook his head.

"She's taken a couple of years off of school and she's working as a sign language interpreter for the deaf. She specializes in all those science classes she studied. She's giving back. Being a good person. I can't even sell a cartoon about squash. They're both so smart and pretty and I don't fit in with them anymore."

Kane felt as if he'd descended into the seventh level of hell. Willow's obvious pain made him uncomfortable and he had no idea what to say to her. The only thing that came to mind was a feeble, "You're pretty."

"Oh, please. You said I was scrawny." She blew her nose and reached for another tissue.

He swore silently. "You were right," he told her. "It was the sweater. You have great…" He raised his hands and lowered them. "You're very sexy. I wanted you, remember?"

She turned to him, her face swollen and blotchy, her eyes red. "Wanted. In the past tense. For a single night. You said that's all it would be and you were right. So I'm good enough for one night, but not to tempt you again."

Couldn't she have just shot him? That would have been easier and less painful, he thought grimly. It was like being trapped in quicksand. The more he struggled, the deeper he sank.

"Don't worry," she said. "I don't want you now. I'm not interested in mercy sex."

"I… You…"

She drew in a shaky breath, then more tears poured down her cheeks. "Dammit, Kane, you could have made a pass at me just now, so I could have turned you down. It's the polite thing to do."

Then she really began to cry, with body-shaking sobs and harsh breaths. He wasn't just in a foreign country—

he'd fallen into a different galaxy. He didn't know how to handle this or her. There were probably words that would make her feel better, but nothing in his experience had taught him what they were.

Women passed through his life without ever touching him. He knew their bodies and their heat, but nothing about their souls or hearts. Willow had been hurt on a fundamental level. While he could understand that, he didn't know how to fix it.

Slowly, feeling both awkward and stupid, he put his arm around her. She turned into him, leaning against his chest, her face pressing into his shoulder. He held her more tightly, feeling the small bones of her back. She was so fragile, he thought. He could crush her without breaking a sweat. Yet in other ways, she was strong and powerful.

Her tears dampened his shirt. He held her close, rubbing up and down her back. He should probably say something, but had no clue as to what, so he stayed silent. Eventually the tears slowed and she drew in a deep breath.

"I'm going to have a fight with my sister," she said quietly.

"Because it's on your calendar for this week?"

He couldn't see her face so he didn't know if she'd smiled, but he hoped she had.

"Because my dad is coming home. Mom called and told me last night. Julie always gets angry and critical when he shows up. He's not like other fathers. He doesn't stick around for long. My mom's okay with that. They're in love, or at least she loves him and she says what she has is enough. I believe her, but Julie doesn't. She says Mom needs more than a husband who visits once or twice a year, stays for a few months, then disappears."

"Where does he go?"

"I don't know. None of us do. It's just what he's always done. The thing is Marina can totally accept him and Julie will never forgive him. They're definitive. People should be definitive."

He ran his fingers through her long blond hair. The cool strands were silky soft and damned erotic. "Why?"

This time she chuckled. "Because it provides order. I'm the middle child, cursed with the ability to see all sides of things. It's annoying for me and those around me."

He touched her chin, forcing her to look at him. Her eyes were the color of the Caribbean Sea. Even puffy, she was beautiful. Her full mouth called to him. Desire flared and he suddenly wanted her with an intensity that hit him like a gunshot.

"Kane? Are you all right?"

"I'm fine."

Shaken, but fine.

What was wrong with him? He'd had her for a night—that was enough. It was always enough. He needed to distract them both.

"Did you like drawing the cartoons?" he asked.

Instantly her eyes clouded. "Of course. It was fun and creative. Sometimes I didn't like the pressure of the deadline. It was very much an every week thing. I was usually late, which isn't good."

"Was it your dream? Did you grow up wanting to be a cartoonist?"

Her eyes cleared as she smiled. "No. It was not my childhood fantasy."

"What was?"

She pulled back and wiped her face with her hand. "I'm sorry to break down like this. You only wanted help with your cat and I've gotten your shirt wet."

She placed her fingertips on the damp fabric. Her touch burned him down to the bone.

He ignored the need and instead focused on the woman. "You didn't answer the question."

"I know. I just…it's so small, you know? Julie's doing big things and Marina's going to save lives or maybe the planet. I'm not like that."

"Why do you have to be?"

"I don't, but if I'm not, do I still belong?"

Her pain made him uncomfortable. He wanted to fix the problem, which he couldn't. He barely understood it. Women and their feelings were a mystery he'd never wanted to solve…until today.

"You'll always be a part of your family," he told her. "Maybe if you were doing what you wanted to do instead of what you thought you should, you wouldn't care about being different."

She blinked at him. "That's good. Do you read self-help books?"

He grimaced. "No."

"I didn't think so. You're not the type. I want…" She drew in a breath and said, "I love plants. I love how they're all so different. I love making them grow, especially the really tough ones. I love how they look and feel and smell and how they all have different personalities."

Personalities? Plants? He told himself to just go with it. This was Willow, after all.

"Sometimes, when they change overnight, it's like magic," she said. "I want to open a nursery."

She paused, then seemed to fold in on herself, as if waiting for an attack. "Dumb, huh?"

"It's not dumb," he told her. "Why couldn't you?"

"I don't know anything about business. I didn't go to

college, I've never even worked in a nursery. It takes money to start a business."

"You could marry Todd. A million dollars is a lot of start-up capital."

That earned him a big smile. "Very funny."

She leaned back against the sofa, which trapped his arm behind her neck, but he wasn't inclined to pull it back.

"Okay, I'll be serious. You get a job in a nursery and learn the business. You go to community college and take business classes."

She turned to look at him. "You make it sound simple."

"Why does it have to be hard? When I was in the hospital and the army recruiter stopped in to see me, I realized it was a way out. I couldn't stay where I was—they'd only come after me again. I already had a fake birth certificate saying I was eighteen, so when I was released, I joined up. If it's important, you do what you have to do. It doesn't have to be hard. Willow, you got me to adopt a damn cat. Trust me, you can make a business work."

"You think?"

"I know."

She smiled then, a warm, welcoming happy smile that made him want to strip her naked and take her in ways she didn't know existed.

Instead he leaned forward and handed her a cookie.

Later, when Willow had left and he was alone with the cat, Kane glanced at the feline who seemed to be watching him with great interest.

"Don't get any ideas," he told her. "I only called Willow because you needed your own space. It won't happen again. I don't like her. I don't like anyone, including you."

The cat blinked slowly.

"Just as soon as your kittens are older, I'm taking all of you to the pound. Just so you're clear."

The cat blinked again and the sound of her purring filled the quiet room.

Six

Willow sorted through the beads on the table in front of her, chose one and picked up her glue gun. She carefully applied the bead to one of the candles she'd finished the previous night and did her best not to grin as Kane paced the length of her small kitchen.

It took him all of three steps before he had to turn around and go the other way. She'd offered him a seat, but he seemed determined to stand during their conversation.

She wouldn't have minded if he didn't look so...uncomfortable. Probably her place, she thought as she glanced around. It was pretty girly—all ruffles and ribbons on the curtains she'd made. There were plants everywhere, along with candles and dishes of potpourri. She had a small collection of china and crystal unicorns on a shelf in the living room. Her furniture there was white wicker with floral cushions.

Definitely not Kane's kind of place.

"I'll be gone two nights," he said as he glanced at a pot holder in the shape of a frog and grimaced. "I'm sure the cat will be fine, but if you could feed her—"

"I'm happy to," Willow told him, holding in her smile. "I'll put out fresh food, change the litter, give her a little attention." She paused and prepared to enjoy the moment. "This means you'll be giving me a key."

"Yes."

"To your house."

"I know."

She picked up another bead. "It will be like we're living together."

He turned and stared at her. "We're not living together."

"I didn't say we were."

"You implied it. You're looking after the cat, that's it. The cat you insisted I keep. I shouldn't have the cat at all."

"But you do."

His mouth thinned. "You're to take care of her and then leave. Don't go through my stuff."

She pretended to be insulted. "Would I do that? Honestly, Kane, when have I violated your personal space?"

"You want a list? I know you," he growled. "You'll snoop."

This was so much fun, she thought happily. He was just adorable when he was grumpy. "I promise I won't."

"As if I believe that."

"Hey, I don't lie. I won't look around."

"I'll know if you do."

He probably would. So what would he do? Put single hairs across drawers and sticky spy stuff on the inside of closets?

"I gave my word," she told him. "I meant it. Take whatever precautions make you happy, but there's no need. I'll respect your privacy."

He eyed her for a second, then put a key on the counter.

She sighed. "This is so sudden. I thought you wanted to take things more slowly."

He gaze narrowed.

She grinned. "I can't help it. You're just so easy."

"Thanks."

She turned off the glue gun, then stood. "I don't mean that in bad way. You're just fun to bug."

"I'm ignoring you now."

"You can't. It's my apartment and I'm in charge. Besides, you'll be interested in this."

She walked into the living room and picked up a catalog from the glass and wicker coffee table. "Look," she said as she waved it. "This is for the spring semester at my local community college. I'm going to sign up for business classes. And I've been looking at getting a job in a nursery." She paused for effect. "I have an interview on Thursday."

His tortured expression relaxed. "Good for you."

"Thanks. I never thought about just taking the steps. I guess they didn't seem possible. But now they are and it's all thanks to you."

"I only pointed you in the right direction."

"You don't want to take credit?"

"No."

"But then I'd owe you."

He stiffened.

She grinned. "Am I bugging you? I don't mean to."

"Yes, you do."

"Okay, a little, but in the nicest way possible. Admit it, Kane. You've never known anyone like me and I'm growing on you."

"Like mold." He folded his arms across his chest. "I see you're feeling better. Back in power and sassy."

"Sassy." She liked the sound of that. It was fun and

sexy. Is that how he saw her? She felt a little zing shoot through her.

"Don't read too much into that," he grumbled.

"Of course not. You don't do relationships." She tilted her head as she looked at him. "What about friends? Any of them hanging around?"

"No."

"No significant other, no family, no friends." Her good mood faded. "That's about the saddest thing I've ever heard," she murmured. Was it really possible that he didn't love anyone—and no one loved him? Her heart began to ache.

"Don't go there," he told her.

"Where?"

"Wherever it is you're planning on going. I like my life."

"Don't you ever want more?"

"No."

He spoke flatly, as if trying to convince her, but she refused to believe him. What happened in the dark of night when he was alone? Didn't he want a friend to share things with? Someone to care? To miss him when he was gone and welcome him home again?

Without thinking, she crossed the few feet between them and hugged him. He pulled his arms free, but didn't touch her. She felt his stiffness, his resistance to the embrace.

"I don't need this, Willow."

"Maybe I do. Just accept it and hug me back."

For a long time, she thought he was going to ignore her or push her away. But at last, she felt his arms embrace her.

She stood holding him, breathing in his tempting, masculine scent, feeling his heat and his strength. He was the most dangerous man she'd ever known, yet she couldn't be afraid of him. He still made her feel safe.

Crazy talk, she told herself. She should ignore it. Except she felt a strong and deep connection to Kane. It was as if some part of him called to her.

Was that real or just her burning desire to rescue the world? Not that he would believe he needed rescuing.

She looked up and met his gaze. The sexual fire there stole her breath away. Wanting swept through her as she imagined being with him again. She became aware of all the places her body touched his and how much better that touching would be if they were both naked.

"You want me," she breathed.

He immediately stepped back. "It doesn't matter."

Was he kidding? "Of course it matters. It's fabulous. Let's go do it."

She grabbed his hand and tried to pull him toward the bedroom, but he didn't budge. She spun back to face him.

"What on earth is wrong with you?" she demanded.

"I have rules for a reason."

"You're stubborn and difficult and your rules are stupid."

"That's only your opinion," he told her.

"But you *want* me," she said. "You totally want me."

"Yes, I do. And I'm not going to do anything about it."

"Kane?" She was trying not to take this personally, but it was hard.

He walked to the door. "I'll be back on Thursday in the early evening."

He was leaving? Just like that? Nothing he did made sense to her. Didn't any of this matter? Didn't *she* matter?

But she wasn't going to ask that last question—her ego was still a little bruised from the cancellation of the syndication deal. Better to not go there until she was stronger.

"You probably don't want me waiting for you," she said.

"You're right."

He was so solitary—it wasn't good. "Don't you ever want to come home to someone? To a bright house and a hot meal and a person who's happy to see you?"

Something flashed through his eyes. She couldn't tell what it was, but if pressed, she would have said a combination of pain and longing.

"I'm not interested in any of that," he said and then he was gone.

Willow stared after him. She might not know anything about being a lawyer or chemistry or even how to run a business, but she did know one thing.

Kane had been lying.

Thursday afternoon Willow pulled up in front of her apartment. She couldn't stop grinning, which was a good thing. Her interview had been amazing. She and Beverly, the owner of the nursery, had talked about plants and gardening and their favorite ways of doing things for nearly two hours. At the end, Beverly had not only offered her the job, but had upped the starting salary by two dollars an hour, with a promise of more money to come.

"You're exactly who I've been looking for," Beverly had told her. "I never thought I'd find you."

Words to make her do the happy dance, Willow thought as she climbed out of her car and walked toward her front door.

But her good mood evaporated like mist in the sun when she saw a familiar motorcycle parked against the side of her building and saw a tall, lanky man standing nearby.

Chuck was back.

Funny how in the past those three little words had always made her heart beat faster and her spirit wonder if this time he finally wanted to stick around. Because Chuck was an unfortunate combination of a man who needed rescuing—like nearly all the other men in her life—and her father—a man who couldn't stay in one place more than a few months.

The combination made him a poor bet for a romantic relationship and therefore nearly irresistible to her.

"Willow," he said as she approached. "It's been a long time. You look great."

"Chuck."

She looked at him, at the familiar too-long dark hair, the catlike green eyes, the sexy smile and braced herself for the emotional meltdown. Only there wasn't one. She felt exactly…nothing.

Willow came to a stop on the sidewalk. Wait a minute. This was Chuck—the one guy she most wanted to be with. The one she'd dreamed about, fantasized about, the one she'd wanted to have kids with.

"You changed your locks," he said, motioning to the door. "I couldn't get inside."

"Yes, I did change them." About six months ago, in a fit of self-preservation.

"Aren't you going to invite me in?"

She didn't have all that much to say to him, but why not? If this new attitude continued, she could consider herself cured.

"Sure."

She opened the door and led him inside. He looked around and grinned.

"Just like I remember," he said. "You've done it up so pretty."

Pretty? "You always said my place looked like a girls-only decorating catalog vomited on the place."

"Did I? I didn't mean it. You have great taste, Willow."

He moved close and put his arm around her. "You're looking good. Sexy."

Sexy? Wait a minute. "Since when?" she demanded. "You said after that one time we did it you thought of me as your sister."

"Nah, that wasn't me. I think you're hot."

Hot? Her? It was the answer to all her prayers. She waited for the rush of relief, the bubble of happiness. Instead she found herself wondering what kind of dirt he was tracking in on her clean floor.

She slipped free of his embrace and moved into the kitchen where she poured two glasses of iced tea.

"I did it, Willow," he said as he leaned against the counter. "I cleaned up my life, the way you always told me to. I moved to Tucson and got a job and saved my money. Whenever I wanted to do something stupid, I'd ask myself, 'Would Willow do this?' and then I'd listen to the answer. I won a bunch of money playing poker and I bought me a Jiffy Lube franchise. They're a great company and I'm doing good. I'm saving for a house, too."

She didn't know what to think. It was too much information all at once.

"Good for you," she said and meant it. She was glad he'd found what he wanted.

"The thing is, I don't want to go back to the way I was," he told her, sounding painfully earnest. "I need you in my life, Willow. I'm a better man with you around. So I was thinking, you could come back with me. We'd live together for a while and if that went as good as I think it's going to, we'll get married. You want that, right? Marriage and some kids? I can give that to you now."

A year ago she would have been melting in a puddle of excitement. Having Chuck finally speak those words—although maybe not as romantically as she would have liked—would have meant everything to her. Now, she felt nothing.

What was wrong with her? Sure, she'd sworn off the whole rescuing thing, but this was Chuck. Shouldn't he have tested her resolve?

"I wish you the best," she said sincerely. "I'm so happy for you and proud of what you've done with your life, but I'm not interested in moving to Tucson."

He moved close and cupped her cheek. "Hey, Willow. It's me."

Then he lowered his head and kissed her.

She waited for the familiar rise of heat and longing, or at least a sense of revenge. After all, Chuck had slept with her and then told her he didn't find her appealing in that way.

She felt the warmth of his mouth and a hint of wanting in his kiss. And that was it. She didn't tingle or strain or even kiss him back. Honestly, what was the point?

He straightened. "What's wrong?"

"Nothing." Which was true, she thought happily. "Absolutely nothing."

"I'm saying I want you in my life," he told her. "You've been waiting for that."

"Apparently not as much as we both thought," she told him, trying not to smile. She felt light and free and totally at peace with herself.

"But…" he began.

She stepped back. "Chuck, I think it's terrific that you've found everything you want. I'm glad I had some small part in that. But you don't need me to be successful. Go find someone you can really love and settle down. That will make you happy."

"But you're the one I want," he said stubbornly.

"Not really. I'm an old habit. I've always rescued you, but here's the thing. I don't do that anymore, which is great, because you don't need rescuing. You're doing fine on your own."

He looked more confused than annoyed. "But I came back for you."

"Which was really sweet of you."

"You're supposed to be in love with me."

"Not anymore." Maybe never, she thought. It was a real possibility she'd mistaken her longing for a fantasy for the real thing.

He swore. "I should have come back sooner."

She hated to think that might have made a difference, but it could have. She shuddered to think she might have actually gone off with Chuck at one time. What a nightmare. However would she have found her way home?

She glanced at the clock on the wall. "I need to get going. I have to be somewhere."

He grabbed her arm. "Is it someone else? Is there another guy?"

If only, she thought, knowing she was completely cured of wanting men who didn't much want her. "No. It's a cat. I'm pet-sitting for a friend."

"If it's about the money," he said, "I'll pay you back."

And pigs would soon be flying across the west side of Los Angeles. "That would be great."

She removed his hand from her arm, then gently pushed him toward the front door. She grabbed her purse and keys on the way.

"Thanks for stopping by. It's been really great to see you, Chuck. I wish you every happiness."

Once they were safely outside, she locked the door behind her and made her way to her car.

"Good luck," she called back to him. "I mean that. I know the right woman is out there, waiting for you."

He didn't wave back or say anything. Willow drove off, made a few turns in the neighborhood, then, when she was sure Chuck was gone, returned to her place.

She ran inside and collected candles and more cookies she'd made. Kane might claim to be comfortable coming home to a dark and empty house, but she knew that wasn't true. She wanted to make him feel welcome. Plus, she was celebrating the fact that she'd been extra good. In all the times she'd gone over to take care of Jasmine and her babies, Willow had never once looked anywhere she shouldn't. She hadn't even flipped through his magazines. For all she knew, she was going to be crowned Miss Privacy Minder of the month.

She drove over to Kane's house and went inside. Jasmine greeted her with a little meow and lots of purring. Willow crouched down and petted her, then gently stroked the kittens. Two of them already had their eyes open.

"Hi, babies," she said softly. "You're getting so big. Yes, you are. Guess who comes home tonight? Kane. Are you excited? I'm excited."

After feeding Jasmine and cleaning out the litter, Willow returned to her car and began collecting her bags. She was on her way back when an unwelcome and familiar sound made her turn.

Chuck drove his motorcycle down the driveway and pulled up next to her. He took off his helmet and walked toward her.

"There's someone else," he said flatly. "You lied to me."

"I didn't lie. I told you I was cat-sitting. Want to see the cat?"

He grabbed one of the bags and opened it. "Candles and cookies. I know you, Willow. There's a guy."

"So what if there is? Why are you surprised? I've moved on with my life, Chuck. You've been gone for months and this isn't the first time you left. Did you think I'd wait forever?"

His stunned expression told her that the answer was yes. How pathetic…for both of them, she thought grimly.

"You always waited," he told her.

"Maybe before, but not anymore. I'm not that person you remember. Things are different for me."

"Who's the guy?"

"We're just friends."

"Like I believe that." He dropped the bag on the ground and stepped toward her. "Who's the guy?"

His face sharpened with anger. She'd never seen Chuck as someone with a temper. He'd always gone with the flow.

He raised his hand and for a second, she thought he was going to hit her.

Kane wove through traffic on his way home. He felt a pressing need to be at his house, which he didn't like. Why did he care where he was? But the desire was there, so he drove a little faster, while telling himself it didn't matter when he arrived. It wasn't as if Willow was going to be there.

Not that he wanted to see her. Or the damn cat. He would admit to some curiosity about the kittens. Maybe they'd grown a little since he'd been gone. Their eyes should be opening. That could be interesting.

He turned down a side street, then hit the remote control device that opened the large wrought-iron gate that led to his place. It was a shorter route than going down by the main house, and more private. He eased his Mercedes forward and checked to make sure the gate had closed behind him.

He rounded the corner and saw Willow standing in front of his place with some guy. It took Kane less than two seconds to read the fear in her body language and the intent in the man's raised hand.

He parked and got out of his car. His movements were deceptively slow, but inside, he felt tension build. The guy looked ready to take on someone and Kane was more than happy to oblige.

"Is this him?" the intruder asked Willow as Kane approached. "Is he the reason you won't come back with me?"

"I won't come back with you because I don't want to," she told him firmly. "I'm not interested in having a relationship with you, Chuck. Now go away."

Chuck laughed. "I don't think so."

Willow looked at Kane. "I'm sorry about this. Kane, this is Chuck. Somebody I used to know."

Chuck glared at her and swore. Although he'd lowered his hand to his side, he was still standing too close and doing his best to intimidate Willow. But she wasn't one to be pushed around. Kane saw her square her shoulders and stare right back at the jerk, as if to prove he couldn't scare her.

"Willow's mine," Chuck said, still glaring at Willow "I'm taking her with me."

Kane felt the slow burn build inside. He stood ready to attack, but without knowing if he should. He didn't mind being annoyed by this ass, what concerned him was the reason—Willow.

He shouldn't want to protect her, but he did. He shouldn't want to claim, yet the need to grab her and brand her with his mouth and his body grew with each passing second. He knew better than to feel anything, ever, yet the emotions would not be denied.

Kane walked toward Chuck. "Is there any part of you that thinks I'm going to let you take Willow anywhere?"

Chuck met his gaze and blinked first. "I, ah…"

"You could try it," Kane continued. "I think that would be fun. Come on. Try it."

Chuck paled and took a step back.

"You were so eager to force her," Kane said. "Were you going to hit her? It looked like you were. Are you the kind of girly man who gets his kicks from hitting women? Because where I'm from, that's lower than low. We use guys like you for wiping up the floor. That could be fun, too."

Chuck raised both hands in the air. "I didn't hurt her. Ask her, she'll tell you."

Kane continued to stare at him. "Get on your bike and get out of here. Never see Willow again. In fact, you should avoid L.A. altogether. Is that clear?"

Chuck nodded several times, then hurried to his bike. Seconds later, he was gone.

Kane stared after him. There was too much boiling inside of him. He should have fought the guy—it would have burned off energy.

He turned to Willow, who studied him. "You're never boring," he said. "I'll give you that."

She smiled. "Welcome home."

Seven

Kane led the way into the house. Willow followed him and closed the door.

"I don't know what happened," she said, both confused by Chuck's behavior and relieved that Kane had shown up when he had. "He's never been the least bit possessive. He was more the needy type and very into himself. Honestly, he's never been all that interested in me. And let me be clear. I didn't invite him here. He was waiting at my place earlier. We talked, I told him it was over and then I left. I guess he followed me. It's just so strange."

"It's not strange," Kane said, looking at her. "You were always available before. This time, you weren't. That made him want you more."

"Talk about twisted," she murmured, suddenly caught up in how good Kane looked. He wore a tailored suit that emphasized his muscles, not to mention the breadth of his shoulders. Now if he'd been the one asking her to run off to Tucson, she would have been gone in a flash.

"It's human nature. We want what we can't have."

Hmm, so was that why she wanted Kane? Because she couldn't have him?

Willow considered the question, then shook her head. No, she had a feeling she would be even more interested in Kane if he were begging her to stay. Not that he ever would. He was a pretty together guy. Now that she knew him better, she had to admit he didn't need much in the way of rescuing—except maybe emotionally and how likely was that to happen?

"He's going to have to get over it," she said firmly. "I'm done with the loser stage of my life. No more fixing guys up and sending them on their way. I'm my own person and I don't need to prove my worth by what I do for others."

He raised one eyebrow. "Read that in a magazine?"

"Uh-huh. Pretty cool. I was thinking of putting it on a pillow."

"Of course you were."

She grinned, then grabbed his hand and dragged him over to the window. Well, *drag* was kind of a strong word. She gave a tug, indicating where she wanted him to go and he did.

"Look," she said. "Flowers. Pretty."

"You're mocking me," he told her.

"Only a little. Okay, these little pots have herbs in them. Basil and rosemary, because of how they smell. I know you're not much for the cooking thing. Always keep rosemary in its own container, because it has designs on taking over the world. Then these two are flowers. Miniature roses. They're surprisingly easy to take care of and I love the colors."

"Okay."

She waited, hoping for more. She knew he wasn't excited about the plants, but could he accept them?

"What?" he asked.

"You could pretend to be interested."

"Would you believe me?"

"I'd try."

He sighed. "They're great. Thanks."

"You're welcome."

She tugged on his hand again. "Come see the kittens. Two of them have their eyes open."

He allowed her to lead him to the other side of the room. Jasmine meowed when she saw him, rose, stretched and jumped out of the box.

Kane bent down and petted her. Willow watched and wished he were petting her instead. Not that she wanted the underside of her chin scratched, but there were other lonely places.

"So how was your trip?" she asked when he'd straightened.

"Fine."

"Coffee?"

He hesitated, then said, "Sure."

Once they were in the kitchen, she poured in water and reached into the refrigerator for the bag of coffee.

"I was very good while you were gone," she said as she measured grounds. "I didn't look in anything. No drawers, no cupboards, nothing."

"Then how did you know where I keep my coffee?"

She smiled smugly. "I saw you get it when I was here before. On second thought, I wasn't good, I was perfect."

"How hard was it?"

She flipped on the coffeemaker. "Pretty hard, but I have

character and backbone. Plus, I gave my word and I try to respect that."

He stared down at her. She felt the intensity of his gaze all the way to her toes. Was there fire flickering there or was that wishful thinking on her part?

"How many other guys have there been?" he asked. "Guys like Chuck?"

Not the direction she wanted for this conversation. "A couple."

He continued to look at her.

"A few," she added. "Maybe more than a few."

"You try to fix them all?"

"Pretty much, but sometimes it works. Look at Chuck. He owns a Jiffy Lube. That's pretty impressive."

"I'm nearly faint with shock," Kane said dryly. "Are you still planning to rescue me?"

"You know, I was just thinking about that. The thing is, you don't really need rescuing. Your life is fairly together. Except for the whole alone thing. That's unfortunate."

"Maybe I like the silence."

"No one wants to be alone all the time. Admit it—you kind of liked having me here when you got home."

"Sure. Pulling up and seeing some guy prepared to slap you was great fun."

"Oh, yeah." She'd forgotten about that part. "I'm sure he didn't mean it."

"I'm sure he did." Kane moved closer. "You're a danger to yourself. You get involved and then you don't know how to get uninvolved. You need to work on that."

She felt the heat from his body. She supposed she could have been intimidated by him—after all he was looming. But this was Kane. He was strong and powerful, but she believed down to her bones all she had to do was say no and he would stop. He was so confident, he could afford to be gracious. Not that he would ever think of himself as gracious and he'd be annoyed to know she did.

"Are you going to fix me?" she asked, meeting his gaze and catching her breath at the fire she saw burning there. The glorious, hungry need was back.

"You're beyond fixing."

"You could try."

"I have other things in mind."

Yeah! She reached over and turned off the coffeepot. "Are you going to give me that speech again? The one about you never calling and how it's only for tonight and to have no expectations because you're only going to break my heart?"

He hesitated so long, she wanted to call the words back. She knew he was violating his rules and maybe pushing him would cause him to have second thoughts. Then he spoke.

"No."

Her heart jumped, her sides began that melting thing and she wanted to rip off her clothes right there in the kitchen.

"Really?" Her voice was a squeak.

"Really."

He leaned in, about to kiss her. She put her fingers on his mouth.

"Would you have beat up Chuck?"

"If he'd touched you."

"You mean if he'd hurt me?"

He gaze sharpened. "No. If he'd touched you."

Then he kissed her.

His mouth was hot and firm and soft and she wanted to give him everything. He wrapped his arms around her and drew her against him.

He was already hard and she squirmed to get closer, to feel all of him, especially his need.

He cupped her face in both hands, then deepened the kiss. His tongue swept inside her mouth, claiming her with an intensity that excited her.

"What is it about you?" he asked, his voice low and thick. "Why can't I get you out of my head?"

"I'm pretty irresistible," she said with a grin.

He raised his head and gazed into her eyes, but he wasn't smiling. "Yes, you are."

He bent down, gathered her in his arms and carried her toward the bedroom. Once there, he set her on her feet and put his hands on her shoulders.

"Tell me if you want this," he said.

He had to ask? How cute. "I want *you*, Kane."

He shuddered, then reached for her. She flung herself at him and when their bodies were pressed together from shoulder to knee, she felt as if she'd finally found her way home.

He touched her everywhere. His fingers explored her back, her hips, before lightly touching her arms. She both longed for the contact and wished he would touch her elsewhere—her breasts, between her legs, the places that ached.

Instead he drew her sweater over her head and leaned in to press his mouth to her shoulders. He licked and kissed and nipped, leaving goose bumps and tingles in his wake. He moved up her neck, along her jaw, then jumped to her earlobe where he bit down and sucked.

She had to cling to him to remain standing. Her legs trembled, her thighs nearly caught fire. Hunger consumed her, making her want to be reckless. She tugged at his tie and managed to loosen the knot, then she went to work on the buttons down the front of his shirt.

Her good intentions faded away when he placed his hands

on her breasts. He cupped her curves and used his thumbs to tease her tight, aching nipples. Her eyes sank closed as sensation washed through her. Oh, yeah, that was good.

Around and around, arousing her until she found it hard to keep breathing. Then he made it more difficult by kissing her.

While his tongue mated with hers, he dropped one hand to the waistband of her black slacks. Seconds later he'd unfastened the button and lowered the zipper. Then his fingers were between her thighs and all coherent thought fled her brain.

There was only the moment and man and the magic he created. The way he immediately found her most sensitive spot and began courting it. He circled and stroked, moving closer, then away. Teasing, exciting until she wanted to grab his wrist and force him to get to it.

But she didn't. The anticipation was too sweet.

He continued to touch her and kiss her. With his free hand, he reached behind her and opened her bra. One-handed—a great trick.

She lowered her arms so the scrap of lace could fall to the floor, then caught her breath as he ducked down and took her right nipple in his mouth.

Exquisite desire coiled through her, pulsing with each gentle suck of his lips. His tongue flicked against her tight tip, perfectly matching the arousing massage between her legs. She felt herself tensing, reaching, wanting.

"Kane," she breathed. "I can't hold back."

Which was, apparently, the wrong thing to say, because he stopped. Before she could protest, he'd taken off her shoes, her slacks, her socks and her panties. When she was naked, he made quick work of his own clothes, grabbed a condom, then led her to the bed.

After she'd stretched out on the bed, he knelt between her legs and pressed an openmouthed kiss against her center.

She remembered him doing this last time—how great he'd made her feel, the ease with which she'd found her release. Now she let herself relax into the sensations he drew out from her.

Need coiled deep within her, making her muscles tense, her body strain. She dug her heels into the bed and thrust herself toward him.

Closer and closer she spiraled. Up and up, with the soft stroke of his tongue driving her nearer to her goal. Waves of heat washed over her, the sound of her rapid breathing filled the quiet of the night.

"Almost," she gasped as he moved faster. "Almost."

And then she was there. Her body shuddered and quaked and she gave herself up to the pleasure. Over and over the contractions swept through her, making her moan and savor and smile. It was good—it was better than good. It was practically a miracle.

She opened her eyes and found him watching her. "You're really good at that," she murmured.

"I'm inspired."

While she'd been basking, he'd put on his condom. She reached between them and guided him inside, then sucked in a breath as she felt another little tingle. Talk about a great way to end the day.

She wrapped her legs around his hips and drew him in closer. He supported himself on his forearms and stared into her eyes as he filled her, then retreated. Over and over, still looking at her, exposing himself as he got closer.

Willow didn't break the contact. She saw the fire of his need and something else. Something dark and broken that called to her. His heart? His soul?

Her heart trembled at the idea of this lonely man sharing so much with her. Had anyone else ever seen inside?

She had no answer for the question, then even the questions were gone as the power of his body brought her once again to the brink. Her muscles tensed as she strained to reach her release.

Each thrust filled her, pushing her closer until she cried out and gave in. Involuntarily she closed her eyes, then he lost himself in her and they were still.

Kane sat in the living room, a drink in his hand. It was well after midnight and the house was still. Even the damn cat was asleep.

A single small lamp in the corner cast more shadows than light, but that suited his mood.

He'd broken his own rules. Rules he'd put in place after caring about someone…a woman…had nearly got him killed. Wasn't being shot in the gut and left for dead enough of a message? Why would he risk this again? Connecting, getting involved only made him weak. He had to stay strong—it was the only way to stay alive.

A logical argument, he thought. Except he couldn't be logical—not when he was talking about Willow.

He couldn't say why she was the one to get to him. Why her and not the one before or the one to come after? What combination of features and body language and scent and sound made him want to forget what he knew was right?

But it was her, and he didn't know how to escape the trap. She haunted him. Even when he was thousands of miles away, he'd remembered her.

He stared at the large package on the coffee table. With his business in New York complete and several hours before his flight, Kane had done something he'd never done before...gone shopping.

The act hadn't been conscious. He'd left his lunch meeting and started walking. But instead of heading for his hotel and then the airport, he'd gone north, toward the exclusive shops with their trendy window displays. He'd looked in them, ignoring clothes and jewelry, looking for what he wasn't sure. Until he'd found it.

A large tote bag covered in plants. It was bright and cheerful and ridiculously expensive, yet the second he'd seen it, he'd known it should be hers. He'd bought it and brought it home and now he was stuck with it.

He should send it back, he thought as he took another sip of his drink. He could pretend he'd never bought it in the first place. Only he wasn't very good at fooling himself.

So what did he do now? Give it to her? He knew what she would think, what it would mean to her. That he thought she mattered, and she didn't. She couldn't. To care about someone meant to risk that person destroying him. He'd already nearly died once because of a woman—he saw no need to do it again.

Willow cut up vegetables for the salad. Marina opened the oven for the four hundredth time and stared at the bread.

"Is it browning? It doesn't look like it's browning," Maria said.

Julie looked at Willow, then rolled her eyes. "You're the science whiz in this family," she said. "So you're the one who should know that every time you open the oven, you're letting out heat. At this rate, the poor thing is never going to brown. Close the door and step away from the oven."

"I know." Marina did as her sister had said. "But I've never baked bread before. I want it to turn out right."

Willow looked at the bowls and measuring cups stacked in the sink. "What got into you?"

"We're having all our favorites for dinner. I thought homemade bread would be a nice addition."

It was Saturday and Willow and her sisters were at their mother's house. Naomi was off volunteering at yet another low-cost clinic with Dr. Greenberg, so her daughters had decided they would provide dinner.

Willow put down her knife and wiped her hands on a towel. She faced Julie and Marina. "I have an announcement."

They both looked at her.

"My comic strip deal was canceled."

"Oh, no." Marina abandoned her post by the oven and rushed to Willow's side. "How horrible. Why would they do that? When did this happen? Are you all right?"

Julie moved close and put her arm around Willow. "This sucks the big one. Want me to sue them?"

Willow let herself soak up the love and concern, then shook her head. "I'm good. It was a shock and I was crushed at first, but now I'm okay with it. I realized this was an opportunity for me to figure out what I really want to do with my life."

"Which is?" Marina sounded tentative, as if she wasn't sure she wanted to know.

"Working in a nursery at first, then later, opening my own. I start a new job on Monday working at this great place. It's huge. They sell to lots of landscapers, so there are regular plants, but also lots of exotics. Beverly wants me to help her with some hybrids, which will be lots of fun. I'm also starting community college in January. I'm going to take business classes. Eventually I want to open my own nursery."

Marina and Julie stared at her.

"It sounds as if you have it all figured out," Marina said admiringly. "I'm impressed."

"Me, too," Julie told her. "This is a big deal."

"It's not yet, but it will be. I've always sort of fallen into things. This time I'm setting out on a specific direction, heading for somewhere I want to go."

"I'm glad," Julie said. "What happened to generate this change?"

"Losing the syndication deal was hard," Willow admitted. "I had to do a lot of thinking about what I really wanted."

Kane had helped. Actually he'd been the one to push her in the right direction, but oddly, she didn't want to talk about him. She'd always been so willing to go on and on about the men in her life, but he was different. Maybe because she didn't fully understand him yet. Maybe because she wasn't sure if they had an actual relationship. Maybe because just thinking about him made the day seem brighter and she wasn't willing to share that yet.

"There's just one thing," she said, patting Marina on the arm.

"Anything," her sister said with a smile.

"Oh, good. Well, I'm going to need you to marry Todd. The million dollars would be really helpful for start-up capital."

Eight

Kane pulled a flash drive out of his shirt pocket and set it on Todd's desk.

"We have a problem."

Todd picked up the flash drive. "I'm not going to like this problem, am I?"

"Probably not. The new start-up has a lot of proprietary software and that's all they have. We lose that and we might as well shut down. Obviously there will be firewalls and employee agreements in place, but that's not enough. Someone with a couple of these in his or her pocket can steal enough to destroy the company."

"Can you make the company secure?" Todd asked.

"Of course, but it won't be cheap and it's going to require a hell of a lot of logistics and processes."

"That's why you get paid the big bucks."

Kane smiled. "So they tell me. It's a challenge. I enjoy a good challenge."

Todd passed back the flash drive. "You're happy here, working with Ryan and me?"

Kane eyed his boss. What was up? Todd wasn't about to get all touchy-feely, was he? "Why do you ask?"

"You're good. We don't want to lose you. I know you get a lot of offers to go back out in the field or whatever you call it."

Black ops. Secret assignments in dark places in the world protecting idiots who shouldn't be there in the first place.

"I'm not tempted," Kane told him.

"Isn't the money good enough?"

"It's okay. Here I get in on the ground floor on start-ups. That's good money, too."

"I'm going to pry here, but don't you have enough to retire a couple of times over?" Todd asked. "You don't have to keep doing this."

Eight million, Kane thought. Per his last statement. He wanted at least double that before he took off for his isolated paradise.

"I like what I do. Besides, I have expensive tastes. I'll be around for a while."

"That's what I want to hear. But you're seriously not tempted by going back into the field?"

"It's a zero sum game," Kane told him. "Sooner or later someone always gets dead. I got tired of wondering if it was going to be me."

"You don't enjoy the thrill of the chase or the hunt or whatever?"

"Not anymore."

"Good to know." Todd studied him for a minute. "How's Willow?"

"Why do you ask?"

"I just wondered. I saw her car there a couple of nights ago. Are you two…"

"No," Kane said quickly. "We're not together." They couldn't be. He didn't do relationships. Yet he'd invited her into his bed a second time. He wanted her to stay the night and he was looking forward to seeing her again. If that wasn't a relationship, what was it?

"It's interesting," Todd said. "Men, women. Look at Ryan, who a few months ago I would have sworn was as much a cynical bastard as I am when it comes to matters of the heart. But not anymore. He's crazy about Julie. I've never seen him so happy."

"Envious?" Kane asked.

"No. I've been burned enough times not to be tempted anymore. I have no plans to get married. When I'm old, I'll get a bunch of dogs or fish or something and leave all my money to them—just to shake things up."

Kane chuckled. "No one is going to believe that."

"I know, but talking about it tortures my relatives. Especially Aunt Ruth. I should be old enough not to enjoy that, but every now and then I have some fun. Still, she's determined to marry me off."

There was frustration in Todd's voice, but also affection. Kane knew both he and Ryan were close to their aunt.

"Julie isn't a threat anymore," Kane said, remembering the offer of a million dollars to one of the Nelson sisters if she would only marry Todd.

"I'm wondering if Willow is, as well," Todd said.

Kane ignored that. "You still have to deal with Marina."

"I don't know anything about her except I'm going to stay away from her."

"She's a lot like her sisters," Kane said.

"You met her?"

"Once." When she'd come to Willow's rescue, bringing cat supplies and food.

"Attractive?"

Not nearly as beautiful as Willow, but otherwise, "Uh-huh."

"Not that it matters," Todd muttered. "What was Ruth thinking, offering them all that money to marry me? If I wanted to get married, I would."

"Maybe she's trying to help things along."

"Push, not help. Still, I'm younger, stronger and more determined. But if you see Marina hanging around here, you'll let me know?"

"Absolutely."

Kane headed back to his office. He walked into the open space to find a well-dressed older woman waiting for him.

"You must be Kane," she said.

"Ma'am."

She rose and walked toward him. "Please. Not ma'am, I beg you. I'm Ruth Jamison, Willow's grandmother."

Because the cats weren't enough of an invasion, he thought as he shook hands and then offered the woman a seat on the leather sofa in the corner.

When she'd refused anything to drink, he perched in a chair across from her. "How can I help you?" he asked, although he had a bad feeling he already knew the subject matter that had inspired the visit.

"You seem like a nice, direct young man, so I'll be direct as well. I understand you're dating my granddaughter, Willow."

Kane opened his mouth, then closed it. It had been a whole lot easier to deflect Todd than this old woman.

"I know her," he said.

"Yes, most intimately, I've heard." Ruth held up one

hand. "I had lunch with Julie the other day and she mentioned something. I'm not spying. I learned my lesson about getting too involved in my granddaughters' lives. I'm staying out of things. It's my fault we don't really know each other and I have to be patient. I can't force closeness in a few weeks. Still, I was curious about you and curiosity isn't meddling."

Kane had no idea what to say to that. Fortunately Ruth seemed comfortable carrying on the entire conversation.

"I'm beginning to think none of my granddaughters are going to want to marry Todd though of course I'm delighted about Julie and Ryan. As I don't know you at all, I'm not clear if you'll be good for Willow or not. Do you think you have any plans to break up soon?"

"We're not… I haven't…" He swore silently. "I don't know," he said at last.

"Pity. Still, if you're a good man, that could work out. Of course that leaves only Marina for Todd and I have no idea how to get them together. Now that he knows my plan, he'll be on his guard."

"I thought you weren't going to meddle."

"I'm not. I'm helping things along. Young people need that sort of assistance. If I waited for nature to take its course, I'd be dead long before I saw any great-grandchildren. No one wants that."

She rose. "It was lovely to meet you, Kane. Take good care of Willow. She's a very special young woman."

Ruth walked toward the door, then glanced back at him. "I understand you have kittens."

"Ah, yes. Three."

"Good. When they're old enough, I'll take one. I've always wanted a cat. Fraser was never fond of pets, but as I only answer to myself these days, I can have one." She sighed. "One of the few advantages of being alone. Still, if I could have him back…" She shrugged. "Goodbye, Kane."

"Goodbye, Mrs. Jamison."

Willow carried the grocery bags from her car to Kane's front door. "I brought food," she said as she pushed past him into the house.

"So I see."

She walked straight to the kitchen and started to make herself at home. After putting the cold things in the refrigerator, she set the bread and wine on the counter, then turned to face her possibly reluctant host.

"I did phone and tell you I was stopping by with dinner," she said, trying not to sound defensive, when she was actually kind of nervous.

"I got the message."

Yes, well, when her call had gone straight to voice mail, she'd decided to take advantage of the situation and invite herself over.

"It's a celebration," she said.

"You mentioned that in the message."

He didn't look all that happy, but then Kane wasn't a "grin like a fool" kind of guy. On the bright side, he didn't look *unhappy,* either.

"I wanted to say thank you," she said quietly. "For helping me through a rough time when I found out I'd lost my syndication deal and for pointing me in a more positive direction." She smiled. "I just finished my first week working for Beverly and I love it." She held up her hands.

He raised his eyebrows. "Ten fingers. Always a good thing."

"No, silly. My nails. Look. I don't have any. Not long ones, anyway. And I'm getting calluses. I spend my day grubbing around with plants. I couldn't be happier and it's all because of you."

He went from not unhappy to uncomfortable. "You would have figured it out on your own."

"Maybe. But it could have taken me forever. This is what I should have been doing all along and I know that now because of you. Hence the celebration."

One side of his mouth turned up. "Hence?"

"It's a word."

"Not one usually found in this century."

"I'm eclectic."

"Is that what they're calling it?"

He was teasing her, which meant he wasn't upset. Kane wouldn't bother to think twice about tossing her out on her butt if he didn't want her here, which meant he did. A warm glow began in her belly and spread out to her ten fingers and toes.

"I was in New York last week," he said.

"I know that."

"Right. You looked after the cat."

She studied him. Something wasn't right. Kane looked…awkward. But he was always confident, always in charge. How was that possible?

"I appreciate that you came over and dealt with her," he said.

"Jasmine?"

"Right. So, I, ah, got you something."

She felt a great shift in the space-time continuum. Her insides fluttered just a little. "You bought me something? Like a present?"

"A thank-you gift."

She felt like a five-year-old on Christmas morning. "What is it? Is it big? Is it something New York-y?

She waited expectantly while he disappeared into the rear of the house. It was all she could do not to follow him and grab whatever it was. But she forced herself to at least pretend to be mature. Still, a present was very cool.

He returned with a massive gift bag, which he passed to her. She set it on the counter and reached inside.

She had no idea what to expect, but it wasn't a beautiful leather tote with floral appliqués done in a rainbow of colors.

"It's gorgeous," she said, not able to believe this was for her. It had to have cost a fortune. The designer name alone caused her to consciously keep her lips pressed together so her mouth didn't hang open.

"I thought with the flowers and everything, you'd like it."

She looked inside. There were compartments for pens and a cell phone and sunglasses. The lining felt as soft as lingerie, while the leather itself was smooth and buttery.

"This is amazing," she breathed, "but it's too everything." She looked at him. "Kane, this is way more than a 'thanks for looking after my cat' gift."

"It's what I got you. If you like it, then keep it."

"Like it? I'll probably insist on being buried with it."

"Good." He smiled. "I saw the bag and I thought of you. That's why I got it."

He'd thought of her? As in she'd been on his mind while he'd been traveling? That little bit of information was actually just as thrilling as the gift itself.

"Thank you," she said. "Seriously, it's so beautiful and I love it."

"Good. What's the wine?" he asked.

Not the smoothest change in subject, she thought humorously. But very Kane-like. Based on what she knew about his life, he didn't buy many women presents. That would require them to be around more than a day.

Did that mean she was getting to him a little? That she was starting to mean something? She was torn between hope and the need to protect her heart.

She handed him the wine bottle. "A lovely Merlot and on sale with my club card, so I'm a happy camper."

He opened a drawer. From it he pulled some fancy cork puller thingie that just zipped the cork right out.

"Cool," she breathed.

He poured them each a glass of wine.

"Were those steaks I saw you putting into my refrigerator?" he asked as he handed her a glass.

"Uh-huh. You have a barbecue on the patio. I know what you're thinking, but meat cooked on a barbecue doesn't count."

"Of course not," he murmured. "Everybody knows that."

She grinned and touched her glass to his. "To our dreams. May they all come true."

Later, when they were finished with dinner and sitting in the living room in front of a fire, Willow curled up in her chair and tried not to read too much into the evening. Kane had bought her a present, they'd shared wine, a bottle of his after they'd finished hers, had a great dinner and plenty of conversation. They were a man and a woman who had been lovers more than once. In some circles, this could be considered a date. While she wanted it to be, she had a feeling Kane wouldn't agree with her assessment.

The problem was, she liked him. A lot. He was all tough on the outside, but inside, he was a soft cream center.

"For a vegetarian, you like a good steak," he said.

"I know it's a flaw. I can be good for months and months, then every now and then I get a serious craving."

"I would have thought you'd lean more toward fish or chicken."

"That makes more sense," she admitted. "But I tend to jump in with both feet. I love steak. And Dodger Dogs, because what's a baseball game at Dodger Stadium without them?"

"A much smaller experience."

"Exactly."

She smiled at him. He didn't smile back, but there was an expression in his eyes—a heat—that filled her with contentment and more than a little need. She had a sudden vision of them making love in front of the fire.

Of course there were logistical problems. With the kittens now climbing around and trying to get out of their box, it was a little too much like having an audience.

"You want me again," she said happily. "Wanting me is one of your best qualities."

"You're assuming."

"Not really. I can see it in your eyes. They get bright with a kind of fire. It's pretty thrilling. I get all tingly inside and start thinking about taking off my clothes."

His gaze narrowed. "You're drunk."

She looked at her glass and didn't have a clue as to how many she'd already had.

"Tipsy, maybe. Extremely mellow." She giggled. "How can you tell?"

"I doubt you'd talk about the fire in my eyes if you were sober. Or getting naked."

"Oh. Good point. You're logical and straightforward in your thinking. I like that. It's so macho. I suspect a cross-section of my brain would look like a kaleidoscope. Very beautiful and intriguing, but not much world order."

"No one wants you to change."

"Does no one include you?"

"Yes."

Ooh, that sounded promising—although promising for what? She'd lost her train of thought.

"You kept the cats," she said, watching the kittens cuddle against their mother. "I'm glad. You need life in your life." She giggled. "I mean you need something else alive in your life."

"Does this happen often?" he asked, pointing at the glass.

"Almost never. I don't like being out of control. It's too scary. But here, with you, I'm completely safe. It's so strange. You're the only person who has ever made me feel special and safe. Like I can resist that."

"Don't trust me, Willow. I'm not one of the good guys."

"Of course you are. You'd never hurt me. Not physically, anyway. Emotionally, I'm not sure. There could be a good trampling in my future, but it will be worth it."

She had a feeling she was saying too much, but she couldn't figure out how to stop talking. Besides, if he wasn't a good guy, why was he trying to warn her off.

He stood and crossed to her chair, then held out his hand and pulled her to her feet. After setting her wineglass on the table, he stared into her eyes.

"We're not dating," he said.

"Of course not."

"This isn't going anywhere."

"Can I hum while you say all this, because it kind of feels like it needs a soundtrack."

He sighed. "Are you sober enough to make a rational decision about staying the night?"

Ah. At last they were getting somewhere good. "No, but I'm sober enough to say take me hard, big guy."

He pulled her into his arms. "That works for me."

Nine

It was, Willow thought happily as she left the bathroom and sauntered toward the kitchen, a perfect day. If this were a cartoon, little forest animals would be running around and collecting her clothes after making a flower wreath for her hair.

"So you're a morning person," Kane said. He stood by the counter, making coffee. He'd pulled on jeans and a T-shirt. She happened to know for a fact there was nothing on under either.

Of course she was a little scantily clad herself. In the absence of a robe, he'd offered a clean white dress shirt. It was ridiculously big on her, but she liked wearing it anyway. Wearing his shirt felt intimate.

"I sometimes enjoy the morning," she said, unable to look away from his face. He was better looking now than when she'd first met him. She wasn't sure if that was because he was more relaxed, or because she was getting to know him.

"Are you tired?" he asked.

"Oh, yeah. You?"

"I'll nap later."

She laughed at the thought of Kane napping and at the pleasure of knowing he felt comfortable enough with her to joke around.

He pushed the button on the coffeemaker, then walked over, bent down and kissed her.

She surrendered to his embrace, letting her body ease into his. His hands slipped under his shirt to rest on her bare butt.

"Again?" she asked as her blood heated.

"You'll be sore."

"I'm a big, tough girl. I can handle it."

He kissed her again and stepped back. "Maybe after breakfast."

He meant coffee, she thought with a grin. Kane didn't keep much food around. He was such a guy, she thought affectionately. But a really good one. Sure he was tough and dangerous, but not to her. With her, he was gentle and kind and funny. He made love to her with a thoroughness that left her quivering from the inside out.

"You're smiling," he said.

"I was thinking about last night."

"Okay."

She laughed. "Now you look like a lion after the kill. Very self-satisfied."

"I didn't kill you."

"I'm not sure about that. I distinctly remember dying a few times...from the pleasure."

The fire returned to his eyes and she felt an answering need inside. But more important than that was his smile.

He relaxed around her. She knew enough to wonder if that ever happened around anyone else.

"So you must be hungry," he said. "For breakfast."

"Starved."

He motioned to the refrigerator.

She rolled her eyes. "Oh, please. I know what's in there. A few condiments and a box of baking soda."

His expression turned smug. "You think you know everything."

"I do. The government often contacts me to help them out of difficult situations because of that." She walked to the refrigerator and pulled it open. Inside she found...food.

She stared at it for a second, then looked at Kane.

"You went to the grocery store," she said.

He shrugged. "While you were still sleeping."

"You have food in here. You hate food."

"I like food just fine. I knew how you felt about eating, and I had a feeling you'd be back, so I got a few things."

She looked at the carton of eggs, the package of vegan bacon, cheese, English muffins, juice, not to mention bread, lunch meat, a bag of salad and cookie dough. This was for more than just a single breakfast, she thought as she closed the door and stared at Kane.

"You thought I'd be back?" she asked, wondering if she could dare read any significance into that statement.

"You're stubborn."

She moved in front of him and placed her hands on his chest. "You're a big, tough guy. You could keep me away if you really wanted to."

He sighed. "Willow, don't make too much of this."

"Stop saying that to me. You invite me in with one hand and push me away with the other. So here's the thing." She sucked in a breath and braced herself for the explosion.

"We're dating," she told him. "You can call it what you want, but that's the truth. We're an item, a couple, a set, a pair. Whatever. You want to keep seeing me and I want to keep seeing you. That's dating. Welcome to the real world."

The fire fled his eyes and his expression hardened, but he didn't back away. So that was something. Then he covered her hands with his and pulled them away from his body.

"There's a reason I don't do this," he told her.

"Do what?"

"Date."

"Okay. Hit me." She smiled. "That's slang for tell me what you mean."

He narrowed his gaze. "I do slang."

"I wasn't sure. You nondaters can be so tricky."

He ignored that. "Getting involved requires trust, and I don't trust anyone. It requires change and I don't change."

He was so wrong, she thought, feeling sad for his inability to see the truth. Whatever he might tell himself, he *did* trust her. He never would have given her the key to his house otherwise. How hard would it have been to take Jasmine and her kittens to the pound? But he hadn't.

As for the not changing issues, from where she stood—which was deliciously close to Kane—he already had changed. The gift he'd brought her from New York. The food in the refrigerator. Hello, all big changes.

But instead of saying that, she murmured, "Don't worry. Dating me is fairly simple. There are only a few rules and you're a pretty bright guy. I think you can handle them."

Then she held her breath because she knew this could go either way. Kane could accept her offer or he could throw her out. Honestly, she had no idea which way it would fall.

He stared into her eyes. "What are the rules?"

Relief poured through her, although with enough happiness to make her float. "Let me just start by saying I'm a fabulous girlfriend. I'm going to spoil you for everyone else."

"I think I can handle that."

"Good. Okay—I want you to call when you say you're going to call, show up on time, not see anyone else."

He still held her hands in his. Now he pulled her close and rubbed her fingers. "I'm not interested in anyone else."

She nearly purred. Talk about exactly what she wanted to hear. "I'm glad. Let's see. What else? Oh, compliments. Compliments are always welcome."

"And gifts?" he asked.

"Not required. But I wouldn't say no." She grinned. "But where you're concerned, I rarely say no."

His eyes darkened with an emotion she couldn't read. "I'm not good at this, Willow. You're asking a lot."

"I have every faith in you."

"What happens when this goes badly?"

"Why assume the worst? What happens when it goes well?"

He released her hand and stroked her face. "Such an optimist. You should get that looked at."

"I have a bubbly personality—it's part of my charm."

"Yes, it is." He kissed her. "Stay right there."

He left the kitchen. She watched him go, then poured two cups of coffee and waited for his return.

When he walked toward her, he held out a business card. "My work number. I wrote my cell number on the back."

She took the card and knew what he was offering— access to his world. Access to him. If things did go badly— as he expected—her having this information could make his life messy. It was a big step for him.

In return, she gave him her heart. She wasn't sure it could be considered a fair trade.

Late Sunday morning Willow stood in front of the second biggest house she'd ever seen. It was three stories of elegant trim and windows and formal grounds. There had to be at least three people on the permanent gardening staff.

Marina joined her and linked arms. "So, what do you think?"

"It's amazing. I can't believe we're related to anyone who lives here. Todd's house is bigger, but we don't really know him, so it doesn't count. You think she has live-in help?"

"I'm sure of it."

"I don't think I'd like that. I'd want to come and go without being monitored. Plus, what about walking around naked? Kind of embarrassing with staff."

Marina laughed. "How much time do you spend being naked in your house?"

"Not much, but I want to keep the option open."

Julie hurried up to join them. "Sorry I'm late. I was, um, busy and didn't noticed the time."

Willow looked at Marina. "I'm guessing she means she and Ryan were doing the wild thing again."

"Oh, yeah."

Julie smoothed the front of her dress. "I'm ignoring you two. Come on…let's go see what our grandmother has in store for us."

As they walked toward the front of the house, Marina sighed. "You're still seeing Kane, aren't you?"

Willow smiled. "Uh-huh. It's official. We're an item."

"Great. So everyone has someone but me. That's kind of depressing."

Julie patted Marina's arm. "You can have Todd."

"Gee, thanks."

The three of them laughed, then Willow pushed the bell by the door.

"Is there a maid?" Marina asked in a low voice.

"In a uniform," Julie whispered back. "You'll love it."

There wasn't just a maid—there was a staff. Someone to show them in, someone else to bring them drinks, a third person to serve the meal.

Willow did her best to keep her attention on the food and the conversation, but she was distracted by the beauty of the "breakfast room."

"So much brighter and less formal than the dining room," Grandmother Ruth had said as she'd led the sisters into it.

If this was informal, Willow didn't think she was ready for anything more grand.

Six beveled glass windows opened onto a beautiful English-style formal garden. There were three crystal chandeliers hanging over the inlaid table and two matching buffets on the wall. The carpet looked antique, the artwork original and the china probably cost more per place setting than she made in a week.

"How are your wedding plans coming?" Ruth asked as the maid set down salad plates in front of each of them.

Julie looked up surprised. "Ah, well, fine. We haven't done much in the way of planning."

"Oh, are you waiting until after the baby's born?" Ruth asked.

Julie touched her stomach. "No, but I've been busy with work."

"And Ryan," Marina teased. "How could details like place cards and vows be more interesting than him?"

Julie grinned. "Excellent point."

Ruth cleared her throat. "I hope this doesn't sound too presumptuous, my dear, but I would be honored if you would consider having the wedding here. The backyard is beautiful, even this time of year, and there's plenty of room for a large tent or two. As an alternative, depending on the size of the wedding, we could hold it inside. There's actually a huge ballroom on the third floor. I never go up there, but it's quite lovely. I know a few wedding planners who could turn the space into a fairyland or whatever else you'd like."

Willow eyed her sister. She'd heard how Ruth had meddled in Julie's relationship with Ryan. But in the end, the old woman had come through, telling her granddaughter she only wanted Julie's happiness.

Willow guessed the offer was as much a way to connect as a desire to see her oldest granddaughter married in her house.

Nothing about this place was her style, but Julie might like it. It was a once-in-a-lifetime opportunity.

Julie smiled at her grandmother. "I'd have to talk it over with Ryan. If he's willing, I'd be very interested in holding the wedding here."

"Wonderful. You will be totally in charge. I won't get involved, except to pay the bills."

"No," Julie said quickly. "You don't have to do that. We want to pay for things ourselves."

"You're my granddaughter and he's my great-nephew. We're all family, dear. It will be my gift to you both."

Marina leaned toward Willow. "Think she'd spring for new cars for us single sisters?" she asked in a whisper.

Willow grinned. "I'm sure they're there for the asking."

Ruth glanced at Willow. "How is your young man? Kane?"

"I, ah, he's good." She tried to figure out if her grandmother should know about Kane. It was possible Todd or Ryan had mentioned she was dating him, assuming they knew. Well, Todd should know. He could see her car parked by Kane's place.

"Interesting man," Ruth said. "Dangerous, which is always exciting and sexy."

Willow nearly choked on her bite of lettuce. Had her sixtysomething grandmother just said sexy?

"He's very wealthy, you know," Ruth added. "An impressive investment portfolio."

Willow's eyes widened. "How do you know?"

"Todd mentioned it. He didn't give me exact figures, but apparently Kane doesn't work because he has to."

Willow disagreed. However much money Kane had now, he didn't think it was enough. Apparently privacy and a secure location didn't come cheap.

Would he really do it, she wondered. Would he really leave everyone behind and go off by himself? The thought of it made her sad—not only because his leaving would devastate her but because she didn't think it would make him happy. Sometime in his past he'd gotten the idea that he had to be solitary. She didn't think that was true anymore, but she wasn't sure she could convince him otherwise.

"He seems very responsible," Ruth continued. "An excellent quality in a man. Although he's a bit of a loner. You'll have to watch that. Some men like that can be turned around, but others can't. Be sure he's given his heart before you risk your own."

Excellent advice, Willow thought. Unfortunately it was about a month too late. Kane pretty much had possession of her heart from the moment he'd fussed over her ankle, taken in Jasmine and her kittens, then freaked when Jasmine went off for a little alone time.

He might have the rest of the world fooled into thinking he was a big, tough soldier, but she happened to know that inside he was warm and caring. He was also the man she loved.

Julie leaned toward her grandmother. "This would be you staying out of things?" she asked with a smile.

"Oh, no. I'm meddling, aren't I?" Ruth sighed. "Old habits and all that. But I do have one more thing before I swear off the habit forever."

Julie laughed. "Of course you do. What is it?"

Ruth turned to Marina. "I would so like for you to meet Todd. I know you have every reason to be apprehensive and so I'll even withdraw the offer of money, if you'd like. Please?"

Marina looked at her sisters, then back at Ruth. "Okay, I'll meet him, but only if the money offer stays on the table. The promise of riches makes it all the more interesting."

"You sure about that?" Julie asked. "What if you like him? The money will get in the way. Trust me, it's a complication."

"Oh, please. No offense, Grand, but what are the odds of that happening? I doubt he's my type. So I'll meet him, just to make you happy, but don't have any expectations."

"You're tempting fate," Willow murmured.

"I'll risk it," Marina said. "What chance is there that Todd Aston the Third is the one for me?"

"Unfortunately she's right," Ruth said. "But I'll still hold on to my grandmother dreams. It's all about family, isn't it? Oh, speaking of family, I'll be meeting your father next weekend and I'm looking forward to that."

"Me, too," Marina said.

Julie only looked annoyed, while Willow wondered what her father would have to say to her this time.

Later, when lunch was over, the sisters left. When they'd reached their cars, Marina turned to Julie.

"Are you really considering having your wedding here?" she asked.

Julie grinned. "Sure. Ryan loves Ruth, so he'd be happy. I'm sure Ruth knows the best party planners around, so that will make things easier. I'm not letting her pay for everything, but other than that, I think it's a great idea. You don't approve?"

"I like the idea," Marina admitted. "The house is gorgeous. I think it's a beautiful venue and if it makes Grand happy, then hey. Why not?"

"Willow?" Julie asked.

"I like the idea, too. Imagine how great the pictures would be. And it is a chance to bond with Ruth. You two got off to a rocky start."

"All forgiven," Julie said.

"Speaking of forgiven," Marina murmured. "Are you okay? About Dad coming home, I mean."

Julie shrugged. "I don't know. I guess. I've been talking to Ryan a lot and that's helped. Mom loves him. I may not understand her feelings, but I want to respect them. He's her husband and our father and in his own useless, selfish, twisted way, a part of the family."

Marina grinned. "As long as you're respecting everyone's feelings."

Julie sucked in a deep breath. "I'm doing my best to keep an open mind, okay? That's as good as it's going to get. In my heart, I'm still angry with him for what he's done to Mom for the past twenty years and I'm furious with her for putting up with it. But it's her decision. Not mine. I love her and I acknowledge that he's my father. That is my peak maturity experience for the day. Anyone expecting more is going to be disappointed."

"You'll get there," Marina said. "Personally I can't wait to see him."

"You always were his favorite," Julie said easily.

"Not his favorite, but we get along. I agree that life would have been better if he'd been the kind of guy to stick around, but he's not. So I accept him for what he is and enjoy the time he's around."

"You're a better person than I'll ever be," Julie said with a sigh. "I have to run. I'm meeting Ryan." She waved and walked to her car.

Marina turned to Willow. "I suppose you want to get back to Kane?"

"Pretty much."

"Wow—both my sisters seriously involved. I suppose that means I need to find myself a guy."

"You have Todd."

Marina laughed. "Right. All I can think is that our lone date will be a night I'll never get back." She hugged Willow. "See you at Mom's."

"I'll be there."

Marina left.

Willow climbed into her car and started the engine. Now that she was alone, she could stop pretending she was excited about her father's return. Her guilty secret had always been that she dreaded his visits. It never mattered what she did or how she tried, he never saw her as anything but a failure.

As a child, she'd tried desperately to make her father

proud of her. Tried and failed countless times. A few years ago, she'd stopped trying. But that didn't mean the hurt had gone away.

Ten

Willow shifted in the passenger seat of Kane's Mercedes. Normally the yummy smell of a leather interior and a dashboard that looked more like a cockpit would have distracted her. If nothing else, she would have tried to justify *how* the smell of leather could be yummy when she didn't eat meat, except on very special occasions when it didn't count.

But this afternoon, she couldn't seem to think about any of that. Instead she fought against the rising need to throw up and wondered if the knot of dread in her stomach would ever go away.

"You're quiet," Kane said as he pulled into the left turn lane and glanced at her. "I've learned that's not always a good thing."

"I'm fine. Okay, not fine, but not awful. Semiawful, maybe. This is all a mistake. Why are we doing this? We shouldn't be doing this. I should have said no or that we were busy or at least that you were busy. Asking you along was a mistake."

She bit her lip and sighed. "I don't mean that in a bad way."

"Oh, no. I'm tingling from the thrill of the compliment."

That made her smile. "You're not a tingle kind of guy."

"You can't be sure about that."

"If I had a lot of money, I'd bet it all. Anyway, the not inviting you was about me. I'm nervous. Besides, you don't do family stuff. Why did you say yes?"

He made the turn. "Because you asked and it seemed important to you."

Under other circumstances his words would have thrilled her. She would have felt an honest-to-goodness flutter right in the center of her chest. But not today. The dread was too big and growing and this was all going to be a disaster.

"It's my dad," she admitted. "He's back and while that's a good thing, it's also…confusing."

"Parents can be that way."

"Do you remember yours?" she asked.

He shrugged. "Not my dad. I never knew him. I'm not sure my mom knew who he was. I have a few fuzzy memories of her. She was strung out most of the time, or gone. She died when I was eight."

He spoke the words easily, as if he'd long made peace with them. But how was that possible?

"Where was Social Services in all this?" she asked. "Why didn't they come get you?"

"I don't think they knew about me. When my mom died, I went out on the streets. I'd been living there most of the time anyway. I was already like a mascot to a few gang members. It wasn't a big step to be accepted by all of them. Besides, I made myself useful. I ran errands—delivering drugs, picking up money."

He might as well be talking about life on Saturn. "You didn't go to school?"

"Not after junior high."

"But you're obviously educated."

"Got my GED while in the army. When I got into basic training, I realized I knew nothing about anything. I started reading in my spare time. Everything is self-taught."

Which was incredible, she thought. He was a sophisticated, dangerous man of the world who'd started with nothing.

Okay—now her pity party had just taken a turn for the worse. Before she'd been worried about what would happen with her father—what he would say in front of Kane. Now Kane was even more amazing and her humiliation would be greater.

She wanted to tell him about her fears and have him put his arms around her and say it didn't matter. Except she wasn't sure he would. In truth, what she really wanted was for him to say he loved her and, to quote Marina, what were the odds of that happening?

But he liked her. He liked her and he was dating her and Kane didn't date, so that was something. She would hang on to that and pray for a miracle. That she could go one afternoon with her father and not have him say anything hideous.

She felt her eyes burning. As tears were the last thing she wanted to deal with, she drew in a deep breath and changed the subject.

"The kittens are really growing," she said. "They'll need a bigger box."

"I'll get one this week."

She forced herself to think about Jasmine and her beautiful kittens and how precious they all were. That was safe. Kittens and chocolate and how Kane touched her in the night.

The knot loosened a little…right until they pulled up in front of her mother's house.

"We're here," she said, hoping she sounded more excited than she felt.

They walked inside. Everyone else was already there and called out greetings. Her father stood in the center of the group, as always.

He looked the same, Willow thought. Still handsome and blond, with a deep tan and blue eyes that were permanently crinkled in good humor.

"You must be Kane," Jack Nelson said with a grin. "I've heard so much about you."

The two men shook hands.

"How's my Willow?" Jack asked.

"I'm good, Daddy." She stepped into his embrace.

His arms were familiar, as was the uneasy combination of longing and apprehension. She knew the hits were coming. It was just a matter of when and where.

She stepped back, but her father kept his arm around her shoulder.

"This is how it should be," he said. "Back with all my girls."

Willow stepped free of his embrace and walked over to her mother.

"How are you doing?" she asked, although she could see the happiness on her mother's face.

"I'm wonderful. It's so good to have him home."

Willow nodded. She noticed Kane talking to Ryan. Julie stood next to her fiancé, holding on to his hand as if she would never let go. Families were complicated.

"Now let me see if I have this straight," Jack said to Kane. "You work for Ryan here."

Kane nodded. "I run security for the various companies Ryan and Todd are funding."

"Ryan says you're the best in the business."

"I know what I'm doing."

"Impressive." Jack slapped Kane on the back. "Good. Good. At least you're not like Willow's other losers."

"Dad," Marina said quickly, taking her father's hand. "Come on. Let's go into the family room. UCLA is playing University of Washington. We can watch our guys kick their Seattle butts."

Willow appreciated the save, but wished it hadn't been necessary. She felt heat on her cheeks and the knot in her stomach had turned to dread.

Her father allowed himself to be turned away. But at the step down to the family room, he glanced back at Kane.

"I'm glad Willow's moving up. I've always worried about her. She's never been as smart or pretty as her sisters. I wondered who would want her. It's good to know I was wrong."

Willow felt as if she'd been hit with an emotional baseball bat. Her face flamed with embarrassment.

Not knowing what else to do, she fled into the kitchen where she picked up a knife and began cutting bread into slices. As she didn't know what they were having or what her mother wanted the bread for, she could really be messing up the recipe. But she had to be doing something. The bread got all blurry and she couldn't see anything. She tossed the knife down and gave in to the tears.

Then her sisters were there.

"He's such a jerk," Julie muttered as she hugged Willow. "This is only one of the reasons I hate him."

"He's not the most sensitive man," Marina said as she hugged them both. "Willow, I'm so sorry."

Willow let their love surround her. It didn't heal the wound, but it eased a little of the pain. Still, the memory of the humiliation clawed at her. What was Kane thinking?

"I should never have brought him," she whispered. "I can't do this."

Instead of answering, her sisters moved away. For a second, she was alone, then strong arms encircled her.

She didn't have to open her eyes to recognize the man. Indecision tore at her. While she needed to be with him, she was too embarrassed to want to face him.

"I'm sorry," she said, forcing herself to look into his eyes.

But instead of censure, she saw something that looked very much like affection.

"You can't pick your parents."

"I know. He's always been like that. Do you want to leave? I could get a ride home with Marina."

He brushed away her tears, then bent down and kissed her. Really kissed her. There was heat and need and plenty of tongue. When they resurfaced, her head was fuzzy and it had nothing to do with feeling bad.

"I want you," he breathed. "I want you naked. I want to make love with you until we're both exhausted. Then I want to talk to you and be with you. Just you, Willow. You know how I feel about relationships, yet here I am. With you. I've known a lot of women and you are unique in more ways than I can count. You are passionate and beautiful and stubborn and giving and you delight me."

The knot disappeared. Her tears dried up and she wanted to crawl inside Kane and live there forever.

She loved him. The words hovered on her tongue, then she swallowed them. Kane was many things, but open to being loved wasn't one of them. It didn't seem fair to repay his kindness with a statement that would terrify him.

But soon, she thought. Soon.

Kane watched the dynamics of the Nelson family and felt more uncomfortable by the second. If intimacy was a dance, then everyone in this house had forgotten the steps. Julie clung to Ryan as if he were the only point of safety. Willow put on a brave face, but he saw the pain behind her big eyes and it made him want to hit something...or someone. Marina seemed the only one able to hang out with her father and be relaxed, while Naomi, the girls' mother, fluttered from place to place in an attempt to make peace.

He'd already berated himself for ever agreeing to join Willow at her less than happy family reunion. He knew better, yet she'd asked and he'd said yes. Because he found it difficult to deny her anything.

He was losing it, he thought. He had it bad for a woman and he knew the trouble that led to. Getting involved could get a man dead.

"Kane!" Jack said jovially. "Come join me in my study."

Kane would rather have been air-dropped into a piranha-filled river, but he nodded and followed the other man through the family room and into a bookcase-lined study. Jack shut the door behind him.

"I love all the women in my life, but sometimes a man needs to get away." Jack grinned. "You know what I mean?"

Kane took one of the leather chairs as his host poured them each a Scotch.

Jack stretched out in the recliner opposite Kane's and raised his glass. "To my ladies. May they always welcome me home."

Kane didn't acknowledge the toast. What was the point

of making trouble? The visit would end and then he and Willow would leave.

Jack sighed. "Do I have a great life, or what? I love this house. I'm always happy to get back here. Naomi's a terrific woman. So warm and welcoming. She understands me. The patience of a saint, that woman. And the girls are special. I'm willing to admit I would have liked a son, of course. What man wouldn't, but maybe it's better this way."

Kane sipped the Scotch. It was single malt, eighteen years old. He knew what the bottle had cost and doubted it had fit comfortably in Naomi's food budget.

"It is better," Kane said casually. "The way you take off and abandon your family every time you get an itch, there could be trouble. A son would grow up and beat the crap out of you."

Jack stared at him. "It's not like that."

"It's exactly like that."

Jack shrugged. "Tell me about your job. Do you like working for Ryan? Weren't you in the military before? Isn't this a little boring for you?"

"I was in Special Forces," Kane said after he put his glass on the small table beside his chair. "Nearly nine years. I specialized in the undetected kill. Get in, get the job done, get out before anyone knows you're there. I was good at it, too."

Jack swallowed. "Excellent. Excellent."

"From there I went into private security. That's the polite word for it. Basically, I was a mercenary for hire. I've survived the most dangerous places in the world. There's a lot of money in that kind of work."

"I can imagine." Jack shifted in his chair. "If I ever need a second career, eh?"

Kane stood and looked down at the older man. "We're

not friends, Jack. We'll never be friends. I don't like you or respect you, but you're Willow's father and as much as I'd like to change that, I can't. You're an ass. You have a wife who worships you, daughters who adore you and that's not enough for you. You want to go play, so you keep leaving them. Of course they keep taking you back, so they have some responsibility in this, too."

He moved toward the door, then turned back to his host. "If it had been me, I would have kicked your butt a long time ago. Grow up. Be a man. You might find you actually like it. But whatever you decide, don't make Willow cry again. If you do, I'll hunt you down like the snake you are and I'll skin you alive. Are we clear?"

Jack nodded frantically and Kane left the room.

He made his way to the backyard, where he was able to breathe for a few minutes.

But his solitude was short-lived. The door behind him opened again and Naomi stepped out.

"I know I'm interrupting," she said. "I won't take long. I heard what you said to Jack."

Kane held in a groan. Just perfect. He looked at Willow's mother. "Do you want me to apologize?"

"Not at all," she said with a smile. "I was impressed. I know Jack was terrified. I might love the man, but I'm not blind to his flaws. Maybe you'll change him, although I doubt it."

"You could stop welcoming him home," Kane said flatly.

"I could, but I won't. I'd rather have Jack some of the time than never at all. That's my flaw. Still, this isn't about me. I wanted to thank you for defending Willow. I've been on Jack for years about how he talks to her, but he would never listen. I think things are going to be different now."

That was something, Kane thought. "Why her? Why not Julie or Marina?"

Naomi sighed. "Willow had some learning problems when she was younger. Nothing serious, but for a while, school was much harder for her. The doctors said it was just because her brain was wired a little differently. Eventually everything righted itself and she did fine. But Jack can't or won't forget those earlier years. I'm not sure why he thinks Willow isn't as pretty as her sisters, though."

"She's not," Kane told her. "She's prettier by a lot."

Naomi's smiled again. "Not that you're biased."

He shrugged.

"I think Jack sees a lot of himself in Willow," Naomi said. "She's always been the dreamer. Or at least she was. Lately she seems to have found herself in more ways than one. She loves her new job at the nursery."

He thought about the army of plants that was slowly filling his place. "I guessed that."

"I always worried about Willow because of the kind of men she chose. So many troubled souls in need of a good rescue. But I see now she was just filling her time until she found the right sort of man." Naomi touched his arm. "You're everything I could have wished for her. Thank you."

She stepped back into the house.

Kane continued to stand on the porch, looking out on the lush backyard, but not really seeing it. Every cell in his body warned him this situation was dangerous and getting more deadly by the second.

That night Kane lay on his back as Willow cuddled up next to him.

"So did you hate every minute of it?" she asked.

He stroked her pale blond hair. "It wasn't so bad."

"The beginning was a nightmare, but later, things got better. I mentioned my new job to my dad and he was actually supportive. I thought maybe the sky was going to fall, but no, he was just being nice. Maybe he's mellowing."

The happiness and wonder in her voice let him know he'd done the right thing where Jack was concerned. Kane would still like to take the man out back and break a few bones, but polite society frowned on that. Not to mention how Willow would react if she found out he'd hurt her dad. Her mixed feelings wouldn't extend far enough to support actual violence.

"Dinner was good," she added, then went on about the meal.

Kane listened to her sweet voice and felt the wanting take hold of him. It didn't matter that they'd just finished making love—he still needed her again.

Needed. When had he ever needed anyone? Needing, like caring and believing and all those other relationship words got you dead.

She pushed herself up on one elbow and looked down at him. She was naked and her long hair veiled her bare breasts. She was an erotic vision. What the hell had he done to deserve her?

"I want to say something," she told him. "I'm going to say it and then you're going to hold me in your arms. We'll turn out the light and go to sleep. You're not allowed to say anything back. I don't want you to. I mean that. This is about me telling you. Okay?"

Dread chased away desire. Wariness stiffened his muscles and made him ready for flight. He nodded curtly.

She drew in a breath, then smiled. "I love you. I have for a while, but I'm finally ready to say the words. I love you."

She lowered herself back onto his shoulder and closed her eyes. "Night, Kane."

"Good night."

He turned out the light and lay there in his dark. She loved him. It didn't matter whether or not he believed her. *She* believed and that was enough.

How had he let this happen?

Damn stupid question, he thought grimly. He'd let her in and she'd made herself at home. Now she had feelings and expectations and he would never be able to take care of either. He didn't want her love. Not now, not ever.

He knew she'd meant the words as a gift, but to him they were little more than a trap. He could feel the metal teeth holding him in place. It was either break free or die. He sacrificed himself or he sacrificed Willow.

He might pretend to weigh the options, but he already knew what he was going to choose, and how much it would destroy her when he did.

Eleven

Willow fixed coffee the next morning while Kane got ready for work. She was both happy and apprehensive. Although she didn't regret telling him the truth about her feelings and was proud of herself for being so brave, she couldn't help the slight quiver of nerves in her belly. Kane hadn't wanted a girlfriend, let alone someone to love him. How would he react to what she'd said?

She poured coffee into his travel mug just as he walked into the kitchen. She held out the mug and allowed herself a momentary eye-party as she admired his broad shoulders and narrow hips in his tailored suit.

"Morning." He kissed her on the mouth, then took the coffee. "I have a meeting at seven-thirty, so I have to run."

"That's fine. I'll feed Jasmine."

"Great." He kissed her again.

She grabbed the lapels of his suit and stared into his

eyes. "About last night," she began. "Are you okay with what I said?"

"You're always going to lead with your heart, Willow. I wouldn't change that."

Then he was gone. It was only after he'd driven away that she realized he hadn't answered her question.

The shooting range stood in a converted warehouse. It was private and exclusive, catering mostly to those with the money to pay for the best. Kane scanned his member-ship card, then headed for the scored target room. After checking then loading his Glock, he put on ear protection and stepped into the room.

He could still hear the sound of gunfire and see the flash of the shots. Ignoring the other shooters, he walked to the end of the aisle and faced his target. But instead of seeing the silhouette of a man, he saw Willow. He heard her laughing as she bent down to pick up one of the kittens, caught the curve of a hip as she danced in his kitchen to some Country song. He felt the soft warmth of her skin and the breath of her sigh as he pleasured her.

He lowered his gun and forced himself to focus. He came to the club a couple of times a month to stay sharp. He liked his time here and looked forward to the challenge. But not today. Today there was only Willow.

He drew in a deep breath and forced her from his mind, then lined up his gun with the target and fired six rounds, one after the other.

George, the manager of the place, walked over. "Hey, Kane. Haven't seen you in a while."

"I know. Been busy."

George eyed the target at the far end of the room. "Did you miss one?"

Kane pushed the button to bring the target closer, then swore. Sure enough, one of the bullets had missed the silhouette completely.

"You're not usually off your game," George said. "I guess we'll be seeing more of you."

Kane nodded and the other man left.

The target fluttered slightly as Kane returned it to its original position, then he stared down the barrel of his gun and knew he was in real danger of losing his edge. As that edge was the only thing that had kept him alive, he couldn't risk that.

He didn't have to ask what had happened—he knew exactly what had changed in his life. Or who.

She loved him. She'd spoken the words with a conviction that left him no way out. He had to believe her and that belief changed everything.

She *was* love. Her entire existence defined the word. She was warm and caring and giving and impetuous. She was also strong enough to have faith—something he'd never had the courage for.

To give her what she wanted was impossible. She wanted him to love her back, to need her, to have her in his life forever. The thought of that filled him with both longing and terror. Only the longing surprised him.

Was he tempted? Did he really think he could expose himself that way, be defined by and connected to another person and still survive? Hadn't facing death more times than he could count taught him anything?

He drew in a steadying breath, then faced the target and fired again. This time the shots filled an area not much bigger than a quarter, exactly where the heart would be. Calmness filled him. He knew what was wrong and he knew how to fix it.

In this world, only the strongest survived. He refused to be anything but the one left standing at the end.

Willow arrived at Kane's with yet another plant. This time she had an ailing orchid. Beverly said it was too late to save it, but Willow was sure she would convince the slender bloom to hang on long enough to get strong again.

As she let herself into the house, she was greeted by three very excited kittens.

"You got out of your box," she said as she set the plant on a table, then crouched on the floor. "Look at you. So big and tough."

They ran to her and began to climb all over her. Needle-sharp claws cut through her jeans and raked her skin. She winced and picked up the biggest offender, a gray and white male, with splotches of orange on his face and paws.

"You're a wild thing, aren't you?" She nuzzled the kitten. He purred and rubbed his face against hers.

The tabby female kitten stood on Willow's thighs and batted at her brother's flicking tail.

"You're all so cute," Willow said. "I want to keep you all."

She couldn't, of course. In theory she couldn't have a cat at all. Not at her place. But if she were to have a change in location...

She stretched out on the floor and let the kittens romp around on her. Jasmine came over to get her scratching. Willow let the kitty love wash over her.

Who knew things would work out like this? A couple of months ago, she'd been intent on giving Todd a piece of her mind. Now her entire life was different. She was happy in her work, desperately in love and moving in a totally different direction. Life wasn't just full of sur-prises...it was very, very good.

She heard a key in the door and smiled expectantly. When Kane walked in, she grinned up at him. "I'm being held hostage by the cats. You're going to have to save me. Think you're up to it, Mr. Big Security Guy?"

But instead of smiling or offering her a hand or even joining her on the floor, Kane closed the door behind him and said, "I'd like to speak with you, please. Can you get up?"

He wasn't smiling. He wasn't doing anything. As she scrambled to her feet, she fought the nagging sense of the familiar. What was it?

And then she knew. It was his eyes. They were empty again. As empty as they'd been when she'd first met him.

"Kane?"

"This is a mistake," he said. "I'm sorry for my part in it. I should never have let you believe there was ever a chance for more. There isn't. I don't want there to be. I am solitary by choice. You can't change that. I'm not interested in what you're offering, Willow. I don't want any of it. Or you."

He spoke calmly, simply and with a clarity that left her bleeding from wounds that would never heal. She couldn't think, couldn't speak, could only try to keep standing.

"I…" she began.

He cut her off. "This isn't negotiable. I'll give you two hours to clear out."

She didn't hurt enough. Willow knew that was a bad sign. There was plenty of pain, but a part of her was still numb. If she could barely survive this, how would she make it when the real ache set in?

"What can I get you?" Marina carried in tea from the kitchen. "Wine? Vodka? A contract on Kane?"

Willow laughed, then sobbed and reached for another

tissue. "I don't want him dead or even hurt. I can't. I love him."

She sat curled up on Marina's sofa. All of Kane's plants were still in her car, but her sister had offered to take in Jasmine and her family until the kittens were old enough to be adopted.

"I'm ok-kay," she said, her voice shaking.

"Oh, sure." Her sister sat next to her and put a hand on her leg. "I can tell."

"It's not that bad yet," Willow told her. "I think it's going to hit me later."

One of the kittens crawled into her lap and curled up, as if offering comfort. Willow patted her.

"It's not his fault," she said. "He t-told me what he was. He was very specific about that. I'm the one who didn't believe him. I just plowed in where I wasn't wanted. Why do I do that? Why don't I listen?"

"We all hear what we want to hear."

Willow shook her head. "It's more than that. I was so proud of myself. I finally felt I'd moved on from rescuing guys, you know? Kane didn't need rescuing. In fact, he rescued me in every way possible." She sniffed. "Isn't that a line from *Titanic?*"

Marina smiled, then stroked her hair. "I'm sure it's okay for you to use it."

"I love sad stories at the movies, but in real life, it really sucks." She blew her nose and reached for another tissue. "I thought I was going to have it all. Isn't that stupid."

"No. Don't say that. It's not stupid. Why wouldn't you have it all?"

Willow sighed. Her body hurt as if she had a bad case of the flu. Her heart ached and every beat seemed almost more effort than it could muster. Her eyes were burning and gritty.

She'd been emotionally beat up and left for dead. The worst part was, she couldn't blame Kane.

"He wasn't wrong," she whispered. "You can't blame him."

"Watch me," Marina said, looking annoyed. "He's a complete bastard. How dare he hurt you like this?"

"But he didn't do anything wrong," Willow reminded her. "He told me the rules and he played by them."

"Why does he get to set the rules? Why not you? Why not me?"

Willow managed a slight smile. "You weren't dating him. As for me, well, I didn't have many rules."

"He changed everything when he agreed to keep seeing you," her sister told her. "He left the scary world he regularly inhabits and entered the world of normal people. Once there, he has to play by our rules and he didn't. Everything was fine until one day he announced he was through and gave no real reason. That's not allowed."

Willow reached for her tea and took a sip. "I told him I loved him. I think that's what set him off."

Marina stared at her. "For real?"

Willow nodded. "He's the one. I've liked other guys and had crushes and all kinds of things, but I've never been in love. Not until Kane. He's so strong and giving and when I'm with him, I feel safe."

She set down her mug and patted the kitten on her lap. "I know being safe doesn't seem like a big deal, but I've never felt much of it before."

"I believe that," Marina said quietly. "I didn't know things had gone that far for you."

"They had. I love him and now he's gone."

She began to cry again.

"Oh, Willow." Marina hugged her close. "We'll figure

this out. I'll kidnap him and we'll keep him weak and thirsty until he realizes he needs you in his life."

Willow hiccuped a small laugh. "If he was naked, I could get into that plan."

"I'm sorry," Marina whispered into her hair. "I'm so sorry. What do you want to do? Eat ice cream? Scream? Throw some plates? Come up with a way to win him back?"

If only, Willow thought. "I can't win him back. I can't make him want to be with me. He has to decide that on his own and I don't think he's going to."

It was dark when Kane returned to the house. He walked inside and heard...nothing.

The cats were gone, the plants were gone, and Willow was gone. He walked through the rooms and saw that despite taking everything he'd asked, she'd still left her mark.

His magazines were fanned out in a circle, which she always did while she was talking on the phone. There was food in the refrigerator and cookies in the large red strawberry cookie jar she'd bought. In the bathroom, the sweet scent of her perfume lingered.

He saw a white shirt hanging on the back of the door. It was his, so she'd left it, but it was the one she wore instead of a robe. He picked it up and held it in his hand, as if he could still touch her.

But he couldn't. She was gone. Just like he wanted.

He returned to the living room and waited for the peace that silence always brought. But tonight there was only the restless need to keep moving. He changed into workout clothes and decided to get in another hour at the gym. Maybe then he would sleep.

It was nearly midnight when he finally crawled into bed.

He was exhausted and yet he couldn't close his eyes. The silence was too loud.

Finally he got up and retrieved the shirt she'd used from the back of the bathroom door, then laid it out next to him. Stupid, he thought. No, beyond stupid. Pathetic.

And then he got it. He missed her. He, who had always prided himself on never missing anyone, missed her more than he could say.

Twelve

Kane gathered his keys and briefcase, then walked to his front door. But before he could open it, someone knocked.

For a second he did nothing. He stood on the tile and listened to the sound of his heart beating. He knew what he wanted, what he hoped, what he could never allow. Willow. But when he pulled open the door, Todd stood there.

"I'm glad I caught you," his boss said. "My car's acting up. Can I get a ride into the office with you? The dealer's going to come pick up my car and they'll deliver a loaner later this morning."

The disappointment was as real and fast as a gunshot. He wanted to howl to the heavens, to demand it be her. But after what he'd said, why would she bother?

"No problem," he told Todd. "I was on my way out."

"Good. I don't see Willow's car. Has she already left?"

"She's gone. We're not seeing each other anymore."

Todd raised his eyebrows. "I didn't know. I thought you two were getting along. That everything was great."

Kane hit the button to unlock his car, then stowed his briefcase in the backseat.

"I won't ask what happened." Todd climbed into the passenger seat. "God knows I'm avoiding women these days. Ruth has been on me until I finally agreed to a date with Marina. What the hell was I thinking?"

Kane didn't have an answer and he didn't want to talk about Marina. She reminded him of Willow and thinking about Willow made him hurt in ways he'd never imagined possible.

She'd changed him, he thought grimly. Silence and solitude had always been his refuge. He'd needed to be alone. Now the evenings and even his life stretched out endlessly before him. It was blank and empty and cold.

But how to change that? Give in? Care? And then what, he asked himself as he turned right. If he let her get close, let her get inside, where would he have to go? How could he protect himself?

"What's wrong with your car?" he asked as a way to distract himself and Todd. Discussing anything was preferable to talking about any of the Nelson sisters.

"Not sure. It just wouldn't start. It's only a few months old. Strange."

Something clicked in the back of Kane's mind. "Did it make a noise at all?"

"Sort of a raspy growl. It turned over a couple of times and went dead."

"You haven't pissed anyone off lately, have you?"

Todd looked at him. "You think it's more than just a car not starting?"

"I don't know. Do you have the dealership's number with you?" Kane asked.

"Sure."

"Call them and tell them not to bother picking up the car. That you'll have it dropped off later. I'll get a guy I know to go by and look it over first. Just in case."

Todd swore. "I don't like the sound of that."

"Better to be safe than—"

Something big and fast moving rammed into them from the side, pushing them into oncoming traffic on the busy street. Kane's car skidded, but he easily kept control. Even as he steered back into the correct lane and avoided an accident, he scanned for the attacker while pulling his gun out of its holster.

He saw it. A silver import. It headed for them again. The sun worked against him, keeping him from seeing the driver.

"Brace yourself," he told Todd, then braked suddenly.

Their attacker shot past them. Kane took aim but before he could pull the trigger, he felt something. A flash of information he couldn't process, a hunch, whatever, followed by the clear and unwelcome realization that Willow wouldn't want him to kill anyone.

He swore, took aim again, only to watch the car crash into light pole and come to a stop.

He drove to the side of the road and called 911. He was out of the car and heading for the driver as the operator picked up. He gave the location of the accident and described what happened automatically, all the while wondering what else she'd changed inside of him and how he would ever find his way back to who he had been.

Kane finished with the police a little after ten-thirty that morning. His car would need some serious body work but it was still drivable. He was about to climb inside when a paramedic stopped him.

"Do we need to look at you?" he asked Kane.

"I'm good. Had my seat belt on."

"So did the kid. Otherwise he'd be dead now."

Kane eyed the totaled wreck being pulled onto a flatbed tow truck. "The police said he is a teenager. That he passed out."

The paramedic nodded. "He is seventeen, a senior in high school. According to his mom, he's a diabetic. Apparently he screwed up his injection this morning and went into insulin shock. When he rammed into you, he was so out of it, I doubt he knew he was driving. You handled the situation like a pro. If you'd let him hit you again, I don't think he would have survived the impact."

The paramedic left.

Kane stood by his car and sucked in a breath. A seventeen-year-old boy. What if he'd shot the kid? Under the circumstances, he wouldn't have been charged. The concealed weapon was legal and Kane was a trained professional. But that would have been cold comfort to the kid's family. And to himself.

Six months ago, he would have fired without a second thought. Today he hadn't been able to. And he knew why.

That night Kane sat alone in the dark and got drunk.

He didn't usually drink to excess, but after today, he figured he'd earned it. Maybe with enough liquor in his body, he could finally forget what he'd almost done that morning. Maybe he could forget about Willow, about how much he missed her.

Maybe. But he had his doubts.

* * *

Willow looked at her boss. "Beverly, it's only been a month."

"I know." Beverly grinned at her. "You should just nod and say thank you."

"Thank you," Willow said and meant it. She'd just gotten a raise and it was a big one.

"You're a find," the other woman told her. "You're a natural with both the plants and the customers. That's rare. Usually it's one or the other. With you to help me, I can expand the way I've always wanted to. You're organized and creative and easy to work with. I don't want anyone to steal you away."

The compliments were flowing so fast, Willow could barely absorb them all. Still, she liked the feeling of pride that welled up inside of her.

"I don't want to be stolen," she admitted. "I love working here. Thanks for the raise."

"You're welcome."

"I'm going to get back to the exotics."

"Great. Do whatever you've been doing. They've never looked better."

Willow waved and walked to the rear of the nursery. She felt good—better than good. If not for the giant hole where her heart used to be, she'd be positively floating.

An hour later, she was elbow deep in soil and nutrients for the growth mixture she'd started experimenting with.

"Hello, Willow."

The low male voice could have caused a shiver in her belly, except it wasn't one she recognized. She turned and saw a tall, handsome, well-dressed man standing inside the greenhouse tent.

Hmm—dark hair, dark eyes and a slightly more than passing resemblance to Julie's fiancé, Ryan.

She sat back on her heels. "Let me guess," she said. "The infamous Todd Aston the Third."

"We meet at last. I understand you want to give me a piece of your mind."

"Is that why you're here?"

"No, but I'll listen if it will make you feel better."

"It won't." Maybe at one time she'd wanted to yell at Todd, but not anymore. She had bigger worries sucking at her energy. "Julie and Ryan are getting married. That's what's important to me."

"Me, too."

She stared at him.

"Don't look surprised," he told her. "Ryan and I have been friends all our lives. I care about him. I want whatever makes him happy and that's Julie."

"Cheap talk."

He gave her a slight smile. "We'll have this conversation again in ten years and then you'll have to believe me."

Ten years? Right. Todd and Ryan were cousins. So when Ryan became a part of the family, Todd was going to be tagging along. Did that mean there would be shared functions? Would she run into Kane at one of them?

The thought was both thrilling and exquisitely painful. To see him but not be with him would be torture. Yet the thought of never seeing him again was worse.

"Are you doing all right?" Todd asked. "I know about the breakup."

Was that the reason for his unexpected visit? Did Kane want an update? Somehow she doubted that. "I'm getting by."

"Kane isn't. He's in pretty bad shape."

Her first instinct was to run to him and try to make

things better. But he'd made it clear he didn't want her help or even her.

She stood and brushed off her jeans. "I'm sorry to hear that, but it's not my business."

"I don't know what happened between the two of you, but I've known Kane for a few years now. He's a great guy. He's careful about who he gets involved with." Todd frowned. "You're the first girlfriend I can remember in his life. So maybe you could cut him a break and give him a second chance."

She stared at Todd. "You think *I* ended things?"

"Didn't you? The way he's been acting, I figured…"

"Sorry, no. He left me. He made it incredibly clear that he wanted nothing to do with me. We didn't have a fight, we didn't disagree, he simply decided it was over."

Saying the words made her ache inside, but there was no point in hiding from the truth.

Todd shifted awkwardly. "I didn't know."

"Now you do." She faced him. "I love Kane. I told him and I think he couldn't handle it. I wish things were different, that he were different, but they are what they are. He doesn't need a second chance with me. He needs to figure out whether he's interested in a first one."

"I'm sorry."

"I'll survive. I come from a long line of strong women." She thought about her family. "Strong women who sometimes make foolish choices when it comes to men."

"If there's anything I can do…"

"There isn't, but thanks." She put her hands on her hips. "Wait a minute. You came here to make things right with me and Kane—why would you bother?"

"I told you. I wanted to help my friend."

"So you're not totally evil?"

"Is that a question and if so, do you expect me to answer it?"

"I guess not. But you surprise me. You were so icky about Julie and Ryan."

"I was *not* icky and I thought Julie was in it for the money."

"She would never do that."

"I know that now."

"You should have given her the benefit of the doubt. It's the right thing to do."

"Not if you have my past."

"Oh, I see. So you're going to punish every woman you meet because you had the poor judgment to pick badly in the past. That's something to look forward to. I'll be sure to tell Marina."

Todd looked both pained and amused by her comments. "You know about our date."

"Oh, yeah. We're all counting the hours."

One corner of his mouth twitched. "Is she more like you or more like Julie?"

"You'll have to figure that out for yourself. But I will tell you that she's incredibly smart, so don't try any of your smarmy crap on her."

"Smarmy crap?" He grinned. "I'll remember that. Leave the smarmy crap at home."

She hated that he was amused. "You know what I mean."

"I do." His humor faded. "It was delightful to meet you, Willow. I'm sorry Kane was moronic enough to let you go. I think you would have been good for him."

She nodded, mostly because her eyes had started burning and she knew where that road led.

She maintained control until Todd had left, then she let the tears fall. She wanted to believe that his visit meant something, but how could it? Kane hadn't sent him. She would bet he didn't even know about Todd stopping by.

Todd had said Kane was in bad shape. Did the fact that he was hurting mean anything? Would he want to fix the problem or simply muscle through it?

Despite everything, she wanted to go to him and hold him until he felt better. But she wouldn't. She couldn't force the man to love her and she was no longer interested in someone who only saw her as a convenience. She'd thought she meant more, but she'd been wrong.

That night Willow curled up in a corner of her sofa and tried to get interested in the movie she'd rented. It was a comedy and it seemed to be pretty funny, but none of the jokes were making her laugh. Maybe because she hurt too much inside.

She reached for the remote control, thinking she would just go to bed and try the movie another time, when she heard an odd noise outside. It sounded like scratching. Or whining. Or both.

She listened and heard the sound again.

She crossed to her front door and pulled it open. A black, fluffy, furry, adorable puppy stared up at her, then yipped.

Delighted, she dropped to her knees. The puppy plunged into her arms and began licking her face.

"Who are you?" she asked as she laughed and tried to hold on to the wiggling buddle of kisses. "Where did you come from? Are you lost?"

"He's not the one who's lost," Kane said, stepping out of the shadows.

Her heart froze. She actually felt it stop midbeat. Her breath caught in her throat and she momentarily lost her hold on the puppy who used her inattention to lunge forward and knock her onto her back.

"Okay, that's enough." Kane stepped forward and grabbed the puppy under one arm. He used his free hand to pull her to her feet. "He gets kind of rowdy."

"I can see that."

She didn't know what to think, what to feel. "Why are you here?"

"Can we come in? He should be okay. He just had his way with a couple of your rosebushes out front, so I think he's safe on carpet for a few minutes."

The only man she'd ever loved, the man who had so clearly rejected her, was talking about whether or not a puppy would pee on her rug?

She stepped back and let them both in. Kane set down the puppy, who ran to her and began licking her bare feet.

She dropped to her knees and gathered the puppy close. "Does he have a name?" she asked because talking about the dog was a whole lot safer than talking about anything else.

She wanted to believe that Kane's presence here meant something, but she wasn't sure. And she hurt too much to hope.

"Not yet. I thought you'd want to name him." Kane crouched next to her. "He's yours. I bought him for you. But he lives with me, so if you want him, you're going to have to come back to me."

She swallowed. Okay, sure, now there was hope, but there was also fear and a broken heart. "You want me back?"

"Want?" He shook his head. "*Want* is such a small word, Willow. I thought I knew what I wanted. Solitude. My peaceful world. I had it all planned out. I was careful—I never got involved. I knew what caring meant and I wasn't going to be a sucker twice. No one got in, ever. Until you."

The hope got a little bigger and brighter. Her breathing quickened.

"I thought I wanted to live on an island somewhere, by myself. I thought I wanted what I had. I did—until I met you. Everything changed after that. Now I want noise and confusion and conversation and laughter. I want candles and plants and food and your mess everywhere."

"I'm not that messy."

He smiled, then reached out and stroked her cheek. The puppy licked them both. "I'm sorry. I'm sorry for what I said and I'm sorry for how I hurt you. The pain in your eyes, pain that I put there, haunts me. I miss you, Willow. I don't just want you. I ache for you. I need you with a desperation that leaves me weak. You made me into a man I never thought I could be. You have changed me as fundamentally as a man can change. It took me awhile to figure all that out. I've never been in love before, so I didn't recognize the signs."

Love? Love!

She released the puppy and reached for Kane. "So you're saying…"

"I love you." He gathered her close and held on tight. "I love you. For always. Through sickness and in health and through babies and houses and whatever else happens. If you can forgive me. If you still love me."

She pulled back and stared at him. "What? Because you thought I might just fall out of love with you?"

She saw the fear in his eyes and knew he'd been afraid of just that. "I hurt you," he said. "I was cruel. I can't excuse what I did. I can only promise I'll never do it again."

He was not a man who gave his word lightly. She trusted him to love her for always, just as she trusted him to be there for her and their children and pets and whatever else might enter their lives.

"I do love you," she said.

"Will you marry me?"

She smiled. "Yes. Do we get to keep Jasmine?"

He grinned. "Of course."

"And at least one of the kittens?"

He sighed. "It's your life, too. You get to decide."

"I hope they like Bobo. He's got some big paws on him. I'm thinking he'll get to fifty or sixty pounds."

He closed his eyes and groaned. "We're not calling the dog Bobo."

"Muffin?"

"It's a boy, Willow. Can he have a little dignity? What about Blackie?"

"Oh, that's original. I'm thinking he looks like a Stan." Kane groaned.

Willow curled up in his arms. "We're going to need a bigger house. Not that I don't love Todd, but do we have to live that close?"

"We'll move. And since when do you love Todd?"

"It's family love. Don't worry. He's not a threat."

"Good to know. We'll buy a bigger house on its own lot."

"With a yard," she said.

"And a garden."

"Ooh, yeah. A big garden. And a big bedroom, because we'll be spending lots of time in it."

"I like the way you think." He stared into her eyes. "I love you, Willow. You've changed everything for me."

"I rescued you." She grinned. "Although I'm retired now. The world will have to get by without my rescuing skills. Except for plants and pets. We're going to have kids, right?"

He began unbuttoning her blouse. "Of course."

"As many as I want?"

"You're the one who has to carry them." He removed her blouse.

She glanced over his shoulder and saw Stan had collapsed on a cushion by the sofa.

"We'll have to be very quiet," she whispered.

Kane stood, then picked her up in his arms and carried her down the hall. "I was thinking we'd just leave the room."

"That works, too."

* * * * *

THE ULTIMATE MILLIONAIRE

BY
SUSAN MALLERY

Dear Reader,

Poor Todd Aston III. His very favourite aunt-by-marriage
offered each of her granddaughters a million dollars if
one of them would marry him. Talk about humiliating.
He doesn't need help getting women. He's successful,
wealthy, good-looking. He could be married ten times
over if that's what he wanted. In his world, women are
only out for what they can get, and what they usually want
is his money.

There's one unattached granddaughter left, but if he can
avoid her, the problem is solved. Except he and Marina
Nelson have agreed to plan a wedding together. There's
nothing like a beautiful woman in a wedding dress to get
a guy's attention.

Marina has no interest in Todd. She agreed to the million-
dollar deal as a joke—honestly, she would never marry for
money. But when she starts to fall for Todd—something
she never saw coming—disaster lurks. Will a man who's
been chased by women all his life believe she's in it only
for his heart?

Susan Mallery

One

"Would you do it if I beg?"

Marina Nelson was careful to keep from smiling at Julie's dramatic plea. Of course she was going to agree to help her sister, but not right away. After twenty-four years of being the baby of the family, it was nice to finally have a little power.

"You know I'm busy," she said slowly. "It's the start of a new quarter and I have a full class schedule."

Julie sighed. "Yes, and your work is very important. But so is this. I wouldn't ask if it wasn't. I really need someone to take charge while I'm on this business trip. We have similar taste and you're organized and I thought…" Julie tucked her blond hair behind her ears and looked sad. "Am I asking too much? I am. I know it's crazy. I'm the one getting married, not you. So I should do the planning. But this trip to China is a once-in-a-lifetime opportunity. Six weeks of Ryan and I working together before we settle in to being married *and* parents."

Marina glanced down at her sister's stomach. Julie was only about three months along and not showing at all. One of the advantages of being tall, she thought humorously—it takes longer to see the bump.

"I can see how a trip to China would be far more thrilling than the messy details of choosing a menu and picking out flowers," she said, still not allowing herself to smile. "Not to mention deciding on a dress. What if you hate what I pick?"

They were close enough in size for the actual gown itself not to be a problem. Any minor tailoring could be done right before the wedding, after Julie got back.

"I won't," Julie promised earnestly. "I swear, I'll love it. Besides, you'll send me pictures, right? We talked about that. You'll upload them into e-mail and I'll write back with my opinion." Her blue eyes widened. "Marina, please say yes."

Marina sighed heavily. "No. I can't. But thanks for asking."

Julie's mouth dropped open, then she reached behind her for one of the small, floral sofa cushions and swatted Marina with it.

"You're horrible! How could you let me go on and on like that? I was practically begging."

Marina laughed, then grabbed the cushion. "There's

no 'practically,' Julie. You begged. You whined. I have to tell you, I was a little embarrassed for you."

Julie sighed. "So you'll do it?"

"Of course. You're my sister. Just give me a list and I'll take care of everything."

"You have no idea how you're helping. Between getting married and our trip and closing on the new house, my life is a nightmare."

They sat in Ryan's study—an uncomfortably modern condo in West Los Angeles. It had a great view and electronic everything, but it lacked color and soul, except for a few throw pillows Julie had contributed. Rather than try to make it homey, Julie and Ryan had decided to buy another house that they both liked. Marina knew that Willow, their middle sister, was going to oversee the minor renovating Julie and Ryan's new place needed, which left the wedding to Marina.

"I think of this project as practice," Marina said with a grin. "I can figure out what I want and don't want should I ever take the plunge."

"Oh, please. You'll get married," Julie said confidently. "The right guy's out there somewhere. You'll find him."

Marina wasn't currently looking, but it would be great when it happened. Assuming she could trust herself to fall in love without losing her soul in the process.

"Until then, just call me the wedding planner," Marina said. "Now, where's that list of yours?"

Julie reached into her purse, then straightened without removing anything. "There's just one other thing."

"Which is…"

Julie drew in a breath. "Okay, so this is Ryan's wedding, too, and he's a little nervous that it's going to be too girly. He wants a vote in what's happening."

Marina didn't get the problem. "Fine. You two can argue all you want, then e-mail me the compromise. I don't care."

"Um, yes, well, that's not exactly the plan. Ryan wants a representative to be with you for all the important decisions. The food, the cake, the band, the decorations, the flowers."

"A representative? Like his mother?"

Marina had never met the woman. No doubt she was perfectly lovely, but another opinion could seriously slow the process.

Julie tried to smile and failed miserably. "Actually, no. More like Todd."

"Todd? As in Todd Aston the Third, all around rich guy and jerk?" Marina couldn't believe it. "Anyone but him," she muttered.

"He's Ryan's cousin and they're as close as brothers. You know that. Todd is the best man and he offered to help. Do you hate me now?"

"No, but I should." Marina sighed. "Todd? Yuck."

Nearly six months ago, the three sisters had been introduced to their maternal grandmother for the first time in their lives. Grandma Ruth had been estranged from her only daughter, the girls' mother, ever since Naomi had run off and gotten married.

Now Ruth was back and she wanted a relationship with her daughter and granddaughters. In addition, she had a burning need to connect her family with her second husband's family through marriage.

In a moment of dinner conversation that Marina was confident would go down in family history, she'd offered each of her granddaughters a million dollars if one of them would please marry Todd Aston the Third, her nephew—or maybe great-nephew, no one was sure—through marriage.

Julie had fallen in love with Ryan and Willow had found Kane Dennison, which left only Marina for toady Todd. Talk about bad luck.

For reasons she was still trying to figure out—maybe it had been a momentary brain injury—Marina had agreed to one date with the obnoxious Todd.

It's not that the guy wasn't good-looking—at least, that's what Marina had heard. She'd never actually seen the man. He was also wealthy and successful in his own right, rather than just inheriting from Mommy and Daddy. Ryan liked him and Marina thought Ryan was okay—especially after he'd shown the good taste to fall for her sister. But Todd?

His idea of a significant relationship was to date the same woman twice in the same week. He went out with models. How could she ever have a serious conversation with a man who dated women who were paid to starve for a living? It violated the female code.

Plus, initially he'd tried to break up Julie and Ryan. Marina thought that was pretty low.

"I'm not asking you to have his baby," Julie said. "Just work with him on the wedding. Besides, it won't be too bad. He's a guy. He'll get bored at the first meeting with the florist and disappear. You'll have to deal with him once. Twice at the most."

"I don't want to deal with him at all," Marina said mournfully. "He's everything I don't like in a man." Talk about emotionally useless. Or so she imagined.

A sound came from the doorway. It sounded like someone clearing his throat. When Marina looked up she found a pretty good-looking guy leaning against the door frame.

He looked more amused than annoyed, but based on Julie's gasp and sudden blush, Marina was willing to go out on a limb and figure this was the infamous Todd Aston.

"Ladies," he said with a nod. "Ryan let me in and said you were meeting in here. I've shown up for wedding duty. I'm also accepting a humanitarian award at the end of the month. Perhaps the two of you would like a shot at writing my bio for the event. It would certainly be entertaining."

"Oh, man," Julie muttered. "I'm sorry. That all came out more harshly than I meant it to."

Marina studied him. He was the walking, breathing definition of tall, dark and hunky. Great face with soulful eyes and the kind of mouth that made a woman dream about being taken against her will. Broad shoulders, a muscled chest and jeans skimming over narrow hips and yummy thighs. All in all, a great package. Too bad Todd's personality was stuck inside it.

He smiled at her. "You must be Marina."

"I am. Nice to meet you, Todd."

"Nice?" He raised one eyebrow. "That's not what I heard. You've already decided I'm an ass. Or is it an idiot?"

She shifted on the sofa, feeling just a tiny bit uncomfortable. "You go out with models. Their airbrushed perfection in magazines make regular women feel bad about themselves."

"Because of that, models shouldn't be allowed to date?"

Logic? He wanted to use logic in a discussion about the objectification of thin, young women in modern society?

"Of course they should be allowed to date," she said smoothly. "I'm simply not interested in someone who's interested in them."

"Right," he said folding his arms over his chest. "Because you assume that if they're beautiful they must be dumb. Therefore I like dumb women."

"I didn't say that, but thanks for clarifying."

His mouth twitched as if he were holding in a smile. "I don't date dumb women."

"You should probably make up your mind about that," she told him.

"I'll get right on it."

"If you two are finished…" Julie pointed to the chair opposite the sofa. "Okay, then. So, we should get started with all this. The wedding."

Todd strolled across the room and took the seat offered, then pulled a PalmPilot out of his shirt pocket. "I'm ready."

Marina looked at him. "You're actually going to participate?"

"Right down to the organic seed we'll be throwing

at the happy couple when they head off on their honeymoon." He leaned forward and lowered his voice. "We don't use rice. The birds eat it and it's bad for them."

She opened her mouth, then closed it. "Someone's been spending a little too much time on the Internet."

"Internet, bridal magazines, whatever. When it comes to wedding planning, I'm your guy." A challenge brightened his dark eyes. "I'm in this all the way. Are you?"

If he thought he could scare her off, then he was in for a wild ride. "I'm in. And just for the record, I define stubborn."

"Me, too."

Ha! No way. He might think he was all that, but Marina was more than willing to take him on and win.

Julie sighed. "I thought you two might not get along, but I never considered this might become a competition. Listen. We're talking about a wedding. My wedding to Ryan. We need help, not a Las Vegas-style show. Bigger is not better. Don't be too creative. Let's just make it low-key and elegant, okay?"

Marina felt Todd's gaze shift to her. She stared right back at him and refused to be the first one to blink. "Julie, have I ever let you down?"

"No," Julie said slowly, as if she didn't want to admit it.

"So trust me."

Julie gave them each a copy of her list. Todd scanned his, then turned his attention back to Marina Nelson.

She was blond like her sisters, only her hair was

darker—more honey-gold. She was about an inch taller than Julie, with the same curvy build. They were obviously sisters and could almost have passed for twins. The main difference—aside from hair color—was the "I'm willing to take you on, big guy" attitude in the set of her chin. Julie was far more agreeable.

Todd had a rule when it came to women—why work hard? There were plenty of attractive females more than happy to come on to *him*. Some of it was due to his success as a businessman, some of it was his looks. Most of it was about the family fortune.

Whatever the reason, he rarely had to go searching for company. His romantic life was an ongoing series of short-term relationships with minimal commitment and effort on his part. That was how he liked things.

Marina was going to be anything but easy and he wasn't even trying to get her into bed. But Ryan had asked for his help, so he would put up with the overly verbal Nelson sister for the sake of his cousin.

He was even willing to admit—only to himself—that he was looking forward to taking her on. It had been a long time since a woman had done anything but let him get his way. Working with her would be good for his character, even if he did plan to win in the end.

"Basically we have the invitations done and that's it," Julie said as she studied her own copy of the list. "Grandma Ruth offered her house for the wedding and Ryan and I agreed it's an amazing place. But there are decisions to be made. It's a winter wedding. Do we want to risk the outside thing? It could be seventy-five or it could be raining."

"She mentioned something about a ballroom," Marina said. "On the third floor. Want us to check that out?"

"I've seen it." Todd kept his attention on Julie. "It would easily hold three or four hundred. A few less if you're interested in a sit-down dinner."

"We are," Julie said, making a note.

"But the guest list isn't nearly that big," Marina told him. "It's about a hundred."

"Ryan said it was closer to two hundred."

Marina turned to her sister. "That many?"

"It keeps growing."

"That's a lot of tables."

"I know. So I need you to check out the ballroom and see how it would be. Is there still room for dancing with all the tables in place? Where would the band go? I'm torn. Being outside would be great, but I'm not sure I can trust the weather, and I won't need to be stressed about one more thing."

"We'll decide that first," Marina said, taking notes. "That will affect all the other decisions. What's next?"

"Flowers, favors—nothing stupid, please—food, entertainment, a photographer and my dress. Oh, and you and Willow have to pick out bridesmaids' dresses."

Ryan was so going to owe him, Todd thought humorously. "Tuxes," he said.

Julie stared at him. "Oh God. You're right. The guys need tuxes."

"I'll take care of the dress myself," Marina said, smiling at him. "The dress is purely a girl thing."

"Do you plan to get a say in the tuxes?" he asked.

"Sure."

He waited while she began sputtering.

"Wait a minute," Marina said. "A bride's dress has to be something special. She's only going to get married once."

"I could say the same thing about Ryan. He'll want to look good and you don't trust me to make that happen. Why should I trust you?" Of course he had no real interest in the wedding gown, but fair was fair.

Julie waved her hand. "I don't care who goes to the bridal shop. Just find me an amazing dress. Nothing fitted at the waist, of course."

That's right, Todd thought. Julie was pregnant.

He knew Ryan was excited about being a father. While Todd never intended to marry, he liked the idea of having kids. The lack of wife would complicate things, but didn't make the situation impossible.

"I can't believe you want a say in the dress," Marina muttered.

He leaned toward her. "Think of all those models I've dated. Some of their fashion sense must have rubbed off on me."

"Did you talk about fashion much?"

"We didn't talk at all."

He heard her grind her teeth together and nearly laughed.

"Willow works for that nursery," Marina said as she ignored him. "I'll ask her for recommendations on the florist front."

"Good idea," Julie said.

"I know a photographer," Todd told her.

Marina widened her eyes. "Does he take pictures of people with or without clothes?"

"Both. You'll enjoy looking at her work."

"I don't care about naked," Julie said. "Does she do weddings?"

"They're her favorite."

"Good. Put her on the list. Marina, nothing too artistic. Just regular pictures."

"Gotcha."

They went over a few more things, then Julie left to find the dress pictures she'd torn out of magazines.

Todd turned his attention to Marina. "I think this is going to be fun."

"Oh, me, too."

"You don't like me much."

"I don't know you."

"You don't want to."

"Actually I haven't decided that. Amazingly enough, you haven't been on my mind at all."

One point for her side, he thought. "You didn't say nice things about me before. I heard you."

She tilted her head as she stared at him. "You have a reputation which, personally, I think you enjoy. But people form impressions based on that notoriety."

"You think I'm shallow."

"I don't think you've ever had to work very hard at anything but your company."

"Still, you agreed to go out with me. One date. You promised. Aunt Ruth told me."

Her gaze narrowed. "It seemed like a good idea at the time."

She might be uncomfortable with the idea of dating him, but he was the one who had to live with the reality of his aunt offering her granddaughters each a million dollars if one of them would marry him. It made him feel like a loser. What the hell was so wrong with him that a woman had to be paid that much money to make a commitment?

Not that he wanted to get married, but it was the principle of the thing.

Fortunately Julie and Willow were both out of the picture, which left only Marina. He would have refused even a single date with her, but Aunt Ruth had looked so happy at the thought and although he would rather face medieval torture than admit it to anyone, he was a sucker when it came to his aunt Ruth.

"It's only one date," he said. "What's the worst that could happen?"

"It will be three hours that will seem like a lifetime?" But there was a flash of humor in her eyes as she spoke.

"The wedding," he said. "We both have to be there, we're both in the wedding party, which means it wouldn't be much fun for anyone else we brought."

She nodded slowly. "We will have just spent all that time arranging the event, so we'll have plenty to talk about."

"We can have lots of champagne."

She grinned. "Always a plan. All right, Todd Aston the Third, I'll be your date for my sister's wedding."

Two

Grandma Ruth's three-story Bel Air mansion was just as awe-inspiring the second time Marina pulled in to the stone covered circular driveway. It was massive and out of place—this was Los Angeles, not eighteenth century England. But the rich lived different lives, Marina thought as she climbed out of her aging import. Lives with live-in staff. Her idea of help at home was a package of premoistened glass cleaning towelettes.

She glanced at the double door leading into the house and decided to wait until Todd showed up before going inside. Okay, sure, she shouldn't be intimidated by her grandmother's maid, but she was. So what? She had other positive attributes she could focus on.

Less than a minute later, a gleaming silver Mercedes

pulled into the driveway. The car was a sporty two-seater model, the kind that cost as much as the national debt of a small third world country.

The guy who climbed out of it was just as impressive. Tall, well tailored and sexy enough to encourage smart women to make some really stupid choices. She would have to make sure she didn't fall into the category. Fortunately he wasn't her type.

"Marina," Todd said with a grin. "I thought you would have already scouted the house and made the decision."

"We're a team, Todd. I totally respect that." Or she would as long as it suited her.

Speaking of suits, his was dark gray, with a subtle pattern in the weave of the fabric. His pale blue shirt contrasted with the deep burgundy tie. While she preferred a more casual look, he wore his power extremely well. She, on the other hand, looked like a college student with a limited budget. Although her skinny jeans had zipped up with no problem, which made this a very good day.

She collected her digital camera and a small notebook, then followed him to the front door. "I have about an hour," she said as she checked her watch. "Then I have to be back at UCLA for a class."

"What are you taking?"

"I'm not. I'm interpreting." She glanced at him. "I'm a sign language interpreter for deaf students. I specialize in chemistry and physics, mostly the upper division classes."

He raised his eyebrows. "Impressive."

"It's not that hard for me. I've taken all the classes

myself, so I understand the material. I have three advanced science degrees. Eventually I'm going to have to pick a Ph.D. program, but I'm not ready yet. I already knew how to sign, so I decided to do this for a couple of years."

His eyes widened. "*Three* advanced science degrees?"

She loved people underestimating her. "Uh-huh. It's less impressive when you know I started college at fifteen."

"Oh, sure. It's practically ordinary. You're pretty smart."

She smiled. "Smarter than you, big guy."

He laughed. "I'll remember that."

He knocked on the front door and when the maid answered, he greeted her by name.

"We're here to see the ballroom, Katie," he told the woman in uniform. "Then check out the backyard."

The maid nodded. "Yes, sir. Your grandmother told me you'd be stopping by. Would you like me to show you upstairs?"

"We can find it. Thanks."

Marina smiled at the other woman, then followed Todd across a huge foyer and up a wide, curving staircase.

"So how big is *your* staff?" she asked as they reached the second floor and walked along a long, carpeted hallway. There were dozens of paintings on the wall and pieces of furniture that were probably impressive antiques, if she knew anything about them.

"Five live-ins, six dailies."

"What?" she asked. She'd only seen his house from a distance—and it had been bigger than this one—but still. "What do they do?"

He turned to her, touched his finger to the tip of her

nose and smiled. "Gotcha. I have a housekeeper who hires people to keep the house clean and take care of the grounds. She comes in three days a week. I'd rather not have any staff, but the house is old and big and I'm not willing to deal with it, so she does."

Okay, one housekeeper *was* better than five live-ins.

They took a second staircase that flowed into a landing that was bigger than Marina's apartment. A wall of ornate doors opened into a ballroom the size of a football field.

She stepped into the center of the room and turned in a slow circle. There were gilded mirrors on the walls and dozens of sparkling chandeliers hanging from the ceiling. The parquet floor gleamed and reflected the sunlight from the windows.

The walls had been painted a neutral pale beige, so any color theme would work.

"We're talking about tables of either eight or ten," Todd said as he pulled out his PalmPilot and pushed a few buttons. "We can fit as many as thirty tables in here and still have room for people to get around."

Marina did the math. "Can we fit twenty-eight tables and still have room for dancing and the band?"

Todd looked at her. "Orchestra. Not band. Julie said elegant. Bands aren't elegant."

Maybe not, but she'd never been to a wedding with an orchestra. "You think the L.A. Philharmonic is available?"

He grinned. "I'd have to check their schedule, but I was thinking of something a little smaller. I have a group in mind that I've heard play at other venues."

Venues? So while the rest of America went to the

mall, the über rich had venues? "What sort of venues would these be?"

"Mostly fund-raisers. A couple of weddings. I'll find out where they're playing in the next couple of weeks and we'll go hear them. They're great. Trust me."

Trust him? Not yet.

She put down her notebook and began taking pictures of the vast space. "I really like this room," she said as she turned slowly to get every angle. "I'll e-mail these photos to Julie as soon as I'm done with class."

"There's more," he said and led her to a series of French doors. He unlocked the first one and opened it, then motioned for her to lead the way.

She stepped out onto a wide balcony that overlooked the property. Although if one couldn't see where the fence line was, did that make it an estate?

The grounds were stunning. She could see the terrace and the pool and the gardens beyond.

"This would give us extra space," he said as he joined her. "A place for people to get some air. We could put lights in the garden for the view."

"I like it," she said more to herself than him. "Anyone can get married in a backyard, but this is incredible. A once-in-a-lifetime opportunity."

She turned back to the ballroom where she could imagine the tables and guests and flowers. Talk about making some memories.

"So you prefer the ballroom?" he asked.

"I do, but it's Julie's choice. Let's go downstairs and take some pictures of the garden so she and Ryan can decide. Once we know which way they want to go, we're free to start making other arrangements."

They made their way back downstairs, then stepped out onto the manicured terrace. It looked more like the grounds of a five-star hotel than someone's home, she thought as she took pictures, not sure how she felt about her grandmother living here.

Something of her confusion must have showed because Todd asked, "What's wrong?"

She pocketed the digital camera and tucked her notebook under her arm. "I keep thinking how strange this is—that a grandmother I never knew about was alive and well about fifteen miles from where I grew up. That this is her world and I can remember times when we didn't have enough money to have meat with dinner."

She shook her head. "I'm not complaining. My mom was great and my sisters and I always had plenty of everything we needed. Money was tight, but that's how it was with most of our neighbors. I'm okay with that. But now, to find out there's a whole other way of looking at things, it's strange." She looked at him. "I'm not explaining myself well and this is more information than you wanted."

"Of course this is different. For what it's worth, Ruth regrets all the years she was apart from you and your family. Her husband, my uncle, was a hard man. He didn't believe in forgiveness. Ruth simply didn't have the strength to stand up to him."

"That's what she said."

"It's true."

Great. So it seemed she came from a long line of women who surrendered heart and mind to their men. All the more reason not to get involved.

He looked at her. "You should try to understand what Ruth went through."

Todd Aston the Third being sensitive? "Okay, now I'm freaked out on two different levels. The contrast between what I'm used to and this, and your emotional perception."

"I'm a man of great mystery."

That made her laugh. "Of course you are. Wealth, power and mystery. You should put that on your business cards."

He led the way around the side of the house toward their cars. "I'm way ahead of you, Marina. I have it tattooed on my back."

She grinned. "I thought you'd have a stick up your butt," she said before she could stop herself.

"They know how to fix that now. Isn't modern medicine a miracle?"

She sighed. "You know what I mean. I thought you'd be…different."

"Unpleasant?"

"Imperious."

"I can be, if that would make you happy."

"No, thanks." She opened her notebook. "Okay, venue research complete. Which leaves us with food, the cake, flowers, a photographer and all kinds of other messy details."

"The dress," he reminded her. "We'll have to look

at something off the rack. There's no time for a custom gown."

She glanced at him, surprised he would know that. "Let me guess. More bridal magazine research? Although somehow I can't see you sitting down with a latte and a bridal magazine."

"I can't have a latte then. Black coffee to combat all the girliness. It's about balance."

Until this moment, she hadn't thought of Todd as a person. At first he'd been just a name, then he'd been the guy who tried to break up her sister and Ryan. Then an annoyance who would get in her way about the wedding. But now…

"Why do you hide who you are behind your reputation?" she asked. "The money thing. The model thing."

He unlocked his car. "I've dated maybe three models in my life, Marina. You need to let go."

"You're right. I will."

"Good." He sat in his car and grinned. "Of course, two of them didn't speak English."

They didn't… Then how… She glared at him. "You had better be kidding. Not speak English?"

He nodded. "I was simply doing my part to improve American relationships with our neighbors." He smiled angelically. "I know a great caterer. I'll set something up and get back to you with the details."

With that he was gone.

Three days later Todd stood in front of the catering office and watched Marina walk toward him. She wore jeans, a UCLA sweatshirt and her hair pulled back in a ponytail. Not someone who dressed to impress.

There was also an air of determination about her that made him anticipate plenty of flying sparks. Planning a wedding might not be his idea of a good time, but so far Marina had been a pleasant surprise. Smart and sexy. He'd been looking forward to seeing her again.

When she stopped in front of him, she put her hands on her hips and glared at him.

"I looked you up on the Internet," she said. "The models in question spoke perfectly good English, albeit with an accent."

"Albeit?" he asked as he raised his eyebrows. "Are we in a Jane Austen novel?"

"What do you know about Jane Austen?"

"Every good useless male who only dates models knows all about chick flicks and Jane Austen. It's required. I not only saw *Bridget Jones's Diary* twice, I've seen the special features. Ask me anything."

She burst out laughing. The sound was light and sexy and made him want to touch her. All of her. Unexpected heat swept through him, startling him with its intensity.

He immediately took a step back, both physically and mentally. He and Marina were on a mission. He was here to protect Ryan's interests and not die of boredom in the process. If tweaking Marina's assumptions about him got him through the day, then he was up to the task. But actually enjoying her company—not a good idea. Getting involved with his aunt-by-marriage's youngest granddaughter wouldn't be very intelligent.

"This place comes highly recommended," he said as they made their way to the front door. "It's supposed to be good food with more choices than beef or chicken. If this is the one we pick, we'll be able to customize the menu. Or in our case, argue over food options."

"You think we're going to argue?" she asked.

"I'm counting on it."

"I'm a pretty agreeable person, but I'm sure you're difficult," she said as he held open the door. "I'll be flexible on food, but not the dessert thing."

"What dessert thing?"

She smiled at him. "That we have dessert. It's one of the great thrills of a wedding. You get dessert *and* cake. How often does that happen in life?"

"Far be it from me to get between a woman and her sugar fix."

"Pretty and smart," she murmured. "How impressive."

"I know." He turned his attention to the receptionist and introduced them.

"I'm Zoe," the woman said with a smile. "We're ready for you. If you'd come this way?"

They were led in to a small room set up like a dining area. The table for six had two place settings at one end.

Zoe seated them, then pointed out the menu printed on a single sheet by the plates.

"We'll go in order," she said. "We'll start with soups, then the salads and so on. Please make notes or write down any questions."

She left and then returned immediately with three small bowls for each of them.

"Lovely presentation," Marina said as she picked the sprig of garnish out of one of the bowls. "Why do they have to put some garden weed on top of a dish? What is it? How do we know where it's been?"

"The not knowing adds to the thrill of the moment."

She looked at him, her blue eyes wide. "Are you thrilled?"

She was close enough that he could see a couple of pale freckles on her nose and hint of a dimple in her cheek. Once again he thought about touching her...and didn't.

"Beyond words."

"Liar," she murmured, then took a taste of the first soup. "Split pea with something else. Not bad."

He tasted it and shook his head. "No, thanks."

They both passed on the creamy mystery soup, while he liked the chicken vegetable and Marina complained it was too healthy.

"We're at a wedding. Do we really have to get our five servings of fruits and vegetables in the first course?"

He poked around the bowl. "Not a lot of fruit that I can see."

"You know what I mean." She set down her spoon. "What about tortilla soup? Or a quesadilla? Doesn't that sound good?"

"You want Mexican food at your sister's wedding?"

Marina's shoulders slumped. "Not really, but I could go for some right now. I should have eaten before coming here. I'm really hungry."

"So you like food."

She narrowed her gaze. "Yes, some women eat. I

eat. Shocking, but true. I also run every day, so I can pretty much eat what I like and enjoy it. Do you have a problem with that?"

"Running with that chip on your shoulder must help with your workout. The extra weight would increase intensity."

She opened her mouth, then closed it. "You're saying I'm a little sensitive about the food thing?"

"Would I say that?"

"You're thinking I'm overreacting because you date models and I don't feel I measure up to their ideal."

"You're doing all the talking."

"I'm not intimidated. Mostly not. Sometimes, maybe a little. But I'd like to point out that these are my skinny jeans. They've fit all week and they look fabulous on me."

"Yes, they do." He'd admired the curve of her hips and her long legs when she'd first walked up. He was willing to take another look, if that would make her happy.

"I don't seek approval from anyone but myself."

"Why would you?"

She smiled. "You're humoring me."

"It seems safest. You have some attitude on you."

"I know. I don't get it. I'm actually a fairly calm person. I'm not sure what it is about you that pushes all my buttons."

"It's because I'm so smooth and handsome," he said as Zoe came in with several salad plates, along with a basket of rolls. "You're uncomfortable."

Marina waited until they were alone to respond. When Zoe had picked up the soup bowls and left, she said, "I'm not uncomfortable. You have an ego the size of Antarctica. You're not that special."

"Of course I am. You researched me. Who was the last guy you researched?"

"The men I know are totally normal. Researching is not required. You make me crazy."

"Then my work here is complete."

She shook her head. "Eat your salad."

He took a bite of the first salad. There were a lot of strange looking lettuces and shavings of things he didn't recognize. Salad was highly overrated, he thought grimly.

"Think about the guys you usually date," he said, enjoying the fact that he could get to her. "Scruffy, poor grad students. When compared to me, they don't have a chance."

She glared at him. "Oh, right. Why would dating the next brilliant man who will change the course of history by improving the world be considered interesting?"

He picked up a roll and leaned toward her. "They're nerds. They're not interesting yet and they're not good in bed. Admit it."

Fury darkened her eyes. She opened her mouth, probably to yell at him. He stuck the roll between her lips.

"Not bad," he said, pointing at the second salad. "I like the blue cheese. What do you think?"

She pulled the roll away and glared at him. "I think you're a pompous, egotistical ass."

He tasted the third salad and grimaced. "So you like me."

"I don't."

"Of course you do. But I was asking about the salads. What do you think?"

She pointed at the one he'd tasted third. "That one works."

He shook his head. "Not a good idea. There's too much garlic in the dressing."

"Since when do you know anything about cooking?"

"I don't." Could he help it that she set him up with one good line after the other? Sometimes a guy couldn't help cutting a break. "But I do know about weddings." He glanced around, then leaned toward her and lowered his voice. "Kissing. Lots and lots of kissing at weddings. You don't want the guests to have garlic breath."

Awareness crackled in the room. He thought Marina might get nervous or change the subject, but her gaze never left his. The humor was gone, replaced by a tension that quickly flared into need.

What would it be like to kiss her? What would her mouth feel like against his? How soft? How hungry? How sexy?

Was she the kind of woman who took charge, or did she like to be convinced? The possibilities were endless and suddenly he wanted to explore them all.

"I think you're overstating the problem," she said. "I don't think the garlic is that big a deal, but if it is, we could simply change the dressing on the salad."

"There's only one way to find out," he said and leaned in farther, then brushed his mouth against hers.

There was heat and need. They competed for his attention. Marina didn't move, but he heard her breath quicken. But before he could take things to the next level, Zoe returned.

"What did you... Oh. Sorry. Should I come back?"

Todd straightened. "No. We know what we need to do."

Three

Marina felt as if she'd been hit by a truck. Well, that wasn't right, she thought as she blinked to bring the room back into focus. Nothing bad had happened and she certainly wasn't squished. But she was out of breath and feeling a little two-dimensional all the same.

Talk about wow. The heat, the tingles, the need to jump Todd's bones and make him have his way with her. All from a teeny, tiny, innocent kiss. What would happen if he kissed her like he meant it?

A dangerous question, she told herself. Todd was nothing like she'd imagined. He was funny and charming. Too charming. She had to remember that any contact with a woman was just a game with him. That he had the emotional depth of a cookie sheet. She should enjoy the superficial attraction for the momentary pleasure and let the rest of it go. He didn't do relationships and she didn't do anything else.

Although technically she didn't do relationships, either. It was the whole fear thing. She didn't want to get lost in a man.

They sampled several entrées, which were okay and the desserts, which were great.

"Are you going to finish that?" she asked, eyeing his barely tasted dish of chocolate mousse.

Todd pushed the bowl toward her. "You're welcome to it."

She dipped her spoon into the creamy, foamy delight and then savored the burst of rich chocolate on her tongue. He watched her, his expression unreadable.

She wanted to think he found her passion for chocolate fascinating, but no doubt he was comparing her normal appetite to his dates' lack of appetite and finding her just a little odd.

"Finished?" he asked when she'd scraped the last of the pudding from the bowl.

She nodded and they walked out to the reception area. After collecting prices and a brochure from Zoe, they promised to be in touch within a couple of weeks, then left.

"What did you think?" Todd asked as they walked to their cars.

"It was good," she said, "but not dazzling. I want to be dazzled. I think the food should be spectacular, not just good."

He glanced at the price list. "Considering what

they're charging, I agree. So we still need a caterer. Do you have any suggestions?"

"I don't cater much, but I can ask around."

"I'll do the same. I'll also check with Ruth."

Ah, yes. Her grandmother. "She does the charity circuit," she said. "At least she's mentioned it. So she should be a great source of information." Marina frowned. "I wonder why she hasn't offered us advice."

"She promised not to meddle," Todd told her. "Don't get too excited—it's not going to last. She's a meddler by nature." There was a tone of affection in his voice.

"So you've forgiven her for coming to me and my sisters and offering each of us a million dollars if one of us were to marry you?"

He winced. "I'm working on it."

"Why?"

He shrugged. "She always had time for me and Ryan. Our parents took off for months at a time and left us behind. Aunt Ruth stepped into the void. When we were with her, it was like family."

Marina didn't know what to say to that. On the one hand, it explained Todd's fondness for his aunt. On the other, this was the same woman who turned her back on her own daughter.

"You're thinking about your mom," he said, surprising her.

"Yes. My mom was seventeen when she fell in love with my dad. That's pretty young. I can understand her parents being upset with her choice, but there are a lot of options between saying it's okay and kicking her out forever. How come they didn't try any of them?" She drew in a deep breath and let it go. "You're going to tell me it was because of Ruth's husband, Fraser. I've heard it all before. He was a difficult man who ruled his house and didn't give anyone second chances."

He was also the only father Marina's mother had ever known. Her biological father, Ruth's first husband, had died before Ruth had even realized she was pregnant.

"My mom was Ruth's only daughter," Marina said. "She should have tried harder. She should have made sure her daughter was all right."

Todd surprised her for maybe the third time in less than two hours when he put his hand on her shoulder and squeezed gently.

"You're right," he said quietly. "She stood by her husband instead of her daughter. Because of that, she spent the next thirty years regretting her decision, but being too afraid to do anything about it. That's got to be a hard way to live, for all of you. She'll never get back what she lost and neither will you."

She blinked at him. "That was really compassionate and understanding."

He scowled at her. "I am capable of rational and emotional thought."

"I know. I just didn't think you'd bother."

"That's flattering."

Now it was his turn to touch him. She grabbed his hand. "I'm sorry. That came out wrong. It's just the way you're presented in the local press and how people talk about you."

Maybe he wasn't a cookie sheet, she thought. Maybe he was actually a jelly roll pan.

The image made her smile, which made his scowl deepen. "You're really starting to tick me off," he muttered.

"I thought you said you had a well-developed sense of humor."

"I do. You're not being funny. Whatever you think about me, you're wrong."

She was beginning to think that might be a possibility.

He pulled out his trusty PalmPilot and pushed some buttons. "We still need a caterer, a photographer, flowers, a cake, a dress, tuxes. It's a long list."

"We'll get through it. I'll e-mail Julie the information on this place. At least we know we're having the wedding and reception in the ballroom. That's something."

"Lucky us."

She stared into his dark eyes and smiled. "Thanks for being so understanding about everything with my grandmother. It helps to talk about it."

"Yeah, yeah. I'll call you and we can set up our next taste testing."

Then he stunned her by bending down and kissing her. Only this kiss wasn't about garlic or proving anything. At least she didn't think it was. Instead it was quick, hot and bone-melting.

His hands rested on her shoulders, holding her in place. His mouth claimed hers with an expertise that made her more than willing to take this wherever he wanted to go. She lost herself in the pleasure of touch and lips and need.

He wasn't what she expected. *This* wasn't what she

expected. She found herself responding to him in ways she hadn't expected.

He tilted his head and brushed her lower lip with his tongue. She parted for him. He swept inside, teased into arousal, then pulled back and straightened.

"See you soon," he said.

What? He was leaving? He was going to kiss and run?

"But you... Why'd you..."

He smiled. "We were interrupted. I like to finish what I start."

To Marina_Nelson@mynetwork.LA.com
From Julie_Nelson@SGC.usa

I can't thank you enough. I really, really owe you for all your hard work. Thanks for taste-testing the first caterer and sorry it didn't work out. But you're right. I want fabulous food at the wedding and so does Ryan.

Interesting about the whole garlic/kissing thing. I hadn't thought that too much garlic could ever be a problem, but at a wedding? You're so right. So, did Todd demonstrate the perils of garlic kissing? ☺ Just kidding. I know he's not your type. Not earnest enough and yet lacking in character. But not totally awful. At least he's cute. Remember that when he starts to make you crazy.

We're having the best time. I can't wait to get more pictures and e-mails from you. Again, you're a total goddess for doing this!

Love and hugs, Julie

Marina opened the cardboard box and reached for the

tape dispenser. After sealing the bottom of the carton, she flipped it over and then looked at the bookshelves in the hallway.

"Does Julie really need to keep all these?" she asked, even though she already knew the answer.

Willow stuck her head out of the bedroom where she'd gone to tackle clothes. "Of course. They're books. She'll keep them forever."

"Does Ryan know what he's getting into? The whole pack rat thing?"

Willow grinned. "She's not a pack rat and yes, he knows exactly what he's getting into."

"Well, I didn't have a clue," Marina grumbled. "Between helping you pack Julie's place, you handling the renovations at their new place and me planning Julie's wedding, she is going to owe us big time. We're going to have to break our legs or something and force both of them to serve us."

"She'll be there every second of our recovery," Willow promised. She held out her left hand and pointed. "Would you hand that to me?"

Marina didn't turn to see the object in question. Instead she stared at her sister's ring finger—or more specifically, at the stunning diamond ring glinting there.

"You're engaged!" Marina yelled. "I'm so happy for you."

Willow laughed, then they were hugging and jumping up and down together.

"It's so beautiful," Marina said, grabbing her sister's hand and studying the impressive cushion-cut stone surrounded by baguettes. "When did this happen? You didn't say anything. How could you not blab the second you saw me?"

"It was hard," Willow admitted. "But I wanted a great reaction and you gave me one." She stared down at the ring. "As to the when, it was just last night. Kane and I had talked about getting married before, when he came to his senses and realized he loved me. But between then and now there hasn't been a word. I was willing to give him time to get used to the idea of just being in a serious relationship."

They moved into the living room and fell onto the sofa. Marina smiled at Willow's happy expression.

"Who would have thought that the strong silent type would turn out to be such a great guy," she said, thrilled that Kane had been the one in a million Willow deserved.

Her sister sighed. "I know. It's a miracle. He's incredible. Last night we were having dinner together. It was really romantic and there was music and suddenly he was on one knee and holding out the ring and saying he wanted to marry me and be with me forever." Tears filled her eyes. "I never thought my life could be so wonderful."

Marina hugged her again. "I'm happy for you. Beyond happy. Delighted. Giddy. There are other words I can't think of right now."

"I'm happy, too," Willow said.

Marina leaned against the cushion. "Two of my sisters getting married. I'll be the old maid aunt, a favorite of the children, but you adults will worry that I'm slowly slipping into madness."

Willow rolled her eyes. "Please. You're too smart for that. But I would say to be careful. Love is in the air and all that."

Marina shook her head. "I'm immune. Which is fine with me. I'm not looking to get married anytime soon."

"What about falling in love?"

"Maybe next year."

In truth, she liked the idea of falling for a guy. But along with the desire to be in love was a healthy dose of fear. Giving away her heart looked a little to much like giving away her sense of self. First Aunt Ruth, then her mother. Marina wasn't willing to be like either of them.

"So, another wedding," she said. "Have you two picked a date?"

"We're thinking spring. Well, after Julie's wedding, but before the baby's born."

"I can help with the planning. I'll be an expert."

"I would love that," Willow told her. "I wouldn't know where to start."

"Just ask me anything. Or Todd. He's actually pretty good at the whole wedding planning thing. Just don't tell him I said that."

Willow shifted so they were facing each other. "Really? He's not awful?"

"No," Marina said, still surprised by that bit of news. "He's actually nice. Funny, charming…I like him. I didn't expect that at all. I thought he'd be a jerk. I really didn't want to work with him on the wedding, but even though we don't agree on everything, I like having him help. It's a big responsibility and I like having someone to share in the process. Plus, he's fairly good-looking. Even if my day is going badly, it's fun to have a little eye candy to look forward to."

"I don't think he's the kind of guy who likes being called eye candy."

"Probably not, but we won't mention it."

Willow studied her. "So this is good?" she asked. "With Julie and Ryan getting married, Todd is kind of in the family now. We'll all be friends?"

"I think so. We'll mock his choice of women when he brings dates, but that will be entertaining."

"Something to look forward to," Willow said. "Todd's not the kind of guy to hang out by himself."

Marina nodded in agreement, but found herself wondering about the other women in Todd's life. No doubt he was seeing someone right now. Who was she? Some socialite or heiress? A high-powered businesswoman? Marina would guess that whoever she was, her wardrobe consisted of more than jeans and UCLA sweatshirts.

Not that she, Marina, was trying to impress him. They were working together on the wedding. Nothing more. Except he'd kissed her. She still couldn't seem to forget the flash of heat and need and desire that had nearly overwhelmed her. And that had been from a kind of nothing kiss. What would happen if he kissed her like he meant it?

"He's actually my date for the wedding," Marina

said. "We both promised Grandma Ruth we'd go on one date and the wedding seemed the easiest."

"Once again I encourage you to marry him so I can have a million-dollar nest egg," Willow said with a grin.

"Kane has money."

"Yes, but that's *his* money. A fortune of my own would be kind of fun."

Marina shook her head. "Sorry. I don't have any big plans to marry Todd. Not even for a million dollars."

"What about five million? I'll bet Grandma Ruth would be delighted to cough up a little more cash."

"Not interested."

Willow sighed. "I thought our sisterly love was supposed to be unconditional. I hate that it has limits."

"Life can be tragic."

Willow glanced back at her ring. "There are some bright spots. I have Kane."

"Yes, you do."

Willow looked at her. "You're next. Things happen in threes. First Julie, then me, so it's your turn."

"I don't think it works like that."

Not that she would say no to her own happily ever after, but there were complications. Falling for a guy meant trusting him completely. While she could see that happening, it also meant trusting herself, which she was a lot less sure about.

Four

Marina sat on the front stairs of her apartment waiting for Todd. As her watch ticked over to the exact minute he was due, his sleek, silver, expensive convertible rounded the corner and pulled up in front of her building.

She stood and sighed. "Pretty car," she said when he stepped out and walked toward her. "Very pretty car." Of course he looked good, too. The man knew how to wear a suit. But she didn't feel the need to share that.

He held out the keys. "Want to drive?"

She blinked. "Excuse me?"

"Drive. The. Car. You're supposed to be the smart one here. It shouldn't be such a complex concept. I've seen you drive. You know how."

She looked from him to the Mercedes and back. "But

it's your car. You're a guy. Guys don't share their cars. Certainly not really expensive ones like this."

"It's just a car, Marina. I buy what I like, but it's not my life." He shook the keys. "Now answer the question. Do you want to drive?"

She snatched the keys from him before he could change his mind. "Absolutely."

But as she made her way to the driver's side, she glanced at him. Sure, Todd had money and if something happened to this car, he could easily get another, but it was the principle of the matter. This wasn't normal behavior. Was he really so secure with himself that he could let her do this without a second thought?

She settled into the leather seat and surveyed the interior. There were the basics she was used to, along with a GPS display, dual zone air-conditioning and a sound system that looked complicated enough to be on the space shuttle.

"It's nice today," he said. "Want to put the top down?"

"Oh, yeah."

She scanned the controls and found the one that took care of the top, then put the key in the ignition and turned to watch the show.

It was a marvel of German engineering, she thought as the top automatically folded down and a built-in cover slipped over it. All without her doing anything.

Then she faced front, adjusted the mirrors, started the engine and prepared to be impressed.

"How fast can I go?" she asked.

"How much are you willing to pay for a ticket?"

"Good point. So where to?"

He pulled a piece of paper out of his shirt pocket. "Today we're taking care of table linens, place settings, tables and chairs, party favors and the tuxes." He glanced at his watch. "We have an appointment at the linen place, so let's go there first."

He gave her the address and she pulled out into the street. The car responded to her every instruction, the engine purred smoothly and she could feel the power hovering just a press of her foot away. The day was warm, the wind wiped her hair around and she felt pretty darned happy.

"I could get used to this," she said as she came to a stop at the light.

"So you're tempted by the dark side?"

She grinned. "More than tempted." Obviously a car like this wasn't possible on her budget, but maybe a used convertible wasn't out of the question. It could still be fun.

She drove to the rental place and resisted the urge to take an extra trip around the block, just for the driving pleasure. Instead she parked and climbed out.

"Thanks," she said, handing over the keys. "That was great."

"Anytime."

"As if you mean that. Still, I'm deeply impressed you let me drive it at all. You're very secure."

"I'm a macho kind of guy."

She laughed. "Not to mention modest. You're extremely modest."

They walked into the rental showroom.

"I called ahead," Todd told her. "They'll have tables set up for us. We can get some idea of what colors work well together and how formal or informal we want things to be."

She pulled her camera out of her purse. "I'm prepared to take pictures."

They walked into the showroom and saw nearly a dozen tables set for dinner. Each table was done in a different color, with coordinating china and a centerpiece.

They introduced themselves to the clerk there, who invited them to walk around and get ideas.

Marina immediately moved toward a round table with a pale pink tablecloth and elegant light yellow napkins.

The plates were cream, trimmed in silver; the centerpiece was a combination of pink and yellow flowers that trailed across the center of the table. Even seated, the guests would be able to see each other and the colors were warm and cheerful.

"I like this one," she said, only to realize she was talking to herself. Todd was across the room in front of a table done in deep reds and purples.

She winced as she got closer. The china was black, the napkins dark and the flowers looked like something out of a nightmare rather than appropriate for a wedding.

"It's elegant," he said when she paused next to him.

"It's scary. I don't think we're going to have many children attending, but what if the ones who did come were terrified?"

He glanced over his shoulder at the one she'd liked. "What if we didn't set the table for an Easter brunch?

Julie said low-key elegant. Bunnies and colored eggs don't fall into that category."

Marina looked at the table she'd loved. "Okay, maybe it's a little pale, but this is awful. I don't like the really tall centerpiece. You can't see the people across from you."

"Which could be a good thing if you didn't like them."

She smiled. "We can't guarantee that will be the case. What about that?"

She pointed to a table done in deep rose, with accents of green. The cream china provided a neutral backdrop for patterned salad and dessert plates. The centerpiece was more botanical than floral and it sat low enough to see over.

Todd studied the settings. "It's not fussy. That's good. The colors are a little girly, but the green's okay. I like the centerpiece."

"It's certainly different," Marina murmured as she got out her camera and started taking pictures. "Rose and green would be pretty colors, with cream sort of blending in."

She snapped pictures of the other tables, but concentrated on the one she and Todd agreed on. Then they went to the clerk at the front of the showroom and asked about a price list.

Todd held out the sheet so they could both see it. The charges were broken down by type of rental, as well as number of units needed. The more rented, the less the cost per item.

"We didn't talk about the glasses," she said.

"Honestly, I can't see Ryan caring. If it holds wine and champagne, he'll be good with it."

"You're not going to argue on general principle?"

"Only to keep things interesting."

They were standing close together. Close enough for their arms to brush. Marina was aware of how much taller Todd was than her and how the heat from his body made her just a tiny bit squichy inside.

She did *not* want to be attracted to Todd, she reminded herself. It was that stupid kiss. If that hadn't happened, she never would have thought of him as more than just Ryan's friend and someone she had to learn to deal with for the next few weeks. He wouldn't have been…a man.

She forced her mind to focus on the project at hand. "Look, they can recommend a florist," she said. "That's good. We need more recommendations. The chair rental isn't too bad. We're going to need chair covers, though."

He swore softly. "They're four bucks each. With two hundred chairs, that's eight hundred dollars to throw a piece of cloth over the chair? Can't they be naked?"

She patted his arm. "No. They look better covered."

"Ryan and I are in the wrong business. If you rent out those covers twice every weekend, even with the cost of the initial purchase and cleaning, you're still raking in the money."

"So invest in the bridal business."

He looked around and shook his head. "It's too emotional. Give me a good high-tech start-up any day."

"But you could expand. Diversify."

"Maybe." He sounded doubtful.

She looked up at him. "So how did you get started?

Do you wake up one morning and think 'Hey, let's be venture capitalists'?"

"Not exactly. Ryan and I had a buddy back in college. He had a great idea for software, but he didn't have the money to manufacture or market it. We decided to finance his business."

"So you used your allowance money for the week?"

He shook his head. "Trust fund money."

"Oh, of course," she said knowingly. "That's where I go when I'm short on cash. It's so handy having that spare billion or two to fall back on."

"You enjoy mocking me, don't you?"

"It's pretty fun."

He folded the price sheet and handed it to her. "The company took off. By the time we graduated, Ryan and I had made our first million."

Impressive, she thought, but she wasn't going to say that to him. "Does the silver spoon ever choke you?" she asked.

He ignored her. "We both paid back out trust funds with interest and never had to tap into it again. Our company has been profitable ever since."

So except for his start-up cash, he'd earned his fortune the old-fashioned way. She would never have guessed. "Make any mistakes?"

"A few. Fortunately they didn't cost too much. Not every new company is going to make it and all the experts in the world can still be wrong. But we have good instincts."

And money, she thought. "No wonder you're considered a hot bachelor. How is it you've survived all this time without being trapped by some determined young woman?"

He smiled, but his eyes were cold and distant. "I've been burned enough times to not trust anyone."

"That can't be fun," she said, wondering if they had the same problem for different reasons. "How can you get close if you don't trust?"

"I don't need to get close to get what I want."

Which made sense, she thought, but was also sad. "That's got to get lonely."

"You don't have a guy in your life. Are you lonely?"

"No." Not exactly. Sometimes she wanted more, but the price of that always scared her away.

"So we're not so different," he said.

"Except for the millions and the fact that you date models, we're practically twins separated at birth."

"You're never going to let the model thing go, are you?"

"Um…not really."

The tux shop was well lit and elegant. Not exactly like those places at the mall. Marina felt distinctly underdressed, especially when the salesperson, a gorgeous brunette in her mid-twenties, stepped out from behind the counter in an outfit that looked as if it cost as much as Marina's rent.

"May I help you?" she asked, her gaze locking on Todd.

"We're here to look at tuxes," he said. "For a wedding."

The woman—Roxanne, according to her nametag—sighed. "Yours?"

"No. I'm the best man. The groom is out of the country. I'm supposed to make the right decision without him."

"I see." Roxanne turned her piercing green gaze on Marina. "And you are?"

"The sister of the bride. I get a vote."

"Wonderful."

Roxanne's attention swung back to Todd. Marina had a feeling it was never going to stray again.

"We have an amazing collection of designer tuxedos," Roxanne said, her voice low and sultry. "They're available for rent or purchase. Does the groom have your build?"

Todd glanced down at himself, then at Marina. "We're about the same size, don't you think?"

Marina nodded. "Pretty much. We want something simple, but elegant. Unfortunately the colors haven't been picked yet, so we're not ready to place the order."

Roxanne continued to gaze at Todd. "That's fine. You can try on whatever you like to see what makes you happy, then come back later."

Marina had a feeling Todd could visit every day and Roxanne wouldn't mind.

The three of them walked over to the display rack of tuxedos. Roxanne eyed Todd's body in a way that made Marina feel that she had stumbled into something intimate, then pulled out several selections.

"There are color choices, of course," Roxanne said. "Traditional black, various shades of gray, a few in other colors such as dark blue."

Todd grimaced. "Black or gray works for me. We're just looking for a regular tux. Bow tie and cummerbund."

"I like vests better," Marina said. Todd looked at her, Roxanne didn't.

"Vests?" He sounded doubtful. "I never wear a vest."

"How often do you put on a tux? Cummerbunds remind me of a high school prom. A vest can be elegant."

He shrugged. "Okay, but then I want a regular tie. A vest with a bow tie makes me feel like a grandfather."

Roxanne ran her hand down his arm. "You're certainly not that, are you?"

Marina held in a gagging noise. "At least try on both," she suggested. "If you hate it when it's on, then you can whine to Ryan."

"I don't whine."

"Oh, please. I've heard you."

Roxanne moved between them. "Let me get your size," she said, whipping a tape measure out of the jacket pocket of her very tailored and body-hugging suit. "Just hold your hands at your sides and relax."

Marina leaned against the counter as Roxanne did a very *thorough* job of the measuring. There was so much touching and cooing that even Todd started to look uncomfortable.

"All right," Roxanne said when she finally finished. "Let's get you into a dressing room and see how things go."

As she went into the back to get the samples, Marina grinned. "I hope she's quiet, because I embarrass easily. If the two of you start moaning, I'm out of here. Oh, give me the car keys so I can abandon you."

Todd gripped her arm. "You're not going anywhere. That woman scares me."

She laughed. "Oh, please. Is the big, bad millionaire frightened by the little girl in the tux shop? Poor Todd."

He narrowed his gaze. "You think this is funny."

"It kind of is."

It would be different if she were in a relationship with him. Then Roxanne's act would be a little disconcerting. But as it was, she could just have lots and lots of fun at his expense.

There was a tiny twinge of something buried inside her stomach, but she wasn't going to worry about whatever stray feeling she might have. It wasn't jealousy. It couldn't be. This was Todd. Someone she could never in a million years care about.

He pulled her into the dressing area with him. "Who's laughing now?" he asked as he jerked open a slatted door leading to a big dressing area, complete with a wooden chair. "Have a seat."

She folded her arms over her chest. "Excuse me? I can't sit here and watch you undress." Her cheeks got hot just from her thinking about it. She lowered her voice. "I barely know you."

"I'm wearing briefs," he said. "What's the problem? Pretend we're at the beach. I'm not going to be left alone with that woman."

He was serious. She wasn't sure if she was shocked or about to break out in hysterical laughter. "You expect me to protect you?"

"Damned straight."

She felt her lips begin to twitch, but she managed to hold in her grin. "All right. If it's that important to you. I'll sit here and watch you try on clothes. But I have to tell you, I'm a little disappointed. I thought you'd be better with women than this. It's another hope dashed. Any more disappointments like this and I'll need therapy."

He glared at her. "I know her type. She's not going to take no for an answer."

"And the big, bad millionaire doesn't want to hurt her feelings," Marina said, mocking him with a baby voice.

His eyes narrowed, but before he could respond, Roxanne appeared with several tuxedos. She came to a stop when she saw Marina in the dressing area.

"You're helping?" she asked in a voice that indicated such a thing could not be possible.

"Absolutely," Todd told her. "Marina has perfect taste."

"He's pretty helpless without me," Marina said with a smile. "Practically unstable."

Todd's gaze lasered in on her face and she had a feeling she might have to pay for that later, but who cared? This was a side of him she could never have imagined and she planned to enjoy every minute of it.

Not only seeing him as someone with flaws and weakness, she thought as Roxanne hung the tuxes on a hook and flounced out of the room, but as someone who was a lot more interesting than she'd first realized.

It wasn't until he pulled off his tie and began to unbutton his shirt that she realized the small detail she'd overlooked. The dressing room was oversized, but still relatively close quarters considering she and Todd hadn't known each other very long and he was about to take his clothes off in front of her.

He'd said to pretend they were at the beach. In theory, briefs wouldn't show any more than swim trunks, but they *weren't* at the beach and a really good-looking guy was undressing. Where was she supposed to look? Or not look?

He shrugged out of the shirt. His broad chest was well muscled and defined. She liked the faint dusting of hair that trailed down to his waistband. But when he reached for that waistband, she found herself suddenly staring at the floor.

"Ryan had better appreciate this," Todd muttered.

"You'll figure out a way to make him pay," she said, noting his socks were dark and looked new.

There was a rustle of movement, then he pulled on the pants from the first tux. Safety at last.

She decided to distract herself from the process by being busy. After handing him his shirt, she slipped the jacket off the hanger and studied the weave of the fabric, then fingered the lapel.

Roxanne appeared in the doorway. "Vest or cummerbund?" she asked, holding out one of each.

"Vest," Marina said, taking it from her and handing it to Todd. "You said you'd try."

He grunted, then slipped it on. Marina admired the way the cut emphasized the breadth of his shoulders and the narrowness of his hips. A faint tingle quivered to life somewhere behind her belly button.

He took a tie from Roxanne and eased it under his collar. After securing the knot, he put on the jacket.

"There's a three-way mirror out here," Roxanne said.

He followed her into the large center area of the dressing rooms. He stepped onto the platform in front of the mirror and stared at his reflection.

"What do you think?" he asked.

"Magnificent," Roxanne purred as she stepped up behind him and began smoothing down the shoulders and pulling at the hem of the jacket.

Marina agreed with the sentiment, even as the other woman's need to touch every inch of Todd got on her nerves. This was a business, not a petting zoo.

Determined to be mature and let Todd handle the situation, she ignored Roxanne and her roving hands.

"I like the vest," she said.

Todd nodded. "Me, too. I see what you're going for. It's less traditional than the cummerbund, but it looks great. We can't order anything until Julie and Ryan pick colors, but we can give them a few ideas."

"We have a Web site," Roxanne said, leaning toward his ear and pressing her breasts into his back. "I'll write down the item number so your friend can go online and see which tux you're talking about. If he looks half as good as you in this, it's going to be some wedding."

Marina held in a groan as Todd sidestepped Roxanne. "Great. Why don't you go get that information now?"

She reluctantly stepped back. When she'd left the dressing room, he turned to Marina.

"You're supposed to be protecting me."

"You're big enough to protect yourself."

"We're supposed to be a team. I'd rush to *your* rescue."

She couldn't figure out what he wanted from her. Did he want her to act like she was jealous? Was this his ego talking? Did he need every woman on the planet panting for him so that he could sleep at night? Or was it something else? Was he seriously uncomfortable?

While she wanted to believe the best of him, his reputation made it impossible. So he was playing her.

Fine. She could play, too. She could make him sorry he'd ever pulled her into his game.

She walked to the edge of the platform and grabbed a handful of his jacket, then tugged until he stepped down onto the carpeted floor. Then she raised herself up on tiptoe, wrapped one arm around his neck and pressed her mouth to his.

She was determined this should be a whole lot more than that brief kiss they'd shared before. She wanted to teach him a lesson. So she kept her lips slightly parted and pressed against him as if she meant it.

After a brief second of shocked stillness, Todd put both his arms around her, hauled her closer and kissed her back. He brushed her lips with his, then took advantage of her invitation and swept inside.

He moved purposefully, a man on a mission. He tasted faintly of coffee and mint—and he knew how to kiss.

The second his tongue touched hers, passion exploded. The feeling was so intense, she half expected the building to shake. There was so much heat and need and pleasure in the way he explored her mouth, teasing, flicking, retreating, returning.

Wanting blindsided her. She couldn't think, so she

reacted instead. She tilted her head and kissed him back. When he moved his hands up and down her back, she explored his shoulders, then his arms. He was all honed muscle and warmth. One of his hands got tangled in her long hair. He tugged slightly, pulling her head back. She let him have his way and was rewarded when he kissed his way down her neck.

The soft, hungry, openmouthed kisses made her want to whimper. Her entire body clenched as her breasts swelled in anticipation. She wanted to be on her back, on any flat surface. She wanted him between her legs, taking her hard and fast and damn the consequences.

That thought—one she'd never had before in her life—stunned her. She pulled back just as she heard the sound of a very irritated person clearing her throat. She turned and saw Roxanne standing in the entrance to the dressing room.

"You two should get a room," the saleswoman said, her voice icy.

"Interesting thought," Todd drawled.

Roxanne turned and left.

Marina stood there, not sure what to think let alone what she should say. Talk about unexpected passion. And awkward.

Several comments floated to the surface of her brain, but they all sounded stupid. Even if they didn't, she wasn't sure she could speak. Her throat was dry and tight and she had a bad feeling her voice would sound breathless.

"Marina," Todd began.

She held up a hand to stop him, then swallowed and forced herself to look at him.

Big mistake, she thought when she saw the hunger in his dark eyes. Her gaze zeroed in on his mouth…a mouth that could obviously drive a woman wild wherever it kissed her.

"I was teaching you a lesson," she said, her voice shaking a little. "At least I was supposed to."

"You're not what I expected, either."

Was that good or bad?

"You're not my type," she continued. "I want to plan my sister's wedding. Nothing else."

She met his gaze. Some of the hunger had faded, but there was just enough there to make her want to throw herself at him and do it all again.

"I agree," he said.

It took her a second to realize he was responding to what she said, not what she'd thought.

"So this never happened," she told him. "Nothing happened."

"Something happened. But we can ignore it—if you prefer."

Which was as close to a good answer as she was going to get, she thought. She left him alone to change back into his street clothes and walked out to wait by the car.

It wasn't the fact that she'd enjoyed the kiss that bothered her. It was that she'd been willing to give herself to him without knowing him. Without deep feelings. Her level of passion scared her.

Todd was a lot more interesting than she'd ever

imagined. Liking him was a surprise. Wanting him, equally startling but there it was. But the two together? No way. They made the situation more than danger-ous—they made it deadly.

She couldn't afford to fall for someone like him. If she did, she would be destroyed. She'd seen it happen. She knew what it cost.

To Marina_Nelson@mynetwork.LA.com
From Julie_Nelson@SGC.usa

What do you mean you kissed Todd! You can't just e-mail "oh by the way, I kissed Todd today" and then hit send. It's wrong on so many levels. You kissed him? On the mouth?

Why? That's so not like you. It's not about the million dollars is it? Please say it isn't. That's not like you, either. Todd? Seriously? How was it? Wait. I'm not sure I want to know.

He's nothing like your type. You always fall for sweet, nerdy guys who are going to save the world. Not powerhouse alpha males with attitude. He dated models. You remember that, right? Are you okay?

On a completely different topic, we love the sage/rose combination for our colors. Go with that, but nothing too matchy-matchy, please.

To Julie_Nelson@SGC.usa
From Marina_Nelson@mynetwork.LA.com

I'm fine. Totally fine. The kiss just kind of hap-pened. It's a long story and I thought he was playing me, so I kissed him. It doesn't mean anything. I wouldn't have mentioned it except I thought maybe he'd say something to Ryan and then Ryan would say something to you and then you'd be mad because I didn't tell you myself. That's all. Although now that I think about it, Todd isn't the type to brag.

As to the kiss, it was just a kiss, you know? Nice. I know he's not my type. You have nothing to worry about.

I'm glad you picked colors. That will help with the planning. I love the rose/green combo, too. And I swear, nothing that matches in a cute way. We'll go for shades and variations on a theme. It's going to be fabulous.

To Marina_Nelson@mynetwork.LA.com
From Julie_Nelson@SGC.usa
   OHMYGOD!! You already know what type Todd is? What else do you know that you're not telling me? What else is happening there? You'd better not fall for him, Julie. I mean it. I'm thousands of miles away and I'd miss everything.

To Julie_Nelson@SGC.usa
From Marina_Nelson@mynetwork.LA.com
   LOL. Don't sweat it. I'm not falling for Todd in any way. You have nothing to worry about.

Five

Todd drove slowly through the traffic around UCLA, then pulled over to the curb. He scanned the crowd of students, then saw Marina talking to a young woman.

Not talking, he reminded himself. Signing.

The two women faced each other, their hands moving in a graceful dance he couldn't decipher. Marina nodded, then glanced over her shoulder. She saw him and waved, then pointed at the car and signed something to her friend. The friend nodded, they hugged, then Marina started toward him.

He watched her walk. In her jeans and long-sleeved T-shirt, she fit in with the other students around her. He let his gaze linger on her swaying hips, then moved his attention to the way her long golden hair fluttered. She looked like a commercial for some sexy product. Buy whatever it was and get a girl like this.

She opened the passenger side door and slid inside. "Hey," she said. "Going to let me drive again?"

"No. Too much power will go to your head."

"So typical," she muttered as she fastened her seat belt. "Why do men feel they have to hold out on women? Don't give the poor females too much responsibility or power. They won't be able to handle it."

"Women control the majority of wealth in this country."

"A fact that makes me smile every time I hear it. I know you don't want me driving because my skill level threatens your masculinity."

"Not for long. I'm in therapy."

She laughed and he joined in. Their last meeting had been at the tux shop, where she'd kissed the hell out of him and had left him wanting more. He hadn't yet decided what, if anything, he was going to do about that wanting. For now it was enough to simply enjoy Marina's company.

As he pulled back into the traffic, he tried to remember the last time he'd wanted to just be with a woman. To hang out and talk and tease without counting the minutes until he could get her into bed.

It wasn't that he didn't want to sleep with Marina—he did. But he also liked her.

When was the last time that had happened? Liking. He'd almost forgotten how that felt. Not that he trusted her. He trusted no woman. But he'd been looking forward to being with her today ever since the last time he'd seen her.

"How did you get interested in sign language?" he asked.

She glanced at him. "I'm embarrassed to admit I first learned because one of my girlfriends had a hunky older brother who was deaf. I was about fourteen at the time. He was older and brooding and I knew that inside he was really deep and fascinating and that he would fall madly in love with me if only we could communicate. I took a beginning sign language class and really enjoyed it, so I kept going."

"What happened with the guy?"

"He turned out to be a total jerk who just happened to be deaf. Still, I'm grateful he put me on this path. I became a certified interpreter. It was a great part-time job for me through college."

She glanced at her watch. "I'm sorry I have to split up our day."

"No problem."

"It's an important class. So I appreciate you being flexible."

"Far be it from me to stand in the way of someone's education."

"Spoken like a true member of the elite."

They were heading over to a different caterer to sample food, then meeting up later at his place to interview a florist.

"Now that Ryan and Julie have picked their colors, we can make some firm decisions," he said. "I let the florist know what the colors were and she'll bring appropriate samples."

"Good. I think the rose-green combo gives us lots of room and areas of compromise. The boy stuff can be green, the girl stuff pink."

"Then everyone's happy."

"Exactly." She smiled at him.

He braked for the stoplight and smiled back. While they were looking at each other he said, "That was some kiss the other day."

Instantly her eyes widened and color stained her cheeks. She jerked her gaze away from him and stared out the windshield. "Yes, well, you said you needed protecting."

He'd wondered what she'd thought about their kiss. Had it been as powerfully erotic for her as it had been for him? Now he knew the answer to that was yes. He also knew she was a little embarrassed and wondered why.

"Not that I thought you really needed protecting," she said, still not looking at him. "You can handle women like that in your sleep."

"I'm more interesting when I'm awake." He drove through the intersection. "I wasn't expecting the passion."

"Just because I'm smart and into science doesn't meant I'm not like other people."

"You're not like other people, but that's a good thing. I'm not complaining, Marina. I like who you are."

"Oh. Good. Not that your opinion matters."

"Of course not."

She glanced at him. "It *was* a pretty hot kiss."

"I agree. I might need to be rescued later."

"I don't think so. You can save yourself without help from me."

"That's kind of cold."

"Live with it."

He chuckled and she smiled. Then she started talking about what Julie had said about the place settings. But most of his attention was on another, more interesting topic. Namely the idea of getting Marina into his bed.

He wanted her. That wasn't the question. He knew they would be great together. He'd learned that the first real kiss told a hell of a lot about chemistry and compatibility and desire. He and Marina had it all times ten. But sleeping together wasn't exactly intelligent.

For one thing, they would be connected to each other for the rest of their lives. Between his aunt by marriage being her grandmother and her sister marrying his cousin, they were in each other's worlds. Having sex would only make a complicated situation more awkward.

For another thing, she wasn't his usual type. She didn't play when it came to men and he didn't believe in getting serious when it came to woman. Better to keep things simple.

But it had been a great kiss. Thinking about it had kept him up much of the last couple of nights and that hadn't happened to him…ever.

Marina stared down at the small plate of pasta in front of her. While she appreciated the artful presentation, she was starting to get a little paranoid.

She leaned closer to Todd and whispered, "Is it just

me, or has every dish been covered with some kind of cream sauce?"

"It's not you," he whispered back. "The salad dressing, that creamy soup, the chicken, the crab cakes."

"Now this pasta," she murmured. "If we picked this place, we'd have to have white as our accent color."

She raked her fork through the perfectly cooked fettuccini. She couldn't complain about the food itself. The shrimp were delicate, the diced vegetables crisp, the sauce a decadent blend of cream and cheese and whatever spices went into it, but still.

"We can leave," he told her.

"Do you hate the food?" she asked.

"No. It's good. It's just…"

"Too much?"

He nodded. "Exactly."

A few minutes later, the dessert samples arrived. Marina managed to hold it together while the hostess explained what each dish was, then began to giggle when the women returned to the kitchen.

Todd raised his eyebrows. "Which will it be? The molten chocolate cake in cream sauce? The berries with cream sauce? The bread pudding with a chocolate cream sauce or the selection of sorbets with a ginger-cream topping?"

She took a bite of the bread pudding. "It's delicious," she said. "Really fabulous."

"I like the food," he said, sounding doubtful.

"I do, too. It's just so rich. My stomach already feels funny. Maybe the owner was a cow in a previous life and all this cream sauce is a way to get back to her roots."

Todd stared at her. "That's odd, even for you."

"I'm searching for an explanation. Okay, I'll e-mail Julie and tell her the food is amazing, but it's cream sauce central. Then they can decide."

They stood. She put her hand on top of her stomach. "Can we stop at a mini market on our way back? I'm dying for a soda to wash away the cream sauce flavor."

"Right there with you."

After her class, Marina drove to Todd's place to meet with the florist. Although she'd been to the gatehouse in back a few months before, she'd never seen the main house up close until today.

As she drove through the open wrought-iron gates, she stared up at the giant four-story mansion. There were dozens of windows and actual gables.

"And I thought Grandma Ruth's place was impressive," she muttered.

The grounds were manicured and endless. When she parked in front of the house, her car looked like a toy that had been left out by a careless child.

Sure, she'd known that the rich were different and that Todd was rich, but until this moment, she'd never realized exactly how rich. She had a bad feeling they were talking billions.

She headed up to the wide double doors, then paused as she glanced down at her jeans. Should she have dressed for the occasion?

Just then the front door opened and Todd stood there. "Take it all in?" he asked.

"Not yet. Do you give tours on alternate Wednesdays?"

"Only for a select few. Come on."

He'd changed out of his suit and was also dressed in jeans and a long sleeved shirt, which should have made her more comfortable. But he looked too good—all hard muscles and sleek sexy male. So between his butt and the elegance of the house, she didn't know where to look first.

She walked onto a marble entry floor and resisted the impulse to step out of her shoes. The foyer was large and oval, with a baby grand piano by the staircase. Right. Because every decent foyer *should* have room for a piano. There were incredible pieces of furniture that were probably antiques and paintings that looked both real and important.

Todd closed the door behind her. "What are you thinking?"

"I'm wondering how many bedrooms."

"More than ten."

"Okay. Good. So do you rent out to large families or simply invite small countries to move in?"

"It depends on my cash flow for the month."

He was joking, but there was something about his expression. Something almost…wary.

"Am I reacting wrong?" she asked. "Should I pretend I'm not impressed and a little intimidated?"

"It's just a house."

She laughed. "It's a really big house and you live here by yourself. That's a little strange."

"I grew up here. It's big and expensive to keep up, but it's been in my family for three generations and now it's my responsibility."

She looked around at the massive chandelier and the fresh flowers. "It's like a really great hotel. Show me the fluffy robe and the room service menu and I'll move in."

"We don't have room service."

She sighed. "Then forget it. Room service is a deal breaker for me." She looked at him. "How do they usually react? The other women?"

"They start by calculating how big a settlement they'll get when the marriage ends."

"Ouch. Not everyone you've dated has been in it for the money. A few of them must have actually liked you."

He chuckled. "You're not very good for my ego. Many of the women I date actually like me. The money is just a big plus." He put an arm around her shoulders and led the way through an arched doorway. "I don't usually show them the house."

"I wouldn't. Not until you're fairly serious. The ones who are in it for money won't be able to pretend anymore and the ones who are will be scared to death."

"*You're* not scared."

They were close enough that she could feel the heat of his body, which made her remember how it had been to be in his arms. How he'd pulled her close and kissed her back and made her tingle all over.

"We're not dating," she reminded him. As far as she was concerned, they never would. Todd was too danger-ous for her peace of mind. She wouldn't have thought she could be scared by a guy, but in some ways he would never know about, he terrified her.

If only he didn't turn her on. Reluctantly she stepped free of his embrace.

They stopped in a large family room. There were two sectionals, a couple of armoires, side tables, a writing desk and nothing about the room felt crowded.

"Nice," she said, appreciating the warm colors and overall comfort of the space. "You have a decorator."

"Of course. I'm a typical guy. If it were up to me, the entire world would be beige."

Somewhere in the distance, she heard the sound of chimes.

"The doorbell," he said. "Probably the florist. Have a seat and I'll let her in."

She crossed to one of the sectionals and sat down. To her right was a drinks cart made of incredibly beautiful inlaid wood. Instead of liquor, there were an assortment of soft drinks, along with ice, flavored water and a few snacks.

"Somewhere a housekeeper or cook is lurking," she murmured to herself as she put ice in a glass and popped the can of her favorite soda. There was no way Todd had put this together himself.

What must it be like to grow up in a place like this? She couldn't begin to imagine. While the house was something out of a movie, she had a feeling it might not have felt very comfortable for a kid. Todd was an only child. This was the kind of house that screamed out for bunches of kids. Had he ever been lonely?

Todd returned with a tiny woman of indeterminate age. He was laden down with armfuls of books and portfolios. She had two baskets with dozens of flowers in them.

"Marina, this is Beatrice. Beatrice, Marina is the bride's sister."

"How lovely that the two of you are planning the wedding together," the other woman said with a smile. She glanced around at the furniture and turned to Todd. "Perhaps some kind of dining room would be better suited?"

"Sure. Right this way."

"Can I get you something to drink first?" Marina asked.

Beatrice glanced at the cart. "Water, please, dear. Bottled if you have it."

Marina filled a second glass with ice, grabbed a bottle of water and trailed after them. As they moved from the family room to the dining room, she braced herself to be both impressed and intimidated.

Good thing, too, because the dining room could easily seat thirty, although the table was currently set with only a dozen chairs. Still, by the way it sat in the center of the room and the number of thick legs clustered together, she would guess there were about eight or ten leaves that fit into it.

Two hutches flanked leaded glass windows, while a long buffet sat in the center of the opposite wall. There were four chandeliers and a fireplace.

Todd set the books on the table, while Beatrice began to lay out dozens of flowers.

"I understand the bride and groom have chosen their

colors," she said as she clustered various blooms together. "That's always helpful. Rose and green will be lovely. However, I have some ideas for something a little different. A twist on the ordinary. For example, here we have dusty-rose colored tulips with green gladiolus. Not traditional, but they look beautiful."

Marina wasn't into plants or flowers, but as she knew what tulips looked like, she could figure out the gladiolus by default. The green petals were amazingly lush and the color was perfect next to the deep pink of the tulips.

"They're gorgeous," she murmured, then looked at Todd. "What do you think?"

"Nice."

She smiled. "Too much girly stuff?"

"I'm not into flowers. This seems fine."

Beatrice pulled out a spiny looking display. "Here we have bromeliad, ginger and anthurium. Again, not traditional, but the colors are perfect and these arrangement could make a charming table."

She handed Marina a ball of flowers in a yellowish shade of green. "Chrysanthemum balls. Very elegant. This sort of thing can be hung from the back of chairs." She thrust a handful of green berries at Todd. "Hypericum berries. A perfect green."

She brought out more and more flowers until Marina couldn't hold anymore. Todd was equally laden down.

Then Beatrice turned to the books. "I have pictures from various weddings. We'll look at them now."

She flipped through dozens of photos, explaining the different flower possibilities.

"You said there would be a separate room for the ceremony?" she asked.

Marina nodded. "There's a perfect room off the main ballroom. We'll set it up with rows of seating, so that space will need flowers, as well."

Beatrice began to talk about what they could do, but suddenly Marina found it difficult to listen. She felt hot and flushed, although at the same time, she felt a chill. Her stomach had taken a turn for the uncomfortable, as well. It seemed to flip over on itself in a way that made her want to gag.

Cautiously she put down the flowers. She'd never been allergic to anything before, but maybe the overdose of pollen was getting to her.

Todd looked at her. "Are you all right?"

Her stomach gave another lurch and she had a bad feeling she was about to throw up.

"Not really," she said, interrupting Beatrice midexplanation. "Is there a bathroom nearby?"

"Sure." He put down his armful of flowers. "I'll be right back," he told the florist and led Marina out of the room.

Down a very elegant hall she was in no shape to appreciate, was a spacious guest bath.

"It's my stomach," she said. "I don't know what's wrong."

"Don't worry about it. I'll handle Beatrice."

Despite the suddenly twisting sensation in her stomach, she managed a smile. "I don't think anyone can handle Beatrice, but you go ahead and try."

"Come out when you feel better."

"Sure. I'll probably just be a minute."

She closed the bathroom door behind her and two seconds later lunged for the toilet.

Marina had no idea how much time had passed. She'd already thrown up twice and had a bad feeling she wasn't done. She felt shaky and weak, hot and cold, and a distinct longing to never feel this horrible ever again.

She sat on the marble floor, her eyes closed and wondered if she had the strength to drive herself home. The task seemed impossible on a couple of different levels. First, she doubted she could make the trip without vomiting again. Second, she couldn't seem to focus on anything but how miserable she felt.

There was a knock on the bathroom door.

"Marina?"

She recognized Todd's voice. Why had this had to happen here of all places? With him around?

"Yeah?"

"How's your stomach?"

"Awful. I can't figure out what's wrong."

"I can. Food poisoning. All those cream sauces."

She remembered what they'd eaten and groaned. "You, too?"

"You bet. I got rid of Beatrice. Come on. I'll take you upstairs to one of the guest rooms. The bathrooms are more comfortable and you can crawl into a bed between events."

She hesitated for a second, then staggered to her feet. Stretching out on a bed sounded really good right now.

She opened the bathroom door and saw Todd looked about as bad as she felt. He was pale, slightly green and there were shadows under his eyes.

"Aren't we an attractive couple," she murmured as he took her hand and pulled her toward the stairs.

"We'll take a picture. We have to hurry. I don't know how long I have."

Despite how sick she felt, she started to laugh. "You sure know how to show a girl a good time."

"Tell me about it. At least it's Friday. You don't have classes on the weekend, do you?"

"No."

"Good. Then you can crash here as long as you'd like. There's a phone in your room if you need to call anyone. There are robes in the closet. I put a couple of my T-shirts on the bed, so you could sleep in something more comfortable than your clothes."

They reached the second-floor landing. She glanced at him. He'd thought of all that while feeling as horrible as she did? Talk about a great guy. "Thanks. You're going way beyond what's expected."

He put a hand to his stomach. "It's going to be an ugly few hours. Basically we have to get all the bad food out of our system."

She didn't want to think about that. "We should—"

Todd cut her off with a shake of his head. "Third door on your right. T-shirts on the bed. Water on the nightstand."

He turned and hurried in the opposite direction, ducking into a door at the far end of the hall.

Marina watched him go, then felt a faint rising in her own midsection. She didn't have much time herself.

She ran into the guest room and found everything as he'd described. There were two clean T-shirts on the bed, three bottles of water on the nightstand and a robe in the closet. But before she could deal with any of that, she ran toward the bathroom and wondered if she could possibly survive the day.

Six

Marina woke up sometime around six Saturday morning. She'd spent quality time in the bathroom until about midnight, then had crawled into bed and slept like the dead. After brushing her teeth with a conveniently placed new toothbrush, she slipped into the fluffy robe and headed out into the vast expanse of Todd's house to find the kitchen.

Passing through the dining room, still littered with flowers, she made her way toward the rear of the house and walked into a kitchen that could easily satisfy the pickiest chef known to man.

She also found Todd there. He wore sweats, a T-shirt and hadn't shaved. There was a slight shifting in her stomach, but this one had nothing to do with the food she'd eaten and everything to do with how delicious the man in front of her looked.

"Morning," she said, doing her best to act normal around the sudden fluttering in her chest. What was wrong with her? This was Todd. A guy she borderline despised. Except she couldn't. Not really. He'd been just as sick as she had been yesterday, but he'd taken the time to get her settled before spending his evening in his own bathroom.

He looked up and smiled. "Hey. How you feeling?"

"Better. My stomach is so empty I can practically hear coyotes howling. You?"

"I wrapped things up about one in the morning, then crashed. I'm going to make an executive decision here and say no to the cream sauce caterer."

She laughed. "I won't fight you on that. I don't think I've ever been that sick."

He nodded at the kettle on the stove. "At the risk of sounding like a wuss, how about some tea and dry toast? I think that's about all I can handle this morning."

"Sounds great. We probably need to hydrate."

He grinned. "That was a lot of fluids coming out."

"Tell me about it." She fingered the robe. "This is nice. Am I the first English speaking female to wear it?"

He leaned against the counter and crossed his arms over his chest. "You were going to let the model thing go."

"I don't remember saying that."

"You should." He looked her up and down. "It's for company, not dates. I don't usually bring women here, remember?"

"But your car is a little small for the wild thing."

He raised an eyebrow. "You're mighty curious about my personal life."

"Men love to talk about themselves."

"We usually go to her place."

"I see. That makes it easier to escape when you feel the need and doesn't push the money thing into their face."

"Exactly."

The kettle began to whistle. At the same time, bread popped out of the toaster.

"Dishes?" she asked.

He pointed to a row of cabinets. It only took her two tries to find small plates. She put the toast on a plate and popped in two more slices, while Todd poured water into a teapot. She glanced over his shoulder and saw fresh tea leaves in a little basket.

"Very fancy," she said. "Yours?"

"Apparently. I e-mailed my housekeeper last night and asked her if I had any tea. She said I did and told me where to find everything."

Imagine having so much stuff, you didn't know what you owned or where it was. Different worlds, Marina thought. Very different worlds.

They sat at the round table by the large window. She nibbled on a piece of toast, then took the mug of tea he offered.

"Interesting house," she said after she'd sipped the steaming liquid. "Kind of intimidating."

"It does leave an impression."

She looked at his face, at the dark stubble shadowing his cheeks and jaw. "How do you know it's ever about you?" she asked. "Nothing about your life is normal. How can you be sure?"

"I'm not. Even you agreed to go out with me after your grandmother offered you a million dollars."

She rolled her eyes. "Oh, please. You know that's just a joke. Although it is fascinating that she does think she has to pay someone to marry you. What does she know that I don't?"

"I'm ignoring the question," he told her.

Marina took another bite of toast and chewed slowly. So far her stomach was staying pretty settled, but she wasn't ready to get wild for a few more hours.

"You have to have been sure sometime," she said. "There have to be some women you trust."

"You don't want to talk about this."

"Are you asking me or telling me?"

His dark gaze settled on her face. "I went to an all-guys boarding school for high school. Ryan and I both did. My first serious girlfriend was a scholarship student at the all-girl school next door. We met at a dance and I fell for her in seconds. She was smart, funny and totally into me."

Marina didn't doubt that for a minute. She had a feeling he'd been the kind of guy a lot of girls would have been totally into.

"Her mother was barely making it, working in an office somewhere. Jenny told her about me. We were each other's first time." His face tightened. "Jenny's mom went to my parents and said that either they would pay her two hundred and fifty thousand dollars or she would bring me up on rape charges. Jenny was only sixteen, so there was a chance the charges would stick."

Marina felt sick again, although this time it had nothing to do with food poisoning. "I can't believe that. How horrible. How old were you?"

"Sixteen. But that didn't matter. My parents paid her off and I learned an important lesson."

She wanted to tell him that he'd learned the wrong thing, that people weren't like that, except she thought for him, maybe they were.

"What did Jenny have to say?" she asked.

"She was upset, or so she said. The week after we broke up, her mother bought her a car. That seemed to help."

He sounded bored and cynical, but talking about the past had to be hurting him. That sort of experience would leave a scar.

"Another woman I was dating came to me and said she was pregnant. I was always careful, but I had no reason to think she was lying. I did the right thing and asked her to marry me. She'd always talked about a big wedding, so I suggested we wait until after the baby was born, so the plans weren't rushed. She freaked at that."

Marina slumped back in her seat and closed her eyes. "Let me guess. She wasn't really pregnant?"

"No. She had a friend who peed on the stick and that's what she showed me. Apparently her plan was to try to get pregnant right away and if that didn't work, to 'lose' the baby right before the wedding. We would both be so devastated by the tragedy that we'd get married anyway."

"I hate that there are people like her in the world," she said. "I know the money makes it difficult, but you have to have had some good experiences with women."

"Some. A few. But I'm never sure. One way or another, I'm waiting for each one to finally admit it's all about the money."

She leaned toward him. "Todd, you're a great guy. You're smart and funny and charming and not half-bad looking."

He smiled. "Wait. I need a moment to bask in the 'not half-bad looking' compliment."

She laughed. "You know what I mean. It's not always about the money. It can't be. There aren't that many horrible people in the world."

"Before Ryan fell for your sister, he was dating a single mom with an adorable little girl. Ryan was convinced he'd found the perfect woman. He was crazy about the kid, wanted them both in his life and proposed. Then I overheard her talking to a friend about how she'd hated having a baby until she realized that most young, rich guys are suckers for a cute little girl. That she planned to stay married to Ryan for a couple of years, then divorce him and live on the child support he would offer to pay."

Her heart ached for Todd. "So what do you do? Never trust? Never care too much? Never put yourself out there?"

"It's working so far."

"But that's so lonely. Don't you want to be in love?"

"Not bad enough to get taken. I can get a woman whenever I want. If I need another heartbeat in the house, I'll get a dog."

Sadness nearly overwhelmed her. On the surface, Todd had everything, but in truth, there were big holes in his life. He was powerful and in charge—the sort of man who thrived on doing. He was also surprisingly kind and caring. And he would never trust a woman enough to truly give his heart.

"What are you thinking?" he asked.

"That we're both seriously twisted. You can't trust anyone else and I can't trust myself."

"I don't believe that," he told her. "You have it all together. Don't you date nerdy guys who are going to change the world?"

"Most of the time. They're brilliant and interesting and…" She bit her lower lip. They were supposed to be talking about him, not her.

"And safe?" he asked, his voice low.

"Maybe. Sometimes. I just…" She took a sip of the tea. "My mom fell in love with my dad the second she saw him. She was seventeen and to this day, she still adores him. My dad isn't a bad person, but he's not the greatest husband and father. He leaves. He just up and disappears for months at a time. We never know when he's going or how long he'll be gone. Every time he walks out, her heart breaks. But she won't tell him he can't come back. She won't let herself love anyone else. She lives a half-life, only truly happy when he's with her."

"You're not like that," he told her. "You're tough."

"You don't know that and neither do I. I'm terrified I'm just like her. That I'll fall for a guy who'll break my heart and I'll let him. I'll say it's okay. Falling in love, really falling in love, seems too much like handing over control of my life. It's not on my to-do list anytime soon."

"So instead of taking a chance, you date guys you're not at risk of falling in love with."

She looked at him. "Do you really want to spend much time pointing out my flaws, because I think you're in kind of dangerous territory."

"I'm willing to risk it. Am I right?"

"Maybe."

"You're always the object of affection, never the one at emotional risk."

"You're making me sound mean and I'm not. I just don't want to fall for anybody until I'm sure I won't be destroyed."

"You can never be sure."

"I refuse to believe that," she said. "One day I'll take a chance."

"Will you?"

She wanted to believe she would. That one man would be worth her step of faith.

"Obviously we both need therapy," she said. "Maybe we could get a group rate."

He laughed. The sound made her feel good inside. Then she yawned.

"Sorry," she said as she covered her mouth. "I didn't get enough sleep last night."

"Me, either." He rose. "Come on. Let's go to bed."

She stared at him. A thousand thoughts raced through her mind. Bed? With him? As in sex? She wanted to be shocked and insulted. She wanted to stand up and slap him. But as images of them together, naked, touching, filled her brain, she found herself just as interested in saying yes.

Todd held up both hands. "Sorry. Poor word choice. Let me start over. Let's go upstairs where we can each sleep in our own beds. Better?"

She nodded, because that was what he expected, but inside, she felt a sharp stab of disappointment. What was up with that?

He waited until she'd risen, then put a hand on the small of her back and guided her out of the kitchen.

"We'll meet up later," he said cheerfully, "and figure out if we ever want food again."

"Sounds like a plan."

At the top of the stairs, they each went their separate way. But as she closed the door of the guest room she couldn't help thinking how much she was wishing he'd meant what he said the first time.

Later that afternoon, Marina stepped out of the shower and reached for a towel. Todd might not invite a lot of lady friends to his place, but he kept the guest room well stocked. In addition to the toothbrush and toothpaste she'd found earlier, there was also shampoo, conditioner, body wash and an assortment of moisturizers.

After slathering on a yummy citrus-scented lotion, she dressed, gave her hair a halfhearted blow-dry and headed downstairs.

She was starving and tea and toast wasn't going to cut it. She figured she could do drive-through on her way home. But first she had to find her host and thank him for everything.

The kitchen was empty, as was the family room. She heard a faint noise, like someone typing on a keyboard and headed in that direction. She located Todd in a panel-lined study that looked like a set out of *Masterpiece Theater.* He was dressed, as well, and looked just as good as he had that morning.

Little tingles broke out all through her body. She felt a distinct flicker of heat and several other unwelcome physical responses.

"How are you feeling?" he asked when she walked into the room.

"Good. I slept more and now I'm starving."

"Me, too. So we both survived our food poisoning."

"Looks that way."

He stood and walked around the desk. "You ready to head home?"

She nodded, even though what she actually wanted to do was throw herself into his arms and beg him to take her. Obviously she was still suffering the ill effects of the bad food.

"Big date tonight?" he asked.

"Not really."

He picked up a folded piece of paper from his desk and offered it to her. "Because I remember you saying you loved Mexican food and there's a great place nearby that delivers. Want to have something to eat before you go?"

She hesitated. Her head told her to get out while she

was emotionally in one piece. The rest of her body—especially the exquisitely female bits—suggested she stick around and see how this might play out.

"We could watch a movie," he said. "I'll even let you pick."

She grinned. "How can I resist that kind of an invitation? What are the odds we'll agree on any movie?"

"There has to be at least one. Something funny."

"But smart, not silly."

"I have that."

"I never thought I'd eat again," Marina admitted three hours later as she stretched out on Todd's sectional sofa in his media room. "But I'm kinda hungry."

Todd sat slumped down with his stocking feet propped up on the suede covered ottoman in front of the sofa.

The fabric on the furniture and the carpeting were the only things soft about this high-tech space. There was a screen that looked as if it belonged in a movie theater, enough speakers to levitate a house, players and recorders and a collection of movies that had made her mouth water. It was man toy heaven.

"A taco, two enchiladas, chips, salsa and a salad weren't enough for you?" he asked as he glanced at her.

She grinned. "Apparently not. I'm kind of in the mood for dessert."

"Then let's go see what's in the kitchen."

He stood and stretched. They were both casually dressed—her in the clothes she'd worn the previous day, him in jeans and a loose T-shirt. As he raised his arms above his head, the hem of his T-shirt crept above the waistband of his jeans, exposing a sliver of skin and his belly button.

It shouldn't have been the least bit erotic. They'd spent the whole night throwing up and doing other disgusting things only a few dozen yards apart from each other. Yet as she watched him, she felt more than a little bit of wanting deep inside.

"You ate a bunch, too," she said as he led the way out of the media room and toward the staircase. "More than me."

"Feeling defensive about your very unladylike appetite?"

"Maybe. I was hungry."

"I won't tell anyone."

She elbowed him in the side. "It's not like I ate with my hands or anything."

He looked at her and raised his eyebrows. "You had tacos. Of course you ate with your hands."

"You know what I mean."

At the bottom of the stairs, she forgot where the kitchen was and went right. He went left and they slammed into each other.

"Sorry," she said as she took a step back.

He grabbed her upper arms and held her steady. "You feeling all right?"

"I'm fine. Just a lousy sense of direction."

His eyes stared into hers. She suddenly felt both vulnerable and incredibly alive. She wanted him to move those hands, to touch her everywhere. Even as her brain screamed out that this was potentially dangerous, she found herself taking a step closer.

She saw the exact moment he felt it, too. There was a sharpening of his features, a subtle tension in his body. Hunger darkened his eyes.

He dropped his hands and stepped back. "Dessert," he said. "We were going to get you some dessert."

"Right. Anything but ice cream."

He groaned. "We're scarred for life."

"I don't think so. I will bravely overcome my fear of cream anything to indulge in chocolate chocolate chip again. It's just the kind of person I am."

He led the way to the kitchen. So neither of them was willing to act on the attraction. Smart, she thought, even as she wrestled with disappointment. Still, there were complications. They were practically related and it wasn't as if he would disappear from her life once the wedding was over. Did she really want to spend the next fifty years sitting at the same table as Todd and have a single night of passion between them? Talk about awkward.

So she ignored the way he moved as he opened the freezer and pulled out an assortment of goodies. There were individual slices of cake, a pie that only needed to be defrosted, then heated, and brownies. In the pantry they found boxes of cookies and some chocolate chips that could work in a pinch.

"What will it be?" he asked.

"Brownies. I'll be putting frosting on mine. I noticed a can in the pantry."

"Because there's not enough sugar in a regular brownie?"

"Exactly."

"Women," he muttered as he pulled the tray of brownies out of the freezer. "We're going to have to microwave these to defrost them."

"I'm an expert at that sort of thing."

She reached for the brownies as he handed them over. But their timing was off and the plastic-wrapped tray slipped through her fingers to crash onto the floor. They both bent over at the same time and bumped heads. Marina slipped and landed on her butt.

"We're a hazard together," she said as she started to laugh. "A complete disaster. I thought both of us getting food poisoning was the worst of it, but apparently not."

He laughed, then sank down next to her on the floor. "You're not like other women."

"I could work on a charming European accent if you want."

He narrowed his gaze. "Let it go."

"Never."

He reached over and tucked a strand of hair behind her ear. "I never thought getting as sick as we did would be fun, but this has been. You don't need to rush home tonight if you don't want to. You could stay."

She knew how he meant the invitation. She could stay in the guest room. It was a polite and well-meaning invitation.

"A sleepover," she teased.

She looked at him, expecting to see an answering

smile. Instead she found heat, desire and a need that made her weak. Then he blinked and it was gone.

Her insides clenched, her heart began to beat faster and her throat when dry. "Todd?"

"I'm trying to be smart here, Marina. I can come up with a hundred reasons why this isn't a good idea."

She pressed her lips together. "A hundred. Wow. I can only come up with about eight."

"I might have been exaggerating." He stood and held out his hand. "Come on. We'll defrost brownies and lose ourselves in the sugar."

"Sounds like a plan."

She put her fingers against his palm and allowed him to pull her to her feet. When she was standing, she found they were really close together. She would have stepped back, but he didn't let go of her.

She let herself get lost in the fire in his eyes. It warmed her and enticed her, and she swayed toward him.

"Damn," he muttered, right before he reached for her.

Seven

His mouth was warm and smooth and when he kissed her, Marina felt heat clear down to her feet. Her toes curled, her thighs trembled, her midsection tightened and her breasts pouted because they wanted some attention, too.

He pulled her close and she let him because she needed to be pressed against the hard planes of his body. She wrapped her arms around his neck and leaned in, making sure they touched everywhere.

He explored her mouth, kissing lightly, gently, but with enough passion to keep her breath locked in her throat. There was a promise in his kisses, a promise that there would be a whole lot more in the near future. As the anticipation was nearly as amazing as what he was already doing, she was willing to wait.

As he continued to tease, rubbing his lips against hers, nibbling, pressing, but not quite taking, she explored the hard muscles of his shoulders and upper back. She ran her fingers through his hair, then raked her nails lightly across his nape.

Wanting poured through her, pooling low in her belly, and her most feminine center ached to be taken.

Finally he tilted his head and touched her lower lip with the tip of his tongue. She parted instantly, welcoming him inside. At the first intimate stroke, a shudder raced through her. Passion grew until her skin felt too tight, too sensitive, too impossibly needy.

She clung to him through deep kisses that touched her soul, through his hands moving up and down her back, until he cupped her rear and she instinctively arched toward him only to encounter the impressive hardness of his desire.

She gasped as she imagined him filling her over and over again. She wanted with a desperation that made her rub herself against him, like a lonely cat. Hunger made her frantic. She'd been very comfortable not dating, not getting involved, not having a man in her life. Suddenly she was starving for contact, for skin on skin nakedness. But not just with anyone…only Todd could scratch this particular itch.

Some of her need must have gotten through to him. Or maybe it was the quick pace of her breathing and the way she clamped her lips around his tongue and sucked. Whatever the method of communication, he seemed to get the message. He moved his hands to her hips, eased them under her long-sleeved T-shirt and rode her curves up to her breasts.

He caressed her with the skill of a man who loves women. Even through the fabric of her bra, she felt the gently but purposefully caress of his fingers. He cupped her, then used his thumbs and forefingers to tease her nipples into a frenzy.

Fire shot through her, diving down between her legs and stirring everything up. She couldn't think, couldn't breathe, could only stand there lost in the pleasure of him touching her. Her only conscious thought was to wonder how much better it would be if she wasn't wearing a bra.

Todd took advantage of her inattention to kiss his way along her jaw, then down her neck. He nipped her earlobe, kissed the sensitive area just below, then traced wildly erotic patterns with his tongue.

The combination of sensations was pretty incredible. She felt herself tensing in anticipation of release that couldn't possibly happen. Not like this. Sure it had been a long time, but she had some pride, didn't she? Shouldn't she at least let him take her jeans off before she gave in to passion?

But as he continued to tease and touch and play with her breasts, she found herself getting closer and closer. Apparently he realized it, as well, because he leaned in and murmured, "We need to get you into bed."

Before she could say anything, he'd grabbed her hand and tugged her out of the kitchen and into the hallway. She hurried alongside of him, eager to get upstairs, get naked and fall into paradise.

They started up the stairs.

"Is sex better on five hundred thread count sheets?" she asked.

He stopped, laughed, then pulled her close. "Of course," he said, right before he pulled her T-shirt over her head and kissed her.

She went willingly into his embrace, kissing him back, needing him more than she'd ever needed anyone.

Even as his tongue stroked hers, she felt him reach for the hooks on the back of her bra. Seconds later, the scrap of lingerie drifted down her arms and onto the stairs.

He broke the kiss and bent his head to take one of her breasts into his mouth. There was immediate heat as he sucked deeply, then circled her nipple with his tongue.

She swayed slightly, then put her hands on his shoulders to steady herself. The powerful pull of his mouth caused every nerve ending to quiver in delight. Between her legs there was dampness and heat and anticipation. More, she thought hazily. She needed more.

But for now, this would be enough.

He used his fingers to mimic the movement of his tongue, caressing both her breasts, forcing her into a higher and higher state of arousal until she knew it would take almost nothing to push her over the edge.

"Todd," she breathed, wanting her release, yet wanting to hang on for a little bit longer.

"Tell me about it," he muttered, then grabbed her hand and pulled her up the last few stairs.

They hurried down the hall and burst into a bedroom the size of lecture hall. She had a brief impression of warm colors, massive dark furniture and a big, comfy, inviting bed.

Finally, she thought as he released her hand and yanked off his T-shirt.

They were barefoot, so it didn't take much manipulation on his part to get them both naked. One second she was topless, then next her jeans and panties were pooling on the floor. His jeans and briefs followed. Then he was easing her back on the mattress and she was in his arms and they were touching skin on skin and it was glorious.

He stared at her, his dark eyes bright with passion. She traced his mouth, then smiled when he gently bit down on her finger.

"I want you," he told her. "You're sexy as hell."

"I find you mildly interesting, as well," she said.

He grinned. "Mildly, huh. So I have some work to do."

"Absolutely." Brave words from a woman on the edge, she thought happily.

"I don't mind getting down and dirty now and then." He shifted so he was next to her, on his side, his hand supporting his head. "Where should I start? Here?" He put his hand on her belly.

While that felt nice and all, it wasn't exactly what she wanted. "Um, no."

"Here?" He ran his fingers from her wrist to her elbow.

She shifted slightly. "Not what I had in mind."

He slipped his fingers between her legs and rubbed her swollen flesh. "How's that?" he asked, his voice low and husky.

It took every ounce of self-control to keep her eyes

open. She desperately wanted to fall into a passionate trance and get lost in her orgasm, but not just yet.

"That works," she breathed as he explored all of her, finding her center and rubbing it.

Tension rose up inside of her. Muscles tensed. She let her legs fall open in a blatant and time-honored tradition of invitation.

"Good. What about this?"

He leaned toward her and stroked her nipple with the tip of his tongue.

It was an amazingly perfect combination. It was exquisite, it was magic, it was more than enough to make her lose control.

She did her best to hang on, to at least take three minutes to come. But he began to move his fingers faster and faster, with the perfect amount of pressure. Then he sucked on her breast.

It was incredible. She pulled her knees up and dug her heels into the bed. Not yet, she told herself. Not yet. Not…

It was too late.

She fell into her release, caught in the waves of sensual pleasure that swept through her. Every part of her sighed in relief as he continued to touch her, easing her onward until her muscles gave out in sheer exhaustion.

Lethargy stole through her. She had to force herself to open her eyes and when she did, she found Todd staring at her.

She'd expected a self-satisfied male smile—one that more than hinted at his expertise and how everything had felt so good because he was so darned talented in bed. Instead he looked serious and intense and instead of smiling, he leaned in and kissed her.

She parted her lips for him and felt the lethargy fade. As his tongue teased hers, passion returned and she found herself eager to have him inside of her.

He was hard…she could feel him pressing into her leg. She reached between their bodies and lightly stroked his arousal. But instead of reaching for a condom and then entering her, he slid down her body, kissing first her neck, then between her breasts, along the center of her rib cage, her belly, before coming to rest at the top of her right thigh. He parted her swollen flesh with his fingers.

While she appreciated the gesture, it wasn't required. "I've already…"

Then he did smile. "I know. I was there."

Her mouth curved in response. "It was great."

"I'm glad. Now let's do it this way."

A man on a mission, she thought as she let her eyes slowly close. Far be it from her to tell him his attentions weren't welcome.

Her stomach clenched in anticipation of his touch. She felt a faint breath of air, then a warm tongue began to explore her.

She groaned as he circled around her still-swollen center. A quick, light brush and then he was gone, caressing the rest of her, getting close, but not actually touching her *there*. It was exquisite torture. It was incredible.

She parted her legs even more and drew back her knees. Heat burned through her as he kissed and licked and sucked everywhere but that one place she wanted the most.

There it was again. One brief moment of exquisite contact, then nothing. One hint of what she could be feeling, then only anticipation.

She began to squirm. She got closer and closer, but knew she couldn't find her release until he focused on that one place. Until he finally—

His tongue brushed her again. She nearly screamed from the glory of the contact, then prepared herself for him to move away. She was an adult and she wouldn't whimper. Only this time he didn't stop. He stayed in that one spot, licking and circling, teasing, arousing, pushing her closer and closer until her climax became as inevitable as the sunrise.

He intensified his attention and she was lost.

The shuddering began deep inside of her midsection and worked its way out. Her thighs trembled, her hands shook and then she was launched into a release so powerful, she truly thought she might never experience anything like it again.

He continued to kiss her, teasing her into coming and coming. She gave herself over to him, letting him take all of her, until the tension finally eased and she was still.

Todd sat up and looked at Marina. A flush stole across her chest and climbed to her cheeks. She was limp, but if the smile was anything to go by, also incredibly satisfied.

Her golden-blond hair spilled across his pillow in sexy disarray and when she opened her eyes, her pupils were so dilated, he could barely see any of the blue.

"Wow," she said, her voice thick and husky. "I don't even know what to say."

He'd been complimented before. Most women made it a point to gush and while he appreciated the praise, he'd sometimes wondered how much of it was earned and how much of it had to do with his bank account.

Marina wasn't like that. Somewhere in the process of planning the wedding, they'd become friends. He liked her. He thought she was funny and smart and sincere. How often could he say that about the women in his bed?

Which made this experience different. He couldn't remember the last time he'd made love with a friend.

She put her hand on his arm and urged him closer. "So far this had been a pretty one-sided show."

At her words, he once again became aware of the pressure of his arousal.

He opened the nightstand drawer and pulled out a condom. After slipping it on, he knelt between her thighs. She reached for him and guided him inside.

Immediately he got lost in the sensation of tight, wet heat. She surrounded him, drawing him in, letting him fill her.

Her scent teased him. He could hear her breathing, feel the light stroking of her hands on his back and sides. For once he wasn't thinking about how quickly he was going to have to get away once this was over. For once he could just enjoy the experience and let the rest of it go.

He pumped harder, faster, in and out, losing himself in the growing pressure. She wrapped her legs around his hips, urging him closer. Her body tightened around him and he was lost.

* * *

"This is not a good idea," Marina murmured, even as she held out her wineglass. "Twenty-four hours ago, I was curled up like a dog on the bathroom floor. I should give my stomach time to recover."

"It has," Todd said confidently. "Besides, you were the one who was going to put frosting on perfectly good brownies. Isn't this better?"

The "this" in question was a bottle of red wine. It was after midnight. She and Todd had made love a second time then dozed off, only to wake up starving. He'd pulled on jeans and had given her a T-shirt to wear, then they'd made their way to the kitchen where they'd found mostly defrosted brownies on the counter.

She inhaled the scent of the wine, then took a sip. It was smooth and dark, with absolutely no bite. "Not bad. Let me guess. You have a wine cellar in the basement."

"The house doesn't have a basement, but there is a temperature and humidity controlled wine cellar."

"Naturally." She thought of the lone bottle of chardonnay she kept in her refrigerator…for special occasions, of course. "And if I wanted a bottle of Dom Pérignon?"

He shrugged. "What do you think?"

That he wasn't what she'd expected. That he was a whole lot better and that made him dangerous.

She took the brownie he offered, then followed him to the sofa in the family room. At some point he must have turned on a stereo because she could hear soft music in the background.

They sat facing each other, the night settling in

around them. She felt a sense of intimacy and connection—neither were very smart.

"Todd," she began, not sure exactly what she wanted to say.

"I know."

"How can you? *I* don't even know what I was going to say."

He set his wineglass and brownie on the coffee table, then leaned in and kissed her. "You're going to say that this is a complication neither of us needs. That we have a wedding to plan and that we're about to become related by marriage—again. That staying friends instead of lovers makes the most sense."

"Okay, yeah, that's probably what I was going to say," she admitted, letting herself get lost in his dark eyes. "Not that tonight wasn't great."

"Agreed."

"And that you're not nearly as toady as I thought you'd be."

He raised an eyebrow. "Toady?"

She grinned. "You know what I mean."

"You mean I'm sophisticated and charming. A man of the world, unlike the boy-nerds you usually date."

"Something like that. And I'm refreshingly intelligent and together, with just a hint of sass and a fabulous grasp of the English language, unlike those stick figures you usually date."

"You are all those things," he said and kissed her again. Then he wrapped his arms around her and eased her onto her back on the sofa.

She stared up at him. "We'd agreed this was a bad idea to continue."

"We'll end things tomorrow," he said as he kissed his way along her jaw.

"It is tomorrow."

"Not until the sun comes up. That means we have all night."

She wrapped her arms around him and gave herself up to his seduction. All night sounded just about perfect to her.

"They're arguing about the color of the shutters," Willow said as she carefully pulled an impossibly tiny plant from the soil and carefully placed it in a plastic container. "I'm sorry I ever mentioned shutters. I don't mind handling the remodel, but I hate it when they start e-mailing me separately."

Marina found herself mesmerized by the quick and expert movements of her sister's fingers. Willow poured in the potting mix, tapped it down, made a hole, plucked a slender plant from the tray and settled it in its new home.

"I'm thinking purple," Willow said. "You know—to match the elephants."

Marina blinked. "What elephants?"

Her sister sighed. "I knew you weren't listening to me. What's going on?"

"There are going to be elephants?"

"No." Willow sighed. "Marina, what's up? You're not yourself. Do you feel okay?"

If she ignored the faint protest of sore and stretched muscles, then she was exceptional. She and Todd had made love past dawn. While she was impressed with his ability to be ready time after time, she was also pretty pleased with her own performance. She would guess that she'd had more orgasms in the last twenty-four hours than maybe in all her previous life.

"I'm fine," she said. "Just a little tired."

"Uh-huh." Willow didn't look convinced. She walked to the door of the back room at the nursery and closed it, then put her hands on her hips and stared at her sister. "Start at the beginning and talk slowly. I don't want to miss anything."

"There's nothing to say." Which was a big, fat lie. "Well, not all that much."

"I'm going to stand here and glare at you until you tell me."

Marina smiled. "You're not actually glaring. It's more of a semiscowl."

"Marina!"

"Okay, okay. I'm fine. Everything is fine. It's just…" She felt her mouth curve up in a very satisfied smile. "Friday Todd and I did some tasting at a caterer. When I went back to his place to discuss flowers with a floral designer, I started to feel really bad. We both had food poisoning. I ended up spending the night there, practically chained to the toilet."

"And *that's* what you're smiling about?"

"No. But Todd was great. By yesterday we were feeling better. He asked me to stay—in the guest room. So we had dinner and watched a movie and then, well…"

Willow's eyes widened. "Ohmygod! You had sex with Todd Aston the Third. I'm going to get a million dollars!"

Marina held up both hands. "Number one, I'm not marrying him, so you can let your dreams of the million dollars go. If you're so hot to open a nursery, talk to Kane. He would do anything for you."

Willow shook her head. "No, thanks. I'm going to raise the money on my own. If you're not willing to marry to get it for me, then I'll get a loan or something. Which, by the way, is so not the point. You had sex with Todd?"

Marina smiled. "I did. It was great. He's nothing I'd imagined. I like him."

Willow moved close and hugged her. "That's great. Yea for you."

"It's not great. It's weird and uncomfortable and we're not going to be together that way again."

Willow stepped back and stared. "Excuse me? You're glowing. I've never seen you glow before. No one walks away from glowy sex."

"I will. We both will. We talked about it and this is the most sensible plan. Look, we're already related by marriage through Grandma Ruth. It's going to happen again when Julie and Ryan get married. Todd is in our lives forever. A relationship with him wouldn't go anywhere."

Willow returned to her plants. "Why not? He's single, you're single. That's an excellent start."

"We don't have anything in common. We're from different worlds. On a more basic level, he doesn't trust women at all. Having heard about his past, I kind of don't blame him. And I'm not totally healthy in that area, myself. I have issues."

Willow collected another plant. "You're not Mom. You're not going to lose yourself in a man."

"You don't know that."

"You don't, either. I know you're too scared to try. You've always chosen safe guys. Guys who adored you but who could never, in a million years, actually touch your heart. You've never risked falling in love, so you can't know what you'll do. None of us want to be like Mom. None of us want to give up everything for a man. So don't. Be strong. Be your own person. But take a chance."

It was really good advice. A sensible person might even consider it. But in this case, Marina refused to be sensible. There was too much to lose.

"Even if I let myself fall for him," she said. "He'd never love me back. He refuses to get that involved."

"There's always a first time."

"Not for him."

"You're wrong," Willow told her. "There's a first time for everyone. Look at Kane. But you have to be willing to take the chance. You can't find perfect happiness unless you're willing to risk the pain. Is a half life of being safe really worth never finding your soul mate?"

Marina thought about their mother. Naomi had only ever loved one man and she'd spent her entire life having her heart broken by him over and over again.

"The soul mate thing is highly overrated," she murmured.

"No, it's not," Willow insisted. "But love does require

faith. If you can't have that, you'll never know. What if Todd's the one? Are you really willing to let him walk away? At least Mom spends some of the time happy. When Dad's with her, all is right with the world. If she didn't have those moments of joy, the rest wouldn't be worth it."

Marina wasn't convinced those brief moments were worth anything. Not when the pain was so great and there was no escape. She'd lived her whole life without a soul mate and had done just fine. It would be a whole lot easier to get over what she'd never had than to risk being destroyed by a man determined to never give his heart.

Eight

Todd checked his watch. He'd arrived a couple of minutes early for his meeting with Marina at the bridal shop, but he wasn't worried about her keeping him waiting. She wasn't the type.

He'd wondered if seeing her again after their long night together would be awkward, but now that he was here, he only felt anticipation. Not a good thing, he thought grimly. She wasn't the type to play the no-strings game and he wasn't willing to accept anything else. Even for her.

So he would forget what happened and look at her only as his cousin's fiancée's sister. A distant acquaintance. Someone he liked, but didn't care about. Wasn't interested in. Wouldn't get involved with.

His good intentions lasted right up until she burst into the bridal shop, looking rushed and five kinds of gorgeous.

"I know, I know," she said as she stepped inside and grinned at him. "I'm a minute late. How you must resent me for treating you so badly. Next thing you know I'll be making you hold my purse while I try on clothes and call you snookums."

He laughed with her and their gazes locked. Within seconds the rest of the world ceased to matter. There was only this moment and the woman in front of him.

Wanting made him hard and need made him step toward her. The sensible part of his brain was outvoted. The only thing that made sense was Marina in his arms.

One of them moved first. He didn't know if it was him or her and it didn't matter. But before he could reach for her, a fortysomething saleswoman walked up to them and sighed.

"How wonderful," she said. "I can always tell when a couple is really in love. You two have brightened my day."

It was like being dropped headfirst in a big, icy pool of reality. He stepped back. Marina did the same and then they avoided looking at each other.

Great, he thought grimly. Now things were going to be awkward. He'd never wanted that. Making love with Marina had been the most fun he'd had in a hell of a long time. Not just the sex, although that had been record-setting. But just hanging out with her. Relaxing, being comfortable.

"We're, ah, not getting married," Marina said with a smile that looked more forced than happy. "I'm Marina

Nelson. You've spoken with my sister Julie. She's the bride who's hiding out in China right now and making everyone else do her dirty work for her."

"Oh, of course." The woman looked between them. "My mistake. I'm Christie."

Todd introduced himself and they all shook hands.

"I have some ideas of what your sister might like," Christie said. "She was very specific about all her no's, which makes things easier. I understand you'll be trying things on and then getting her feedback?"

Marina nodded.

"That's fine. Usually we don't allow brides to take pictures until they've actually put a deposit on the dress, but Julie made special arrangements with the owner, so we're good on that. You have a camera?"

Todd patted his suit jacket. "Right here."

"Good. All right, Marina. Let's dress you up like a bride. I understand you and your sister are about the same size and height?"

The two women disappeared down a hallway. Todd found a comfortable chair and a table full of financial and sports magazines. A few minutes later Christie appeared and asked if he would like anything to drink.

He accepted the offer of coffee, then settled in to read. But he couldn't seem to concentrate on the article. Instead he remembered Marina's teasing expression when she'd first walked into the shop and felt a return of the pleasure he'd felt at that moment.

What the hell was up with that? he wondered. Liking her wasn't one of his rules. Wanting more was even worse. He knew the danger inherent in the situation…the betrayal that would follow. It always had. No woman was to be trusted.

But for the first time in years he found himself wanting to break his own rules. To see if maybe, possibly, Marina was different, even though he knew she couldn't ever be.

Marina fingered the incredibly soft fabric of the wedding gown. Except for the basics, like cotton versus leather, she knew nothing about material. Only that whatever this one was, she wanted it in her life always!

Christie came into the dressing room and smiled. "You look beautiful."

Marina grinned. "I know you say that to all the brides, but right now, I don't care. I feel amazing. I love how this dress feels and moves."

Christie fastened the buttons Marina couldn't reach, then held open the dressing room door. "Come see how you look."

Marina had come in wearing jeans and a T-shirt, feeling frazzled, rushed and weird about seeing Todd again. But dressed in this flowing confection of a dress, she felt beautiful and girly and like a princess. Even the borrowed high heels, compliments of the salon, had fit.

She stepped in front of a three-way mirror and gasped. The dress was perfection.

The fitted, strapless bodice clung to her and made her look impressively chesty. At the waist, the dress cascaded down to the floor in layers and layers of fabric, each row shaped and draping like a flower petal, including the three or four foot train.

There was a hint of pearl in the fabric and it made her skin glow. The style would hide Julie's pregnancy, but was still elegant and to-die-for.

"Wow."

She glanced up and met Todd's gaze in the mirror. She smiled and spun in a slow circle.

"You like?" she asked.

She couldn't tell what he was thinking but she definitely liked the way he had to swallow before speaking.

"Incredible. Both the woman and the dress."

Man, did he have all the good lines, she thought, feeling herself react to his words and his presence.

Christie moved in and began tugging on the dress. "The style is flattering to many body types, although if your sister is built like you, then this should work perfectly. She needs one that's ready to go and this one is available. We'll clean it and get it altered right before the wedding. Can you move in it all right?"

Marina took a couple of steps. The dress swayed gracefully. "It's so fabulous."

"Good," Christie said. "Now let me put up the train and we'll see if you can dance in it."

Dance? Marina looked at Todd again. "Can you dance?"

"I'm practically a professional."

"Liar."

"Try me."

Christie looped the train, fastening buttons and hooks until there was an impressive bustle in the back. Then Todd stepped close and swept Marina into his arms.

She told herself none of this mattered, that it wasn't real. She was helping her sister, nothing more. Yet as they danced to an imaginary song, she felt something stir deep inside of herself. Something dangerous and wonderful and more than a little scary.

She made the mistake of looking into his eyes and found herself wanting to get lost there. His fingers tightened on hers. She shifted slightly closer. The layers of the beautiful dress kept her from feeling his body against hers, which was a serious drag.

"So lovely."

The comment came from an only slightly familiar voice. Marina looked up to see her grandma Ruth standing in the entrance to the bridal salon.

"Hello, my dears," the older woman said as she approached. "I know, I know, I'm not to meddle, but when Julie e-mailed that the two of you would be here this afternoon, I couldn't resist."

Todd released Marina and walked over to his aunt.

"Ruth," he said in obvious affection, then bent down and kissed her. "Watching Marina trying on wedding dresses isn't meddling."

"I'm sure Julie will be delighted to have one more opinion," Marina told her, then hugged and kissed her grandmother as she did her best not to feel or look guilty. She stepped back and turned in a slow circle. "What do you think?"

"That you're very beautiful and so is the dress." Ruth smiled at Todd. "Have you taken pictures?"

"Not yet. We were seeing if Julie could dance in the dress."

Was it Marina's imagination or had Ruth's eyebrows gone up just a little?

"An excellent idea," the older woman said. "I'm sure Julie appreciates your thoroughness."

Marina had the sudden thought that somehow her grandmother had guessed she and Todd had slept together. Heat burned on her cheeks as she tried to convince herself that wasn't possible. No one knew. Well, Willow and eventually Julie and maybe Ryan, but no one else.

Marina posed while Todd took several pictures, then she escaped back into the dressing room. She eased into a second gown, this one also strapless, but with a lace bodice and shirring across the waist. The skirt, a stunning, smooth silky material with an inset of embroidery and lace, fell in a sophisticated A-line that spilled into a train.

Ruth stepped into the dressing room. "Another winner. Julie's going to have a difficult time choosing. But that's the problem to have. Here, dear, let me help you with the buttons."

"Thanks. There are a lot of them."

Ruth stepped behind her and began fastening the cloth-covered buttons. "You and Todd looked very special together, dancing. While I always hoped one of you girls would fall for him, I'll admit I thought it was little more than the dreams of an old woman."

Panic welled up inside of Marina. "You're not old," she said by way of a very pitiful distraction.

"Thank you, dear, but that's not the point. I offered you and your sisters the money as a way to spur competition, but I see now I only needed to let nature take its course."

Marina's mouth opened, then closed. Her brain froze and she had no idea what to say.

"We're not a couple," she managed to say at last. "Seriously. We're barely friends. Semifriends, really. Acquaintances. We're helping with the wedding and that's all. We haven't even had our first date yet. That's not until the wedding."

Ruth finished with the buttons and stepped out in front of Marina. "Apparently a date isn't required. You look very beautiful."

Marina muttered something unintelligible, then hurried out of the dressing room as fast as she could on borrowed three-inch heels. Instead of stepping in front of the massive mirror, she hurried to Todd's side and grabbed his arm.

"She knows. My grandmother, your aunt, knows. She knows we had sex and I'm telling you right now, I can't stand it. I'm totally humiliated and you need to be, too."

Todd looked unconcerned. "She doesn't know. She can't."

"Want to bet?"

Ruth stepped out of the dressing room and Marina moved in front of the mirror. They discussed the dress like rational adults and she did her best to keep from blushing. She even managed a smile while Todd was taking pictures.

"I'll send these to Julie," he said.

"Great. I think she'll really love them."

Which all sounded normal, but what she was thinking was more along the lines of *get me out of here.*

Todd obviously didn't believe her, because he continued to joke with Ruth, right up until his aunt said, "I suppose a double wedding is out of the question."

Todd looked at Marina, then back at his aunt. "You mean Willow and Kane?"

"No, dear. You and Marina. There's obviously chemistry. Of course a relationship requires more than that, but passion is wonderful. I had it with your uncle every day of our marriage." She gave a little laugh. "Well, not *every* day, but most of them."

Marina resisted the need to cover her ears and hum loudly so she wouldn't hear anymore. Todd swallowed hard and muttered, "There's an image I'll never get out of my head."

Ruth sighed. "You young people. Never wanting to know about the older generation. You should be happy to know your uncle and I had a wonderful marriage all those years."

"I'm thrilled," Todd told her. "Details not required."

Ruth smiled. "That's all right. I've waited a long time for you to find the right girl and now you have."

Marina swept past him and headed for the dressing room. He followed on her heels.

"I told you," she said as she presented him with her back so he could unfasten the buttons. "But no. You wouldn't listen. You knew best. My *grandmother* knows we had sex. Do you know how humiliating that is?"

"It's worse for me. You never met my uncle, but I knew him all my life. Now I have a picture of the two of them…"

Marina spun to face him. "You're not taking this seriously enough. Ruth knows. She's talking about double weddings. She might tell my mother. I do not want to have a conversation about my sex life with my mother."

He touched her cheek. "Then don't. Look, telling Ruth wouldn't be my first choice, but she guessed. So what? We know what we want and don't want from each other. It's no big deal."

Apparently not for him, she thought bitterly, wondering if maybe he was right. If maybe she was overreacting.

Ruth stepped into the dressing room. "I have to leave, so you two enjoy yourselves. I hope it all works out. Truly I do. Not just because of what I want, but because all that money will really make a difference for your family, Marina. Sweet Willow can buy her nursery at last."

Then Ruth was gone, but Marina barely noticed. Instead her attention was riveted on Todd's face—on the way his features tightened and the distance she saw in his eyes.

He physically took a step back from her. "I'll leave you to get changed."

Then she was alone in the dressing room. Alone and angry and confused.

Why had Ruth had to mention the money like that? For a woman who was so set on getting them together, she'd picked the one way guaranteed to keep them apart. If Todd had a button, it was women wanting him for his money.

She wanted to stamp her foot in frustration. Talk

about unfair. She wasn't the least bit interested in his millions or billions or however much it was. The bet about marrying him was a joke. He had to know that.

Except why would he? Given his past, he would think the worst because the worst had always been true.

"It doesn't matter," she told herself as she stepped out of the dress. "We don't have a real relationship. We're just friends."

Friends who slept together.

But sex wasn't love and there was no way she was falling for him, so what did it matter that he thought badly of her?

Yet somehow it did matter and when she left the bridal salon a few minutes later, it was with a tightness in her chest and a sick feeling in her stomach.

To: Marina_Nelson@mynetwork.LA.com
From: Julie_Nelson@SGC.usa

Let me just say, for the record, that I'm stunned that you would sleep with Todd Aston the Third and not tell me. Even worse, I had to hear about it from my GRANDMOTHER! You slept with Todd? You slept with TODD? While I'm out of the country and we're so many time zones apart that I'll never hear the details?

I know you're telling Willow everything. I hate being left out. In time I'll forgive you, but know for now the sisterly bonds between us are stretched to the limit.

To: Julie_Nelson@SGC.usa
From: Marina_Nelson@mynetwork.LA.com

When did you become such a drama queen? The sisterly bonds? Someone's getting just a little too carried away by all this.

I'm sorry you had to find out from Grandma Ruth. I was going to tell you myself, but I didn't want to put that kind of information in e-mail. Obviously I'm the only one who worries about that sort of thing.

It was one time, or at least one night. It happened by accident. I'll explain the details later. They're actually kind of funny. But the point is, we're not a couple. We're friends who happened to sleep together and we have no plans for it to happen again.

To: Marina_Nelson@mynetwork.LA.com
From: Julie_Nelson@SGC.usa

That's it? That's all I get? How pathetic. I want details. And FYI...people don't accidentally sleep together. It's a conscious act/decision. You're not fooling me here, kid. So what's really going on?

Marina stared at the e-mail before answering. What *was* going on with her and Todd?

To: Julie_Nelson@SGC.usa
From: Marina_Nelson@mynetwork.LA.com

We're just friends. I swear. I like him, which I never thought would happen, but liking isn't anything more. Yes, we slept together, but there won't be a repeat performance and after this wedding is planned, we'll see each other at family events a few times a year and that's all. He's not the one. He's just a guy.

A special guy, she admitted to herself as she sent off the e-mail. But still, just a guy.

"I'm running late," Belinda yelled as Todd stepped into her photography studio. "Have a seat and I'll be with you in a bit."

He smiled at the receptionist, then made his way back to the large open space where she did most of her work.

Belinda, a petite redhead who dressed like a gypsy, stood in front of a camera and stared at the adorably dressed twins sitting on a bale of hay.

The identical little girls wore pink and white dresses and their dark hair had been carefully curled and styled.

"Okay—heads together," Belinda said with a grin, "but no bumping. Just touching at the top."

The girls complied.

"Now think about Christmas morning. What it's like to be awake but know it's too early to go downstairs. Remember how excited you feel. There are so many presents and soon you'll get to rip open that shiny paper and see what you got. It's so fun, but you have to wait. Think about that."

Both girls smiled, their eyes bright, their faces alive with anticipation.

Belinda snapped several pictures.

"She's good."

He turned and saw Marina had walked into the studio.

Their last meeting had turned awkward, thanks to Aunt Ruth. He waited for some feeling of discomfort, or a need to be anywhere but here. Instead anticipation swept through him and made him want to pull her close.

"The best," he said. "How are you?"

"Good. Busy with classes, but that's fun." She looked at the twins. "Adorable little girls."

"I agree."

"Really? You want kids?"

"Sure. A lot. I've always wanted my own baseball team."

She winced. "That's too many. But three or four would be a nice number. How do you plan to get these kids?"

He glanced at her. "I have no problem with having a family. It's having a wife I object to."

"So you'll adopt?"

Her eyes were the color of the sky. A perfect shade of blue. He liked how he could read her moods and how she wasn't intimidated by him. When this was over, maybe they could stay friends…assuming he got his burning need to make love with her again out of his system.

"Adoption is a possibility," he said. "But I would like a couple of biological kids to carry on the family name."

"Inherit the family money," she teased.

"That, too."

"So what will you do? Hire someone to carry the kids? Rent a womb, so to speak?"

He shrugged. "Maybe. It's an option."

Marina's eyes widened and her mouth dropped open. "I was kidding."

"I'm not. Everything is for sale."

"No offense, but that's really icky."

"Why? Surrogate mothers aren't uncommon. I'd have to be careful."

"Sure. What was I thinking?" She folded her arms over her chest. "It's a complicated choice. After all, the biological mother contributes fifty percent of the gene pool. Plus some scientific studies suggest intelligence is inherited through the mother."

"Which explains why a lot of successful guys who are more concerned about a beautiful woman than one with brains or character end up with disappointing children."

Disapproval radiated from her like fog. It surrounded him, trying to chill him, but he was unmoved. It was his life and he could damn well do what he wanted. If that meant kids without a wife, then that was his choice.

"You sound really cold-blooded," she told him.

"I'm being practical."

She drew in a breath, then released it. "Given your past, I understand your reluctance to trust anyone, but there's still a part of me that says you *can* have it all. You can fall in love, get married and have your kids the old-fashioned way. No contracts required."

"Is that what you want?" he asked.

"Sure. There's something wonderful about being a part of a family."

"You don't seem to be in a hurry to find Mr. Right."

Marina nodded. "I know I have my issues, but I'm willing to take a step of faith."

"Cheap talk."

"I'll get there. Eventually."

Would she? He doubted it. They might be very different, but they both had a fundamental lack of trust when it came to love. She was afraid of losing herself, the way her mother had, and he was determined to be more than a meal ticket.

"It takes faith," she told him. "One day I'll find someone who makes the leap worthwhile and then I'll jump."

Todd looked skeptical. "I hope he's there to catch you."

The photographer finished up with the children, then came over and hugged Todd, then introduced herself to Marina.

"I've never been hired from China before," the older woman said with an easy grin. "This could be fun."

"We'll e-mail Julie and Ryan some samples, if that's all right with you," Todd told her. "Marina and I will pick out a few."

"Sure. Great. I have my albums over here. I'll show you a big selection, then point out which ones are available to be sent digitally."

Marina watched the easy rapport between Belinda and Todd. "How did you two meet?" she asked.

Todd groaned, but Belinda laughed. Then she patted him on the cheek.

"Todd's parents hired me to take his picture for his sixteenth birthday. It was all very formal and solemn."

"So humiliating," Todd muttered.

Marina grinned. "That portrait wouldn't be in the sample albums, would it?"

Belinda shook her head. "He'd kill me if I put it

there, but maybe I can scan one of the proofs and send you a copy."

Marina leaned close to Todd and rested her head on his shoulder. "I would love that."

"You send it and I'll never forgive you," Todd told Belinda.

"Of course you will."

They spent the next half hour going over Belinda's samples. Her pictures were incredible. Romantic without being mushy, clear, artistic, yet timeless.

"She captures personalities," Marina said as she pointed at a wedding picture. "Look at the bride's smile. You can tell she's kind of wacky but fun."

"Yeah and he's crazy about her."

Looking at the happy couples made Marina feel a little empty. She wanted what they had—love and trust. Someone she could count on, no matter what. But this day wasn't about her.

"Any of these would be great," she said. "Let's just give Belinda Julie and Ryan's e-mail address and she can send whatever she wants. They're going to love her work."

They returned to her studio to tell her.

"Sure, I'll send a big selection," Belinda told them. "But before you go, let me snap a couple of pictures of you two. Having a familiar subject can be really helpful."

Todd looked at Marina who shrugged.

"I have a few minutes," she said, not exactly sure what Belinda was talking about.

"Good. I'm all set up for my next appointment. That will make this go quickly."

Belinda pointed at a muted backdrop done in blues and grays. There were lights all around and a camera in front of the backdrop.

"Stand in the middle," Belinda told him. "Close together. Let's try a traditional pose. Todd, put your arms around her waist. Marina, put your hands on top of his."

They did as they were told. Marina did her best to ignore the heat of Todd's body and the way his nearness made her thighs tremble. The longer he held her, the more she ached for him.

"Big smiles," Belinda said. "Come on, don't make me do the Christmas morning speech a second time today. It gets old. Think about something great. I know. The last time you had sex."

Involuntarily she glanced up at him only to find him looking down at her. She remembered everything about them being together that night. His touch, his laughter, the way he'd made her respond in ways she hadn't thought possible.

"Perfect," Belinda called. "Keep looking like that. Okay, now think of something funny—like Todd in a chicken costume, complete with a big chicken tail."

Marina felt her mouth twitch as she got the image in her mind. Then she started to laugh.

"Gee, thanks," he told her.

"You'd make a great chicken."

"My life is complete."

Marina was still laughing when Belinda told them they were done.

"I'll e-mail these pictures to Julie and Ryan, as well,"

she said. "I'm holding the date, so if you could let me know in the next week or so, that would be perfect."

"Will do," Todd promised.

"Thanks for everything," Marina told her. "You're amazing."

"Words I live to hear."

Marina followed Todd outside.

"We're still on for the wedding this Saturday, right?" he asked as they stopped by her car.

"You mean the wedding we're crashing? I'm braced."

"We're there to hear the orchestra. That's not crashing. We won't eat anything. It will be fine."

"I've never crashed a wedding before," she said. "That will make this very special."

"You'll like it."

She waved, then climbed into her car. He did the same and drove away first. But before she started her engine, she thought about what he'd said about having kids without a woman in his life. While she admired his desire to have a family, she was also sad at how he was limiting himself by refusing to trust anyone.

Ironically they were opposite sides of the same issue. He trusted himself, but no one else. She trusted everyone *but* herself. They both needed to take a leap of faith, but could they? And if they didn't, would they ever find their heart's desire?

Nine

Late Saturday afternoon Todd drove through Westwood toward UCLA. Marina had called earlier and asked him to pick her up on campus, instead of at her place, for their appointment to listen to the orchestra. She'd given him directions to one of the frat houses.

Now he found the correct street and turned right, then looked for the address. He spotted Marina before he saw the house. She stood on the lawn with a tall good-looking guy and they were gesturing at each other.

As he watched, the guy pulled Marina close and hugged her. She laughed and kissed his cheek.

Something dark and cold coiled low in his belly. He narrowed his gaze as Marina spoke using sign language. She obviously knew the other guy really well. But what the hell were they talking about?

They continued to gesture rapidly, then Marina turned, saw him and waved. The guy looked at him, hugged her again and turned back to the house.

As she walked toward his car, Todd was torn between being unreasonably pissed off and admiring the way her dress outlined her curves. He'd only ever seen her in casual clothes, so the high-heeled sandals, dangling earrings and upswept hair were a change.

"I'm ready for my night of crime," she said as she opened the passenger door and lowered herself onto the seat. "I thought about bringing masks so no one would recognize us, but then I was afraid we'd really stand out."

He ignored the humor and stared at the big house. "You date frat boys?"

"Date? Uh, no. That was David, one of the people I sign for. He's a senior, he has a hot date and his car died a couple of days ago, so I'm loaning him mine. Normally I wouldn't, but he's planning on proposing, so that seemed like a good cause to support."

He turned his attention to her and saw a combination of humor and exasperation in her eyes.

"I just wondered," he said defensively. "Frat guys have a reputation."

"Sure. That was the only reason for going all primitive on me."

"Primitive? Not my style."

Not ever. That would require jealousy and jealousy implied caring. While he liked Marina, theirs was a friendship.

"You're weird, Todd," she murmured. "You know that?"

"Not weird. Charming, handsome, sexy, mysterious."

She eyed him. "I'll give you complicated, but nothing else."

"You just don't want to admit how much you're attracted to me."

"As if."

But as she spoke, her gaze lingered on his mouth. He felt a rush of heat and need that had him shifting uncomfortably on the seat.

He pulled into traffic. "The reception is in Beverly Hills," he said. "We'll go in, smile politely, offer congratulations, listen to the music, then leave."

"Whatever you suggest," she told him. "You're the professional criminal. This will be my first time."

"We're just going to listen to music, that's not against the law."

"Criminals always have an excuse. Does Ryan know about your lawless ways? You guys are business partners—he should probably be protecting his assets. Next thing you know, you'll be pilfering."

He deliberately kept his expression stern. "I do not pilfer."

"Sure you don't. You're practically sainted. If your aunt Ruth could see you now."

Speaking of Aunt Ruth. "Did she call you?"

Marina looked at him. "My grandmother? No. Was she going to?"

So he'd been the only one. "No. Don't worry about it."

"You can't just bring up something like that and then drop it. What happened?"

"She's called me a couple of times since she dropped by the bridal place. There were a few unsubtle hints about us taking things to the next level."

Marina winced. "She wasn't talking about us sleeping together again, I'm guessing."

"Not exactly." Although his aunt had mentioned the whole "passion" issue several times, taking the conversation to a place Todd never wanted to go again.

"You're probably not going to think this is good news, but she also blabbed to Julie, who probably told Ryan."

He glanced at her. "Your grandmother told your sister we had sex?"

"Oh, yeah. I had a couple of very shouty e-mails from Julie. She's afraid she's missing out."

And he wanted a family why?

"What did you tell her?" he asked.

"That I'd share all the details when she got back." She smiled at him. "We're very close."

He had a feeling she was kidding. Or maybe that was wishful thinking on his part. Women did talk and he had no idea what they said to each other. Like every other normal guy on the planet, he didn't *want* to know.

"I'm sorry Ruth is being a pain," he said. "Can you ignore her or should I say something?"

"As I'm not the one she's calling, ignoring works for me. Are you going to have problems ignoring her?"

"No." He loved Ruth, but she didn't get to tell him

what to do. He knew she wanted him married and that wasn't happening.

"That sex thing was probably a mistake," Marina said quietly. "It's good we're never doing it again."

He thought about how great they'd been together. How much he'd enjoyed pleasing her, tasting her and touching her. How easily they'd talked and laughed. How much he still wanted her.

"I couldn't agree more," he said firmly.

The hotel was like something out of a movie, Marina thought as she and Todd strolled down wide, well decorated hallways to the ballroom overlooking the private garden.

They managed to slip inside without anyone asking them questions or accusing them of being there without an invitation, although she felt as if everyone in the room knew they were imposter guests.

"Relax," Todd said as he slipped an arm around her waist. "There have to be at least three hundred people here. No one will notice us."

"Okay, but no eating or drinking. We probably shouldn't even sit down and take a real guest's place."

He smiled a her. "You're not much of a rule-breaker, are you?"

"Only under very specific circumstances. Like the no more than four items in a dressing room rule. That one I'm good to break."

They circled the ballroom, avoiding the tables clustered at one end and staying toward the dance floor. A waiter came by and offered some kind of puff pastry treat. Todd reached for it, but she pushed his hand away.

"We're not supposed to eat," she told him, her voice low and insistent.

He chuckled. "You're making this too much fun."

"We're not here to have fun. This is serious. Okay, they're setting up to play. This is good. We can listen, then leave."

"Coward."

"I'm ignoring you." She watched the small orchestra seat themselves. "You're right—there aren't too many of them. So what are you thinking? The alcove in Grandma Ruth's ballroom?"

"Or that space between the pillars. The sound would be better coming from there."

"Good point. I just wish they'd start."

A well-dressed older couple moved toward them.

"Kitty and Jason Sampson," the woman said as she reached for Marina's hand. "How good of you to come."

Marina froze. They were caught!

But Todd smiled smoothly and responded. "Everything is lovely. Very impressive. Such a happy day."

Kitty beamed. "Isn't it? We're so delighted."

"Of course you are," Todd told her.

Jason leaned down and kissed Marina's cheek, then slapped Todd on the shoulder. "Thanks so much for joining us today. It means a lot."

"We wouldn't have missed this for anything."

The Sampsons left.

Marina waited until they were out of earshot, then

covered her face. "We're going to hell. I can hear them etching our names on our chairs."

"We get chairs in hell?"

She glared at him. "You know what I mean."

"Nothing happened. We were polite and gracious. In five minutes, Kitty and Jason won't remember us. Come on. You can handle this. Look, the orchestra is about to start."

"Maybe. It's not that I *want* to feel guilty," she began.

"Then don't. Come on. We'll lurk in the corner and stay out of trouble."

As he spoke, he grabbed her hand and pulled her to the side of the room. While his touch was totally casual, her body responded as if he'd just ripped off her dress and thrown her down on a table. Make that a bed…in a very private place, because her reaction was anything but outrage.

She melted from the inside out. The need to be with him nearly overwhelmed her, which was five kinds of crazy. They'd only been together that one night. Even though it had been a great time, it shouldn't have made that much of an impact on her.

Still, she found herself wanting to be with him, but not just in a sexual way. She wanted to be in his arms, talking and laughing. Watching him smile, listening to his voice and hearing his unique perspective on the world. She wanted…more.

"Better?" he asked as they stopped in a corner of the room, close to the orchestra but out of the flow of guest traffic. "We're practically acting like spies, hiding behind this potted tree." He fingered a leaf. "Do you know what this is?"

"Not a clue. That's Willow's area of expertise. It looks real, though." She allowed herself to relax. "Yes, this is much better. I can feel my guilt easing."

"Excellent."

He smiled at her. The answering quiver deep inside had something to do about his proximity, but not totally. Some of her reaction was just about him.

What was up with that?

Before she could figure out an answer, a waiter stopped by and offered them each a glass of champagne.

"The bride and groom will be here in a few minutes," he said. "This is for the toast."

Marina pulled free of Todd and tucked both her hands behind her back. "We can't," she whispered.

Todd took the two glasses and thanked the waiter. When the two of them were alone again, he offered one of the glasses.

"We have to," he told her. "Not toasting the bride and groom would be tacky and rude."

She bit her lower lip. "This is a very slippery slope. Okay, we'll raise our glasses, but we can't drink."

He grinned. "Right, because after we put the glasses down, someone else will gladly finish off the contents? Face it, kid. You're in this for a glass of champagne."

Marina sighed. "Maybe we can find out Kitty and Jason's favorite charity and make a donation."

"You're such a lightweight," he told her as he put his

arm around her waist and pulled her close. "I like that about you."

The quiver intensified.

A man who was probably the best man walked up to the microphone in front of the orchestra. "Ladies and gentlemen, will you please join me in welcoming Mr. and Mrs. Alex Sampson."

Everyone cheered as the bride and groom entered the room.

"A toast," the best man continued. "To a couple who defines love. May each day be better than the one before."

He raised his glass. The guests all did the same. Marina winced, then raised hers and took a tiny sip of the illicit champagne.

Todd leaned close. "Dom Pérignon."

"Really?" She took another sip. It was really nice. And honestly, if the families could afford that high-end champagne for the crowd, then maybe two stolen drinks weren't that big a deal.

"I'll accept the champagne," she murmured, "but we're not staying for dinner."

"Absolutely not. Just for one dance."

The orchestra began to play. The bride and groom stepped onto the dance floor and moved together.

Marina ignored them and instead focused on the smooth music. It was definitely more elegant than a DJ, but not really stuffy.

"Good choice," she told him. "I like the orchestra. Now let's go."

"Not so fast." He took her glass from her and set it

on a small table next to them. Then he led her toward the dance floor.

"What?" She tried digging in her heels, but it was a hardwood floor and that was not going to happen. "We can't dance."

"Why not? Everyone else is."

Sure enough several of the guests had moved into the center of the room and had joined the bride and groom. Marina decided that one dance wouldn't hurt. It wasn't as if they were eating anything. So she relaxed into Todd's arms and found out that he had yet another talent she'd never considered. This was even better than their spin around the bridal shop dressing rooms.

"You're good," she said after he'd twirled her around and then neatly caught her. "Lessons?"

"Years of them."

He pulled her close as the music slowed in tempo.

She rested her head on his shoulder. He had one of his hands on the small of her back. They pressed together in a way that was both sensual and enticing.

"We'll leave after this song," he said, speaking directly into her ear.

"Okay."

"You want to get something to eat?"

"Sure."

"Takeout?"

She raised her head and stared at him. Passion turned his eyes to the color of night.

He touched a finger to her mouth. "I know what

you're going to say," he told her softly. "That we agreed we couldn't do this again. That it would be a mistake for a lot of reasons. If that's what you want, I won't ask again. I've spent the past week telling myself why I have to let this go, but I can't. I want you, Marina."

They were words that would have cracked a wall a whole lot tougher than hers. "You had me at 'takeout,'" she whispered. "Let's go."

They went to his place because it was closer. The seventeen-minute drive seem to last forever, possibly because Todd spent much of the time nibbling on her fingers. The combination of teeth and tongue and lips was amazingly arousing. More than once she'd been tempted to tell him to pull over and they could just do it in the car.

She held back because it was daylight, she wasn't into being an exhibitionist and because a night in jail wasn't on her to-do list for that day. Of course Todd hadn't been, either, but she did try to be flexible when offered a wonderful opportunity.

They reached his house and piled out of the car. He opened the front door, pulled her inside, slammed the door shut behind her, flipped the lock and dragged her into his arms.

She went willingly, already anticipating the heat of his kiss.

He didn't disappoint. His mouth was firm and hungry and he tasted like great champagne. Even as they touched and strained and did everything they could to climb inside each other, he swept his tongue into her mouth and began that passionate dance.

He circled her, teasing, exciting. She met him with moves of her own and then closed her lips around his tongue and sucked gently. He groaned. She felt his hardness press against her belly. She was already wet and swollen. Her breasts ached. Deep inside she clenched in anticipation of what was to come.

He pulled back slightly and nudged her backward. "Bed," he murmured against her neck. "Up. Go."

The instructions would have been funny if she hadn't been so eager. She forced herself to break free of his erotic kisses and hurried toward the stairs.

Before climbing, she kicked off her shoes. He did the same.

Halfway up, they stopped and kissed again. As he stirred her soul, he reached for her zipper and pulled. She pushed off his suit jacket, then began to loosen his tie. He pulled his shirt free.

While she wasn't usually overly aggressive in bed, Marina didn't think of herself as shy. So she took a step back, shrugged out of the dress and let it fall to her feet.

Underneath she wore a lavender lace bra and matching panties. Todd's breath caught audibly. She reached behind herself, unfastened her bra, let that fall, as well, then turned and ran up the stairs.

It took him a second to follow, but when he did, he caught up quickly. At the second-floor landing, he lunged for her, grabbing her and pulling her to a stop. She laughed and spun toward him.

He was standing a step lower. He tore off his tie, unfastened his shirt and tossed it down, then leaned in and took her right nipple into his mouth.

He sucked and licked and circled until she could barely keep standing. She had to hold on to his shoulders and even so, her legs shook. The deep tugs caused an answering response low in her belly.

When he moved to her other breast, she felt herself starting to lose her balance. He must have sensed it, too, because he put his arms around her waist and lowered her to the top of the carpeted stairs.

She went willingly, wrapping her arms around him and enjoying the feel of his hot skin.

He raised his head. "We *will* make it to bed," he told her.

"I'm in favor of that plan."

He smiled. "But first…"

He reached for her panties and pulled them off in one quick movement. Then he shifted down a couple of stairs, urged her to part her legs and kissed her between them.

The intimate caress took her breath away. She had to brace herself on her arms to keep from falling over and even that wasn't enough. Not with her already shaking in need.

He was as good as she remembered. Exploring, circling, stroking, licking, driving her to the edge, only to back off just enough to make her whimper.

Over and over he touched her with his tongue and his lips. He drew her higher and higher, pushing her forward, then letting her fall back. He made her pant. He nearly made her scream.

She lost track of the world and everything in it. There was only this moment and this man and what he was doing to her.

Her muscles clenched tighter and tighter. She could feel herself swelling, pushing close. Her orgasm was tantalizingly out of reach. Close, so close, but not yet there.

Then he began to flick his tongue over her center in an age-old rhythm. At the same time he inserted first one finger, then two. He filled her, pushing up as if to caress her from the inside, as well.

One stroke, two…and then she was lost.

Her release claimed her with an unexpected force. She lost control and cried out. She came again and again, riding the magic of his tongue, his fingers, his whole body. Pleasure claimed her, marked her, then eased her back into reality.

When she finally surfaced, he sat next to her, smiling.

She sat up and sighed. "Go ahead. Gloat. You earned it."

"I will in a second. Meet me in my bed, okay?" He stood.

"Where are you going?"

"It's a surprise."

He hurried down the stairs. She watched him go, still basking, then realized she was sitting naked on his stairs and she had no idea if this was housekeeper day or not. Which got her moving.

She found her way to his large bedroom and had

barely pulled back the covers when he walked into the room carrying two champagne flutes and a bottle of Dom Pérignon.

She laughed. "You did say you always had some on hand."

"I did."

While he opened the bottle, she climbed into bed. He poured them each a glass, took off the rest of his clothes and joined her.

"To unexpected surprises," he said, touching his flute to hers. "You more than qualify."

She opened her mouth, then closed it. She couldn't speak, couldn't move, could barely breathe. It was as if she'd been flash-frozen.

And then she knew why. Looking at Todd, at his handsome and now familiar face, listening to his voice, sitting in his bed after he'd just taken her on an amazingly sensual journey, she suddenly realized what she'd been ignoring all along.

He was perfect.

Well, not perfect. The man had flaws. But he was everything she'd ever been looking for. Caring, warm, smart, into family, affectionate, challenging, determined and not the least bit intimidated by her big brain.

Perfect.

And somewhere along the way, she'd fallen in love with him.

Ten

A night of incredible lovemaking managed to distract Marina from her unexpected realization. The next morning she ducked out early, claiming a very legitimate meeting with Willow. She was terrified that she wouldn't be able to keep acting normally around Todd. How could she when her brain was practically rotating from shock?

In love with Todd? How? When? She wasn't supposed to fall in love with anyone, and should the unexpected happen, did it have to be with a man who would never, ever, under any circumstances, trust a woman?

She made her way home where she showered and changed. As promised, David had dropped off her car in the night and left the keys in a planter by her front door. She collected them on her way out and drove to the bridal salon where she and Willow would pick out a couple of bridesmaid dresses to e-mail Julie.

"Nothing yucky," Willow said after Marina pulled in next to her in the salon parking lot and climbed out of her car. "Nothing too frilly, and nothing you have to be tall to look good in. I don't know if you've noticed, but I'm not tall."

Marina pretended surprise. "Since when?"

"Very funny. You know what I mean. So many clothes look fabulous if you're as tall as a giraffe but the rest of us mortals end up looking dumpy. I refuse to be dumpy at my sister's wedding."

Marina grinned. "No dumpy dresses, I promise."

"You'd better. I don't want to be outvoted by the two tall sisters."

"Trust is an important part of our relationship."

Willow narrowed her gaze. "I don't trust anyone with legs as long as yours." They walked into the salon. "I saw the wedding gown pictures. It looks great."

"I'm sure Christie will bring out the dress Julie picked," Marina said. "It's strapless, so I was thinking we could go that way, or do spaghetti straps. Nothing long."

Willow rolled her eyes. "Thank goodness. I have so many long dresses from other weddings. And the bride always said 'you can take it up.' Right. Because there are so many places I can wear a lime-green flocked short dress. Speaking of green, I know that's one of the colors, but come on. We're blond. We're doing shades of rose, aren't we?"

"Oh, yeah. Green reminds me too much of recent attack of food poisoning. I'm not wearing it."

"See. This is how it should be," Willow told her. "Sisterly solidarity."

Christie walked toward them. "Morning ladies. You must be Willow. I'm Christie."

They shook hands.

"Ready to try on bridesmaid dresses?" Christie asked. "I've been e-mailing Julie and she has a few suggestions."

Marina looked at Willow who groaned.

"Good suggestions or bad suggestions?" Willow asked, her voice small.

Christie smiled. "Good ones. I think you'll be pleased. Oh, Willow, did you want me to bring out Julie's dress so you can see it?"

"If you don't mind, that would be great."

"I'm happy to." Christie looked at Marina. "Maybe we can do the preliminary fitting, if you have time this morning."

"I'm available."

"Excellent. Now if you two will come with me, I have the dresses Julie liked picked out."

They followed her to a room on the side that was filled with bridesmaid dress samples. Two dresses were displayed on the wall. One was strapless, fitted to the waist, then flared gently to the straight hem. There was an overlayer of some sheer fabric that was scalloped at the hem. The second dress was a slip style, with a little bit of lace at the bodice and tulip hem.

Willow fingered the material on the second dress and smiled. "I think both of these work. What do you think?"

Marina nodded. "Neither are scary. I give Julie points for that."

"Good." Christie pointed to a set of dressing rooms on the far wall. "There's one for each of you inside. Why don't you try them on. I'll be back in a few minutes."

"Which means Julie e-mailed our sizes," Willow murmured when they'd slipped into the dressing rooms. "Does her level of organization ever worry you?"

"Not too much." Marina pulled off her T-shirt and unfastened her jeans. "They have shoes here that we can try on. Just to see how the dresses look in heels."

The door to her dressing room opened. Willow stepped inside and closed the door behind her.

"Okay," she said flatly. "What's wrong?"

Marina stared at her. "Nothing. Why? I'm fine."

"You're not fine. You're..." She frowned. "I don't know. I can't put my finger on it, but fine isn't applying. Are you upset? Did something bad happen? Do you need Kane to kill someone?"

"While I appreciate the offer, and I'm sure he does, too, I'm good. Really."

Willow folded her arms over her chest. "I'm not leaving until you confess everything."

"There's nothing to..." Marina sighed. "I'd been so determined to act normal, too."

"You didn't quite make the goal." Willow's mouth twisted. "What happened? Is it Todd? Did he hurt you?"

"No. Of course not. He didn't do anything wrong. It's just…"

Willow moved closer and touched her arm. "You don't have to talk about it if you don't want to."

Marina managed a smile. "Oh, sure. Say that now. I just… We…" She swallowed. "I'm in love with him."

Willow continued to stare at her. "And?"

"And nothing. Isn't that enough? I'm in love with Todd Aston the Third. How crazy is that?"

Willow grinned, then hugged her. "Not crazy at all. It's great. You're in love. You're single, he's single. You're amazing, he might be someone the rest of the family can tolerate. What's the problem?"

Marina sank onto the bench in the room and covered her face with her hands. "I'm terrified. What if I'm just like Mom? What if I get lost? What if I let him treat me horribly and I pretend it's enough because it's better than being without him?"

Willow sank down next to her. "What if you don't?" she asked as she put her arm around Marina. "What if you're strong and grown-up and you just let yourself be happy?"

While she appreciated the support, happy didn't seem like much of an option. "He has issues."

Willow rolled her eyes. "Of course he does. All men do."

"His are complicated. He doesn't trust women. At all. Ever. No female trusting by the rich guy."

"Sounds simple to me," Willow said. "Fine. He doesn't trust. I'm sure other women have taught him that. But what have you ever done to make him not trust you? Nothing. So it may take some time and a little work, but you'll bring him around."

Marina wished it was that easy, but something in her gut told her that Todd wasn't going to be convinced by a lack of action on her part.

"Have you always been this optimistic?" she asked.

"I think so," Willow told her. "I'm the middle child. It's my job to see both sides of things. Although in this case, I'm only seeing yours. Have a little faith. I doubt your feelings are one-sided. You're pretty amazing. He's lucky to have you in his life."

"I don't think I'm the problem. He is and I don't know how to fix that."

"You don't have to. That's his job."

Marina looked at her sister. "I'm not like Mom, am I? Falling for a guy who can't commit?"

"You're nothing like Mom. You are your own person. Have a little faith in yourself."

Faith sounded easy enough, but Marina wasn't sure how to put it into play.

"You okay?" Willow asked.

Marina nodded. "We have dresses to try on."

A few minutes later they met by the large three-way mirror.

"This is not flattering," Willow grumbled as she tugged on the spaghetti straps of her dress. "The tulip hem thingy makes me look short."

"You are short," Marina teased. "But the dress isn't the right one. We both looked better in the strapless one. I hope Julie doesn't mind that the waist is so fitted."

Willow grinned. "You mean she'll be bitter because her tummy is growing? Hmmm. I hadn't thought of that. But it's okay. She can be bitter for a while. She's getting a baby." She smoothed the front of her dress. "After Kane and I get married, we're going to try for children right away. I'm really excited. I feel like I had my first taste of pregnancy the first couple of weeks I was on the pill."

"Bloated?" Marina asked sympathetically. "That's why I'm not on it. Plus, I felt yucky."

"Me, too. But the yucky part passed. Good things, too, because of the whole condom problem."

Marina stared at her. "What condom problem?"

"You know. That they're not a hundred percent. If used perfectly, in controlled studies, they're like ninety-seven percent effective. But in real world use, it's a lot lower than that."

Willow kept on talking, but Marina wasn't listening. Less effective? As in more chance of getting pregnant?

All she and Todd had used were condoms. She wasn't on anything else and he'd never asked. Not that there was a whole lot more he could have done, but still.

She touched her stomach and tried to relax. So they weren't a hundred percent. She and Todd had only made love a few times. Nothing could have happened. Not really. Could it?

Two and a half long hours later, Marina finally escaped the bridal shop. She'd had to suffer through the wedding gown fitting, which Willow had stayed for. In the end she, Marina, had gotten away only to drive to a drugstore and buy two different pregnancy tests. She was positive she was fine, but a little scientific evidence never hurt.

Now she counted out days on her calendar and had to admit that maybe she was a little late. Just by a couple of days, but still.

Her chest tightened until she found it hard to breathe. Pregnant? She couldn't be. Not that she didn't want kids, but not now. Not like this.

She remembered all the horror stories Todd had shared. If she were pregnant, he would think she was just like the other women in his life. He would never trust her.

Scared, shaking and terrified of the outcome, she opened both boxes and took the test. When the needed time has passed, she stared down at two plastic sticks and groaned.

One said she was pregnant, the other one didn't.

"Just so how my day is going," she said, fighting tears of frustration. "I have to know."

She grabbed the first of the boxes and dialed the 800 number for customer service.

"Hi," she said, when a woman answered. "I took one of your pregnancy tests a few minutes ago. I also took another brand. Your test says I'm not pregnant and theirs says I am. Who should I believe?"

"Oh, no," the other woman said. "That's not good. How late are you?"

"Just a couple of days."

"Okay, you have a couple of choices. You can buy more tests and see what they say, or you can wait. I know it's hard, but that would be my advice. Wait about a week and take the tests again. Your final option is to make an appointment with your doctor."

Marina thanked the woman and hung up. Going to her doctor wasn't an option. He was practically a friend of the family and her mother worked in his office. That was a little too close to home for this situation. She could find another doctor, but by the time they fit her in, at least a week would have passed anyway. Waiting and taking the tests again made the most sense.

But being sensible didn't ease the knot in her stomach to make her breathe any easier. Pregnant? Was it possible?

She was torn between the maternal thrill of a baby and the horror of knowing what Todd would think about her. That she'd tricked him.

Needing to talk to someone, she picked up the phone and called Willow.

Her sister's cell went right to voice mail, which meant Willow was probably with Kane and they were practicing for making babies of their own.

Restless and still needing to talk, Marina walked to her laptop and turned it on.

To: Julie_Nelson@SGC.usa
From: Marina_Nelson@mynetwork.LA.com

Hi. It's the middle of the day here, so I'm thinking it's the middle of the night there. Which is a serious drag because I really need to talk. Not that we will, and I don't want you to call. It's about a billion dollars a minute and I'll be in class most of tomorrow. It's just...

Okay—don't be drinking your morning coffee when you read this. I'm late. As in...late. So I got a couple of pregnancy tests and took them. One says I'm pregnant, one says I'm not. The lady at the company suggested I wait another week and retest, which really makes sense. Except wait a week to know? How is that possible?

I want kids. I really wouldn't mind being pregnant—except for Todd. He's not a trusting guy and while I don't blame him, I can't begin to imagine what he would say if I told him I was pregnant. He would think I was trying to manipulate him or trick him. It would be awful.

Even worse...and you can't tell anyone about any of this, but especially what I'm about to say. I think I'm in love with him.

Marina paused in her typing, then sighed.

No. That's wrong. I know I'm in love with him. I've been in love with him for a while now. Maybe from the beginning. I'm excited and scared. I mean, what if I'm like Mom? But what if I'm not? What if I can't be strong? So that's a good possibility. But this is Todd. Would he ever trust me enough to have a real relationship? Is he even interested in a real relationship? And if he could be, being pregnant will ruin everything.

So that's how my day is going. E-mail me back

when you can. I feel better now that we've "talked." Thanks for listening.

* * *

Marina didn't sleep much that night, which made her morning class on the physical aspects of Inorganic Chemistry class tough. She did her best to clear her mind of all that was currently going on in her life and pay attention to the lecture. She seemed to do okay, because Jason, one of her deaf students, only frowned at her twice.

When class ended, she made arrangements to meet him in the lab later that week, then walked toward her car. As she moved through the crowd of students, her mind swirled and dipped and raced in a hundred different directions.

What if she was pregnant? How would she tell Todd? What if she wasn't? Would she be sad?

She felt her emotions being ripped in two. She loved Todd and would be thrilled to be having a baby with him. But with his past, she doubted they could ever get past his inherent mistrust of all women, including her. So the most sensible thing to hope was that there was no baby. Except she couldn't quite bring herself to want that.

Sleep, she thought as she walked across the parking lot. She needed sleep.

What she got was a familiar expensive convertible pulling up next to her. The driver's window rolled down and a very angry-looking Todd stared at her.

"Get in," he said flatly. "We have to talk."

Eleven

He knew. She could read it in the coldness in his eyes.

Marina wasn't surprised. There was no way Julie wouldn't have told Ryan, and Ryan and Todd were as close as brothers.

"I'll follow you to your place," she said, knowing there was a very good chance that any conversation with Todd right now wasn't going to go well. Better to be able to leave and not have to wait for him to drive her anywhere.

He opened his mouth, but before she could speak, she added, "I'll follow you there. You should at least trust me that much."

"Why?" he asked bluntly. But he also closed the window and drove a few feet forward so she could back out her car.

Twenty minutes later she drove onto the familiar circular stone driveway in front of the massive house she'd actually grown to like. But as she climbed out her car, she felt an uncomfortable combination of apprehension and panic. Based on all that she knew about him, Todd wasn't going to handle any of this well.

They walked inside without saying anything. She figured that she should probably be the one to start the conversation, but she didn't know how. Nor did she know what he knew. Which might be a good place to start.

She followed Todd into his study and set her purse on one of the leather chairs in the book-lined space.

"Did Ryan give you a recap or just forward my mail?" she asked, suddenly remembering her confession of love. Surely Julie hadn't shared that with her fiancé.

"He gave me the facts." Todd's dark gaze dropped to her midsection. "That you think you're pregnant."

She couldn't figure out what he was thinking from his tone. So far, his body language seemed controlled enough, so she should be feeling better. Except she wasn't. There was a coldness, a bitterness, that seemed to steal all the warmth from the room. Despite the pleasant temperature, she found herself shivering.

"I don't know if I am," she said. "He told you about the two pregnancy tests?"

Todd moved behind his desk, then turned to face her. "Let me be clear. I've been manipulated by women far more experienced than you, Marina. You will not win this game."

She felt as if she'd been slapped. "I'm not playing a

game. How could I be? I'm not like that and you know it. You know *me,* Todd."

"Do I? You're the one who's in this for a million dollars."

She stared at him. "Don't be ridiculous. That's just a crazy idea of Ruth's."

"She offered to take the money off the table, but you told her no."

Coldness eased down her spine. "I was kidding. It was a joke."

Nothing in his expression hinted that he believed her. The walls seemed to close in a little.

She took a step toward him. "This is crazy. We've become friends. We've laughed together, we'd talked about our hopes and dreams. I'm not some manipulating bitch out for the money. Dammit, Todd, I didn't trap you. You wanted us to make love, too. You were a more than willing participant."

He opened a desk drawer and pulled out a pad of paper. "If you continue to claim to be pregnant, I'll want the condition confirmed by an independent test performed by a doctor of my choosing. I will be there for the test, as will my attorney."

"Claim to be pregnant?" she asked, her voice low and shaky. "I'm saying I don't know. How much more honest can I be?"

He ignored that, too.

"If you are pregnant, I want paternity determined by a DNA test upon birth. If I am the father, we'll have to negotiate some kind of custody arrangement." He stared at her. "I wouldn't count on winning that battle if I were you."

It was like being locked in a freezer. The chill made it nearly impossible to breathe.

She closed her eyes as she remembered his words about wanting children, but not a mother. Was that really his plan? To take her baby?

"This isn't about me," she told him. "None of this is. This is about your past. You're making me pay for what those other women did to you."

"Did my aunt offer to withdraw the million dollars?" he asked.

She couldn't win. He wouldn't let her. "Yes."

"Did you tell her to keep it on the table."

"Yes."

There was no point in explaining she'd been kidding. That she'd never imagined even liking him, let alone falling for him.

"It's like asking for the moon," she said, even as she knew she was wasting breath and energy. "Sure, I said I'd take it but it was like accepting an offer to raise the Titanic. It's not going to happen. The money isn't real."

She took another step toward him, although with a giant desk between them, it was a pretty useless gesture.

"I wanted to give my sister a great wedding," she said. "Just like you wanted to give that to Ryan. We had to work together. At first I didn't like you very much, but then we became friends and it was great. That's all, Todd. Don't make it ugly now."

"Give me one reason why I should trust you."

"You can't argue trust. It has to be earned over time. Tell me one thing I've done to violate your trust."

"I can give you a million of them. You getting pregnant only confirms what you wanted all along."

Horror swept through her. "It was a joke," she began, then stopped. What was the point?

She grabbed her purse and pulled out her cell phone. Ruth's number was in her address book. She hit Send.

"Hi, it's Marina," she said, when Ruth had answered. "I need to tell you I'm not interested in the million dollars. Whatever happens, I don't want it."

Her grandmother sighed. "You never did want it, dear. I knew that."

"Todd doesn't."

"Oh, yes. He can be stubborn. But he'll come around."

Marina stared at his stern expression, at the starkness in his eyes. "I'm not so sure about that."

"I know he seems like he's too much work, but he'll be worth it in the end. Have a little faith."

"I'll try." She hung up.

Faith. Was there enough of that in the world?

"It doesn't mean anything," he told her. "You know you can get even more money from me."

And then she got it. She couldn't win. That was the point.

"If it wasn't the pregnancy concern, it would have been something else," she said, more to herself than him. "You're determined to never trust me and people always find what they go looking for. If you expect the worst, you'll find it."

She drew in a breath. "Someday I'll appreciate the irony of this situation. I've been so worried about being like my mother. I've been terrified I'll lose myself in a man. I never stopped to think about the danger of falling for someone who couldn't love me back. In my head, I was the one with the big problem."

She shoved her cell phone into her jeans pocket and grabbed her purse. "But I'm not. I was willing to risk it with you. I was scared and worried, but still willing to take on that next step. I never stopped to think all my fears didn't matter. Because you're not willing."

His expression didn't change. She wasn't sure why she was explaining herself, except maybe for some kind of closure.

"The only way to convince you I'm not in it for the money is to not be pregnant and never see you again," she said. "I can't do anything about having or not having a baby, but I can get out of your life. If I really am pregnant, we'll work something out. Something fair. You're not going to simply take my child. If I'm not, then we only have to deal with each other at the wedding and then stay out of each other's lives."

She walked to the study door, then turned back. "I know you're scared, Todd. I'm scared, too. But after falling in love with you, I'm willing to face my fears. Maybe I'm not the one for you. Maybe you don't want to care about me, and that's fine. But if you never care about anyone, the bitches of the world win. They might not have you, but they've sure made sure no one else will, either. It's a hell of a way for you to live."

* * *

He waited until he heard the front door close before walking out of the study. The emptiness of the house pressed down on him, but was nothing when compared to the fury he felt at her betrayal. If there was one woman he was going to trust, it would have been Marina. Only she'd turned out to be just like the rest of them.

Pregnant, he thought grimly. Fine. If she wanted to play that game, he would play it right back. He would take the baby and start the family he'd always wanted. She would be compensated, but nothing else.

She was, he acknowledged, a good genetic candidate for his child's mother. Intelligent, healthy, determined. He would hire a nanny and be a father.

It was a plan and he always felt better when he had a plan. But not today. He had a hole in his chest and it burned.

He wanted to throw something. He wanted to put his fist through a wall. He wanted her not to be like them. He wanted to trust her.

Which he couldn't.

He might have given her a second chance if she'd confessed and then begged for his understanding. If she hadn't said she loved him. Because that was the biggest betrayal of all. To use the one thing he truly wanted to manipulate him. That he could never forgive.

Marina knew she would probably drown in her tears. They came and came, pouring down her face as sobs ripped through her body. The pain was more intense than anything she'd ever experienced. It was as if she'd been cut off from the very air she needed to survive. Only she didn't die. She just hurt and cried and prayed to feel better.

Willow held her and soothed her with soft sounds. Not words. There were no words.

"How do I stop loving him?" Marina asked, her throat raw, her body battered. "Tell me how."

"I don't know," Willow admitted softly. "But we'll figure out a way."

Nearly a week later, Todd walked into the florist to finalize the order for the flowers. While he wanted to make sure the wedding looked good for Ryan and Julie, most of his attention was on the fact that he was going to see Marina again.

He'd expected her to call and she hadn't. So what did that mean? She'd claimed to love him and then she'd disappeared. If she loved him, shouldn't she be trying to get him back?

He wanted her to be trying and it really pissed him off that she hadn't once been in touch with him. As he'd been the point of contact with the florist, he'd been forced to call Marina to set up their appointment. Even more annoying, he'd been disappointed when he'd gotten her machine.

He'd done the right thing—leaving a message rather than trying again later. But she hadn't phoned him back and now, as he stood surrounded by flowers, he found himself looking forward to seeing her again.

He knew he shouldn't. He knew she was screwing with him, but that didn't stop the anticipation from rising inside of him.

She walked in, right on time for their appointment.

Even as he held himself still and didn't say anything, his body reacted to her nearness. She was beautiful, in a stern, pale kind of way. His fingers itched to get lost in her long gold-blond hair. He ached to touched her all over, to listen to her voice, to hear her laugh. He wanted to lean in and inhale the scent of her body.

Damn. What was wrong with him? He knew better. Look at what she'd done.

Except what had she done? Thought she might be pregnant? As she'd pointed out, he'd been more than willing to sleep with her. They'd used protection, but it didn't always work. Weren't they equally to blame for what happened? Did he really believe that Marina was trying to trick him?

"I have a class in an hour," she told him. "So why don't you go head and make the final selection on the flowers?" She handed him a few printed out e-mails. "These are Julie's ideas for her bouquets. I'm sure Beatrice can come up with something beautiful."

"You're not staying?" he asked, knowing he sounded like an idiot. Oddly he'd counted on them spending the afternoon together.

"No. I can't miss class. I know the wedding is next week, but everything else is taken care of. Julie and Ryan will be back this weekend."

She glanced around, as if checking to make sure they were alone, then she lowered her voice. "The mixed message has been resolved. I'm not pregnant."

"You took the tests again?"

"I didn't have to."

There wasn't a baby. Nothing about her expression told him what she was thinking, but he was shocked to feel the ache of sadness sweep through him.

Sad? Why should he be sad? Because he'd secretly wanted a baby with Marina?

"I'm sure you're relieved," she told him. "I know I am. Not that I wouldn't have loved to have a baby. Just not with you."

Her words did what they were supposed to. They cut through him, wounding.

"Under the circumstances," he began.

She shook her head. "I'll accept you being upset. Anyone would be. I'll even accept that you have issues, but there is no excuse for what you said and how you treated me. You threatened to take my child. You accused me of lying deliberately for financial gain. You made judgments and decisions before you knew all the facts. You were wrong about me, Todd. So very wrong. I was never in it for the money."

She squared her shoulders. "The thing that hurts the most is that I think you knew you were wrong, too. I think you secretly did believe me, but you couldn't admit it. So you attacked. That's not something I can get over. I suppose the only bright spot in all of this is that I was wrong about you, too. I was wrong to think you were special. I was wrong to think you were the kind of man I could fall in love with."

And as she had before, she walked out and left him alone.

But this time was different. This time as she left, he realized the enormity of what he'd lost. That despite the pregnancy, his past, her worries and all that had happened between them, that he'd fallen in love with her.

But he realized it too late. As he'd once told her— what had happened was unforgivable.

Twelve

Twelve

Tuesday after work, Todd sorted through the mail. There was a large, stiff envelope with no return address on the bottom of the pile.

He opened it and removed several photographs. The pictures they'd taken at Belinda's studio. Samples, to send to Julie and Ryan. Apparently Belinda had decided to send him copies.

He pulled out the eight-by-ten pictures and studied them. Marina stood in his arms, staring up at him, her mouth curved in a smile. He stared down at her with an intensity that made him wonder what he'd been thinking.

There was an ease in their pose, and a connection. The camera had captured what he'd never allowed himself to see before—how he and Marina seemed to belong together.

There was something else in the pictures. Something in her blue eyes. Love.

He flipped through the six photographs, then carried them into his study and sat behind his desk. After turning on the lamp, he laid out pictures and let the images speak for themselves.

There was a hint of laughter in one, sexual need in another. A smile that spoke of a shared secret.

The pain slammed into him with the subtly of a lightning bolt. It cut through him, leaving him exposed and bleeding. Something dark and ugly surrounded his soul and began to squeeze the life out of him.

He'd lost her. He'd been so sure he would never want anyone that he'd made the decision to let her go before he'd even known what it was to have her. He'd assumed she wouldn't matter, couldn't be special. He'd cast off her gift of love without being aware that it could change him forever.

Now, alone, he felt the loss of her. He ached to hear her laughter, to see her smile, to touch her, hold her. He wanted her to need him—not just in bed, but in her life. He wanted her to miss him, to grow old with him. To love him.

He returned the pictures to the envelope. She'd made it pretty damn clear that she wasn't interested in him anymore. That she didn't love him.

He closed his eyes for a second, then opened them. Marina wasn't someone to give her heart lightly. Was it possible that she'd just been able to turn off her feelings or had she been bluffing because anything else hurt too much. Was there still a chance?

He pushed to his feet and realized it didn't matter about chances or hopes or wishes. He'd always been a man who worked his ass off to get what he wanted. If he'd been willing to give that much to something as meaningless as a business, what more would he be willing to do to convince the only woman he'd ever loved to take a chance on him?

Marina was making coffee when she heard a knock on her front door. She instantly thought it was Todd, crawling back to beg her to give him another chance. The visual would have been funny, if her reaction hadn't been so incredibly sad. Even knowing what he was and how badly he'd handled the situation, she desperately wanted to give him another chance. Which made her a huge weenie.

But it didn't stop her heart from fluttering in anticipation as she pulled open the door. And while the person standing there wasn't Todd, it was nearly as good.

"Julie! You're back!"

Marina reached for her sister just as Julie grabbed for her. They hugged and screamed and danced in front of the open door, then Marina stepped back to study the changes of the past six weeks.

"You're barely showing," she said, staring at her sister's nonexistent bump. "But you look so happy."

It was true. Julie's face glowed with contentment.

"I am happy," her sister told her. "Ryan and I got back last night and I wanted to come see you first thing. How are you?"

Marina led the way into the apartment. "I'm good. Fine."

Julie didn't look convinced. "You can't be fine."

"Okay—how about I'm adjusting? Would that work?"

"Maybe." Julie hugged her again. "Are you sorry about the baby?"

"Yes and no. I was excited at the thought of being pregnant. Terrified, but excited. Then when Todd freaked, I knew having a child with him would be a big mistake. He's not ready to trust anyone. I can't have a relationship with a guy who's so willing to think the worst of me. I certainly can't have a baby with him. So not being pregnant is a good thing, right?"

Marina did her best to speak calmly, to be logical and rational and sensible about the whole thing. But in truth, her heart hurt. She missed Todd, she missed the baby, which was insane and she didn't know when she was going to be able to get back to her old self.

"Oh, Marina," Julie murmured. "I'm so sorry. About all of it. I shouldn't have asked you two to work on the wedding."

Marina took her hand and led her to the sofa. They plopped down at opposite corners.

"You had nothing to do with this," Marina told her honestly. "Todd and I are totally responsible for what happened. I thought I was safe from anyone like him. He's so not my type."

"Apparently he is," Julie told her.

"Tell me about it. The thing is, we were attracted, we acted on that attraction and I screwed up. I thought it was more than it was. It ended badly, but at least I know the truth about him. I won't spend my time missing a man who can never be what I need."

"So you're over him?" Julie asked, sounding doubtful.

"I'm working on it. The good news is if I fell in love with him, I can fall in love with someone else. It will just take a little time."

"As easy as that?"

"I don't think it will be easy." She thought about Todd, about how he made her laugh and how they were more alike than she ever would have guessed. "I miss him. I'll miss him for a long time, but I'll recover, and then I'll move on."

To what? Another man? She couldn't imagine ever caring about anyone the way she cared about Todd. Worse, even though she would never admit it to another living creature, she finally understood her mother. In truth, she, Marina, would also settle for a small piece of Todd rather than having no part of him at all. Thank goodness no one was giving her the option.

"What about the wedding and the rehearsal and the rehearsal dinner?" Julie asked. "Will that be too awful for you? Would you rather not come?"

Marina shook her head. "It's your wedding. Of course I'll be there. I love you and I want to see you and Ryan get married. Plus, hey, I have a whole lot invested in the event."

"But Todd…"

"I can handle it," she promised, hoping it was true. "It's one evening and one day. I'm tough. Don't worry about me. Just focus on yourself and your happy day. You're marrying Ryan."

Julie smiled with so much love, she lit up the room. "I know. I can't believe I was so lucky to find him. Thank you for all you've done. Thank you for making my wedding perfect."

Marina had to blink several times to fight tears. "Don't thank me yet. You haven't seen anything. You did say you wanted a jungle theme for the reception, right? Because we found the cutest little stuffed giraffes for wedding favors, not to mention a 'sounds of the jungle' CD to play at the reception."

Julie swallowed hard. "You didn't. You wouldn't."

"You'll have to wait and see."

The rehearsal dinner was held on the Thursday before the wedding. Marina spent most of the afternoon in hot curlers in a feeble attempt to get her long hair to be something other than straight.

She usually didn't bother, but today she felt compelled. Probably because she was going to have to spend several hours in Todd's company and she was bitter enough to want to look good enough to make him feel bad. Not exactly her proudest moment.

She was also scared about seeing him. At the florist, she'd been able to keep the meeting short and maintain control. While the wedding rehearsal itself didn't worry her, the dinner was another matter. It was just going to be family—Julie, Ryan, Willow, Kane, Todd and herself, their mom, Ruth plus Todd and Ryan's parents.

That meant a small table and lots of conversation. Everyone would notice if she was too quiet or if she and Todd weren't speaking. It could be awkward and embarrassing. Plus her mother didn't know anything about her relationship with Todd...unless Ruth had shared that information with her, as well as Julie.

Marina groaned at the thought, then slipped on her dress and zipped it up the back.

The dark blue fabric brought out the color of her eyes and the fitted style made her feel especially skinny. She'd already finished her makeup so all that was left was her hair.

She took out all the curlers, then bent over at the waist and began to finger-comb the curls. When they were loose and, hopefully, sexy-looking, she stretched out her arm to grab for the hairspray, but instead encountered a hand.

She immediately screamed, jerked into an upright position and took a jump back.

Todd stood next to her dresser in her bedroom. Her messy bedroom with the unmade bed and clothes scattered everywhere. Although when compared with how fast and hard her heart pounded in her chest, she wasn't sure that mattered.

She had a brief impression of how great he looked in khakis and a silk shirt, then remembered her hair and clamped both hands on top of her head.

"What are you doing here?" she asked. "How did you get in? Couldn't you have knocked?"

At least she was dressed, but jeez. Talk about a shock.

"I knocked several times, then tried the door. It was open. You okay?"

No, she wasn't. She risked a glance in the mirror and saw her hair didn't look too bad, so she lowered her hands to her sides.

"You shouldn't leave your door unlocked," he said.

"You drove all the way out here to tell me that? Fine. I shouldn't. I don't normally. I don't know why I did today."

Distraction, she thought. She'd been distracted at the thought of seeing him, and now that he was standing in front of her, she knew why.

She still loved him. Despite everything he'd said and all that had happened and how much she should know better, she loved him. Right this second, she wanted to throw herself into his arms and have him tell her that they would work it out. That what had happened before had been nothing more than an icky misunderstanding. Not that Todd would ever say "icky."

"Why are you here?" she asked.

"I wanted to talk to you," he told her. "There are some things we have to clear up."

Right. The rehearsal dinner. "I'm fine with it," she said, hoping she would be. "Yes, it will be awkward with our family there. I've been thinking about everything and I think we can pull this off. It's not like we were dating for years. No one really knows. Well, my sisters and Ruth, but they won't say anything. We planned the wedding together, nothing more."

His dark gaze settled on her face. "Is that all that happened?"

"It's all I'm going to admit to."

"I'm giving a toast tonight. At the dinner. I would appreciate it if you'd listen to it and tell me where I can improve it."

He wanted her advice? Even worse, she was pathetic enough to be willing to give it.

"Fine. Read away."

He pulled a piece of paper out of his shirt pocket and unfolded it. "The Bible tells us that love is kind. Scholars tell us that love can change the course of history. Scientists tell us that love is chemical. Poets tell us that love is eternal. But true love is so much more than that. It's about believing and risking. It's about committing to always being there for one person and believing that person will be there for you. Love is about hanging on through the roller-coaster ride of life. Love is having faith, in yourself and the person you love. For Julie and Ryan, love is who they are."

His words wrapped around her like a hug. She wanted to both laugh and cry, but mostly she wanted to go to him and tell him that no matter what, she would always love him. That's what love was for her. How had he known?

Instead she said, "It's lovely. They'll be deeply touched."

He took a step toward her. "I mean it. For a long time I didn't know what to say about them getting married.

I thought Ryan was a fool for trusting Julie. Eventually she won me over and I was happy for him. But not envious. I never wanted what he had…until now." He smiled wryly. "Not Julie—the in-love part."

"Good to know," she managed to say even though her throat felt tight. What was he saying? That he cared? That he wanted to care? That she mattered?

"You know my past," he said. "You know why I hold myself back, never really getting emotionally involved. You know what I'm afraid of." He shook his head. "I can't believe I just admitted I'm afraid."

Neither could she. "I do know why."

"When you said you were pregnant, I thought you were just like them," he said, staring into her eyes. "I was angry, but more at me than at you. I was angry at myself for wanting you to be different. For wanting to believe you hadn't tricked me. I said a lot of things I shouldn't have said. I was wrong. Because you're not like them."

Her eyes filled with tears, but she blinked them away. He took a step toward her.

"Marina, when you told me there wasn't a baby, I was devastated. I want to have children with you. I love you. I want to marry you and grow old with you. I want to live with you in that damn house of mine and have you change everything in my world. I want to believe in forever."

She was already on the emotional edge, barely able to believe he was actually speaking these words to her.

Then he stunned her by dropping to one knee, taking her hand in his and asking, "Can you forgive me? Can you give me another chance? Will you take that step of faith and believe in me? Will you marry me?"

She didn't mean to burst into tears, but she did. She also managed to nod and that must have been enough because then Todd was standing and pulling her close. She went into his embrace and knew she would always feel safe when she was with him.

He held her tightly against him. "I love you," he whispered into her ear. "I think I've loved you from the first. It was safe to be friends and so I let down my guard. One day I woke up and you were a part of me. I'm so sorry for what I said, how I reacted."

"It's okay. I understand." She looked at him and smiled through her tears. "I love you, too."

He wiped her face with his fingers. "I'm glad you didn't change your mind."

"I wanted to, but I couldn't. I seem to be a one-man woman."

"Thank God."

She laughed and so did he. Then he kissed her. At the first brush of his mouth, her whole world righted itself.

"We need to get to the rehearsal," he said when they came up for air. "But first…"

He pulled a small box out of his slacks front pocket. "This belonged to my grandmother. If you don't like it, we can pick out something else."

He opened the box and she gasped. Nestled in the velvet lining was a sparkling diamond ring. A huge, round center stone was surrounded by other diamonds. The light glinted off the facets and nearly blinded her.

"It's beautiful," she whispered, "but it's really…"

"Big?" He grinned. "We Astons don't do anything by halves. It's about eight carats total."

"Wow."

"Too much?"

"I'll adjust."

He slipped the ring on her finger and it fit perfectly.

"It was meant for you," he said just before he kissed her. "I love you, Marina."

"I love you, too." She gave herself up to his embrace, then pulled back. "Does this mean there's going to be a Todd Aston the Fourth?"

"Probably."

"I can live with that." She glanced down at her ring, then pulled it off her finger.

He nodded. "After the wedding?"

"If that's okay. I don't want to take away the spotlight from Julie and Ryan."

"I'm good with that. We have our whole lives to celebrate."

He set the box on her dresser and she put the ring into the box. Then they walked out together.

"I have some very specific ideas about our wedding," he said as she collected her purse. "Color schemes. Place settings."

She laughed. "So you think we should plan it together?"

"We did a good job on this one. We're a great team."

"Yes, we are."

* * * * *

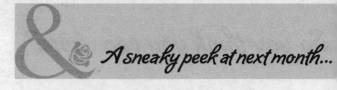

A sneaky peek at next month...

By Request

RELIVE THE ROMANCE WITH THE BEST OF THE BEST

My wish list for next month's titles...

*3 stories in
each book - only*
£5.99!

Available at WHSmith, Tesco, Asda, Eason, Amazon and Apple

Just can't wait?

*Visit us
Online*

You can buy our books online a month before
they hit the shops! **www.millsandboon.co.uk**

0912

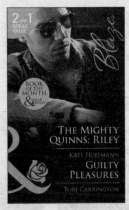

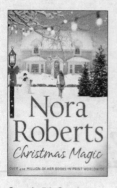  

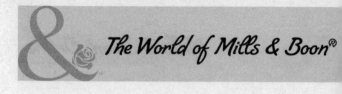

The World of Mills & Boon®

There's a Mills & Boon® series that's perfect for you. We publish ten series and, with new titles every month, you never have to wait long for your favourite to come along.

Blaze

Scorching hot, sexy reads
4 new stories every month

By Request

Relive the romance with the best of the best
9 new stories every month

Cherish

Romance to melt the heart every time
12 new stories every month

Desire

Passionate and dramatic love stories
8 new stories every month